GHOST LETTER

A Mystery by Helen Currie Foster

This is a work of fiction. All incidents and dialogue, and all characters, with the exception of some well-known historical and public figures, are products of the author's imagination and are not to be construed as real. Where real-life historical or public figures appear, the situations, incidents and dialogues concerning those persons are used fictitiously and are not intended to depict actual events or to change the entirely fictional nature of the work. In particular, any legal predicaments and analyses are fictional and not intended as legal analysis or advice. In all respects, any resemblance to persons living or dead is entirely coincidental. Coffee County and Coffee Creek exist solely in the author's imagination, where they are located somewhere in the Texas Hill Country between Dripping Springs and Fredericksburg.

Printed by CreateSpace, An Amazon.com Company
Available from Amazon.com and other online stores.
Available on Kindle and other devices.

Library of Congress Control Number: 2016900293
CreateSpace Independent Publishing Platform, North Charleston, SC
Copyright 2016 Helen Currie Foster. All Rights Reserved
Design by Bill Carson Design

For Larry, Sydney and Drew

OTHER BOOKS BY
HELEN CURRIE FOSTER

Ghost Cave

Ghost Dog

Ticking Away

"So, it's mine, right?" Bryce shifted impatiently—unusual for him. He'd asked her legal opinion, though, and Alice resisted being rushed, even (or especially) for her friend.

"Depends." She scrutinized the fragile yellowed letter. April afternoon sunlight streamed through Bryce's office window. Bryce had hung the CLOSED sign on the door and hurried her back to his office. "If you bought the nightstand at an auction—"

"Yep."

"—and you signed the usual auction document saying you took the item as is and with its contents—"

"I did."

"—then it may be yours—"

"Right!" Bryce sat up straight, then relaxed back in his antique desk chair.

"—unless it was taken from someone. Stolen."

"Huh. How am I supposed to know that?"

"Just the risk any buyer takes. You don't get title to stolen property."

The letter lay between them on Bryce's mahogany desk— carefully chosen, like all his inventory at Coffee Creek Old Style, a mecca for Texas antiques mavens. Nearby lay a yellowish fabric packet, about ten inches square, from which Bryce had pulled the small envelope that had held the letter. Next to it was a small faded green silk bag, embroidered with flowers.

Alice ran her fingers lightly across the yellowish packet, faintly aromatic. "Is that oiled silk? I've never actually seen any before, just read about it."

"Yes, it certainly is," said Bryce. "And inside that oiled-silk packet were the letter and that little embroidered bag."

"How did you find them?"

"The packet was under a piece of black oilcloth covering the shelf inside the nightstand when I winkled it out this morning. You know, the shelf where you'd have put the slop jar, back before indoor toilets. When I previewed the nightstand at the auction yesterday, it seemed unusual for the oilcloth to be wrapped and glued around the entire shelf. In these old nightstands there's usually just a square of oilcloth stuck to the top of the shelf."

"So you suspected your nightstand came with something extra."

"That shelf felt a little thick to me. But"—he glanced up, eyes rounded in innocence—"I loved the nightstand instantly. Simple lines, all cherry, mid-nineteenth century, but battered, neglected. It was apparently stored in a root cellar on a Medina County ranch, so at least the wood was not as dried out as it might have been, but just look at the poor old thing. Still, the price was right." He smirked. "I outbid the usual suspects at the last minute."

"But the letter. What's so special that you wanted me to see it?" Gently flattening the small folded letter, entirely covered on both sides with angular handwriting, Alice slowly deciphered the following:

Saturday, April 12, 1919

Dear Father,

Our Air Service squadron finally made it back to Kelly Field in San Antonio last week. We griped about being sent to Coblenz to keep the Germans "surrendered" after the Armistice, while everyone else got orders for home. But some good news: I'm starting a job training pilots at Kelly Field. Not sure for how long, given that Congress doesn't understand airplanes are the future. I get no leave until Saturday when I plan to ride my Indian motorcycle, safely retrieved from storage, west to Blue Pool, then back south to the ranch. I'll get there by suppertime and stay for church on Easter. Father, I'll be asking your blessing on my marriage to Susana Navarro, who has waited for me through this war. I want you and Miss Ella to come to our wedding in San Antonio on April 26. Susana wants a church wedding. I'm waiting for Judge Brackett to return and draft up adoption papers for my little Alejandro so there will be no question about his status. He's mine. You will love the little boy as I do. I dreamed of this the entire year in France, and of being in the little cabin at Blue Pool and working my land up there. It won't suit for cattle but I believe goats will do well.

Please kiss Aunt Dee for me and thank her for sending the book. I almost cried when I unwrapped that old friend, which I'm bringing back, battered but intact. Tennyson got me through some tough spots. Tell her I'm bringing her new poems by two Brits, Siegfried Sassoon and Ivor Gurney. Hurrying to catch the mail to Madrone, and trusting this finds you well, your loving son Alex.

P.S. Love to dearest Bonnie. Hello to Willy. He must be full grown!"

"Who is this?"

Bryce turned over the envelope. In larger script it was addressed to Alastair Drinkman, Drinkman Ranch, Madrone, Texas. Glued in the corner was a small orange six-cent stamp picturing a biplane. Alice peered closer. "Wow! What a cool stamp!"

"Yup. That's the Curtiss Jenny, 1918. It's a great color, but only worth about thirty bucks. Now, if it were the upside-down Curtiss Jenny, which was red and blue—it could be worth at least half a million. But . . . no such luck." Alice never ceased to be amazed by Bryce's encyclopedic memory for antiques, stamps, coins, and the way he could make old objects spring to life. "But look at the address, Alice!" he said, pointing.

"Drinkman Ranch, in Madrone. Medina County, right? Are you thinking this means the Drinkmans as in the Drinkman Foundation? Aren't they based in Medina County?"

"That's exactly what I think."

The Drinkman family funneled millions through a PAC called Preserve Our Heritage. POH funded handpicked candidates nationwide, with special emphasis on anti-immigrant platforms and a tom-tom beat of antigay rhetoric. POH's meteoric rise to political fame in the past decade paralleled the rise in Drinkman income, fueled by horizontal shale drilling on family holdings that extended beyond the Hill Country counties into South Texas. POH's latest initiative supported broadcasts by TV and radio talk-show hosts across the country on the Drinkmans' closely held network of stations. So far, no one had found shale deposits in Coffee County, to Alice's relief; she often suspected places were cursed, not blessed, by their natural resources.

"How do you know it's the same Drinkmans?"

"Just look online. The POH website is very proud of the Drinkmans' Texas genealogy. In fact, it showcases Alex Drinkman's service as a pilot in the Great War."

On the envelope flap Alice saw, in faint small letters, *"Given me by Alastair Drinkman, June 15, 1919. Adecia Bond."* She tapped the letter. "Interesting. Who is Adecia Bond?"

"I believe Adecia Bond is Alex's mother's sister, whom he calls Aunt Dee. Texas Cemeteries Online shows her as buried in Woodville, in East Texas, in 1924, next to her husband, who died in 1910. But here's the thing, Alice. Poor Alex Drinkman never made it home. He died April 19, 1919. He was killed crossing Madrone Creek."

"Oh no." Alice thought of the young man who loved poems and Susana Navarro. What irony, to survive the perilous skies of the Great War, to make it almost home . . .

"But don't you get it? Look who he was in love with! Doesn't the Navarro name ring a bell?"

A wild surmise struck Alice. "Not—as in Sandro Navarro?" He was a rising star in San Antonio politics.

"Yes! Susana was his grandmother!"

"And Sandro is leading the charge for immigration reform. And if I remember, he supported same-sex marriage in Texas."

"The same!"

Alice knew Bryce's fixation on immigration reform. The border issue was fraught; her South Texas cousins regularly scanned the horizon with night-vision glasses, fearing illegal drug mules were crossing their ranch. But Bryce still talked about the young Mexican man who had traveled back and forth from Acapulco to Coffee Creek for years, doing any work he could find. He helped build Bryce's Coffee Creek ranch house, pulled fence, built stonework, graded the driveway. But travel between Texas and Acapulco became more and more risky. After his last trip home to visit his children, he died in the desert trying to get back north. Bryce occasionally sent money orders to the family in Acapulco. "I never saw anyone more honest or more hardworking, Alice!" Bryce blamed anti-immigrant rhetoric he heard on talk radio shows, like those on Drinkman-owned stations, for such deaths, saying, "Why can't we have work permits?" Bryce hated the antigay slurs as well. "Whatever happened to the Texas we knew back in the eighties and nineties, when people didn't get a microscope out to look at your private business?"

Alice looked down at the letter. "So if our returning soldier had lived, and married Susana as planned, then 'little Alejandro' might have inherited some of the Drinkman fortune?"

"Right. How would the Drinkmans feel about that? And if he had, 'little Alejandro's' son Sandro might not have such an uphill battle if he runs for president. I think the San Antonio newspapers could have some fun with that, don't you? I'd like to see POH squirm. But wait, Alice—there's more!" He nodded at the little embroidered bag.

"I'll bite. I've bitten. What else?"

"First, a bandana." He lifted the flap, glanced at Alice, and gently pulled out a folded bandana, frayed and faded to a ghostly red.

"Whose?" Alice breathed, watching him unfold the first crease.

"Just wait." Bryce pointed at a scrap of paper protruding from a fold, labeled in tiny print "*Alex, from his body. Adecia Bond, 19 Apr. 1919.*" Alice couldn't help herself. She leaned over and sniffed the bandana. Old, old, old cotton, old air still caught in it, sweet faint old sweat, the unmistakably unique and individual smell of the nape of the neck of a young man who had worn it on horseback, in airplanes, on his motorcycle, through a heartbreaking spring, sweaty summer, and icy winter, who had wiped his face with it, folded and refolded it, before climbing back on his motorcycle to head home. For whom it was a comfort. A smell of himself, a piece of home.

"Adecia Bond, again," Alice said. "So she kept not just the letter, but his bandana." Alice herself still kept, in the far back of her closet, two old cotton dress shirts of her father's, which still held, oh so faintly, the barest presence of the man. She couldn't seem to give them away. "And what's that?" A bit of gray silk stuck out of the next fold.

"Look." Bryce gently pushed back the bandana, revealing the piece of gray silk. He lifted the silk to reveal a curl of dark hair, tied with a faded piece of ribbon, again labeled with tiny black letters: "Alex."

"Whoa," said Alice. She felt a shock—electricity from far away. Even after death, hair carried a secret blueprint: scent, curl, texture. Even after skin and body were long transmuted, hair remained, individual and distinct. She could not touch this hair. Alex Drinkman wasn't here to defend himself against the fingers of intrusive strangers, strangers fingering his bandana.

Alice felt Alex Drinkman standing near them, like a hologram shimmering in the shadows on this April afternoon. She imagined someone—his aunt?—mourning a body which smelled faintly of sweat and dried blood and creek water, then snipping a lock of hair. She had shocked herself by doing just that when her own mother died. Into the back of her office desk drawer she'd pushed a small box with an envelope holding a snippet of silvery curls. Why? She'd never told her children or siblings. It seemed—primitive. Certainly didn't bring back the beloved one. Didn't even bring back the memories she wanted, but only memories of the deathbed, of being present at the end. The action itself, snipping the hair, was a hopeless attempt to hold onto the beloved, who had already departed.

Bryce was pushing back the next fold.

"Bryce. Is that blood?" Two quarter-size brown spots, smeared at the edges, stiffened the faded cloth.

"That's my thought."

"Lord, it's like a movie." She looked up at him. "But we should be careful, and not touch the hair, or the stains." Alice was now thinking of the Navarro heirs, of DNA.

Bryce looked up, raised his eyebrows, then nodded, and used the pencil to refold the gray silk over the lock of hair. "But we're not through." He unfolded the last fold of the bandana to show a slim scrap of paper, rolled into a cylinder. He unrolled it, holding one corner gingerly, the pencil helping. Alice saw, shining in the late sunlight, two long, narrow, pointed brass bullets. One was slightly deformed, with a small brown stain. The other looked clean. On the inside of the paper, she read—in the now-familiar tiny printing, *"From Alex's boot and my Tennyson. A. B. 19 April 1919."*

"See why I wanted you over here?" Picking up the pencil, Bryce pushed the bullets back into the paper cylinder, refolded the bandana, pinched it by a corner, and slipped it back into the green embroidered bag. Alice and Bryce stared at each other. Then he put the green bag into the oiled-silk packet.

"Let's have some iced tea," Bryce said abruptly, shoving back his chair. "This is getting a little too real, no?"

Alice followed him into the kitchen of the old turreted stone house that served as his shop in Coffee Creek. Bryce pointed at the crockery cookie jar and a Depression-era glass plate. "Put some of those gingersnaps on there, Alice. I just made them this morning." He bustled around, loading a tray with napkins, fresh mint and lemon in a crystal bowl, glasses full of ice, and a pitcher of tea. "Sugar bowl is right there, and don't forget the iced-tea spoons." Alice dutifully gathered sugar, spoons, and cookies and followed him back to the office. They sat opposite each other. The oiled-silk packet lay on the desk. Ticking like a time bomb.

Alice used the sterling iced-tea spoon to muddle the mint in her tall frosted glass. "So elegant, Bryce."

"I can have iced-tea spoons if I want. Get over it."

She bit a gingersnap—crisp on the outside, just slightly softer in the middle. "Delicious," she said. But she was not hungry, thinking of the bandana, hair, bullets. And blood.

"You know Cassie always made cookies for the customers. It's her recipe. I still use it."

Cassie had been Bryce's partner in the Coffee Creek antique shop until her disappearance ten years earlier. The past fall, after narrowly escaping death herself, Alice had guessed where Cassie might be found.

"Here's to Cassie." Alice solemnly clinked glasses with Bryce. "I wish I'd known her. Why do the good die the wrong way? Or at the wrong time?"

"You and the Greeks. We all want to know. We want the 'why.' Take this poor soldier Alex Drinkman. I've been digging into what happened to him, Alice. In a manner of speaking. He was shot dead, but no one knows who did it."

Alice set down her glass. "Was there an investigation?"

"Of sorts. You'd be amazed what you can find in the county history records. A newspaper account says he died on a sandbar in Madrone Creek. He was found by the foreman at the Drinkman ranch, who was riding home after delivering a herd of cattle to San Antonio. The foreman saw the motorcycle turned over just off the low-water crossing, then saw him lying on a sandbar downstream. There may be more but it's on microfiche and I'm waiting for it. So's that reporter, Rose Rayburn, from the San Antonio Express."

Rose Rayburn? Alice had heard her on public radio, reporting from prisons, courtrooms, dangerous locations. In a broadcast with fellow journalists about investigating financial crime, she'd detailed the precautions she took to protect her work from hackers. "Never put anything online," she'd said. The other reporters agreed, describing their care in shielding their computers from Internet attacks. Alice, remembering a Roseanne Rayburn a few years behind her in high school, had been curious enough to find her picture online. Yep, same intelligent eyes, same crinkly blonde hair, same skeptical smile she recalled from high school. They hadn't been friends then, but Alice had come to admire the low-key, unemotional, concise but densely factual reporting Rose delivered on public radio. When had she joined a San Antonio newspaper? Alice sat back and fixed Bryce with her sternest stare. "Okay. What's up? Why did you ask me to come see this letter? And what is Rose Rayburn's interest?"

"Alice, I want you to represent me. Defend my claim to this letter, if anyone challenges it."

"Just your ownership, that's what you mean?"

"Right. That's all."

"But how will anyone even know you have it? Wait a minute, did you tell that reporter?"

Bryce fidgeted, stirring the long silver spoon round and round his glass. "I did tell her about it," he admitted. "And I sent a copy to Sandro this morning before I called you. We were friends in college."

Ah. The cat was out of the bag. She laughed.

"Bryce, why don't you pick on someone your own size? Taking on the Drinkmans—you realize that if Sandro's family has a legitimate claim on even a fraction of the Drinkman fortune, the implications are huge, for both families? Good grief!" She frowned. "But if you've already sent a copy to Sandro Navarro, have you also thought he may need to have the DNA tested—the hair, the blood? I'm assuming you wouldn't object, even if you consider the letter—and presumably everything in that oiled-silk packet—yours now. What's your thought on that?"

"Hmm. No. Well, of course if he needs to do that, it's fine with me."

"Where are you keeping the letter? And the packet?"

"Well, I wondered—can you keep it all in your safe? Seems like it would be safer than mine."

"Yes. But you need to be sure *your* insurance covers it too, given the size of the fight you're picking. Right away. And I'm going back to the office. Want to look at the law a bit. And you could get me a copy of your bill of sale for the nightstand and the auction house's paperwork. May I see the nightstand?"

Old, battered, it sat quietly in the antique linens area of the shop, door open, old tea towels stacked inside on the formerly oilcloth-wrapped shelf where a chamber pot could stand. An ordinary hiding place, as in "The Purloined Letter." But now the letter had escaped.

Alice slipped the auction documents and the oiled-silk packet into her backpack and headed for the front door. Bryce unlocked it, flipped the CLOSED sign back to OPEN, and walked out with her onto the porch. They sniffed the spring air, a little cooler and heavier as the day wore on.

"What a beautiful day. Thank you, Alice. And if that reporter calls, will you talk to her? I . . . um . . . I already gave her your number."

Alice rolled her eyes. "Depends on what she wants to talk about. But I will put your letter and everything else in the safe."

"It would make me feel better. In fact, I already feel better." Bryce smiled his lopsided smile, waving from the stone porch.

But I don't, she thought, walking down the sidewalk toward her office. The image stayed with her: Alex Drinkman, shot at his most vulnerable, slowly guiding his motorcycle down the creek bank on a low-water crossing, then dying on a sandbar as Madrone Creek purled past, carrying faint traces of his blood downstream. Late sun lit up the Coffee County Courthouse, all creamy limestone and domed cupola with a clock that nearly always told the exact time. Four o'clock. She rounded two sides of the courthouse square and turned into her own office in the old Puryear house. Cool inside and very quiet; her secretary, Silla, was rustling around in the back. Alice sighed and unlocked the double doors of the conference room closet to reveal the tall ornate Victorian safe she'd bought from the old Coffee Creek Cowman's Bank. It now sported up-to-date locks and was bolted to beams beneath the floor. She slipped the oiled-silk packet into a mailing envelope, sealed it and marked it "Coffee Creek Old Style," and locked it in the safe. Then she relocked the double doors to the closet.

Something still nagged at her mind. What had Bryce said? She walked into her office, plopped down at her desk, gazed at the pictures of John and Ann, her precious children, exploring their Scottish roots in their college year abroad in Edinburgh. She was eager to have them home, have a semblance of normal family life for a change, instead of wondering whether they were home from the pubs, whether they had studied enough for exams. Alice jiggled her mouse and pulled up the online record of Texas court decisions. The adoption papers. Intent to adopt . . . wasn't there an old case . . . but also new legislation? She started scrolling down the list of case names.

Silla swung in with a note, red ponytail bouncing. "Call Congressman Navarro's San Marcos office on this number and ask for Carey Norville. He wants to speak with you."

Well. Carey Norville—she'd read that name before. He was a well-known political operative. Navarro must have serious ambitions. To her surprise, Alice got through immediately.

"Ms. Greer. I'm Carey Norville, campaign manager for the congressman. I got your name from Bryce Sheridan."

"Ah."

"The congressman says he and Bryce go way back and that Bryce says mighty good things about you. We want to know if we can engage you, perhaps on a limited basis, about this letter of Bryce's. He sent the congressman a copy."

"What do you have in mind? I need to be sure there's no potential conflict with Bryce. He's not formally a client, but he is a friend."

"Understood. What we want is to understand the law, the lay of the land. What rights, if any, does the congressman's family have? His dad is still alive, you know. Alejandro Navarro. The Alejandro, it appears."

"No, I didn't know."

"He's at least ninety-three, and a war hero. World War II."

"Didn't know that either."

"We need to know what, really, are the chances of Sandro's family, or Mr. Navarro, being declared an heir to the Drinkman fortune, or some of it."

"That's impossible at this point, to give you odds. I need more history and more legal research. I'd rephrase the question—what are Mr. Alejandro Navarro's chances of being declared heir to Alex Drinkman, and what might that mean?"

"Of course. And as you can imagine, we'd like to know what jurisdiction we'd be in."

"Do you mean whether the suit would be in the congressman's district or not? Depends on your facts. Possibly more than one county may be involved."

"Ms. Greer, the 'odds' question, as you call it, is very important. I don't know your views on the congressman?"

"I'm a supporter."

"If he or his family were to file some sort of proceeding, I'd damn sure want it to be close to a laydown."

"You don't want him to look . . . whiny? Litigation-happy? Trying to get something he didn't work for?"

Norville expelled a deep breath. "Yep, you got it. If there is a good chance of serious money, that's one thing. If it is a small chance of small money, or years of litigation with an uncertain outcome, I'm not sure that squares with Sandro's passion about being a public servant, having a servant's heart, and wanting to use his resources to make life better for other citizens. So, Ms. Greer, if we're going to run into big headwinds on the money, I'd rather not try to go after it."

Well, she'd wait to hear what her client thought—he's the one who mattered. If she decided to represent him. "So," Alice summarized, "what you want first from me is an assessment of what might happen?"

"Right. Including what courts we might be in, and our chances. Especially our chances."

"I think you're talking initially about an application for determination of heirship. And with his dad still alive, my initial thought is for Sandro's father to file as heir to Alex Drinkman. But again, let's get the facts nailed down and clarify some of the legal issues. And I warn you, those may be challenging, given the Texas Supreme Court's 2010 decision in the *Kenedy* case. Meaning *The John G. and Marie Stella Kenedy Memorial Foundation v. Fernandez,*" Alice said.

"That's a mouthful."

"The petitioner, in her mid-seventies, filed suit in 2000 after hearing she was the illegitimate child of a man whose will was probated after he died in 1948. Will contests over his sister's estate were settled in 1975, and his wife's estate was closed in 1987. The family said she'd waited too long; she said she wasn't notified of the will contests. But the Texas Supreme Court said the discovery rule—the 'I just found out' rule—did not apply: when an heirship claim is brought after the dead person's estate has been administered, or after the dead person's property has been sold to a third party, courts apply a four-year statute of limitations."

"Doesn't sound good," said Norville. "A lot more time has passed here." Alice didn't think he sounded too unhappy. Norville shifted gears. "Could the client be—could you address your communications to me at the Navarro for Congress PAC?"

"I'd be more comfortable communicating directly with the client or clients. I'd require their consent and access to them anyway. It's their rights which are involved."

"It's all privileged, right? Can you copy me on the communications?"

"That needs to be discussed with the clients. We should be cautious. We don't want to waive attorney-client privilege. Also, before any work is done I need to clear conflicts, and know who the client or clients are, who the contact persons are, and who the adverse parties will be."

"You'll want a retainer?"

"Yes."

They briefly discussed terms.

"I'll get someone to wire the retainer. Can you start immediately on the research?"

"As soon as we finalize the engagement letter. But we're rushing. Since their consent is critical, when can I meet with Mr. Navarro and the congressman?"

"Can you come by our San Marcos office tomorrow morning at ten? You and I can talk more. Then you could meet Sandro and swing by the fundraiser at noon tomorrow at La Rotonda. It's a big one—should be fun. And you can meet Mr. Navarro there."

Well. Always nice to get a new gig. A change from conservation easements and ranch sales, at least.

*****

Her desk phone rang.

"Alice MacDonald Greer? Rose Rayburn here. Bryce says he told you I might call? And that you might still be in?" A cheerful voice, intense, busy. Alice heard road noise.

"Yes. Still here. And you are actually Roseanne Rayburn, right?"

"Yes! Of course I remember you, Alice! You were so smart and grown up in high school! I was just a lowly freshman!"

"Oh, right." Alice laughed, warming to the idea of a reunion with Rose, though thoughts of the long tiled corridors of high school still made her break out in hives. "I didn't know you'd left DC. Did you leave the national radio scene for the San Antonio newspaper?"

"I did. Sounds crazy, and it is. I fell in love with a guy from San Antonio. May I come by, just for a bit? I want to give you some background on the Drinkmans, and ask a couple of questions."

"What are you interested in?" Alice would need to avoid disclosing any specifics about her clients—actual or potential.

"Actually, I've been looking at the Drinkman enterprises for a couple of years. It's part of a broader investigation. The Drinkmans have a lot of irons in the fire besides those radio stations they own. Contributions, contracts . . . But I have some questions for you on Texas inheritance laws, if you would be so kind. And I have some information you may want. Or need."

"On?"

"Oh, various things . . . various people. Can you give me a few minutes? I'm almost to Coffee Creek. You're right on my way— I have a meeting tonight in Austin."

Alice felt great reluctance to discuss the letter until she understood more of the lay of the land. She would take refuge in client confidentiality. But Rose sounded bright, convincing, funny— though circumspect on the phone. "I'd be delighted to see you. Here or elsewhere?"

Rose quizzed her about locations and they opted for the Beer Barn. Alice hung up. No reason not to meet Rose again. No husband waiting at home—Jordie, the tall Scot she'd married after law school, had disappeared three years ago, when the oil company helicopter went down somewhere over the North Sea. No children waiting for supper—John and Ann were probably out playing music at some Edinburgh pub. No Ben Kinsear, the law-school beau with whom she'd recently reconnected—he was at a rare-books convention in New Orleans. Alice sat alone, facing a lonely drive back home, where only the burros would be waiting. The desk clock ticked, and shadows outside her window lengthened. She turned back to the computer and was soon lost in old cases on intestacy, adoption, heirship, reading terse century-old legal opinions by long-dead justices. Suddenly the computer calendar beeped. Time to head for the Beer Barn.

Play with the Big Boys

Alice stood waiting in the Beer Barn parking lot by its lit-up portable sign. Today's message: "We're all down here 'cause we're not all there."

A blue Ford Focus whirled into the gravel lot and parked in the first space. Alice recognized Rose Rayburn immediately—same big intelligent eyes, same blonde hair (now more stylish), same hurrying walk. White tee, jeans, loafers. And a remarkably beautiful small computer bag in soft chestnut leather, the long strap slung across Rose's chest. Italian? Alice wanted to touch it.

Instead she stuck out her hand. "All these years! Great to see you."

Rose's eyes didn't leave Alice's, absorbing—what? Alice wondered. "So glad you suggested this place. I moved the Austin meeting to tomorrow so we could visit. And I'm starving!" said Rose.

As they pushed through the Beer Barn's tall swinging doors the fragrant haze enveloped them—incense compounded of hickory smoke from the wood-fired grill, chiles toasted on an iron comal, and thousands of bubbles popping in bottles and glasses, releasing the yeasty magic of beer to the air.

"Starving!" Alice echoed. She claimed two seats at the non–"aces and eights" end of the horseshoe-shaped bar. Mindful of the sad demise of Wild Bill Hickok, who had violated his own rule in the Deadwood saloon, sitting with his back to the door, Alice always tried to sit with her back to the wall, where she could see the whole room, bar, tables, dance floor in front of the stage. In the same way, she liked that her house had a long view of the access driveway, liked the view out the back down a bluff, again so she could always see what was coming. She considered her preferences substantiated by anthropological studies of human habitat choices. Not weird at all that she arranged her desk the same way. Not weird at all.

A local band was warming up, wandering across the stage checking pedals, tuning, rearranging instruments. Jorgé Benavides, one of the three owners locally known as the Beer Barons, stepped onstage. To her delight, the Beer Barons had become Alice's clients. She'd helped steer them through a takeover effort and smear campaign organized by a moneyed local, later indicted for murder. Jorgé surveyed the band's progress, jumped back down. Just a low-key Wednesday night.

Rose settled on her barstool, surveyed her surroundings. "Perfect."

"Well, you asked for background noise. Do people really try to overhear your conversations?"

"You'd be surprised. Ever looked at the spy stuff in the catalogs you find on planes? Cameras that look like pens, directional amplifiers, and so on? I've seen those and all kinds of ridiculous gadgets. Investigative reporting—you've got to protect what you're learning. Get it down, bit by bit. Don't share it till you're ready to roll. I've seen reporters get hacked, bugged, cars broken into, computers stolen, you name it." She shook her head. Alice noticed Rose had not removed the beautiful bag, still wore it as she sat on the barstool.

"Computer?" Alice pointed at the soft leather. "Or tape recorder?"

"Sometimes both. But lately I've gone acoustic. Analog."

Alice raised puzzled eyebrows.

"I mean non-digital. Handwritten, typescript, hard copy, stashed. Oh, of course I use my little laptop, but I've learned to keep the work printed and separate, never all where someone could hack me and delete everything. On this last project, I've tried new tricks. You can get pretty creative with where you stash your files, too," Rose added. "You play with the big boys, you need a different playbook."

"You're making me nervous. Some lawyers go totally digital, notes, everything, but I have paper files too." Alice had grown up on carefully maintained paper files for estates and real estate work.

History (so-called because he was finishing his PhD in history at the University of Texas) swooped up in his bartender apron. "Hi, Alice! What can I get for you ladies?"

"Flat Creek Bock for me," said Alice.

"Iced tea, here."

Alice inhaled her beer, bubbles generating the millennia-old ether that comforted humans. Great discovery, fermentation, she mused.

"And to eat?"

Alice ordered her current favorite, the Pancho Villa, with roasted chile salsa and guacamole. Rose asked for Beer Barn Number Five with hickory-smoked barbecue sauce.

"Okay," said Alice. "You've got me curious. What did you want to know about inheritance laws? Remember, I can only talk to you on a general basis."

The intelligent eyes considered her. "You've seen the letter?" Alice just looked at her. "If Alex had signed the adoption papers, little Alejandro Navarro would be an heir?"

"That's not general!" said Alice. "Let me ask you a question. Have you seen any will from Alex Drinkman?"

"I haven't seen one. How would that work?"

"Speaking only generally, if someone has a valid will, property passes under his will. If not, you'd look to state laws of intestacy." And, she said to herself, I'd have to look back at 1919 and see whether there was even any administration of his estate. Because if not—

"What if he was murdered?"

"I'm speaking generally here, Rose. In some states there's a slayer statute that can preclude a murderer from benefiting. The Texas statute is limited, so a court might impose what's called a constructive trust to prevent an unjust result, always depending on the specific facts." And, she said to herself, did Alex's murderer benefit, as by getting Alex's share of something? What did Rose know? "What do you know about who shot Alex Drinkman?"

"Alice, are you interviewing me?" Rose laughed. "I don't know who shot him, but I've been wondering how to find out. I called Medina County to see if there was still an open case file. No answer yet. I've only visited Drinkman headquarters once. I got kicked out, but when the receptionist was walking me down the hall for the interview she took me past big glass cases of Drinkman-ia, historic stuff. There were pictures of their first oil wells in the thirties, the Pearsall play, and old ranch photos. And in one case, I saw Alex Drinkman's pilot's uniform, complete with scarf and helmet, and his sidearm and holster. There was a picture of him, too—he was a handsome man. And," she sipped her iced tea, "another case held guns. I wanted to see those especially but by then the guard had me firmly by the elbow and was hustling me out."

History bustled up with heavy white oval platters. "Extra guacamole for you," he told Alice. Rose had gotten fries, hand-cut and glorious. She tasted one, rolled her eyes, shook her head, tried another, and picked up her burger. Hickory sauce oozed down the sides. Rose delicately licked the dripping sauce. "Ooh, not too sweet. It has some bite!"

Alice heard a ringtone somewhere—same as hers, but not from her own purse. Rose sighed, put down the hamburger and wiped her fingers, then ferreted around in her back pocket. "Sorry," she said. "Just got to check this call." She looked at the phone screen, then slid off the barstool. "Alice, eat my french fries while they're hot. I'll be right back, just need to call this guy back. May be a breakthrough here. Might get an answer to the big question from him—my secret 'innie' at Drinkman." She smiled a lopsided smile.

"What does he do?"

"Oh, supposedly he drafts copy for the horrible hate-radio talk shows. He says it's like writing commercials—pick a theme, make up a half lie, have someone repeat it all day in a rich fruity authoritative voice. Yech. But he says he thinks someone wants to bring me a document."

"Well, watch out."

"It's okay, he seems like a nice guy. Harmless. Should only take a sec." She ran toward the front doors.

Well. Alice ate half her burger, stole a couple of Rose's fries, sipped her Flat Creek beer, rejoicing in a cosmic fusion of primordial elements—fries, meat, smoke, chile, beer. History walked over. "Is she coming back? If so I'm going to cover her plate for her."

"Yep. I'll just go check. And I'm not through either."

Alice walked to the doors, peered out. Rose was pacing ten feet away, talking on the phone. Then she swung round. Alice saw her nod, and lip-read her "okay" as she hung up. Rose glanced up, saw Alice. "I've gotta run pick up a document."

"From your 'innie'?"

"No, no, someone else. Not on this letter deal. He's about ten minutes away." She raced for the Ford Focus, calling, "I'll be right back."

Rose backed up and exited the Beer Barn lot onto Hays Street, which led east toward town, then veered into the post office parking lot, heading for the outdoor mailboxes. Alice watched her push a big envelope into the mailbox. Out of the corner of her eye she saw a silver pickup parked just outside the Beer Barn's other entrance on Travis, the driver, head down, on his phone. As she turned to go back into the Beer Barn, intent on her hamburger, she noticed the pickup was also crossing the parking lot, turning onto Hays.

Back inside, the band, over long slow compelling bass notes, slid into Count Basie's "How Long Blues," an Alice favorite. Alice snitched another of Rose's fries and checked her watch. Seven o'clock. Through the bar crowd she saw Jorgé walking toward her, accompanied by a black-and-white dog with startling blue eyes. "Pardner!" She leaned down, patted the dog's ears.

"He's gonna be a dad. Lily's having puppies." Lily, a lovely spaniel, had been the official Beer Barn dog until Pardner had joined her after helping Alice discover the fate of his missing owner, a singer-songwriter. Pardner thrived on guitar music. "But listen, Alice! We were going to call you tomorrow. We've got an idea."

"We" meant Jorgé and his partners, Bill Birnbach and Bill Benke, who called each other "Other Bill."

"We want to open a mini-brewery." Jorgé's eyes sparkled.

"But where? Not here?"

"On my land. Family land, outside Coffee Creek. You available in the morning?"

They brainstormed an agenda: arcane state beer regulations, brewery requirements, real estate issues, trademarks. Alice patted Pardner. Jorgé gazed at Rose's plate, paper napkin on top. "Cold fries, warm iced tea. Where's your friend?"

Alice shook her head. Almost eight. She felt unsettled, like she'd been dumped by a date. Irrational. Silly. She didn't really know Rose Rayburn anyway. She checked her phone. No message. She stood up.

"Leaving?"

She nodded.

"See you at your office."

She drove home in the April moonlight, listening to the local "roots radio" station. Yeah, a little Dr. John on piano, that'll cheer a girl up. Some. And as she crossed the low-water crossing on the creek road, she thought of Alex Drinkman on his Indian motorcycle, bandana on his neck, throttling down for a run across Madrone Creek.

She read herself to sleep and woke at five. Still no message from Rose. Well, drat the woman.

Chapter   Three

Let the Games Begin!

A lice grabbed her yoga mat and headed into town for the 6:00 a.m. class. She was almost there, admiring the stars beginning to fade before sunrise, when her cell phone whirred—incoming text. Bryce's: "I'm in shop hiding. Some guys broke in. Call police. Don't call my phone!"

She mashed the accelerator and sped around the courthouse square, turned onto Pecan Street and pulled up at Bryce's. Hands shaking, she called 911. "Slow down, ma'am," said the Coffee Creek dispatcher. Alice took a breath, gave the address and Bryce's message, and said, "Hurry!" Then she pelted up Bryce's steps, yanking at the front door handle. Locked. In the gray predawn light she read the sign in the glass sidelight by the door: "CLOSED UNTIL MONDAY—GOING TO MARKET!" She shook the door handle. "Bryce!" She knocked the antique dolphin doorknocker long and loud and listened—no sound within.

Two houses past Bryce's shop sat a shiny black Audi, the four linked rings glinting in the light from the lone streetlight on the block.

Alice grabbed the handle and shook the front door again, hoping to disrupt whatever had alarmed Bryce. Out of the corner of her eye she saw a man walk briskly from the rear of Bryce's shop toward the Audi. He moved like a cat—a cat with dark slacks, dark turtleneck, dark hair—and pulled open the driver's door. License plate! thought Alice. As she ran down the porch steps the dark man looked back and their eyes locked. Alice was so rattled she only remembered the last four digits on the license plate. The Audi moved quickly up the street, then stopped for another man, in dark clothes, with a blond crew cut, who ran, limping slightly, from between two houses, yanked open the front passenger door and jumped in. The Audi sped off.

Alice ran back and banged again on the front door. Behind her a Coffee County Sheriff's Department sedan slid up and a burly uniform, burdened with the weight of the world and his equipment belt, eyes saying it was the end of his shift, padded up the steps to stand next to her.

"Officer, can you open this door?"

He smiled a tired smile, fiddled with the lock, and opened the door. "Police!" he called.

"Bryce!" Alice called.

From the dark hall Bryce materialized, barefoot, in pajamas.

"I slept in my office last night," he said, without preamble. "You know, that little bedroom off the office, used to be the maid's room. Somehow I just felt I should be here. Then I woke up to hear drawers slamming in the office, right next to me! Of course I didn't have a gun in there, only my phone. And I tell you, I was too scared to open the door, or make a sound."

"So you never saw whoever it was? Were there two? Three?" asked the patrolman.

"It sounded like two pairs of feet were walking around, and I only heard two voices. They weren't shy about talking. Didn't know I was here, obviously."

"I saw one of them pretty well, getting in the car. And got a glimpse of another." Alice described the two men.

"Hmm. Did they see you?" asked the patrolman.

"The first one did. He gave me a long look." Again she saw the still face, the long stare. "Don't want to meet him again." The patrolman called in the partial license number she gave him.

She and the patrolman followed Bryce through the antique store, heading for the office. Alice looked longingly at the coffee pot on their way through the kitchen.

"Hey, Bryce?"

He stopped. "Oh heavens. Just a second." The coffee grinder whirred. She inhaled the grateful odor of Bryce's special blend. "No rush," he said. "Now that those guys are gone."

With the coffee brewing, Alice and the patrolman followed Bryce to the office door. He scanned the room as she peered past his shoulder.

"Sir, how does this look to you?" asked the patrolman. "What were they after in here?"

"God, what a mess." Bryce turned slowly, surveying the drawers of his desk. "Well, the drawers are all empty. I'm guessing they went through every folder. See that stack of empty folders over there? And look at the books. I'll bet they went through every one." His books—ledgers, daybooks, tomes on antiques, travel books—were off the shelves, roughly stacked by the wall. "If I reshelve them I can see if anything's missing but I'll bet nothing's gone. It's the papers that are gone."

"It is a mess, but it looks awfully systematic," Alice said.

Then Bryce looked at his laptop. "Hey, it's closed." He shook his head. "I never close it. But at least they didn't take it. That would be a disaster, with all my pictures of inventory."

"You don't store it just on the cloud, do you?" asked Alice.

"Well, I do, but I also back up that computer. Maybe not as much as I should." He started to open the laptop—the patrolman waved him back.

"Not yet. We'll dust for prints."

Alice felt a chill. "Bryce. What if your computer's closed because they—whoever—just copied all your files?" Alice had seen enough trade-secret litigation at her former firm to worry about copied computers. She and Bryce stared at each other. "The info that Rose sent? Emails?" asked Alice.

The patrolman swung around, eyes narrowed. "What do you have that these people want?"

"An old letter. But it's not here. I mean, it's not kept here, so they couldn't find it."

"And how did they get in? Don't you have a security system?"

"I don't know, and yes I do," said Bryce. "I don't know why it didn't work. The little box in the hall where you set the alarm looks dead, I mean, the light is not on like it should be."

The patrolman nodded and made a note.

"Meanwhile, if you don't mind, I don't want to meet your colleagues in my pajamas. Okay to get dressed?" Bryce headed to the little bedroom.

Alice gave the patrolman her card and headed outside. Pink and blue sky, fresh smells, early sun spangling the windshields of cars parked at the Camellia Diner and the courthouse across the street. A small-town morning. But the black Audi crawled like a tarantula across her consciousness, as she thought of the small yellowed letter with its orange stamp, ticking quietly away in her safe.

As she drove slowly past the Camellia Diner, Alice saw from the corner of her eye a blue Ford Focus, parked in the lot behind the diner. Alice was still irritated that Rose had just disappeared without the courtesy of a phone call or text to say her plans had changed. Was that her car? Curious, she parked her truck by the courthouse and walked across the street and down the driveway past the diner windows—no Rose inside. She peeked in the car. A woman's jacket lay abandoned on the passenger seat. Looked about Rose's size. Was Rose planning to eat breakfast at the diner? Or walk across the street to do some records research in the courthouse? She touched the hood—cold. And (she checked the clock on the cupola) it was only seven fifteen. She noted that the driver's seat was pushed back, all the way back. But Rose was only about five foot five. Gingerly she pulled the driver's-side door handle. Locked.

Alice found her cell phone and dialed Rose's number. In a few seconds she heard a faint ringtone somewhere close. She walked toward the back of the car. The ringtone got louder.

Alarmed, Alice backed away and called George Files, a Coffee County detective whose office was in the old jail by the courthouse. "I'm worried about someone who didn't meet me last night when she said she would. Rose Rayburn."

Pause. "We don't have a missing persons report. You think something happened?"

Alice explained that Rose, an investigative reporter, had disappeared from the Beer Barn.

"Maybe she got a better offer."

"Maybe, but here's her car by the Camellia Diner, and her cell phone seems to be ringing in the trunk. I don't like this!"

In two minutes she saw the Coffee County Sheriff's Department sedan cruise around from the other side of the courthouse. Files slowly emerged, eyes tired, staring at the Ford Focus.

"What'd you touch?"

"The hood. It felt cold."

"Doors?"

"Driver's-side handle—I pulled it. Locked."

Files peered into the driver's side.

"She's about my height," Alice offered. "But look where the seat is."

He nodded.

"And . . ." She dialed Rose's number again. In the morning quiet they heard a faint ring.

"The trunk," said Files.

Then they heard a muffled thump.

Files pulled something from his pocket, busied himself at the driver's side, unlocked the door. With his key ring he poked the trunk-lid button.

The trunk lid rose gently. Alice followed Files to the rear of the car. Rose lay on her side, trying to turn her head back to look at them, intelligent eyes glazed, mouth covered with duct tape, arms and wrists and ankles and legs taped and then taped to the metal supports inside the trunk. Dried blood plastered down the hair at her left temple and was smeared over her ear and neck.

"Oh, God!" said Alice.

"Mmph!" said Rose.

"Don't touch that lid!" said Files to Alice. "Hands down." And to Rose, "It's okay, it's okay. Hang on one minute! We'll get you out." He called for backup, an ambulance and a crime scene team. He cut the tape attaching Rose's body to the trunk's interior and lifted her gently to a sitting position. Then he carefully removed the duct tape from Rose's mouth.

Rose's face turned very pale. "I think I'm gonna throw up."

"Don't. Just sit there for a minute. You're probably concussed."

"Okay."

Alice closed her eyes and took three deep breaths. Files looked over at her. "Come on, you know scalp wounds bleed like a stuck pig," he said.

Alice took another deep breath. Then she looked again at Rose. "Hey."

"What?" said Files."

"Last night her computer was in that leather bag." The bag, still across Rose's shoulder and body, lay limp, empty. "A little laptop."

"But she still has her phone." Files noted.

Rose reached for the pocket she'd been sitting on. "It's in my back pocket."

"Who hit you?"

"I didn't see who it was. I was to meet them—him—here at the Camellia Diner, in the parking lot. When I got out of the car, someone hit me. Then I don't remember anything."

"Tall person? Short?"

"My impression was there was someone big behind me. I didn't see him. It was a him, though, I'm pretty sure. I remember before he hit me that he smelled like that Old Spice bodywash stuff."

"Any other cars here in the parking lot?"

"I don't remember. I don't remember. Oh—I got out of my car to walk around to the front of the diner in case I had mixed up the directions. Because there was no one back here."

"I'm thinking that's why the driver's seat is pushed back," said Files. "Someone searched inside the car. I'm puzzled why someone would work so hard to get her computer, but not take her phone, and leave her alive?"

Investigative reporter, thought Alice. Someone wanted her work.

The Coffee County ambulance, flashing lights but no siren, rolled up. EMTs helped lift Rose out of the trunk after checking for broken bones. "We're gonna take you over to the hospital, get you checked out," said the EMT. "Get that head looked at."

Rose gingerly touched her bloody hair, the dried blood on her cheek and ear and neck. "It's probably not a great look?"

"Not your best," said Alice, trying a small smile.

"I'll come see you in a bit, over at the ER," Files told Rose.

The ambulance, lights flashing, rolled off.

"What do you know about this, Alice?"

Alice told Files that Rose was investigating something that related to the Drinkman fortune but had been tightlipped about the topic. She'd left the Beer Barn to pick up a document, saying she'd be back in a few minutes. Then—radio silence.

Alice promised Files she'd be at the office or reachable on cell. She walked back to her truck, by the courthouse square. A little deep breathing, that's what she needed. The sun was now above the trees, lighting up the silent bronze statue of an anonymous veteran, ever on guard by the steps to the Coffee County Courthouse. Her favorite live oaks, solid, ancient, sent their generous horizontal branches across the courthouse lawn. The live oaks had kept their glossy dark leaves all winter, then suddenly dropped them in a tearing hurry, rushing to replace them with pale new growth and a flurry of gold catkins, now littering the sidewalks. Alice normally drank in each minute of the too-swift Texas spring, reveled in the cool scent of each narcissus, the latent power of each tightly furled bud on the bold iris stems, and of course the ridiculous charm of the bluebonnets. A patch of late bluebonnets still ran riot around the feet of the bronze veteran. But now all was awry. Again she saw Rose Rayburn, taped into the trunk.

She beat down the black anxiety shapes. Grumbling, they sank back but remained crouched, ready to spring. Get a grip, Alice!

She drove the short block to her office, marched up the entry steps and stalked inside. Silla stuck her head into the hallway, red ponytail swinging, and stared at Alice's yoga clothes. "We going casual Thursdays now? Really casual?"

"Never made it to yoga. That Rose Rayburn got herself conked on the head and left all duct-taped in her trunk. At the Camellia Diner!"

"You're kidding!"

Alice shook her head, thinking of the blood on Rose's hair.

"Because there's a big envelope from her on your desk. It was at the post office this morning. Also, we got an email that your retainer for the Navarro matter arrived. And here"—she pushed a sheet of paper at Alice—"here's your invitation to the Navarro fundraiser at La Rotonda today. You'll have to change and leave here pretty quickly if you're supposed to meet Carey Norville first."

Fortified with coffee, Alice sat, back to the wall, at her antique partner's desk. A large manila envelope, thoroughly taped shut, lay on the desk. She could work on the Beer Barn mini-brewery plans, or the easement for the ranch sale . . . Curiosity abounding, Alice picked up the manila envelope. She grabbed a sterling paper knife, gift from a favorite courtly older client, and ceremoniously waved it in the air before slitting open the top of the envelope. She pulled out a handwritten note and a smaller brown envelope, ostentatiously sealed, metal clasp folded shut, envelope flap glued down, the entire envelope taped thoroughly. The note, on heavy cream cardstock, read: "Alice, now that you're on board. Let the fun and games begin!" Signed: "Rose." Taking up the knife again, Alice opened the other end of the inner envelope, bypassing the clasp, tape, and glue. "Let the games begin," she muttered.

Chapter Four

The Slow Reveal

Rose Rayburn had sent Alice a ten-page single-spaced printout of her notes on the death of Alex Drinkman and subsequent history, with phone numbers, notes of phone calls and interviews, and, stapled separately, copies of ancient newspaper articles and probate records. Her handwritten notes decorated both. Alice had Silla make a working set for herself and copies for Mr. Navarro and for Bryce (though she wondered if Rose had already sent him a set). She put the originals back into the envelope and locked them in the safe. Alice also asked Silla to scan a copy into her computer. She leaned back in her chair and stared at Rose's marginal annotations, the exclamations, the notes to self: "Back-check this," "Also check Bexar County," "Texas State Historical Assn?" "Blue Pool?" and last, "Golf course?"

Alice had an hour before heading to the fundraiser to read what Rose had sent. First page: a printout listing new recruits into the new US Air Service. And there he was, Alexander Drinkman, shown as enlisted June 1917. That was shortly after news of the Zimmermann telegram enraged Texans and pushed President Wilson into declaring war. Alice, curious one afternoon about why two great-uncles, both just graduated from Austin College, chose to leave Texas to fight and die in France, had recently discovered the astonishing saga of the Zimmermann telegram. On the first day of World War I, the British had cut Germany's transatlantic cables, so that German messages had to travel by wireless. In early 1917 the British had intercepted and decoded a cable which Arthur Zimmermann, the German foreign minister, sent via the German ambassador in Washington to the president of Mexico. Germany proposed an alliance, including "an understanding on our part that Mexico is to reconquer the lost territory in Texas, New Mexico and Arizona." After reading that saga, Alice was convinced that the prospect that Mexico, with German help, might reconquer "lost territory in Texas" was what sent her great-uncles racing to join up. And she could imagine similar discussion occurring around the Drinkman dinner table, before Alex signed up to fly with what later became the new Air Service. And if there had been no Zimmermann telegram? She'd wondered about that, staring at the faces of her great-uncles among the photographs in the online alumni page titled "Fallen War Heroes: World War I."

Next in the stack were microfiche copies, black around the edges, from the Medina County probate court. Alice read carefully, slowly, looking at a will dated June 1914, written in the same clear strong hand that had signed it: Alastair Drinkman. So the dad's will must have been filed for probate—when? She peered at the notation. Was it August 1919? Part of the microfiche was so dark she could only guess at the date. Witnesses: Dr. A. B. Cleburne. Mrs. A. B. Cleburne. She mentally tsk-tsked over one paragraph of Mr. Drinkman's bequests:

> I bequeath to Ella Kendrick Drinkman, my wife, during her lifetime and for her use, one-third of the income from my real property holdings. However, should one or both of my beloved children Alex and Bonnie predecease me without marriage or lawful heirs, then I direct that such child's share of those real property holdings go in fee instead to Ella Kendrick Drinkman and her heirs.

Alice hoped Mr. Drinkman had drafted that himself, and that no professional had had a hand in it. But lord, figuring out decades later what was community property and what was not, what separate real property Alastair Drinkman brought to the marriage, what Ella Drinkman would have been entitled to and what she wouldn't, would be an accounting nightmare and a legal war of attrition. Assuming any heir tried at this date to challenge what the other heirs had gotten.

Mr. Drinkman had also been pretty generous:

> I bequeath to my late wife Adeline's sister Adecia fifty (50) of my silver eight-Reales Mexican coins in gratitude for her selfless care for me and my children following Adeline's death.

> I bequeath to our foreman, Ron Freeman, the remaining ten (10) of my silver eight-Reales Mexican coins in gratitude for his work.

I further bequeath to the Presbyterian Church of Madrone, Texas, my two city lots at the corner of Center Street and the San Antonio Road adjacent to the church.

Next: a microfiche of a 1917 newspaper clipping describing the departure of the aero squadron pilots from San Antonio to the Great War. Alice pictured dogs barking, flags fluttering, the crowd waving, smiling, crying, and the soldiers, excited, nervy, waving back from the train windows until the whistle blew, and off they went, heading east toward a troopship that would carry them straight into danger. Alice wondered how many of those pilots were still alive in November 1918 to hear the news of the Armistice.

Next page: another clipping, April 1919. Dry account: Capt. A. Drinkman was shot at Madrone Creek late on April 19, 1919. He was found by R. Freeman, the foreman at the Drinkman Ranch: "There was about six inches of water flowing over the low-water crossing. When I started across, I saw a motorcycle on its side in the shallower water downstream, just off the crossing, and recognized the name on the saddlebag. Then I saw a body on the sandbar further downstream, and I went to see if I could help." The report stated that Drinkman said only "Tell Susana" before he died in the foreman's arms. The foreman said it looked like Drinkman was shot in the stomach, with flesh wounds in his right arm and leg. "Drinkman was the only son of A. Drinkman and his deceased wife, Adeline Drinkman, and served as a pilot in France and Germany."

Alice imagined the motorcycle, swerving, skidding off the low-water crossing into the rock-strewn waters of the creek after the sudden shot, the stricken rider somehow crawling to a sandbar. Someone lay in wait for him, she thought. Someone lay behind the brush or trees on the opposite bank and carefully sighted and shot him at his most vulnerable moment, chest and abdomen exposed, just as he came down the creek bank, shifted into low gear and throttled down to guide the motorcycle across the low-water crossing. The rider was headed west, headed home, not expecting trouble. Alice imagined the late sun sharp in his eyes, so he couldn't see the light glinting off someone's rifle. Wonder what kind? After the Civil War, then Reconstruction, then the Spanish-American War, and the end of World War I, who knew how many rifles stood in gun cabinets in that part of Texas.

Then a printout from Texas Cemeteries Online, including a photograph of the Drinkman cemetery plot in Madrone, at the Madrone Presbyterian Church.

Next, a blurred microfiche copy of a deed, transferring a Medina County parcel from Bonnie Drinkman Walters to Ella Kendrick Drinkman. Was the date 1982?

And another deed, also 1982, from Ella Kendrick Drinkman to Bonnie Drinkman Walters.

Finally, looking very contemporary after the microfiche copies, came court pleadings in a lawsuit filed in 1986. Adele Collins had filed a petition as executor of the estate of her mother, Bonnie, against the heirs of Ella Kendrick Drinkman, including Willy Drinkman's son—Will Drinkman, head of the Drinkman Foundation—and Will's son, Warren Drinkman. Fascinated, Alice scanned the claims with their dry, unkind legalese: ". . . did fraudulently conceal the value of the transferred rights and property . . . breached a fiduciary duty of full disclosure to petitioner . . . knowingly concealed facts material to the petitioner's decision to sell the transferred rights and property."

Ouch. That would hurt your feelings. She read further. Adele Collins contended the Drinkmans knew but had failed to tell her mother that oil had been discovered immediately adjacent to the parcel they had persuaded her to trade to them, in exchange for a larger parcel further from the new Taylor-Ina oil play in Medina County. What had happened to the case? Alice couldn't find a record of judgment in the stapled copies. Maybe the litigation was still languishing in Medina County District Court.

Next-to-last page: huh. Photograph of a glamorous Fiesta Week ball in San Antonio, with Will Drinkman and his son, Warren, the men in tuxes. Warren looked like a blurred copy of his father. Both had broad shoulders, a high narrow forehead, big eyes. But Will Drinkman, unlike Warren, looked dangerous. She frowned. At some point she'd have to deal with Will Drinkman.

Last page: classified legal notices of state contracts out for bid. One, just one, bore a faint checkmark in the corner: "State of Texas Detention Facility Supplies." What did that have to do with the Navarro letter? Meant nothing to her. And whose checkmark? Rose's? Alice squinted up and down the classified columns—no other marks. She shook her head. Maybe included by accident.

Phone call. "Alice? Alice, I heard about Rose." Bryce's voice shook. "You don't think my sending that letter to Sandro caused— did—something to—to—God, that poor woman."

She stood by the desk, cradling the phone, considering. A butterfly's wing. Butterfly effect. Chaos theory. Who knew what the letter had caused? But he was human and horrified. "I wouldn't think so. I don't know what happened to her. Or who was involved, or why. Letting Alex Drinkman's heirs have a copy of that letter seems right, not wrong."

She stared out the front window of her office. A purple iris trembled in the April wind. "But we need to talk."

"Okay. Would you mind coming over here? I've got a customer coming by."

Silla stuck her head in, raised her eyebrows at Alice's yoga clothes, and pointed at her watch.

"Okay. I'm going to change and stop by Bryce's for a second. Silla, could you look at the Coffee County property records and see what you can find about Alex's deed for Blue Pool? Assuming there was one."

"Sure."

Ready for the Navarro fundraiser, Alice headed out. Two minutes later she and Bryce stared at each other across Bryce's kitchen table. Alice took a deep breath.

"Bryce, two things. First, you have to tell me everything you know. Don't hold back. I know you like to have your secrets—we all do—"

"But Alice . . ."

"Hey, I've seen you do the slow reveal. With your sales pitch, with your great stories. One little detail at a time—plop! Into the pool it falls, the ripples widening, then quieting. Then—plop! Another detail. But this time, no slow reveal. You've got to tell me what you've learned. Or guessed. Or surmised."

"Okay. You sound like Files. I told him everything too." He blinked. "I think."

"Well, you didn't tell me you'd contacted Carey Norville."

"I just told him you were the best, that you could get things done."

"I appreciate that, but you also said you wanted me to defend your ownership of the letter. I've said I'll help the Navarros unless there's a conflict with you, so you need to tell me what you want and what you know. I mean, this could turn out a way we don't want. What if the Drinkmans prove the letter was stolen?"

"But the aunt's note on the envelope says Mr. Drinkman gave it to her, told her to take it!"

"She could have misheard. Or she could have lied, though I don't know why. Even if she had a right to the letter, did the Drinkmans steal her nightstand? Or commit an act of conversion by refusing to deliver it when asked? Or instead did she abandon it? Waive her rights? Drive away and leave it at the Drinkman ranch? And it's not just the letter; it's everything in the oiled-silk packet. It will be much better for us to have the original letter and have control of the items to be sampled than to have to fight for access to them, or be accused of disclosing private information."

"You mean, that they might really have a right to the nightstand? But I paid for it!"

"They'd probably have to prove it was stolen. Your sales documents look fine. But I'd be remiss not to tell you this might not come out the way you want. If you don't think you can stay friends with me when I'm telling you hard stuff, things you don't like, or if this goes south on us, tell me now. The Navarros want me to help them, as you suggested, but I'll be asking them to waive conflicts with you."

"No problem. We're in it together." He nodded at her, smiled a lopsided smile. "Even if you're telling me what I don't want to hear. Friends forever."

Damn. Well, it was true. She had adored Bryce since their first real conversation, about his partner, Cassie. "Okay."

A voice trilled from the front of the store. "Bryce? Yoo-hoo!" Bryce, making an apologetic face at Alice, headed out of the kitchen. Alice slipped past Bryce and his customer, already in deep enthusiastic conversation before a handsome pecan-wood pie safe, and started for San Marcos.

C h a p t e r   F i v e

Put a Spoke in Their Wheels

Alice was ushered immediately into Carey Norville's office at Sandro Navarro's campaign headquarters in San Marcos. Navarro's district, carefully gerrymandered by the Texas legislature, stretched from the outskirts of Austin west to Hays County and next-door Coffee County, then south, including part of San Antonio, and nearly to the Mexican border. Of necessity he had offices in Austin, San Antonio, Pearsall, and this one in a strip center near the courthouse in San Marcos, where political consultant Carey Norville was running his hands through his silver hair, leaving it stuck in tufts above the glasses perched on his head.

"You are good to come so soon. Sandro can meet you in a few minutes. You'll have to wait to meet his dad, Mr. Navarro, but he'll be looking for you at the fundraiser at La Rotonda."

"What's he like, Mr. Navarro?"

His eyes twinkled. "He made me feel like standing up straighter, the first time I met him."

"Ah."

"He's a smart guy. Grew up in west San Antonio. I've never heard him discuss it, but the word is he had quite a war record, as a fighter pilot in the Pacific. He used the GI Bill to finish college with a degree in actuarial science and went to work for USAA, the big insurance company here. He stayed forty years. Married his high school sweetie, who was a lovely woman. She died about fifteen years ago. Sandro was their only child."

Well, that makes it cleaner, thought Alice. Always unbecoming to have siblings disagree on the legal strategy. "Tell me about Sandro and his family."

"Sandro's wife, Ninfa, died just three years ago. Long battle with ovarian cancer. They have two kids—neither of them shrinking violets, either."

Alice raised her eyebrows.

"Isabella's twenty-five. Very smart. She's finishing her PhD in public health at Yale now, after working at some public health clinics out in New Mexico. She's pretty doctrinaire sometimes"—he grinned—"you know what I mean. It's great to be young, right? But she's very smart, very serious." He fingered his tie. "Pretty outspoken, wants to save the world. Right now."

Alice nodded. So hard, being young, and painfully learning how slow the world was to decide it wanted to be saved.

"And then there's Tomás. A little more problematic, but he's got a good heart, I think. I hope."

"Problematic?"

"You'll meet him. Very handsome. Great smile. Drives too fast. Spends too much money—Sandro had to confiscate his credit cards. Sandro says he has no concept of frugality. He's also all over Facebook, Instagram, Twitter, wherever. He even makes the grown-up society pages, since he somehow gets invited to everything. I'd say he's a little immature, a little unwilling to take responsibility. And a little impulsive."

He pushed over a clipping from the society pages of the San Antonio Express-News, pointing to an extraordinarily handsome young man, smiling in his tux, framed by two glowing young women, each holding champagne flutes with one hand and clutching the young man's arm with another.

"So your job includes keeping him out of trouble?"

He blew out his breath. "I'd say instead, keeping the trouble out of the papers. He's a good kid, ultimately. I think. I hope. His dad keeps him on a short string. Otherwise Tomás would be driving lord knows what, something even faster and pricier than his little Beemer."

"School?"

"If we can keep him in there, he's at Trinity, down in San Antonio. From time to time he says he wants to run for office. We'll see. Maybe I'll be long gone by then."

"And Sandro? You don't think he faces serious opposition this fall?"

"The guy with the most money—from the Drinkmans, by the way—is Bobby Scanlon. But some little birds are telling me Bobby has problems. Serious problems. He's a lawyer, you know. He was referring clients to a buddy who's a stockbroker without telling the clients about his secret contract with the broker to get kickbacks. That hasn't hit the papers yet. But it will. Also he was involved in getting clients some shaky contracts with state agencies. I hear the legislature may be planning to take a hard look at those. Who knows, the attorney general might get involved. So, my prediction is that Scanlon will be toast well before November."

"And what's your long-term vision for Sandro?" Alice seized this opportunity to hear a guy with forty years of political experience assess his candidate. "How do you see his chances if he runs for president?"

Norville didn't answer for a moment, then apparently decided this was a serious question. "Right now, I'd say he could win. I'm not saying it wouldn't be close. But look—he's a widower. That's got appeal to the public—and to a consultant like me, it means no wife issues. Nice blank canvas to work with. And a sympathy vote. The truth is, Ninfa was a wonderful wife and mother, fought the good fight but lost to cancer, and he's still single. He doesn't do the playboy thing; he's very careful, always. Again, that's restful to a consultant. And he's got the kids in a pretty good place." He thought for a moment, shrugged. "I dunno, maybe getting married wouldn't be so bad for him. Might be tough for a new wife, unless she's used to politics. Still, in terms of the election, Sandro's a bright, honest, hardworking widower with two kids, in pretty good shape. That's pretty easy duty for a consultant. But if you are really asking seriously?" He looked at her again.

"I am," said Alice, wondering where this would go.

"Seriously, this is a huge moment for our country, if we could get him elected. I think he's got the chops for it all—foreign policy, military—you know he was stationed in Kosovo back in 2001? Just before he ran the first time."

"So you're serious about him. This guy."

"I am. Funny word, serious. This may be my last gig, Alice, and I intend it to be a good one. If I could get this guy elected—well, all the other stuff you have to do as a consultant, and I'm not saying what it is, it would all have been worth it. And I think my mama would be proud of me." Sideways grin in the lined face.

Interesting.

He went on, lines of determination around his mouth. "Look,

Alice. I'm not married. I have no children. So maybe there's no need for me to care about the world. But I still do. I've seen a lot of politicians come and go. This one is different. He's—he's essentially good. That sunny face you see? The man is about pursuing good. We need him, Alice. And miraculously, he is probably electable. So that's my dream, that's why I hang on. If we can win this next election, it's no pipe dream to say he can run for president." He patted his head, looking for his glasses, folded them, stuck them in a pocket. "First Mexican-American president. Let's get it done. Then I'll die happy." He looked at his watch. "Sandro should be in the conference room. Let's go."

Down the hall they went, past scuttling staffers, arguing at computers, breathlessly talking on phone banks, saying thank you, would you, could you, thank you. Norville knocked at a closed door and, without waiting, entered. "Sandro, meet Alice Greer," he said. "Alice, I'll see you later." He smiled and left.

Alice's impression of Sandro was of warmth. Warm hand, warm face, warm brown eyes. A staffer brought them coffee.

"I enjoyed meeting Carey Norville," Alice said. "When you've read about someone for several decades!"

Sandro nodded agreement. "You don't know how lucky I am. I fought to get him. He knows everyone. Has such credibility. And it's not just longevity. People respect Carey Norville. I've seen it over and over. The higher-ups I need info from, say on defense issues—well, it's always a time crunch getting to talk to the right person at the Pentagon, or State Department. But they respond to his calls, they respect him. So it's much easier for me as a mere congressman, especially a minority congressman, to get a briefing when Carey's making the contacts. And that's not all. If you're in the House, you're constantly having to raise money. Carey's got serious dollar value. He knows the contributors, especially in Texas—he's got deep roots here." He stared out the window. "I think I would have lost without him, when I first ran for the House. I wouldn't think—wouldn't even consider—running for anything else if he wasn't on board."

Alice changed the subject. "I know you're heading to your fundraiser shortly. I want to talk to you, and your dad, too, about this letter. Your dad's the proper party to apply for heirship. What does he think about the prospect? It could be a very hard fight, as I expect you know. Right off the bat, I'm worried about the statute of limitations." She knew that Sandro, a fellow lawyer, would understand.

"Yes. After *Kenedy*, right? But isn't the legislature changing that somehow?"

"Right. The bill says a proceeding to declare heirship of a decedent may be brought any time, but this provision only applies where the decedent dies after the bill's effective date. Before the effective date, the old law applies. Whatever that may be."

"Well, that makes it interesting," said Sandro. "Also, the opposition will be very tough. I've only met Will Drinkman once. Do you know him? The current head of the Drinkman Foundation? Not a cozy guy. He's pushing eighty at least, but the word is he still runs a tight ship, still keeps his finger in all things Drinkman. I heard recently that now he's supposedly letting his son, Warren, run some of the money in a separate division, and Warren is supposedly desperate to try to show his daddy he too can make deals, but I also heard Will Drinkman still questions Warren's capability. And Will really enjoys having a great deal of money. Or, perhaps, all the power that having a great deal of money gives him. He won't be interested in sharing either one—money or power. So if he's running the show—watch out."

"We'll see. How do you feel about Alex Drinkman's letter?"

"Amazed. Amazed, to sit here and think that he's my grandfather! That he loved poetry and loved Susana Navarro, my grandmother! A man I never knew. Weird feeling." His brow furrowed. "But I'm also angry about it."

Alice cocked her head.

"Not the letter itself, but what followed. I'm angry that all that love went unrecognized. Disregarded. After that letter arrived, did anyone contact my grandmother when Alex Drinkman was found dead in the creek?"

"I wonder that too. There's a lot we don't know."

"I've always been so proud of my grandmother, my Tejano heritage, the Navarro name. The Navarros have been in this part of Texas since about 1740. It's confusing now to think about having to be proud of an Anglo forebear. But . . ." He held up his hands, looked at his palms. "It sounds like I may have his DNA, don't I? Didn't even know it, but his chromosomes . . . and hers . . . Alex Drinkman knew 'little Alejandro' was illegitimate and so he planned not only to marry Susana but adopt him so there would be no doubt about his status?"

"I think so," said Alice. "Belt and suspenders? Back then, here and some other places, illegitimate children couldn't inherit from the biological father unless the parents later married. It wasn't until 1977 that the Supreme Court said it was unconstitutional to discriminate against illegitimate children. But states can still make an illegitimate child jump through hoops to inherit from the biological father, so long as the hoops support a permissible state interest."

Sandro nodded.

"If, and it's a big if, we were to win, what would you or your family do with more money? Would you still run for office?" Alice asked.

"Of course. Of course I would. And what I'd do with more money—well, that depends if there's enough money to do what I would like to do." He took a deep breath. "Buy the Drinkmans' damn chain of radio stations. Or set up my own."

"Interesting thought."

"They broadcast their paranoid negative talk shows all over my district. I'd like to buy 'em out. Change the programming. Send out something positive, something to build us up, not tear everyone down. Get the truth out. And make room for debate, so people could get three hundred sixty degrees of information and form their own opinions." He smiled at the surprise on Alice's face. "Plus, those stations make a bundle from ads."

The conference room door burst open and a slim handsome black-haired boy was halfway to Sandro before he checked, glancing at Alice.

"Tomás!" said Sandro. "You could try knocking!" He smiled a small smile. "Alice, please meet my son, Tomás."

The boy smiled, shook Alice's hand, looked back at Sandro. "Um, Dad, when you get a minute—"

Sandro nodded. "I'll come find you." Tomás hesitated, then, with Sandro's eyes on him, nodded and left.

"Maybe the other thing I'd do is pay off Tomás's credit cards. You have kids?"

Alice nodded. "Always exciting." She waited a beat, then began again. "My secretary called me from the Coffee County Courthouse while I was driving down here. She says she found a deed showing Alex Drinkman as record owner of a small ranch that's partly in Coffee County, and the legal description says it includes 'a spring-fed pool commonly called the Blue Pool.' I'll be amazed if it is still in his name; surely someone filed an affidavit of heirship or some other document. But she's checking."

The congressman lifted his chin, cocked his head. "I'd heard of the Blue Pool before I read the letter. And you know what? I would like the Blue Pool. Add that to your list." He smiled.

"The place where Alex Drinkman wanted to settle with your grandmother."

"Yes." He shook his head, mouth turned down. "You ever read the San Marcos paper?"

"Occasionally."

"I saw an article last week saying that some Drinkman outfit has applied for a groundwater permit to send water from the Blue Pool Ranch to a proposed big new resort outside Coffee County. This outfit wants to drill wells at the ranch and pipe water across miles of hill country to sprinkle on golf courses. Golf courses! Know what that will do to the Blue Pool?"

Alice nodded. The limestone aquifers were so permeable, and could drop so quickly, that springs that flowed furiously after big rains had recharged them could go silent when the water drained away. And the Blue Pool could shrink, dwindle, dry up.

"It'll dry up the Blue Pool. Instead of that magic spring, which drew Native Americans for thousands of years, and which drew the settlers for what it was, water in the wilderness—instead of that magic, reliable spring, the Drinkmans will be spilling its clear, clean, secret water onto golf courses and into condos and toilets and flushing it all into some package treatment plant and back into some dry streambed. Blue Pool will go dry. Be a mudhole. Shrink to an insignificant puddle. Kill the turtles, invertebrates, fish."

"Sounds like you don't think the groundwater district will impose some permit limits to protect the spring," said Alice.

"Oh, it could. But you know it won't. I'll bet the Drinkmans made sure when the little groundwater district was created that it wouldn't have much power. The district is seriously outgunned."

Alice nodded. She knew many groundwater districts were given very limited powers when created in the twentieth century by their own specific legislation. Most were notoriously underfunded when it came to carrying out the complex statutory assignment handed to them in the twenty-first century: to dole out pumping limits on permits so that their aquifers would not be permanently damaged and future descendants could still thrive. But underfunded districts in the face of the major droughts of the twenty-first century were, as the congressman said, outgunned. Still, she also hadn't expected such passion over invertebrates from an elected official.

Navarro was still on a roll. "The Drinkmans will pepper that groundwater district board with studies. They'll have geologists prancing around with PowerPoints and charts. The district will be too scared to put serious brakes on the permit." He shook his head. "But what really gets me is the Drinkmans being so heartless as to rape the Blue Pool and throw it away, just like that! To trade that unique spring for a golf course! It's such arrogance—to play God, to take away some beautiful piece of nature just because you can. Makes me sick."

Whew. Alice blinked.

He stood up. "That would be worth going after, saving the Blue Pool. I'm happy to mess with the Drinkmans on policy issues any day. Yeah, I get warmed up over that. I'll smile at them and challenge their selfish, shortsighted hate-mongering. But my gut? My gut wants the Blue Pool. So if I'm Alex Drinkman's grand-boy, I'm willing to fight for the Blue Pool."

"We'll need to think through the steps, depending on what the property records show. We'll have to figure out whether it's wise to file an application for heirship, or perhaps an action to recover real property. It all depends on the facts. We'd probably need to figure out local counsel who could help us in certain jurisdictions. You have some ideas on that?"

"We'd have some ideas."

"And—maybe intervene in the Blue Pool permit proceeding?"

He raised his eyebrows, grunted appreciatively. "I like it. Great suggestion. That'll put a spoke in their wheels."

"Maybe. We don't want to miss a deadline, though. We'll want to check the district procedures."

"Oh, right."

Alice looked back at him, considering. "What would you do with the Blue Pool?"

He nodded. "That's a big issue too. What would I do? Make it into my own private luxury enclave? Or a nature preserve? Guess it could be ruined if it was public with no controls, with thousands of swimmers a day, trash, footprints, cars, erosion. But if we fight for it—and get it—I don't want to be selfish. And yet we all know the Hill Country can't support the same development as the flatlands. It'll be ruined if we cover it with houses and concrete and fast food. What a conundrum."

Alice sometimes felt guilty, as a privileged person in the Hill Country, wanting tourists to come, but only in limited quantities. She would allow them to stay at a beautiful B&B, admire the wild animals, native plants, and limited parking—and then go home.

"'Pave paradise,' right?" he sighed.

"You'll figure out some creative solution. Rather, your dad will. It would be his decision, of course. He might come up with a conservation easement."

"You do that, don't you? Conservation easements?"

"Yes." Alice had worked to protect cave art, artesian springs, old architectural and archeological sites. Some of her clients cared deeply about such things.

He glanced behind Alice toward the door, then, smile in place, asked if there was anything else he could help with. A staffer, without knocking, was smiling around the corner of the door behind Alice. "The mayor's here. Then it's time to leave for La Rotonda, in ten minutes."

"Got to go, then. But thank you for coming." Navarro extended a warm hand to Alice.

"Keep yourself safe," she said to him.

He stopped shaking her hand, just held it. "Ah. I hadn't thought of that."

"Well, you should."

"I guess Rose Rayburn should have too?"

"You heard about that?" Alice wondered how.

He didn't volunteer. "And you found her?"

"Saw her car and thought it was strange for it to be where it was." And isn't it strange for you to know about her already, Sandro, unless . . . Then she thought of something he needed to know. "There's been another break-in in Coffee Creek already, at your friend Bryce's shop, by folks looking for the letter, we think. They looked . . . serious."

"Professional, maybe?"

She nodded.

Navarro raised his eyebrows, exhaled, ran a finger around the inside of his collar. "Life in the fast lane."

"So, take good care." Alice moved toward the door.

Navarro raised a hand. "I'd like you to head up the legal effort here. I know you may need to work this out with Bryce—"

"Yes."

"—but can you help us too? Work together?"

"Yes, assuming we understand any conflicts and get them resolved. And we may want to put an agreement in place to protect our communications," said Alice.

Sandro Navarro was a lawyer too. He understood joint defense agreements and limits on representation. But she'd be firm about her role.

C h a p t e r   S i x

Flying Past

Alice loved La Rotonda, the century-old hotel on the edge of San Marcos where the congressman and mayor were combining a fundraiser with the announcement of a new transportation grant for San Marcos. A smiling doorman held open the giant, deeply carved wooden doors from Mexico, waving Alice into the lobby with its dark polished Saltillo tiles, inset with bright Talavera tiles. People already were milling around the lobby greeting each other, or talking in little groups. To her left a smiling pudgy silver-haired man in ostrich cowboy boots and expensive tailoring was holding forth to a well-dressed couple. "Got my start here, working as a bellboy in high school. Met every politician in town." He had an engaging smile, a dimple on one cheek.

"And now you're here, checking out the opposition." All three laughed. Pudgy Man was sporting the Texas lobbyist uniform, wasn't he? She watched him walk over to speak to Tomás Navarro, just walking back from the bar with two glasses of wine and a bright-eyed blonde.

Alice stood for a moment, watching Tomás listen intently to Pudgy Man, then dodged through the crowd toward La Rotonda's famous hand-carved wooden bar. Since 1912 it had helped customers discover they'd gained some swagger. They could slide onto a cowhide-covered barstool, or rest a boot on the brass rail, all the while admiring themselves in the twelve-foot antique mirror with its ornate silver frame. Down the hall past the bar was the circular ballroom where Sandro and the mayor were scheduled to speak. Alice especially loved the ballroom, where she'd danced with Jordie at a friend's fairy-tale wedding reception long ago. She remembered twirling across the romantic room, lit by enormous Mexican pierced-tin wall sconces that sent sparkles of light across frescoed walls, covered with vividly painted birds and jungle foliage, all beneath a high domed ceiling topped by a cupola. Just below the dome, a columned gallery circled the wall, giving access to the upstairs rooms. A small musician's balcony of graceful black wrought iron hung on one wall, accessed from the gallery. Alice remembered mariachi players up there in huge sombreros and blue uniforms sparkling with silver braid—irresistible music, gleaming cornets, the huge guitar.

But now no Jordie, no dancing—instead, money and politics. Alice could just hear Sandro Navarro's laughing voice, echoing down the wide hall that led into the ballroom: perfect pitch, perfect timing.

"Restroom?" she asked the bartender.

"To your right, but watch out, the light bulb just went out in the hallway."

Alice dodged down a short dark hallway discreetly perpendicular to the bar, and slipped into the women's restroom. She dabbed on lipstick and peered into the mirror. Acceptable . . . not really made-up though, compared to the glossy ladies milling around outside. Alice always felt she'd never grasped the finer points of decorating her face. Oh well.

Exiting into the dark hallway she stopped, surprised. At the far end of the bar stood Carey Norville, one foot on the bar rail, his side to her. Talking urgently to him, and facing her, stood Pudgy Man. Both men checked the mirror above the bar for a long moment, then returned to their conversation. Why wasn't Norville in the ballroom tending to his candidate? The two men again looked around, then leaned toward each other. Alice stood still. "Man your age, ought to think about long-term security," said Pudgy Man. He smiled at Norville, the dimple showing. "Consider my proposition."

Norville put his glass down, started toward the hall leading to the ballroom. Pudge elbowed up next to him. Alice shrank back in the darkness. Their voices were louder. "We'll see. By the way, you don't really think your boy Bobby Scanlon has a chance in hell of making it out of the primary in May, do you? Even with all that Drinkman campaign support? I'm hearing news may come out about some curious public contracts, involving interesting products and interesting agencies, and the possible 'conflicts of interest' involved . . ." Norville waggled his fingers, indicating quotation marks. "Might be of interest to our voting public, wouldn't you agree, if someone's engaged in 'milking the public'?"

"Be very unwise for anyone to air any such irresponsible allegations," hissed Pudgy Man. No dimple in sight. "Very unwise. You with me?"

"Be very unwise for your boy to challenge mine. Very unwise."

"Maybe it's all right for you, you've got some mailbox money. Some of us have to make a living on our own. You know?"

Alice stared, fascinated. To her, "mailbox money" often meant oil and gas royalty checks from mineral interests in parcels hither and yon across Texas. Thousands of Texans got them. She guessed Pudgy Man had missed out.

Norville smiled at Pudgy Man and turned toward the ballroom. "Coming?"

Pudgy Man followed, two steps, then stopped. He had red patches on his cheeks. "We'll talk," he said. Alice shivered at his tone.

"Always," said Norville, and walked away. Pudgy Man stood for a moment, then adjusted his belt and walked slowly back to the bar.

Alice waited ten seconds and then walked briskly around the corner. She caught up with Norville just inside the ballroom and greeted him.

"Who was that? He looked familiar."

"Who? Where?" Norville swiveled his eyes around, stared at her.

"Pudgy guy with silver hair and a nice suit and ostrich boots. He looked familiar but I can't place him."

"Oh. Kelly Cosgrove. Old political consultant, pretty far right. We're old rivals."

"You've known him a long time."

"Oh yeah. We've been on opposite sides of several battles, as we are now, with Scanlon. Old Kelly likes to try to pick my brain. Gotta watch him too, he's no dummy. I just wish he'd see the light. No luck yet, though. He's in bed with the Drinkmans. On retainer now, I'm thinking. He doesn't seem to have a political gig right now other than Scanlon, but he seems to be making some money."

Deftly done, thought Alice, but what were you really talking about with him?

Noise and people, perfume and laughter surrounded them as they edged into the crowded ballroom. Norville took her elbow. "I want you to be sure to meet Alejandro when he comes in. First, though, let's meet one of Sandro's big supporters. I'll bet she doesn't know yet that his dad may try to take part of the Drinkman fortune. Not sure yet whether or how that could impact her—maybe you'll tell me. She's Adele Collins, from Woodville. Her mother was Bonnie Drinkman Walters, Alex's sister. Based on that letter, Adele and Alejandro would be first cousins. Keep your powder dry, Ms. Greer, would be my thought, but you know best."

He beelined toward a group that opened to admit him and Alice, bringing them face to face with the very intelligent face, beautifully made-up, of a tall silver-haired woman wearing no jewels but her wedding rings, which were extraordinary. She kissed Norville on both cheeks.

"Carey. So good to see you."

"Now, ma'am, let me present Alice MacDonald Greer from Coffee Creek. She's a lawyer there and one of Sandro's supporters." The intelligent eyes took her in; the gracious hand was extended.

"I always wanted to go to law school," she said, holding Alice with her eyes. "I wish you'd come to Woodville for tea and tell me what it was like." Alice found herself agreeing to call.

Norville cocked his head toward the open space in the middle, where Sandro Navarro and the mayor stood elbow to elbow. Sandro was beginning the announcement. "This grant will help thousands of citizens in this district get to work sooner, and get home when there's still time to visit with their kids, and get home more safely." Cheers. "This grant will help this district and will help voters get to the polls next November!" More cheers. "It's uphill from here, but we're aiming for the top! *Arriba! Gracias!* Thank you!" Big cheers. Balloons went up. A "Navarro for President" banner was lowered from the rails of the little musician's balcony. On a big screen on another wall, the campaign video started rolling. Norville and Navarro were circulating, smiling, shaking hands, cementing relationships, soliciting contributions.

A tall man, now stooped, with a shock of white hair carefully brushed except for the errant cowlick at the crown of his head, stood against a wall near Alice, hands in his pockets, watching the room. He was elegant in a white shirt, bolo tie, blue blazer, gray slacks, beautifully polished old boots. Alice was drawn by the broad forehead, the leathery brown face the color of a mailman's pouch, and especially by his stillness, his calm watchfulness.

Suddenly Tomás, slim in his edgy black suit, dashed up. "Abuelo!" Alice heard. "Ooh, *muy papasito!*" He grinned, waving one hand at the old man's immaculate style, bowing to him. Then he glanced up, saw Alice. "Ms. Greer! Please come meet my grandfather!"

Alice extended her hand, stared into the old man's eyes. And she did find herself standing up straighter. "Glad to meet you, Miss Alice." His handshake was firm. "Hear we're going to ride the river together. Looking forward to a good ride."

"I'd like to meet with you. Do you have some time this week?"

"Tomorrow? Sunday? Seize the day! Especially at my age."

"Abuelo, they want us upstairs for the big photo op. My suggestion to use the balcony! Ready?" The old man smiled. Arm in arm the two started toward the far wall of the ballroom. Only then did Alice notice the old man had to swing one leg stiffly forward. Injury? Stroke? But no cane. Head high, the old man swung forward, arm in arm with his grandson.

The two Navarros joined a small knot of men heading for the stairway that led up toward the gallery. Alice saw Norville's white hair in the group. A reporter and photographer, slung with camera equipment, stopped next to Alice. They wore *San Antonio Express-News* identification tags. "We need to be right below the musician's balcony, if you want decent audio," the photographer told the reporter. The two bustled over to the area below the balcony and set up their equipment.

It occurred to Alice she could video the announcement herself, and send it to John and Ann, her precious children, far away in Edinburgh. She suspected they thought their widowed mother had no life. Well, she would show them. On the side of the ballroom opposite the musician's balcony she found the alternate staircase to the gallery, next to the hallway leading back to the bar and lobby, and darted up. Yes, perfect. The round gallery, with its arches looking down at the packed ballroom, felt suddenly quiet, removed from the hubbub below. To her left, pushing a three-foot-wide yellow wool dust mop, came a thin middle-aged Hispanic man in a La Rotonda jacket and hat. He smiled at her and nodded ("*Señora*") as he moved past, polishing the gleaming tile, the dust mop leaving behind a faint trace of lemon oil. She smiled back, wondering, as he passed, would he vote? Walking left to right on the opposite side of the gallery, an elderly thin man with a strong jaw disappeared behind the wall that held the doors to the musician's balcony and the second staircase leading down to the ballroom.

Holding her cell phone, she planted herself directly across from the little musician's balcony. It seemed to be several steps down from the gallery, like an opera box, with a door behind it. Now the door into the musician's balcony popped open. First one through was the mayor of San Marcos, beaming and waving at friends below. Next came Sandro Navarro, positioning himself in the center of the first row at the right side of his friend the mayor, his warm smile lighting up the balcony. On the tier behind Sandro stood Mr. Navarro, swaying just a bit. Alice saw him quietly slip his right arm into Tomás's left, then stand steady. And last to walk in, standing on the stairs to Tomás's right, and just at his level, was Carey Norville, a modest smile on his lips. Planning the future, Alice thought. Imagining the presidential race his boy could make. The crowd cheered. Alice saw the janitor stop pushing his dust mop around the far side of the gallery to her right, staring at the scene. He felt her eyes and waved at her and she saw him disappear and reappear after he passed the musician's balcony, heading off to her left. The mayor waved for quiet. She set her cell phone on video, lifted it to her eyes, and started filming. She admired Sandro's smile, and Mr. Navarro's white hair and straight shoulders in his navy blazer, and watched Norville, also in his navy blazer, leaning over and craning his neck to the right, surveying the crowd below with his shrewd eyes. He waved once at someone off to his right. Then Sandro began speaking. The crowd hushed, listening to the voice rise and fall, perhaps imagining how convincing it would sound on TV ads the coming fall; their money would be well spent. She saw the janitor's jacket again, across the gallery to her left, now pushing back toward the musician's balcony. Sandro was thanking a long list of people, smiling, encouraging, strong. The mayor grinned from ear to ear when Sandro reminded him how successful the transportation grant would be for San Marcos. Almost the mayor's turn to talk—Sandro's sunny face warmed the crowd and he turned toward the mayor. At that moment Norville jerked, lurched forward over the low rail, his left hand reaching for Sandro, his right grabbing at air. Sandro held the balcony rail with one hand and clutched wildly at Norville's blue blazer as it flew past, but he missed. Tomás's right arm was outstretched, his face a mask. One horrifying image—the body in the air—then a sickening thud. Carey Norville landed hard on the tile floor, scattering photographers and equipment everywhere. Sandro and the mayor stood frozen, mouths in wide *o*'s, both gripping the balcony rail.

Alice stood transfixed, breath stuck in her throat, staring at the melee below. Norville lay splayed on the Saltillo tiles, his eyes open, unseeing, blood slowly leaking in little rivulets from the back of his head, his neck at an odd angle. Two doctors had already pushed through the crowd to kneel by him. Multiple people were punching their phones, one shouting, "I've got EMS on the way!" A shocked circle stood around the mess of tripods, cameras, Norville, mouths agape or covered with trembling hands, eyes riveted on the scene before them.

Across the gallery people hurried forward, backward, some leaning over the gallery rail, some hustling toward the stairwells on either side. Sandro, the mayor, Alejandro, and Tomás still stood frozen in the musician's balcony. A blue-uniformed policeman opened the door and pulled out the mayor and Sandro, followed by the old man, impassive, and the grandson. Alice realized the phone was in her hands, still filming—what? The floor, now. She turned it off, sick at her stomach. Thirty feet to her left Kelly Cosgrove, whitefaced, mouth a little open, stood clutching the rail and staring down at Norville's body.

Downstairs a policeman plucked a handheld mike from a photographer's hand and asked for quiet. The crowd hushed. He said no one should leave; he explained that each person would need to provide name and contact information, and should let the police know of any detail, whether important or not. An interview table was being set up out in the lobby, he said. Each person should stop and leave the data needed before leaving the building. He asked if everyone understood.

In the resulting hush Alice heard a disembodied whisper at gallery level. "We even going to get paid for our time? Someone else got in first and screwed it up! And what's the fat man looking at?" She turned her head to the right. Fifty feet away stood two men part way around the gallery, staring across at Kelly Cosgrove—a dark-haired man, a blond man. Blue shirts, dark suits, ties. How could she possibly have heard them? The blond man's mouth moved and she again heard the whisper, "Light duty for sure. Let's slide out." They turned and headed back toward the musician's-balcony staircase. She stood, shocked. She had heard them as clearly as if they stood next to her.

Shouldn't she follow, see where they went? She dashed down the staircase just behind her, emerging in the ballroom. No sign of them. Was there a service entrance? Sure enough, on the far side she saw the swinging doors that must lead to the kitchen. Alice pushed through, and saw two dark coats just heading out the exit past the kitchen entry. She ran down the hall, stuck her head out the exit door. A dark Audi SUV was already pulling out, too far for her to see the license. Damn. Why weren't the police watching this exit? Just then a patrolman came out of the kitchen.

"You missed two guys," she told him, and described them.

"It's pretty chaotic around here," he said.

Sure the large elegant women's facilities off the ballroom would be packed, she headed for the dark hallway by the bar, hoping the little hidden restroom would be empty. No one was visible—but the acid smell of vomit burned her nostrils. She peeked under the closed stall door. Loafers. They looked like Rose's.

"Rose?" The sound of flushing. The door opened. Rose came out, looking apologetic, and splashed her face, rinsed her mouth at the sink. Her face was pale.

"Were you in there? When—when he fell? I didn't see you," Alice said.

Rose wiped her face with a paper towel. "I was there. Downstairs with everyone else."

"I was upstairs watching Sandro. Are you okay?"

"Just—made me sick, that's all."

"Who wouldn't be, after being bashed on the head? And now

seeing this?" But what was it, tugging at Alice's brain? The shadows under Rose's eyes, her pallor. "Are you—?"

Rose looked back.

Well, it was none of her business. Or maybe investigative reporters were not so hardboiled after all. She changed the question. "Are you here as part of your—your investigative project?"

Rose blinked. "Well, in a way."

Looked like that was all Alice was going to get.

Rose wiped her hands dry, tossed the towel in the wastebasket. Her hand shook a bit. Then she said, "I hate this throwing up. I have a pretty good poker face. But I can't keep from throwing up."

"No wonder, given what just happened."

"Yes." Rose nodded slowly. "Oh, yes." Dry-eyed, face set, she said, "I'm heading to San Antonio. Take care, Alice."

On the way out, after standing in a line of shocked whispering guests, Alice stopped at the police table and left her contact information. She found her truck and headed for Coffee Creek, unable to get out of her head the image of Norville, grabbing for Sandro, falling, falling. How had that happened? And why? Was there a connection between Norville's death and the break-in at Bryce's shop, or Rose getting whacked on the head? Did Norville's death affect Alejandro and Sandro Navarro? How?

With the familiar gut-crunching onset, she detected that the responsibility monster had stalked up again, was crouching on her shoulder, breathing down her neck. It looked like taking care of her new client meant retracing some of Rose's tracks, trying to confirm what Rose had learned, traveling some of the same ground, but with an eye to resolving Alejandro Navarro's odds of becoming a Drinkman heir—including trying to learn who killed Alex Drinkman the afternoon before Easter 1919.

She stopped at the office to grab Rose's notes, thinking she'd read them at home. And she knew she had to try to enlist Adele Collins as an ally, and make an exploratory visit to the Drinkman Fortress.

Warm blue fragrant twilight washed over her as she walked back to the truck. What smelled so good? Periwinkle iris, blooming in the small flowerbed between her yard and the dentist's office next door.

Spring! But Alice felt disgruntled in every way. Stolidly, reliably, the tan pickup started without a murmur of complaint. Yet even this middle-aged beige Toyota pickup, so basic, so reliable, was suddenly unsatisfactory. Trying hard to fence out of her mind the image of Norville falling, falling, she tried one radio station, then another. Nothing suited. It was spring, she was alive, she needed escape, needed a road trip—and shouldn't she be driving something entirely different? Sure, the truck was practical for hauling hay for the donkeys, but how would she look with wind in her hair, in—for instance—a convertible? A navy blue Fiat convertible with red pinstripes? She'd seen one breezing down the windward side of Oahu once, heading for the blue-green Pacific, and thought, Could I? With red leather interior? Of course, if she parked a convertible under the pole barn at the ranch, it would be full of catkins and cedar elm leaves in five minutes unless she put the top up. What was the point then? She envisioned a cloud of caliche dust settling on the navy paintwork. Maybe she should get over it—she should love the truck, like Guy Clark loved the old blue shirt in his song "Stuff That Works." But he had not included a plain boring beige Toyota pickup in his list of Stuff That Works, and his list had more style than her plain boring beige . . . Oh well.

Almost home. She turned off the creek road from town, waited for the solar-powered gate to open, started down her long gravel drive. She'd left no lights on. Her cell phone rang. Kinsear's voice— "Alice!"

"Hey! How's New Orleans?"

"Don't shoot. I'm not in the Big Easy. I'm sitting on your porch."

"Ah! I see the Land Cruiser."

She pulled under the pole barn and slid out, lugging her briefcase.

"I'll take that." Kinsear grabbed it with one hand, hugged her with the other, leaning down for a kiss. And another kiss. He dropped the briefcase and settled in for a third. Alice sniffed the center of his chest. A good smell, one of the best—a little peppery, leathery, soapy, with a dash of pheromones and the old-fashioned cleanliness of an ironed cotton shirt. Yep, smelled like Kinsear. She tiptoed, kissed him below his ear.

"I thought you'd be in the Big Easy until Saturday? What's up? Not a good book show?"

"Well, it is possible to pay attention to the news in New Orleans. It is possible to glance online, say, early this morning, and notice a reporter of no small fame has been assaulted in little Coffee Creek, Texas. And that her fortunately still-alive body was found in her car trunk by a lawyer named Alice MacDonald Greer."

"Oh." Alice hadn't thought that that news would go beyond Central Texas. She hadn't thought to look online. "Uh-oh." She thought of her clients, wondering if they felt their lawyer should be less involved with discovery of bodies.

"Not only that, but that there was some indication the reporter was looking into the Drinkmans. Sounded more interesting than the book show, though I did score a few treasures on the first day." He nodded toward his ancient Land Cruiser. "A first edition of a Civil War journal published by the LSU Press. Couple of nice first editions—J. Frank Dobie included. Then I read the news. I called Silla, who said you'd be working all afternoon. Then I took a chance and drove back."

"I'm really, really glad." He doesn't know yet about La Rotonda, she thought. "I am just really, really glad to see you." She told him about Norville's plunge over the musician's balcony.

He hugged her hard, and looked at her. "That happened at a fundraiser? Tough way to get attention for your candidate."

"I liked Norville."

Alice unlocked her front door. The air was alive with the buzz of crickets and the scent of jasmine. Two pots were blooming on the porch, the little ivory blossoms glowing in the blue evening light. She looked at the porch rocking chair. Kinsear had left his e-reader there, had been reading in the dusk. Tactfully, he'd left his overnight bag out of sight.

"I love this house," he said, kicking off his shoes by the door, walking in stockinged feet across the big Saltillo tiles into the kitchen. "It reliably has cold beer in the refrigerator. Something to count on."

"And red wine." Alice pulled out a half-full bottle of Syrah and handed a cold Flat Creek Bock to Kinsear. "You're probably still dreaming of oysters and po'boys. But what about tostadas for supper? I know I have tortillas." She foraged in the refrigerator, pulled out tortillas, cheese, and fresh jalapeños, and, to her relief, after rummaging through the vegetable crisper, one lime. Kinsear found a can of refried beans in the pantry and thoughtfully fondled two avocados and a tomato from the counter basket.

"If you'll make your guacamole with lime and cumin, I will make the famous, nay, fabled Kinsear refritos."

"Deal." She began heating one small iron skillet with oil for the tortillas and handed him another skillet for his beans. He sautéed his chopped onions, added the canned beans and busily sprinkled in chili powder and cumin, tasting frequently. Alice finished frying the tortillas and they assembled their tostadas, Kinsear judiciously adjusting the ratio of beans, cheese, and sliced jalapeños. They slid them into the oven. Alice finished mashing and seasoning the guacamole. After a few minutes they peered through the glass oven door.

"Is there a poem about how the cheese melts in yellow glory around the long green slivers of jalapeño? Okay, Alice, let's eat!"

"On the screened porch?"

They sat on the porch, with candles, tostadas, wine, beer. In the east the moon had just topped the trees on her fence line. Alice popped another bottle of Topo Chico and watched the fat bubbles rise in the water. She told Kinsear about the bam-bam-bam pace of events—Rose Rayburn's disappearance, the break-in at Bryce's, and finding Rose in her car trunk, minus her computer. Then he asked to be told about Norville again.

"Did he trip? Did he fall?"

"He just suddenly flew over the rail. Like he was propelled. I don't know how."

"I don't like you being tangled up with this mess."

"But I can't see how Norville has anything to do with Alejandro Navarro and the Drinkman connection."

"Maybe, maybe not. You were all there, and Norville's dead."

Well, she couldn't deny that. "You can stay?" she asked, finally.

Kinsear had to juggle any visit to Alice with responsibilities to his two teenage daughters. One was in boarding school in Austin, one a freshman at UT. They were often, but not always, home on weekends. Kinsear's housekeeper stayed with them when he was out of town.

"Yes. I want to hear more about this Drinkman deal, too."

"Let's walk down the road."

Alice loved a last walk down her driveway, the caliche gleaming white under the waxing moon, almost full. The burros had set up camp for the night, off in the pasture under a clump of live oaks, detectable only by their white muzzles.

"So, Bryce just wants me to protect his ownership of the letter, which was hidden in a nightstand he bought at the big antiques auction outside Boerne along with some other items." She didn't want to mention the other items right now. "His idea is that the guy who wrote the letter was murdered before he could marry Susana Navarro and adopt her little boy— which he believed was indeed his little boy. And Bryce sent a copy of that letter to our congressman, Sandro Navarro."

"Why?"

"Bryce wants to discomfit the Drinkmans—he always despised their antigay rhetoric. But short term, his thinking is that given their opposition to any immigration reform, they would be mortified by the possibility that the Drinkman fortune is partly the Navarro fortune."

"But what's he getting you into? Those people play hardball, Alice. If they don't want to do hardball themselves, they hire it out."

"I told him it may not go the way he wants. Letter and nightstand could both turn out to have been stolen. I agreed to defend his ownership, if it's challenged."

"That's not what I mean. There's a difference between defending his ownership and getting in the middle of a pissing match between the Navarro campaign and the Drinkmans!"

Alice prickled. "Well, I was also asked by the Navarro campaign to figure out whether Alejandro Navarro, the congressman's father, is Alex Drinkman's heir. I said I would represent him assuming no conflict with Bryce. So I'll do what I need to for these guys!"

"I know. But look—Rose Rayburn is already bashed on the head and two guys who sound like pros have broken into Bryce's shop."

"I do know that."

"And you can argue it's unrelated but the campaign manager for your client's son has just been pushed—or has flown—off a balcony."

Alice nodded.

"And are you off the hook with the police? Is Bryce?"

"What do you mean, me? Or Bryce?"

"Oh, I can think of some scenarios where the police might think the putative owner of the letter could be motivated to shut Rose's mouth. She might have had evidence that conflicted with Bryce's ownership," Kinsear retorted.

Ah. That articulated a worry she'd felt ever since the envelope arrived. And what was she to do with Rose's information? Was it privileged? And the repercussions? She drew a big breath, blew it out. Looked at the moon. They turned around to walk back to the house. Low in the southeastern sky, Scorpio waved its spectacular tail.

"Let's think of something else."

"Let's do. I have some possibilities in mind." Kinsear stopped at the Land Cruiser for his overnight bag. They turned the lights off—porch, living room, kitchen, hallway, as they headed back to her bedroom. She opened the sliding doors so they could catch the southeasterly breeze and hear the night noises. Far down the hillside by the creek she heard the odd little whinny of a screech owl, singing to itself, or to a friend. Yes, there was the answering whinny. "Come here," he said.

"You come here."

He did.

Stone Faces

On Friday morning early she heard the creek rushing through the rocks and brush at the bottom of the hill. Kinsear had made coffee and was standing on the deck, staring down at the blue-green glint of clear water. She joined him. A hill country stream in the spring of the year. Irresistible. Alice suddenly realized that if she did not go get in that water immediately, there would be consequences. Her soul would dry up, or something wonderful would never happen—it all depended on being in the creek, immediately. "Hey! Let's go!" she said.

They tugged on bathing suits and river sandals, took tin camping mugs of coffee, grabbed her rattiest towels, headed down the hill. A great blue heron flapped up as they picked their way down through clumps of Indian grass to the gravel bar just above the little waterfall. Kinsear pointed across the creek to a smallmouth bass, suspended in the clear water, guarding its circular nest in the streambed. Alice stepped in. Cold! Oh, not that cold. She slowly walked upstream, water lapping deeper and deeper on her thighs. At the edge of the big pool she paused, then took a breath and gave herself to the water, paddling slowly upstream toward the curve in the creek where the water had carved a grotto at the waterline under the limestone cliff. On the bank a red-eared slider turtle plopped into the water and disappeared. Alice turned over and floated on her back, kicking gently to keep her place next to the little grotto. She closed her eyes. Birdsong. What? Titmice. Maybe a painted bunting. She never could remember birdsongs. Kinsear was splashing upstream. Idly floating, she wondered if he'd find this spot as magical as she did—her grotto retreat. When she stood up, she'd feel on her feet the colder uprush of the little spring beneath the cliff. And from the rock itself, water was sliding, glittering down the cliffside. Green maidenhair fern, nothing but a dried clump in last summer's drought, now nodded up and down the cliff, the dainty green leaves wet, roots somewhere deep in the water filtering through the stone.

She floated, floated. Hostess duties? She peered sideways—Kinsear was floating too. A kingfisher darted above them, heading downstream, swooping up, down, up.

Violence of kingfishers, violence of humans. Rose Rayburn,

bashed on the head, blood in her hair. Hate talk on talk shows, out in the empty quarters of the country. Norville, splayed on the floor, blood seeping from his cracked skull.

But the water rustled. A fish tickled her thigh. Cedar perfumed the air, water perfumed the limestone—she swore limestone had a scent. This beauty, this blue-green oasis, this source of life, multiple and multifarious, fish-bird-insect-amphibian-algae-moss-fern, was a perilous beauty, with vultures prowling above, heron waiting below, owls hunting and coyotes howling at night, caught rabbits squealing—so much hidden life and death, striving and serenity, amid beauty, sheer beauty. And for this moment she was alive in her beloved hills with their hidden water.

We need the secret blue-green water, thought Alice. We so desperately need this water amid the dry lands. It's what keeps us living here, in the face of drought, flood, icy January, scorching August. It's why we stay. And it's what Alejandro Navarro is willing to fight for.

She dived under, watched a passing fish, stood up, inhaled. Waded over, gravel underfoot, and kissed Kinsear.

"Better?"

She nodded. "Not baptized, exactly—more of a ritual bath after being too close to death."

"Sort of a mikvah?"

She laughed—the creek was indeed a sacred ritual, for her. Like the dried maidenhair fern that waited on the cliff all summer, waiting for water to reach its roots again, she felt alive after submerging in the creek. Purified, as by a mikvah? Reminded, rather, of life.

Kinsear followed her up the steep bluff to the house. She knew he had to get back to Fredericksburg after the out-of-town jaunt to the rare-books convention. Saturday was busy—his shop assistant would be watching out the window, anxious for him to show up. And she'd see him late Sunday when he came to the eclipse-watching party at Bryce and John T's. But when they reached the porch, with the sun warming their wet chilled skin, the process of tugging off their bathing suits slowed them down, slowed them down. Sent them back to the bedroom.

Alice did wonder, from time to time, where she was going with

Kinsear. Conventional thoughts didn't work—whose house? Whose town? Whose job? She batted the thoughts away. She liked her life. Didn't she? She and Kinsear kissed good-bye, then kissed some more, in the driveway. Then in the back of the Land Cruiser.

She really couldn't believe she'd done that. Don't tell the children.

* * * * *

By midmorning, sedately at her desk, she'd made an afternoon appointment with Adele Collins. The Coffee County Groundwater District called. "Ms. Greer? Your office asked me to tell you when the board is going to hear that drilling permit application for the golf course, on the Blue Pool property down at the south end of the county."

"Oh, right. Have you set it?"

"Yes, it will be the third Thursday night in May, at our regular meeting."

"I have some opposition to file."

"You need to get that to us at least a week before the meeting."

Alice looked at her phone. Good grief! "That's less than three weeks away!"

"Yes ma'am."

She looked up Mr. Navarro's number, trying to envision introducing him to a semicircle of puzzled board members sitting on the dais in the hearing room at the groundwater conservation district offices. Imagined herself saying, "Mr. Navarro is sole heir to Alex Drinkman, and hence rightful owner of this property. The current permit applicants are not entitled, and cannot show they are entitled, to pursue this permit." Result: lightning bolts and brimstone in the hearing room.

"This is Alejandro Navarro."

"It's Alice Greer. How'd you like to come to a groundwater hearing? I think I'd like folks to see who they're going to be dealing with."

"I'm all yours. But you'll have to drive."

Alice had thought about what else she needed to file, and where. The county of Alex Drinkman's domicile was where, theoretically,

80

she'd have to file a petition in the probate court for determination of a right of inheritance for Alejandro Navarro as the biological child of the decedent. Was that Medina County? Might not be too friendly a venue. But was Medina County really his domicile? Had Alex actually lived at Kelly Field in San Antonio, which was in Bexar County? That was his return address on the envelope carrying his letter. Any advantage would help. Note to self: need to call her favorite local counsel in San Antonio right away. Somebody who wasn't already representing—and wasn't afraid of—the Drinkman interests.

But more thought was needed. Silla had called Medina County and found there was no record that anyone had ever probated any will purporting to be Alex Drinkman's. Furthermore, no one had ever filed for administration of Alex's estate. Alice wasn't surprised there was no will; she thought it more probable that Alex had asked the judge preparing the adoption papers also to draw a will for him, but had not lived long enough to sign it. But she was surprised that no one had been appointed to administer whatever estate he had. Instead, the Drinkmans had either forgotten that he owned property, or had just treated his property as their own. Silla had looked at the Coffee County and Blanco County deed records on the Blue Pool property and found no deed or any other recorded document after the 1916 deed to Alex Drinkman. She'd also checked the tax records: only in the past year had the property taxes been paid, by "Drinkman Realty Management." Alice suspected that since Alex's property apparently lay on the boundary between Coffee County and Blanco County, both counties had lost track of it. She also suspected that the Drinkmans had started paying property taxes on it about the time they had discovered it might be a good groundwater source for their proposed golf course development, and that they would need to fix the title problem. She was also beginning to think, after looking at the facts in the cases deciding that the four-year statute of limitations might bar an heirship application, that what she could file instead was an "action to recover real property." A couple of cases said the four-year statute did not bar actions for the recovery of interests in real property, even though as part of such a proceeding, the party seeking to recover land would have to provide the same type of proof needed to establish heirship. Please throw me in the brier patch, thought Alice: filing an action to recover Alex's Blue Pool property in Coffee County was right down her alley, and in fact right down her street. Coffee County was her turf. Maybe she'd have to file in Blanco County too, since the Blue Pool property straddled the county line, but surely the courts would consolidate the two filings into one case.

She tried to explain some of this to Alejandro Navarro. "Mr. Navarro, you know Alex Drinkman was sure you were his son." She wasn't yet sure what Mr. Navarro thought about the letter.

"It makes some sense. I can't say it feels wrong to me. But I think I would like to know."

"Well, it looks like no one ever probated a will signed by Alex Drinkman, which should have happened if he had a will. So we assume he didn't have one. And it also looks like no one was ever appointed to administer his estate, which is what you would do when there is no will. If there had been an administration of his estate, the heirs would already have been determined."

"So who inherited, if he didn't have a will?"

"Since he wasn't married, his children. If no children, his father and mother. If only one parent, half to the parent and half to his siblings, if I remember correctly. So normally we'd have to file a proceeding—let's call it an heirship case—to get you declared his heir. We'd submit DNA evidence as well as the letter, and you'd better expect the Drinkmans to fight us every step of the way. In particular, they'll argue that this lawsuit called the *Kenedy* case means it's too late for you to file, because the statute of limitations is four years."

"Does that mean we can't go forward?"

"I don't think so, because there never was any administration of Alex's estate. But if recovering his land is your main goal, an option is to file an action to recover real property, which is apparently not barred by the four-year statute of limitations. We'd still have to prove that you are Alex Drinkman's heir. Going this route might be faster and less risky, but you'd be trading away possible dollars, as you're only seeking his land. You might be able to add other claims later, but we can't be sure at this point."

"What about protecting Blue Pool?"

"Looks like the Blue Pool property is still in Alex's name. So we should also intervene in the groundwater permit proceeding, arguing that the Drinkman have no ownership of the Blue Pool property and therefore can't drill for groundwater on it."

"All right. I'm counting on you."

Alice hung up, reminding herself that Silla ought to check property records in Medina, Blanco, Hays and perhaps other counties for anything still in Alex Drinkman's name. If the Drinkmans had misplaced one piece of property, they might have misplaced another.

Also, reinforcements would be useful. Could she enlist an ally for this man?

* * * * *

Heading for Woodville, Alice dodged most of the lunch-hour traffic around Austin and headed east, never her favorite direction. Road trips west were a decided preference; Alice generally held to Thoreau's view: "Eastward I go only by force; but westward I go free." Still, she passed fields still splashed orange and blue with paintbrush and bluebonnets. "All the Blue Bonnets Are Over the Border," she hummed. Jordie had convinced her the name came from the blue tams of the Scottish mercenaries. And maybe Alex Drinkman still found bluebonnets when he travelled west from San Antonio just before Easter 1919. She turned off Highway 190 and found a short gloriously leafy street with the fabled house of Alex Drinkman's—what?—niece, Adele Drinkman Collins, the redoubtable descendant of Alex's sister Bonnie. Assuming Alex had no will, his sister Bonnie was also a potential heir—depending. Alice started up the old brick sidewalk toward the old brick porch, with its four white columns and its upstairs sleeping porch stretching across the front of the house. The front door stood open. She could see through the entry hall with its old Persian rugs all the way to the French doors at the back. A classic old house, with a classic old smell—lavender, dust, a wisp of mildew, a wisp of Pine-Sol—and a strong sense of old books. And the smell of baking from the back. She tapped at the open door.

A raw-boned woman, dark skinned, erect, came from the back,

wiping her hands on a dishtowel. Disconcertingly direct gaze. Alice stood as tall as she could.

"Miss Adele is expecting you." She waved her through long folding doors to Alice's right.

There stood Adele Collins, the distinguished woman with skeptical eyes whom Alice had met in the ballroom at La Rotonda. "Well, Alice, I didn't know we'd get to meet so soon after this terrible business about Carey Norville. Such a tragedy." She called toward the tall woman at the door, "Estelle? Can you bring tea?" and then took Alice's elbow and led her into the quiet living room that ran the depth of the house. Chintz couches, lamps from the fifties. Comfort, calm, bookshelves. Silver-framed photographs on end tables, the mahogany tabletops wavy with years of polishing. Was that Bill Clinton with Adele Collins? It was. Ralph Yarborough, back in the day? It was. Adele Collins and Lady Bird Johnson? Yes. On the wall, a lifetime award from the Nature Conservancy. So, a major donor on many fronts. Well, Alice knew about that from the Internet.

Adele waved a thin hand at the lantern-jawed man waiting for them. "My lawyer, John Frierson. John, this is Alice Greer from Coffee Creek."

He extended his hand. "Pleasure. How do you find Coffee Creek, after practicing in Austin?"

Ah, he'd done some homework. She hadn't had the advantage of knowing his name. But she recognized him: she'd seen him striding along the gallery across from her at La Rotonda, minutes before Norville's plunge. "I do get very interesting clients. Didn't I see you at the fundraiser yesterday, at La Rotonda? Upstairs on the gallery?"

"Oh." He seemed surprised. "I was up there just for a moment. An old friend wanted to talk."

Estelle and the tea entered. Silver teapot, sliced pound cake on a doily, perfect fine-grained texture, a little extra moisture in the middle of the slice. The aroma made Alice close her eyes. She would try not to gobble it up and look longingly for a second slice. Instead she picked up the thin old crazed teacup, gold edges slightly distressed, cradled it in her left palm, inhaled the sweet tannic odor, sipped. She smiled at the two faces quietly observing her from their chairs—

both ensconced in a familiar, settled way. They've sat in those chairs together on many occasions, she realized. She wondered what the long discussions and shared silences had produced. Alice returned her teacup gently to its saucer, deciding to plunge.

"Ms. Collins, I represent Alejandro Navarro, son of your uncle, Alex Drinkman. He is the 'little Alejandro' mentioned in the letter I forwarded to you."

"Sandro Navarro's father?"

"Yes. Oddly, a pilot in World War II, like his father in World War I."

"And now after money."

"He has never had the joy of knowing who his father was until now. He's over ninety and wants to claim that relationship."

"He wants the money."

"Based on our research there was no administration of Alex Drinkman's estate. We find no record of any distribution of his real or personal property, for example, to his father or to your mother, his sister. Do you know otherwise? Do you know whether she ever received anything from his estate, whether money or real or personal property?"

A pause. Adele Collins had not considered this possibility—that something might have been withheld from her.

"I never heard that."

"After Alex was killed, I understand your mother left the ranch. Can you tell me why, if you know?

"Only distant rumor. After Mr. Alastair had his stroke, but before he died, she and my great-aunt Dee left the ranch and moved to Woodville, and then that fall she went straight to the Texas State College for Women."

"Surely she could have traveled to college from the ranch. Do you know why her aunt took her to Woodville?"

"The family story was that Aunt Dee was upset about a horse my mother was riding—looked like its cinch had been cut. Probably mere rumor. But my mother fell and broke her arm. And she was a good rider."

"Who did Aunt Dee think had cut the cinch?"

"I wasn't there, Ms. Greer. And you're just speculating."

"Who was she riding with that day?"

"Willy Kendrick."

Alice blinked. Then a little click. "Miss Ella's son. Mr. Alastair's—stepson? So, your mother's stepbrother."

"Yes. He changed his name to Drinkman later, you know." Adele Collins looked at the ceiling, considering—maybe—what more to tell Alice. "Family rumor was that he was sweet on my mother, wanted her to marry him."

Interesting. Alice's turn. "Do you know the terms of your grandfather's will?"

"I think part of his estate went to my mother. Ella got the rest. His second wife."

"The terms of the will on the real property holdings were that Ella Kendrick would have—from memory—'during her lifetime and for her use one-third of the income from my real property holdings. However, should one or both of my beloved children, Alex and Bonnie, predecease me without marriage or lawful heirs, then I direct that such child's half of my real property holdings pass in fee instead to Ella Kendrick Drinkman and her heirs.'"

Silence. Frierson uncrossed and recrossed his thin legs, then leaned slightly forward. "You are saying that someone would be motivated to kill Bonnie before Mr. Drinkman died. Poor drafting."

"As you know, Mr. Frierson, people don't always think of all the ramifications when they're trying to dispose of their lifetime's accumulation of wealth. Loving people can forget about—oh, original sin. Greed. Longing."

He nodded, awarding her a dry little smile. "So after Mr. Drinkman's death, the land holdings would have been divided equally between Bonnie and Ella Kendrick Drinkman. But you are suggesting that Alex's estate may not have been administered when he died, may not have been included in that division?"

"That's one thing I wonder about."

"And?"

"I wonder who killed Alex Drinkman. Who shot him on his motorcycle as he rode down onto the low-water crossing at

Madrone Creek."

Frierson lifted his head and stared past Alice, eyes unfocused. Was he thinking how it was, the young man, muscles guiding the motorcycle down the ramp, water rushing past, ears full of the sound of the creek, eyes squinted shut against the setting sun, trying to make it home for supper?

"And who cut the cinch. If that happened."

No one answered her.

"May we shift to another subject? Do you know whether your Aunt Dee received any of Alex Drinkman's belongings? As you know, he mentioned in the letter that he was bringing her back a book and also some new poems by Sassoon and Gurney. Those could have been in the saddlebag on the motorcycle."

Adele Collins shook her head.

"Another question. Before you received the copy of Alex Drinkman's letter to his father, which we sent you, had you ever heard of it? Ever known the story of his letter to his father about Susana Navarro and little Alejandro?"

After a pause, Adele Collins shook her head again.

"Not even from Aunt Dee? No mention of a letter, or anything else?"

"I wasn't there."

"Of course not. But no family history of anything Aunt Dee said or did about Alex's death? Did she see his body?"

Stone faces.

"Or write anything about his death?"

This time Adele Collins blinked. But shook her head.

Alice took a breath. "I want you to know about Mr. Navarro, and what he hopes for. He is a very fine man. You saw him at La Rotonda, Ms. Collins. He served this country with courage and has reared a family that seeks to do good in this world. Belatedly, after no one in the Drinkman family ever reached out to him, he has learned the identity of his father. He knows now that his father wanted him. That means a great deal to him. You know Blue Pool is the property where Alex Drinkman proposed to bring his bride and son. Mr. Navarro hopes to save it from a drilling permit requested by the Drinkmans to pipe water from that property to a proposed new golf resort."

Her listeners sat unmoving, still stone-faced.

"Mr. Navarro will oppose that permit on grounds that the property does not belong to the current Drinkman interests."

Frierson leaned forward again. "When Alex predeceased Mr. Drinkman, Bonnie should have gotten half of Alex's estate. She could lay claim to Blue Pool."

"No." Alice stared back. "If Alex was intestate, his property should have gone to his child. His son."

"You have no proof Navarro is his son."

"I will have proof."

"We'll dispute it."

"Will you? Why? Tell me why you would not want Alex Drinkman's son"—she looked at Adele Collins—"your first cousin, in fact, to inherit what was wrongfully withheld from him? Tell me, if Alex was killed and someone gained from his death, why you would take steps to compound that wrong? Tell me, if Bonnie Drinkman felt she had to leave her father—her ailing father, who had had a stroke—and you may agree that a daughter would not likely do that absent an overpowering reason—tell me why you would choose to side with those from whom she apparently fled?"

They sat silent. Outside flowers nodded. Somewhere a floorboard creaked. Adele Collins glanced at Frierson, then looked for a long moment at Alice. "I think we might support you in opposing the groundwater permit. Or at least not oppose you. That's aligned with my interests as well as your client's. I'm not interested in seeing that water used on a new golf course."

"Perhaps you would favor me with a copy of anything you file," Frierson added.

"Of course. Thank you both for your time. And for the tea." She stood slowly, shifting her notebook to her bag, and extending her hand first to Adele Collins. Then to Frierson. His dry old-man's skin was cool, bony, a little rough. "I'll be in touch."

"Yes, we'll be expecting to hear from you." Adele's clear eyes did not blink.

Alice left the dark cool hall, feeling the weight of years of stories, of emotion, of anger, of grief, of plans, wars, elections, deaths. Come on, Alice! Don't let your imagination run riot. She controlled her pace, trying not to hurry, trying not to heave a sigh of relief as she reached the brick porch with its tall columns. The sense of being watched by speculative eyes faded as she walked down the old brick sidewalk. She threw her bag in the truck, blew out her breath, and heard herself say aloud, "Good lord!"

And what had she learned? That the house held a formidable intelligence; that Adele protected her reputation for percipience and virtuous enterprise; that she was not a woman to cross; that she enjoyed her own power and her ability to affect lives and enhance her reputation by focused use of money. So, mused Alice, would she want to share?

She headed west, threading through the growing waves of Austin traffic. Woodville was deep East Texas, southern more than southwestern, home of tall pines, timber industry, and (Alice truly hoped and believed) maybe still an ivory-billed woodpecker, hiding somewhere deep in the Big Thicket, calling with the booming voice she'd heard on a scratchy recording. But Austin, with its Balcones Fault, the "balconies" of hills west of the Colorado River, still thrilled her. Despite the ever-growing traffic she still felt she'd reached home when she hit the "Austin City Limits" sign. She felt unencumbered here—which was odd, given the ties of family, profession, friendship, and inner compulsions and compunctions that (she had to admit) she felt always bound her. At least, in Austin, people didn't think she was crazy.

Frierson. She would call him in the morning, see if she could glean more from him, winkle out the additional questions that he and his client had discussed after Alice left. Also find out what old friend he was talking to on the second floor of La Rotonda. Maybe he would proffer a fact or two, about Aunt Dee hustling Bonnie off the ranch, maybe her arm in a sling, leaving behind . . . the nightstand, and who knows what else. A book?

That night Alice lay awake as moonlight crept across the floor. How to stymie the golf course water permit? If she moved to intervene in the groundwater permit hearing, and if the groundwater district refused to stop the permit proceeding, what then? And what about the heirship evidence she would need to file an action for the recovery of land? Shouldn't she go ahead now and get DNA tests on Alex's hair and Mr. Navarro's? What if the Drinkmans somehow succeeded in getting the letter back, with the lock of hair and everything else in the oiled-silk packet? Or what if the Drinkmans disputed the results? What if they claimed, for example, that the chain of custody for the DNA samples was disastrously flawed or the samples were hopelessly contaminated? Well, in that case perhaps she could persuade a court to permit exhumation to allow samples from Alex's body. But—and here she sat straight up in bed—what if the Drinkmans disinterred Alex's body? Spirited his coffin away? Nothing prevented them from doing that right this minute. She flopped back on the pillow, thoughts whirling. What did she even know about Alejandro Navarro? He was a client, but she'd seen him for twenty seconds. Sure, an impressive war record, but—she was about to go to the mat for this man. Was he worth it? She had to do something. She had to do many things. She took a deep breath. Try the deep breathing. Three good breaths, lengthening each exhalation. Then one big breath and an exhalation as long as the three earlier exhalations together. If it was good enough for Navy SEALs training, maybe it could calm an anxious lawyer.

At five she woke, surprised she'd slept. But her ideas had rearranged themselves in order. Armed with coffee, she started drafting. At seven she called a sleepy Bryce and explained. The oiled-silk packet and its contents were his, at this point. She told him what she needed to do with the contents. He agreed. She called Alejandro Navarro. Yes, he'd like a road trip to Blue Pool. Sunday was fine. He went to mass on Saturday night. Okay, then.

Chapter Eight

A Little Reminder Scar

A lice needed to know how Alejandro Navarro really felt about going after his father's property. She tested out that question on Sunday morning, on their scouting expedition to Blue Pool, to inspect what would be one of Mr. Navarro's future land holdings if all went according to plan. His grandson Tomás dropped him off at the Antler Café, for an early lunch, then waved, smiling, at Alice and roared away in a shiny little blue BMW.

Mr. Navarro ordered sweetened iced tea and a small chicken fried steak, explaining, "The large chicken fry overlaps the entire dinner platter. You want to live long, stay a little hungry. My motto. Except when tempted." When the waitress set down his platter, he smiled up at her. "Could you bring me a little more of that cream gravy?" As he spooned it over the last crusty morsel on the plate, he saw Alice's smile. "I was tempted," he said.

Alice toyed with her cheese enchiladas. "We may have a shot, on Blue Pool," she said. "I don't think we have a good shot at claiming what Alex would have gotten from Alastair Drinkman's will, if he had lived. I suppose a court might impose a constructive trust if we could really prove who shot Alex." At the words "impose a constructive trust," Mr. Navarro's eyes had glazed over. "But for discussion purposes only, imagine you got, I don't know, a hundred million dollars or more—what would you do with it?"

He looked up at the antlers propped around a shelf on the wall, his eyes unfocused, then laid his fork down. "Not a damn thing."

"Oh?"

He shook his head. "Nothing different. Wear the same clothes. Drive the same car. Go to mass at five on Saturday. Bet a little money on the Spurs."

"But Sandro? The grandkids?"

"Sandro could use a super PAC, I guess. But Tomás and Isabella? Got to think that through. Would Tomás just run through it like—like water through your fingers? I don't like for people to be motivated by money. I worry about Tomás; he loves that playboy life. But I also worry about Isabella. She'd get courted by some gold-digging boy—he'd pretend to be interested in one of her orphanages or whatever she's doing—and she wouldn't know he was just after the money until it was too late. She thinks everyone is as altruistic as she is. Little idiot." He shrugged, sighed. "Not sure, Miss Alice. I'd like to give the grandkids each a present. Like ten or fifteen thousand a year. Nice, a cushion, but not life-altering. Sandro—there, too, I'd put part in a foundation he could run, and part in a super PAC. That doesn't change his life. Might help him do some good in his district, for example."

"What about the radio station idea? Buy up a chain of radio stations, like the Drinkmans' chain? Put out a different message, he said."

"Hadn't heard about that. I'd have to think."

"Pie? Coconut cream, peach?" sang the waitress, swooping down to refill their iced teas.

Alice shook her head. Mr. Navarro grinned up at the waitress. "Coconut, biggest slice you have."

"'Stay a little hungry'?"

"I said, except when tempted!"

He spooned up the last of the gravy. "You know, I do worry about my boy Tomás. He needs something to run. He'd be good at it if he really tried."

"You mean like radio stations?"

"Maybe. He can sell. He can talk. He needs to find himself a cause besides getting his next date. But he can't just have all that money—he'd never finish his growing up. Think about it, Alice. What was your first job?"

"I was sixteen. Working in the office at a church retreat center. Inside, not much to do, boring—but I knew I was lucky not to be assigned to the cafeteria. All the kids thought the bosses were so mean, so stingy, so strict, especially on the girls. My father came out for a conference. I and my buddy Steve told him we wanted to leave, we were being mistreated. He rocked back and forth on his heels and then asked, 'Didn't you sign on for the whole summer?'" Alice lifted her shoulders and smiled. "Still feel that question—didn't you sign on for the whole summer? Maybe that's what I feel for clients."

Navarro's smile cracked open. "I want something like that for

Tomás! Your dad still around? Could he make that same speech to my grandson?"

Alice's father had died so young and so suddenly, she and her brothers and sister still couldn't talk about it. She just shook her head.

"I'm sorry."

"So, do you go after anything but Alex's Blue Pool property? Any land he owned back then? And what if we prove a family member shot him?

"I'd want revenge on the person who killed my father."

"It'll be a long shot." She grinned. "Bad pun. Terrible."

"Don't you have the bullets? The Drinkmans don't know that yet, do they?"

"Right." They nodded at each other. That was another issue Alice knew she needed help with. What kind of rifle shot Alex Drinkman? There might be thousands of similar rifles just in Central Texas.

* * * * *

"This road looks like the county just paved the existing goat track," muttered Alice, inching over the top of the hill. A sign announced "limited sight distance." Very limited. "You couldn't see a semi-trailer coming up the other side."

Mr. Navarro had directed her towards a Catholic Charities youth camp that he said was downstream from the pool. "They'll let me in, don't worry," he said. They were deep in cedar-covered hills on a two-lane blacktop road with no center stripe and more curves than the Kilgore Rangerettes.

"So where do you think we can best get a view of the pool?" asked Alice.

"You mean since the Drinkmans won't let onto the property?"

She glanced at the old man in the passenger seat. "I did tell their lawyers we were coming to look at Blue Pool. They said no; they would call the sheriff if we trespassed. I said since you owned it, it would not be trespassing. They said if we cut any fence we'd be arrested."

"Who told you that?"

"I pushed their counsel to call Will Drinkman and supposedly he said 'hell no.' But here's something interesting. Looking at the Internet, the fence is pretty new. If you look at the 'earth' view, you can still see dirt piles where the fence posts went in."

"Well." He lifted his head, looked out the windshield at the cedar-covered hills whirling past. "Is that important?"

"Could be, if they try to claim they've adversely possessed this piece of property. I think they just fenced it when they started looking for a groundwater source. That's when they started paying taxes. And since the property's not too big, sort of an odd shape, lies on the county line, and only has an easement across someone else's property back to the highway, it's been ignored."

"I don't understand how someone can just ignore property they think they own."

"Oh, you'll find situations like this in rural areas. But this one has a twist, with the death of Alex Drinkman."

"I've actually seen the pool before from the air," said Alejandro Navarro suddenly. "Back in 1934. I was learning to fly at Kelly Field, for Tobin Aerial Surveys company in San Antonio. They did aerial mapping for the oil companies."

"In 1934?"

"Well, I fudged my age a little. Maybe a lot."

Alice looked at him, one eyebrow raised.

"I got to solo finally. Took off south but then headed west and got out over those hills and thought—I want to see that Blue Pool."

"You already knew about it from the church camp?"

"Oh yeah. Catholic Charities sent some of us poor kids out for a week when I was about ten. That was the first time I'd really been out of San Antonio. It was so quiet! But then loud, with frogs, with crickets, and then quiet again. And the water. The stream was clear as clear. I'd never seen anything so amazing. There was a little spring, a seep really, came out the side of the hill up above the creek. Ferns growing in it. We climbed up there, and I was fascinated at the clear water sliding down the hill—like magic—into the creek. And then the creek! We swam—well, we splashed. None of us could swim.

We were lucky we didn't drown."

Alice slowed for another sharp uphill curve. "So how did you see the Blue Pool?"

"We trespassed. One day, late on the last day of camp, I got a wild hair. I ducked under the water bar, you know, the big screen between the church property and the next property upstream. Me and Joaquin, my big buddy. We sneaked under and waded upstream, trying to stay under the cedars on the bank so we wouldn't run into the old guy who owned the piece just upstream, before you actually get to Blue Pool. The sisters had warned us about him. Anyway, we came around a curve and there it was. So beautiful. Like a big blue eye staring at heaven. Not that big, really, but so beautiful. It's an amazing color, you know? That clear blue-green? Up on one side there are big cliffs curving around it, then the little waterfall, the rapids that came on downstream. And it was so quiet."

"Then what?"

"We'd started back down the stream so we wouldn't be late for supper and we heard that unmistakable sound, unforgettable, someone racking a pump-action shotgun. Someone yelled at us. 'You little wetbacks, get the hell off this property!' We were dashing down that creek, trying to get back under the water bar. I never ran so fast in my life. Whoever it was fired that shotgun, too. I got a pellet in my calf. We pried it out with a pocket knife and never told Sister, though."

Alice thought about someone shooting at the "little wetback" who, not much later, would be risking his life, flying for his country.

"So, later?"

"I took off in that little plane, solo flight, and instead of doing what I was supposed to I went straight west out over the hills and went a little bit north, a little bit west, then suddenly, there it was. The Blue Pool. I circled it and circled it again. I made another run west and then came back in low and flew over it as slow as I could without stalling. Then I flew back to the airfield. I caught some flak from the instructor but he didn't rat me out." He stopped, staring through the windshield, perhaps seeing something long ago. "So in the Pacific, going up for another run over New Guinea, I'd think, 'Be smart, Alejandro. Be careful, be smart. Don't let these Zeros get in your blind spot. Be the hawk, ready to dive, ready to pounce. You are coming back and you will see the Blue Pool again. Maybe have'—well, I didn't let myself think about actually owning the Blue Pool, but I thought about having a place with water like that, one day. And by some miracle I did make it back."

"Did you have a name on your plane?" Alice was thinking about old photographs of crews around their fighters.

"Oh yeah. The Hawk. Halcón, I called her."

"How did you wind up in the Pacific?"

"Well, of course I wanted to be a fighter pilot. Didn't everyone? That wasn't easy if you weren't white. But a manager at Tobin spoke up for me and helped get me into the Army air force. And I got to hunt Zeros."

Alice slowed. She'd spotted the entrance to the Catholic Charities camp. They bumped down the road, hand-painted wooden signs directing them to Administration, Chapel, Picnic Area. "Turn left," directed Navarro. "Down the hill." They bumped slowly down to a small parking area, bordered by logs. Water glinted through the trees.

Alice stood on the stone platform by the water, tugged on her river shoes, and rolled up her pants. Navarro slipped off his shoes and rolled up his slacks. He was wearing his socks. They inched into the chilly clear water. How could he walk on this rocky bottom? She took his arm as they pushed slowly against the water, and there it was—the water bar. Big brown steel pipes held a tall screen of heavy hogwire, ten feet above the water, and another couple of feet below. She could see the hogwire had been cut below the water, leaving long sharp spikes, so that anyone crawling beneath it would be scored by the wires. They stared upstream. "This is what you and Joaquin crawled under?"

"An earlier version of it."

She pointed at the sharp wire ends visible below the clear blue-green water.

"Yeah. I got a little reminder scar on one shoulder from that."

They stood, breeze on their faces, looking far upstream where, shadowed by the cypress trees bending over it, the water turned and disappeared behind the cliffs. Alice felt the pull of the stream. No wonder those boys wanted to turn the corner, find the pool.

Navarro stood staring up at the top of the cedar-cloaked hill to their left. "Let's climb up there. See that little trail?"

She and the old man made their way to the bank and up the trail, part caliche, part limestone, part gravel. He did not slip in his socks, swinging the stiff leg up, slowly covering ground. She had to stop to get gravel out of her river shoes. "Design defect," he commented.

Breathing hard, they made the top, a classic church-camp hilltop, cleared of brush, with a few rough benches circling a slightly lopsided cross made of cedar poles, propped up by a cairn of limestone rocks. Kum-ba-yah space.

Swinging the stiff leg, Navarro walked to the edge of the bluff. "There it is."

Around the curve of the stream ahead, she saw blue water, reflecting the sky. The high cliffs circling one side looked sacred. Far above a hawk circled.

"Worth going after," he said. He looked at Alice, silent for a moment. "Can we get it?"

"We're going to try."

She and Mr. Navarro inched back down the trail to her truck. Mr. Navarro slipped his loafers on. They turned back down the bumpy gravel drive through the Catholic Charities camp.

"So you're basically okay just going after Alex's land, right? Not a share of the Drinkman fortune?" she said. She was still mindful of what Norville had told her: Sandro's chances would suffer if his family got entangled in long-running litigation over weak claims.

"I've done all right for myself. I'm proud of what I've built. Just me, Alejandro Navarro. No silver spoon, no leg up from a rich daddy."

"Right. And then you have your children."

"Yes. At my age, I feel like some old tree from the Psalms, from Proverbs. My roots have been watered. Sandro and my grandchildren stand by me like . . . like . . . oh, I don't know. Trees. So I could be satisfied. But there are two things that make me go forward."

She glanced at the profile, the strong nose, the grizzled eyebrows. "Yes?"

"First, now I know that my father wanted me. He wanted me! Now I know he was a young pilot, and I know what that's like—I can imagine him being scared shitless, and then feeling like lord of the world for a few minutes after he bested some German—it's like I am in his mind, seeing what he saw through the clouds, starting his plane into a dive. And now I know he loved my mother. And wanted to have me near him. I have never known any of this before, never. And now I know he was taken away from me before I could even live with him. That—I am still thinking about. And second? Second . . . I want my children to have that Blue Pool. Pure emotion. I just want it."

He thumped Alice on the shoulder. "And I trust you."

Oh boy, she thought. Oh boy. I hope so, because getting you declared Alex Drinkman's heir is going to be a wild ride.

She braked as she pulled up the gravel drive to the highway, ready to turn north toward Coffee Creek, where Tomás had promised to pick up his grandfather. As she sat there, the truck idling, she saw the helicopter. It rose out of the valley near Blue Pool, then slowly turned above the highway, moving toward her truck. It hovered, then peeled off in a circle, then changed speed and moved slowly behind and then back around her. Then it regained speed and headed south.

"What was that about?" Alice fumed.

Navarro squinted up through the windshield. "Private," he said. "Bell Huey Two. Civvy version of the old UH-1."

Good grief, thought Alice, I can't see that far.

He pursed his lips. "Wonder if it's the Drinkmans' private chopper. Wonder what they're doing out at Blue Pool today."

"Probably thinking about their new golf resort."

He laughed, a dry and satisfied little hmmph. "Gonna put a spoke in their wheels."

Alice nodded. She devoutly hoped it would be a strong sturdy spoke.

Chapter Nine

Take Dead Aim!

On Sunday night, just at dusk, Alice pressed the buttons to open the steel gate and then bounced across the cattle guard onto Bryce and John T's drive, rolling down her window to sniff the spring evening air. She wondered if Kinsear had already arrived. She wanted to introduce him to these friends, and he wanted a tour of Bryce's book collection, so Bryce and John T had invited them out for a doubleheader: to eat a potluck supper and watch a total lunar eclipse from their deck. It was Alice's first visit to El Rancherito, as they called their place, since they'd finished moving in. Alice was curious to see it. She could hear bells tinkling up the hillside: John T's Nubian show goats, she surmised. She was not that keen on the smell of goats, personally, but you had to keep your ag exemption somehow.

Bryce and John T had found a hundred acres downstream on Coffee Creek, several miles from Alice's place, at a point where the creek had carved the hillside steeply, and had situated their house right at the edge of the cliff. She backed her truck under the long pole barn between a tractor and Kinsear's ancient Land Cruiser and lugged her contribution—a refrigerated bag containing four gallons of different flavors of Blue Bell ice cream—down the gravel path. The porch lights were off; a lone solar lantern on the pathway provided a faint green glow in the blue dusk, lighting the way to the entry porch next to the garage. The garage doors were down. No lights showed anywhere. If she hadn't seen Kinsear's SUV she would have wondered whether she was showing up for dinner on the wrong night. Was it already time for the eclipse? She thought it wouldn't start for another fifteen minutes.

Alice pushed open the wood-and-carved-glass door. "Hello?" She walked down the dark stone-flagged entry hall. A faint gleam of stainless steel guided her right into John T's tidy kitchen. Still no lights. She unloaded the sweating cartons into the freezer. Where were those boys? She walked into the living room, still visible in the evening light from the tall glass doors opening onto the deck to her left. Out there stood the telescope. Cocked and loaded for moon, she assumed. Then she heard a rumble of male voices down the hall that angled off to the right from the far side of the living room. "Hello?"

"Alice! Is that you?" John T's comfortable bulk emerged from the hall, swaddled her in a warm hug. "We're in the armory, showing your beau the toys." Alice followed, wide-eyed. The dim hall light above made shadows on ivory walls hung with iron, dark wood, dull steel, sharp blades. Weapons. Maces! Spears! Pikes! Was that a trident? Old smoothbore muskets. Swords. Shields. Bryce stood next to Kinsear, who stood awkwardly in his therapeutic foam boot, recuperating from a vicious pickup basketball game the day before at the local Y. Head lowered, he was listening to Bryce, who was patting a flintlock pistol and volubly discussing the courtesies and strategies of duels. "Now this"—Bryce hefted an iron mace, lifted it down from its hook, gingerly poked the sharp spikes protruding from the ball— "this is my personal favorite. Really it's called a morning-star flail." He gently swung the spiky ball, the hand-forged iron chain creaking. "I've practiced a little but I always worry the chain might break. Don't know why I worry, though—those fifteenth-century smiths did strong work." He hung it back, gently.

"How did this sneak in here?" Alice pointed to a black braided whip. "Zorro thing?"

"Hey, that's a gen-u-wine mule skinner's whip, nearly twenty feet long. Spanish. Mexican, rather. For the mule trains that ran from Texas down into Mexico, back in the day. You know, running the Yankee blockade for cotton, and such."

"You practice with that too?"

"I've tried. It takes some forearm strength to get it out there twenty feet, where the mules are."

Alice was drawn to a glass shelf holding shimmering four- and five-pointed stars of handmade steel, beautifully dangerous. She reached out. "How do you throw these?"

"Hey, be careful! Those are like scalpels! You throw them—well, not sideways like a frisbee. No." He demonstrated. "Hold them vertically, more like you hold a dart. Maybe wearing those mesh metal gloves John T uses when he slices vegetables on his mandoline. Since the last accident."

"Good lord," breathed Alice. She picked one up, touched the delicate point, lifted it cautiously, experimented with how to hold and throw it without slicing her fingers.

"Put that back, Alice. Don't want you bleeding on the cocktail napkins. John T just ironed them. Speaking of which, come back to his treasure room and I will pour you an Acapulco Mule."

"Treasure room? And some kind of mule? Lead on."

Past the master suite, at the end of the ivory-walled weapon-shadowed hall, John T opened the door to a windowless room. It felt cooler. She heard a low hum. John T closed the door and turned on the light. Shelves lined the walls, holding baskets, beaded moccasins, pottery, arrowheads. Alice saw kachinas, masks, drums. On a table in the middle of the room stood a pitcher, glasses, and a plate of devilled eggs. John T handed out drinks and napkins. "We've still got about ten minutes before the eclipse starts, so I thought we would have cocktails in here and I could give you a quick tour of my treasures. This room is all light and climate-controlled. It had to be, especially for the baskets and the leather items." He explained that they were all from New Mexico, gathered in his long-ago days as a landman for the oil companies.

"The Hopi pottery is on that shelf. This shelf is Navajo." Each piece had a card indicating provenance, dates, artist. "The baskets are mainly Apache. Aren't they beautiful?"

Alice nodded, awed by the sophisticated artistry, the patient and demanding handwork. She sipped her drink. "Whoo. John T, you call this a mule because of its kick?"

"Yeah, it might have a little backswing. It's three parts tequila, one part lime juice, ginger beer to taste. You've got to pick a decent ginger beer, too."

"And not forget the salt on the rim," said Kinsear, staring back at the blank eyes of a dance mask. "Are you still collecting?"

"Nope. I just enjoy these. When I'm in Santa Fe I always try to stop by the Indian Arts Research Center, learn a little bit more. There's a professor there who's been out here to see my collection. He's taught me a good deal. Someday I'll give these away. Got an invitation to show them next year in Santa Fe and I just might do it, too. I want to keep learning."

"Speaking of artistry," Kinsear said, holding up half a devilled egg, "what's the spicy touch here?" Kinsear was a notorious recipe hound. "Sriracha?"

"You got it. You know, I like the Southern devilled eggs, with candied dill pickles minced fine, and I like the fancy ones with little bits of smoked salmon and homemade mayonnaise, but lately I'm drawn to a little more spice in these babies."

Bryce looked at his watch. "Hey, I don't want to miss the dragon's first little bite out of the moon. I'm going to go check if the eclipse is starting." He swung open the door and started down the hall. Alice, musing over an Apache basket by the door, saw him come to a sudden stop at the end of the hall, swinging his arms back at them in the universal signal—Quiet! Stay still! Silently he backed up and lifted the mace off the wall, holding the spiky globe in his left hand, handle in his right.

John T, moving very quietly for a big man, moved up beside him. "What?" he hissed. Kinsear and Alice moved up by John T as well.

"There are two men in our study."

"Where are your guns?" Kinsear whispered.

"Locked in the study. Not handy."

John T lifted a pike off the spear rack, then, nodding to each other, he and Bryce charged into the living room. Kinsear limped along behind, brandishing a small bamboo Filipino fish spear and the Zorro whip. Alice grabbed a throwing star in each hand. Between the bulk of John T and Kinsear, she caught a glimpse of two men in black, holding flashlights, coming out of the study next to the living room. When they saw Bryce they moved quickly toward the entry hall.

Bryce darted across the living room to cut off their escape. "Oh no you don't!"

The men—one dark, one blond—reversed course and dashed toward the open doors to the deck. Blond Man vaulted left over the deck railing onto the ground. Dark Man ran down the steps that led off the deck along the cliff-top path. John T thundered after him, waving his pike, with Kinsear hobbling behind, fish spear held aloft. Bryce ran onto the deck and went left over the railing. Alice, thinking there must be a getaway car, ran out the front entry into darkness.

The solar lantern had quit; the eclipse had begun; no night birds sang. The Milky Way sparkled above, and the moon had lost its symmetry. Chalk up bite one to the dragon.

She crept down the steps and along the pathway. At the end of the pole barn she could just make out a black SUV, lights out, quietly easing forward onto the drive, then slowly reversing toward her. Was it an Audi? She could not tell. Off to her right she heard grunting and thrashing on the slope below the pole barn, a thud and a cry and then more thrashing, just below the hilltop. Blond Man edged between her truck and Kinsear's and panted down the drive toward the black car ten yards ahead. Standing in the dark, Alice thought, Take dead aim! and hurled her first, then her second throwing star. No response, no anguished cry. Instead, she heard two separate metal clinks on the gravel drive. So she'd missed. Apparently untouched, Blond Man covered the last few yards and leaped into the backseat. The SUV again resumed backing slowly toward her. Was it waiting for Dark Man? What was the license plate? Praying the dome light in her truck would stay nonfunctional, Alice slipped along the cliff side of the pole barn to her truck, opened the driver's-side door, reached under her front seat, and pulled out the heavy Verey flare gun. Creeping forward, she held the gun with two hands and aimed for the sky. The gun bucked and roared and a satisfying green whoosh erupted overhead. Alice memorized all seven symbols on the license plate as Bryce panted up the slope beside her. "That mace is just hell in the trees," he said. "Doesn't work worth a damn. Where's the other guy?"

And to their left Dark Man appeared, thudding around the front of the house. He was tugging awkwardly at something trailing from the back of his left arm. Raising his mace, Bryce took out after him but Dark Man managed to climb into the far side of the car. He was still trying to pull the door closed when the car leaped forward, then began lurching down the drive, *going ka-whomp, ka-whomp, ka-whomp*. It listed toward the back left.

"Flat tire?" said Bryce. "You think they've got a flat tire?"

"Well, I did throw a throwing star. Two. I'm thinking that car backed over one."

"Great work!" crowed Bryce. Alice did not mention she had been aiming at Blond Man and completely missed her target.

"Hey! Need some help back here!" Kinsear shouted from the cliff side of the house. Bryce and Alice turned and ran around the front of the house, dodging the fence around John T's vegetable garden, heading for the cliff at the back. Glancing back, Alice took one more look at the taillights bouncing crazily across the cattle guard (was that a rim hitting? she hoped so), then hurried after Bryce, stumbling over clumps of grass as she ran.

Kinsear knelt by the slope. Alice groped in her pocket for her cell phone and shone the flash down. Fifteen feet below, John T teetered on a boulder that jutted from the cliff face. He was leaning in, clutching the rocks protruding from the cliff face.

"I don't see a good way up," called John T. "Maybe I'll just stay here tonight and you can lower my dinner down on a rope. And coffee in the morning. Only"—the boulder teetered—"I might spill the coffee."

"Hold on!" begged Alice. Below John T stretched a steep rocky slope terminating over a hundred feet down at the creek below.

"Try this." Kinsear unfurled the Zorro whip. "Let's give it a shot."

"Not sure if it will reach around me," John T called. But holding onto the cliff face with one hand, he managed to loop the end of the whip around his belt in front and, trying to stay balanced, tied it, knotted it, yanked it tight. "Hope that holds." Then, holding the knotted thong with both hands, he began walking his feet up the outcrops on the protruding limestone cliff. Alice held her breath. Would it hold? Bryce braced Kinsear while Kinsear held the whip, hauling in the slack. As John T neared the top Alice dug in her heels and held Kinsear's shoulders while Bryce reached down and hauled John T back over the edge, all of them tumbling backward in a heap. They whooped in triumph, then paused. A crunching sound below—the boulder let loose and bounced heavily down the slope.

"Yikes," said Alice.

"John T had that guy in a pretty good hold but then the guy did some sort of judo move and threw John T over the edge," said Kinsear.

"I'm glad to be here and not there," said John T. "What about supper?" Then he paused. "Wait—do you smell smoke?"

They pounded back up the stairs onto the deck and through the living room and out the entry. Off in the pasture flickered a long low smoldering line of flame, growing, growing. Bryce and Alice raced into the pasture, stamping out flames in the burning grass, Kinsear hobbling behind and stamping with his nontherapeutic boot. John T hauled the hose from his vegetable garden as far as it would go, shooting water, splashing Alice and Bryce and Kinsear. Finally no more flame was visible. They stood together, panting, waiting for a night breeze to blow the flame alight again. Had they doused it? The acrid smell of wet ash stung their nostrils. They waited a few more minutes.

"Umm. Sorry," said Alice. "Guess it was the flare gun." She didn't say "again," not wanting to admit to these three men that she'd once lit her own pasture on fire, trying to see another intruder's license plate.

As the men stood watching the pasture Alice scanned the driveway with her cell phone flash. She could only find one throwing star. "Ha," she muttered to herself. "Ha." The other one had gotten the tire.

"Well, I guess the dragon has almost eaten the moon now," Bryce said. "This is not exactly how I planned to watch it." They looked up. The Milky Way was brilliant, sparkling from horizon to horizon. Only a silver sliver of moon was left, the rest an umber memory. Back in the house they turned on the lights and looked at each other. John T's hands were scraped from hanging on rocks and his arms were bruised and abraded from wrestling on the cliff path with Dark Man. Bryce had leaves in his hair, a swelling bruise on his face and a long bloody scrape on one arm. Both glowed with pride—householders defending their turf.

"Hey, John T, your little stunt with the Zorro whip?" said Bryce. "That was a real cliff-hanger." He waited for a response, then raised his eyebrows.

They all rolled their eyes. Alice couldn't help laughing, in sheer relief.

"Sorry about your antique fishing spear," Kinsear said. "I couldn't find it anywhere."

"Not sure, but I believe it's out front. The dark-haired guy was trying to yank something off his arm when he ran to the car," said Alice. "Maybe you winged him."

"Oh my. That spear's got some sharp little barbs on it. Pulling it out might be pretty painful. Which makes me happy," Bryce said.

John T bustled around the kitchen, pulling bowls of cold shrimp and homemade red sauce out of the refrigerator. Alice arranged more devilled eggs on the devilled egg plate. Kinsear poured wine. Bryce lit candles. Out on the deck, they lifted glasses to the now-dark moon, a deep umber, and took turns peeking through the telescope.

"Wait! We forgot to call the police!" said Alice.

"Oh yeah. I'll do it." Bryce called the Coffee County Sheriff's Department, repeating the entire license plate as Alice called it out. "No sir, they're gone. Think the car had a flat tire so maybe you can find it. We would have called sooner but we had to"—Put out the grass fire? Effect a cliff rescue?—"we had to find one of our party. No, nothing was taken, at least as far as we know." Finally he hung up. "Well, the police will start looking. Alice, do you agree they look like the same guys you saw outside the shop?"

She nodded.

"Well, it felt good to terrorize someone else for a change, after the indignity of having to hide in the bedroom while they ransacked my office. I guess they still thought no one was home, that we'd gone to market. Oh well. Alice, let's eat."

So they sat beneath the brightening moon as the dragon slowly relinquished its hold, retelling their stories, laughing aloud in relief. Comrades in arms. Comrades in odd old arms, of varied provenance.

Chapter Ten

Looking for Nuclear DNA

On Monday Silla bounced in, red ponytail embellished with a purple ribbon. "When did you get here?" she said. "Looks like you finished the whole pot of coffee!"

"We've got to pounce." Alice handed Silla her drafts. "First, we need to file an action for recovery of real property here in Coffee County, for the Blue Pool property. There's an alternate claim for trespass to try title. We'll include an affidavit from Mr. Navarro, as well as an affidavit as to what's on file in the property records. We may have to file in Blanco County too, since the ranch crosses the property line, but file in Coffee County first; then we'll ask that the cases be consolidated."

Silla nodded.

"Second, we're filing an application to intervene in the Coffee County Groundwater District proceedings involving the Blue Pool permit application, saying that the permit applicants have no right to drill for groundwater since they don't own the land. That one's probably on the fast track, since it has to be filed at least a week ahead of the hearing."

"Easy, we just file that at the groundwater district office. I'll get started on these. But Alice, you know you told me to check the nearby counties as to Drinkman ownership and anything Alex owned besides Blue Pool?"

"Right."

"It took me a while. Mr. Alastair Drinkman bought quite a bit of property beginning in 1910 and he didn't limit his purchases to Medina County. In 1916 he bought a big ranch in the north part of Frio County, and deeded a half interest to Alex Drinkman. I could not find any subsequent deeds. And guess what? It included the mineral interests, and they've never been severed."

"Really?" Alice's ears pricked up. There was a good bit of Eagle Ford shale production in Frio County. "You didn't find any mineral leases, I assume?"

"Nope. Of course I looked. But if I read the legal description right, the drilling in Frio County might be getting fairly close to this ranch." Silla, whose family was from Oklahoma, kept tabs for her extended family on their scattered mineral interests. Even for old stripper wells, there was often enough oil and gas production that the royalty checks provided a welcome boost to the family budget.

"Well, then let's go ahead and file another action for recovery of real property in Frio County." She began worrying. "As soon as we can! Now that they've seen the letter, the Drinkmans may start filing affidavits of heirship saying they own Alex's property!"

Silla brought in the deeds she'd found, and marched out with Alice's drafts.

Alice sat at her desk, stewing over whether she'd picked the right procedures. She'd never dealt with a case exactly like this. She called David Frohbel, her real estate and probate lawyer buddy in Fredericksburg, to brainstorm, first confirming he had no Drinkman clients.

"I'm trying to decide if I should also file, in Medina County, a request for administration of my client's father's estate, or maybe an application for determination of heirship, asking the district judge to declare that my client is the decedent's heir."

"And you're worried that the opposition—I assume the Drinkmans—will claim the four-year statute bars even a request for administration, or the application?"

"Yes," said Alice. "I think they'll argue we're time-barred. I don't think so, of course, but they'll argue it's a frivolous position and ask for sanctions."

"You can deal with that. But if you're just going after land, is all you need your application for recovery of land?" asked Froebel.

"I'm worried or I wouldn't ask you," retorted Alice. "It's possible, but doubtful, we could ask for more than land."

"You might want an accounting of mineral interests, or royalty payments," said Frohbel.

"Theoretically, but the minerals haven't produced yet. And our decedent apparently owned one small lot in Madrone, in Medina County."

The line was silent while the two brooded, separately.

"You know, if it were me, I'd think about getting local counsel in Medina County."

"I was thinking of asking Mark Tompkins." No one knew better the arcane mores and customs of the Bexar County Courthouse and its judges. She hoped he could manage next-door Medina County as well.

"Good choice."

"Also I'm thinking at some point we should ask the court to rule that Alejandro Navarro is entitled to control his father's remains, and include a motion for temporary restraining order forbidding any disturbance of his body."

"Alice, are you thinking about exhumation?"

Alice didn't answer for a moment. "I guess I could also do that in the action for recovery for land, though." She sighed. "Thanks, David. Always good to talk to you."

"You've done the same for me many a time. And you'll notice I couldn't give you an answer."

"Tell Isabel hello." And Alice hung up, feeling somewhat better.

Next, Alice called Alejandro Navarro and told him she'd be sending to Sandro's office a draft affidavit concerning his heirship for the Blue Pool property. "You'll need to sign it before a notary and get it back to me. Let me know of anything incorrect, or anything that bothers you, so we can fix it."

More coffee needed. And more thinking. She needed a criminal mind. Well, a criminal defense mind. Mr. Navarro had authorized her to get another lawyer to help if she thought it was needed. She picked up the phone again.

"Tyler? Alice. I need to pick your brain about DNA testing."

"At this hour of the morning? I'm not adequately caffeinated yet. Can you come over here?"

Alice liked visiting Tyler Junkin's office, in an old house like her office. He had toys everywhere—pool table, jukebox, a furry trout with fangs hanging over the toilet in the restroom. Maybe that was to relax his terrified clients. Or maybe he threatened the recalcitrant ones with the trout. Or a pool cue.

Tyler had gained a pound or two around the middle, but his eyes and his brain were sharp as ever. "You look worried," he told her. "Don't fret. DNA testing has made huge leaps in the last few years. What're you trying to do?"

After, again, making sure of no conflict, Alice plunged in. "I have a lock of hair from a man who died in 1919. I want to prove he's the father of my client."

"Where is the hair?"

"Tied in a ribbon in a bandana in an embroidered bag in an oiled-silk packet in my safe."

"Where's it been?"

"Um, under some oilcloth in an old nightstand."

"Where? Since when?"

"Um. Some question about since when. Facts are murky."

"Do you have any evidence the hair is from the father?"

"Alex Drinkman, that's his name. Well, not to say evidence. Someone wrote 'Alex' on the label."

"Someone? How can I cross-examine 'someone'?"

"It was folded into a bandana that was labeled 'Alex, from his body.'"

"Labeled by whom?"

"Um. The bandana and the lock of hair were in the embroidered bag that was in the oiled-silk packet with the letter from Alex Drinkman to his father."

"But he didn't put them in there."

"No, of course not, but . . ."

"And where has this envelope been since . . . 1919?"

Alice nodded. "Yep. I see what you're saying." The scope of potential Drinkman challenges to these filings was expanding by the minute.

He went on. "To whom was the letter addressed?"

"His father, Alastair Drinkman."

"But how did the letter get into the nightstand? Who put it there? Why is it not in the possession of the recipient?"

Alice blew out her breath. "Time for some creative thinking, Tyler. I need to find the best DNA lab I can afford, with someone who can help us on these chain-of-custody issues, if that's what they are. I'm terrified we'll contaminate the sample or make the results uncertain."

"Hair alone is not a guaranteed result, Alice. If someone just cut a lock of hair, you aren't going to have the hair follicle, and that's what you'd want for DNA testing. For samples from two males, you're looking for nuclear DNA for Y-chromosome testing."

"Just hair won't work?"

"Well, I'm not saying it won't work; you'll be within a range of probability, but nothing like you would with a hair follicle. Got anything besides the hair?"

"The bandana. It has blood on it."

"Whose blood?"

She glared at him. "Alex was shot! It's his blood!" But was she sure?

"Well, with blood, again it's going to depend on how deteriorated the sample is. Now if it's been in a hot attic in West Texas for eighty-some years, you're possibly screwed."

"I heard the words 'root cellar' . . . maybe we have a shot."

"Maybe. Anything else you can think of?"

Alice shook her head. What else could she come up with?

"Look, Alice, you're going to want the best lab you can possibly get."

"I know."

"I can give you names. Now, how soon do you want the results?"

"I was going to go ahead and get an action to recover land on file, which will require a determination of my client's right to inherit that land. And we're intervening in the groundwater permit hearing."

"In advance of the DNA results? What if they come back—contrary? Or just indeterminate?"

Alice felt nauseous. She desperately wanted to file both right away, to protect Blue Pool from the threatened drilling permit. But to win, Alejandro Navarro must show that he was Alex Drinkman's son and heir. What if the letter was wrong? A hoax? What if Alex Drinkman thought "my little Alejandro" was his son—but he wasn't? Wouldn't it be nice to get definitive test results back and know for sure, before filing? The last thing she wanted was to make Alejandro Navarro—with his proud war record, his family, his long career—look ridiculous. Worst case: what if DNA results were a clear negative?

But the groundwater district required that the intervention be filed soon. Did she have time to get DNA results?

Tyler went on. "I know of one accredited lab in Austin that can tackle hair shafts without a root, or a bloodstain on cloth, and seems to get good results. That lab's pricey. And you know whatever you come up with will still be challenged."

"Still, we could start there. How can I be sure we don't screw up—contaminate—the sample before we send it?"

"I'd call and get them to walk you through it. They understand. They add a fee when their test has got legal implications."

"Tyler, thanks. I'm going back to the office. I've got to talk to the client. And the lab. I'll call you in a bit."

Back at the office, Alice first called the Austin lab. An employee promised confidentiality, then outlined the time needed and the costs for rush results. After listening to the circumstances, the employee also strongly recommended that the lab handle the taking of all samples, and urged Alice to bring all material to be sampled, and Mr. Navarro, to the lab. "Saves time and money in the long run," he said.

Alice got both Sandro and Alejandro Navarro on the phone. She outlined the need for haste and the risks haste posed.

"I don't want to look like an idiot if the letter—if there are problems with the letter and the DNA!" said Sandro.

"Well, nor do I," said his father. "Can we get a quick read on some of the DNA? The hair and the blood, maybe?"

"Based on what the lab said, we could ask for a rush and at least have some results with a good level of confidence fairly soon, depending on the state of the samples," said Alice. "But at the groundwater district we ought to get at least a bare request to intervene filed by next Monday, and that's before we're likely to get any results. I could try filing just the request to intervene, and then we could supplement with the affidavit and the results before the final deadline. Another reason I want to get the DNA samples done is that I worry about—well, what if someone steals the letter and the bandana and the hair? What if someone steals Alex's body from his grave, so we can't double-check? Might be far-fetched, but we've already had two break-ins."

"I'd like a little more certainty before I sign that affidavit you mentioned." Mr. Navarro's deep voice. "But I agree we need to go ahead and intervene to stop that permit, right away."

"Okay. We'll go that route. We're also going to need a sample from you, Mr. Navarro. I think just a cheek swab."

"You want to do that today?"

"Yes."

She heard a whispered conversation in the background.

"I'll be at your office in—what, an hour? No, less than an hour. Tomás is driving me."

"Okay. Just don't get killed before I get that cheek sample, okay? We'll drive you to the lab from here."

Alice found Silla. "Silla, here's the lab address. It's in Austin on North MoPac. Can you bring Mr. Navarro? I'll go ahead and take the rest of the material in and meet you there."

And the cheek swab reminded her of something nagging at her brain . . . no, she couldn't retrieve it. But she needed to.

* * * * *

"Whew." Silla wiped her forehead with a tissue. "Okay, Alice, what next?"

The lab had all the samples.

"So, we go ahead and file a motion to intervene in the permit proceeding, at the groundwater district. We attach an affidavit reciting the state of the records and that the Drinkmans have no title. Then we supplement—or fold—when we get lab results. If the results are promising we'll file the applications for recovery of land immediately."

Alice sighed. Her law practice had never before included racing to a faceless building on North MoPac to hand over precious artifacts to a gloved lab tech who violated a lock of hair belonging to her client's possible relative by moving selected strands into the sterile container specified by the DNA protocol. The tech had assured Alice she would carefully follow DNA lab protocols for the bandana, with its bloodstains, and the bloody bullet. The tech had assured Alice that yes, the bandana would be returned. So would the bloody bullet. Mr. Navarro, rigid in a chair, had opened his mouth for a cheek swab. The DNA lab manager came out personally to assure Alice that the lab was well prepared to handle such samples and would provide expedited results for a hefty fee. But she warned Alice that while DNA results could be obtained from even partially degraded material, like the blood on the bandana, the value of the results could be questioned by contamination or deterioration, given the storage history of the material. "And I don't know that the hair will help, since we don't appear to have roots. But we'll certainly look at it." Fingers crossed, thought Alice, fingers crossed the lab report will show definitively that Alex Drinkman and Alejandro Navarro are father and son. Fingers crossed the report will come back fast enough to fend off issuance of a groundwater withdrawal permit for the golf course. And so, fingers crossed, Blue Pool would not wind up sucked dry, its blue-green reflecting eye shrunken, diminished, ruined.

* * * * *

"Drink," ordered Tyler Junkin, sagging into the chair at her antique tea table and pointing at the cabinet.

He knew where Alice kept the Talisker.

She put a cube of ice in one crystal highball glass (she eschewed ice in hers), and tilted the bottle. She poured just a capful of bottled water into hers—"to release the flavor," as Jordie always told her.

"Perfect peatiness," she told Tyler. "Just peaty enough."

They sat at Alice's tea table, each thinking separate worries.

"What if"—each said at once.

"You first," said Tyler.

"Okay." Alice leaned forward. "We have a hole card. If the results are not definitive, there is something else we can try."

"Besides hair? Besides blood? What are you thinking, we exhume the body under cover of darkness and chop off a little of one of his femurs? Or possibly a bit of tibia?"

"We could. Surely it's a crime to meddle with buried bodies, but it is Mr. Navarro's own father, or so we hope to prove."

"You might seriously consider a graveyard raid. Maybe some of the hair . . . maybe some still has follicles? Or teeth. Teeth with roots?

Also, femurs are quite useful."

"Could we? That graveyard is in a very small town." Alice said. "People might notice."

"Streetlights?"

"Maybe not. But anyway, Tyler, what about the envelope?"

He stared back.

"Alex Drinkman licked that stamp. Surely he did. And the envelope flap too, don't you think?"

Tyler nodded, lifted one eyebrow in appreciation.

"But as you are already thinking, that's destructive. Or at least I expect it is. Would mess up our exhibit for testing by the other side."

He shook his head. "I'm not so sure. I think the lab would try to steam the stamp off, and also steam open the flap."

"Maybe we could offer it as our hole card for court-supervised testing, if these first results are not definitive."

"I like that idea. Let's get this initial testing done and depending on the results, we can either go forward with the stamp and the envelope ourselves, or under agreed court order."

* * * * *

Tyler had left. Silla had left too, but not until she warned Alice: "Remember, you have that ranch closing next Tuesday morning and you owe documents back to the title company and the lawyer on the other side. They're on your desk." Sitting in blessed quiet, Alice flopped down at her big partner desk, stared out the window for a while, trying to clear her mind of DNA uncertainties. Then she took a deep breath, called her buyer client, called the seller's lawyer in Houston, worked out some issues, and plunged back into the reassuringly familiar world of real estate transactions. She finished marking up the documents and emailed them to the seller's lawyer. Ball's in your court, she thought. Such a great feeling.

It was very quiet. The old hall clock ticked loudly. Alice felt a tension between her shoulder blades that gave her the nagging sense of something undone. What?

She got up, walked into the hall, looked in Silla's workroom, checked the lock on the back door leading out of the kitchen. Locked. Walked into the conference room. Ah. The closet door was wide open, revealing the safe . . . the safe holding the oiled-silk packet, still holding the letter, the envelope, the lock of hair. What if . . . what if someone broke in? Set the office on fire? Oh, don't be ridiculous, she thought. Then she remembered a prior break-in, when a rogue lawyer was looking for her client's documents.

Maybe a safety deposit box. Maybe hide the ticking time bomb in the vault at Madrone Bank? It was already nearly five. The bank had closed at four thirty. She would do it tomorrow, first thing. Very first thing. On the way to the office. She unlocked the safe, removed the mailing envelope with its oiled-silk packet inside, relocked the safe, and then locked the conference room closet and the conference room itself, pocketing the keys.

Now she knew she would worry every second until the oiled-silk packet with its contents was in the bank vault. She had to do something. Her briefcase? Too risky. Her purse? Too risky. She slipped the mailing envelope containing the packet into her yoga backpack, grabbed her purse, locked up, headed to the driveway, started the truck, and realized she'd forgotten the briefcase. Am I losing my mind? Early Alzheimer's? She threw open the door, unlatched her seatbelt, and, on second thought, grabbed the backpack and stalked off toward the office, leaving the truck idling. Inside she grabbed the briefcase from the chair where she'd left it. The phone rang—lawyer for the seller, with a couple of questions about timing and escrow on a tax-free exchange. Good. She hung up, remembered the briefcase again and headed for the front door.

That night Alice slept with the backpack, slipping one leg into the shoulder straps. Made it hard to get up in the night and pee, but she was terrified of losing the letter, like it was a baby, a child, a piece of Alex. She even moved it to the bathroom and showered with the glass shower door open, where she could see it. Then straight to Madrone Bank she drove, clutching her safety deposit box key.

Now to wait for those results from the DNA lab.

Chapter   Eleven

An Abuse of Process

At midmorning on Monday Alice finished her comments on a conservation easement. Done! She was marching to the kitchen for celebratory coffee when the phone rang. Deep voice, measured. "Ms. Greer? My name is Jonathan Whiteside. I represent Oak Motte Links, LLC."

The applicant for the golf course groundwater permit. "So you are with Black and Whiteside in San Antonio? Are you the Whiteside?"

"Um, that's my dad." Aha, he was faking his grownup voice. "We have recently begun representing Drinkman interests. You filed an intervention last Friday in our permit application before the Coffee County Groundwater Conservation District."

"Right."

"It's not right. It's an abuse of process. You don't have any proof that this—Mr. Navarro, whoever he is—is an heir of the Drinkmans. Your petition's just a bare assertion of lack of ownership by my clients. I'm calling to tell you to dismiss it." The measured syllables, the deliberately and artificially deep intonation.

Tell me to dismiss it? *Tell me*? *Señor*, you are making a grievous error. Now she was standing behind her desk, holding the telephone like a hammer.

"Actually, *Jonathan*, it's your application that's an abuse of process. Oak Motte Links has no right to the water it's asking for. If you want to talk about a bare assertion of ownership, that's yours. And we're confident we will establish that your cupboard is bare." Heart pounding. Such arrogance.

The voice rose to tenor range. "I'm calling as a *courtesy* to tell you we are seeking a temporary restraining order to prevent you from interfering with the permit. It's set for hearing tomorrow."

"Tomorrow? I assume you're talking about Coffee County, of course." He'd better be or she'd challenge jurisdiction.

"Yes. Before Judge Sandoval. He can hear us at four thirty."

Oh lord. She still had no results back from the lab tests. And she had a probate hearing tomorrow afternoon to prepare for. "Tomorrow is not convenient and there's plenty of time before the hearing on the permit application, so your status quo is not at risk. I request that you move the TRO hearing to a date next week. I'll arrange my calendar to make that possible."

"Nope. That's not convenient for us. Four thirty tomorrow."

"Professional courtesy would dictate otherwise."

"We're going to be there at four thirty, whether you're there or not. This is all the notice you'll get."

Little twit. She hung up and fired off a letter documenting that while tomorrow at four thirty was not convenient, she had offered to be available any time next week. She had Silla email and mail it. She'd have a copy delivered to the court too. What did she know about Judge Sandoval? Brand new to the bench—just elected last November. Republican. Had practiced law in Austin and then moved to Coffee County, like Alice had. And hadn't she seen him once at Rotary? She had. Well, it was Monday.

But she hadn't planned to go. With a sigh, Alice got the ritual red sweater out of the office coat closet and donned it in the office bathroom. Her friend Red had given her the sweater and insisted Alice wear it when she first hauled Alice, new to Coffee Creek, off to a Rotary lunch. Alice had finally started keeping it at the office. A few months earlier, she had forgotten to wear the red sweater to a Rotary meeting and the woman at the desk handing out nametags hadn't recognized her. Ritually garbed, off she went.

Jorgé Benavides stood right at the entrance to the Rotary meeting room at the Coffee Creek Drop Inn, glad-handing like he was running for office. He hugged Alice.

"You running for council?" said Alice. "Usually you're so—buttoned down! Reserved!"

"Let's go grab food. I was just doing a little meet 'n' greet, reminding people how they love the Beer Barn. Just in case we get to build my dream place."

She looked a question at him, then followed him to the buffet. Barbecue today. Well, she needed fortification. She decorated the sliced brisket with the sauce labeled "Heat: bath temp" and then topped it off with "Heat: sauna." No potato salad, plenty of coleslaw, a cautious and judicious amount of beans. Jorgé had put pork ribs on his plate next to a few brisket slices.

"*Pork ribs?*"

"Pork's moving in, Alice. Pretty soon you're gonna see some pork shoulder on this buffet. Beef's getting pricey right now." He shook his head. "End of the world."

Alice agreed. She hated change. Besides, she could not, absolutely could not, eat pork ribs with her fingers at Rotary. Grease on cheeks, bits caught in teeth. "Jorgé, do you know Judge Sandoval?"

"Bernie? Of course. See him at church all the time. He comes to the Beer Barn now and then, maybe not so much since he got elected."

"I'd like to meet him. I have a hearing coming up."

Wise brown eyes looked at her, eyebrows lifted. "Watch this."

Jorgé shouldered his way back toward the buffet, where he captured a portly man carrying a plate of coleslaw and beans and brought him back to their table. The table filled immediately, with introductions all around—bankers, George the surveyor, a council member.

"Judge, that's pitiful. Coleslaw and beans?" George pointed at Judge Sandoval's scanty plate.

"Well, I have to tell you, I've gained ten pounds since getting elected. Sitting on the bench is—it's sitting. Couldn't get a more sedentary job than sitting. If the coleslaw diet doesn't work, I'm going to water."

Jorgé introduced Alice. "Our lawyer, Judge. Saved the Beer Barn when it was under serious threat last winter." Judge Sandoval smiled, stuck his hand out.

George the surveyor put his fork down. "Hey, Alice. Can you come talk to our surveyor chapter about the new title policy tweaks? I heard you gave that talk to some lenders. In case you can't tell, I got stuck with being program chair."

"Be glad to." And conversation became general. Good. She'd done nothing untoward, said nothing *ex parte* about the case, but Judge Sandoval would recognize her tomorrow in his courtroom.

On the way back to the office Alice stopped at Madrone Bank and retrieved the letter. She called the DNA lab and explained. She and Silla wrapped the package, using packing tape on every square inch. Silla drove it straight to the lab. "Yes, I got there fine, yes, the lab signed for it," Silla said when she returned from the errand. Then she cocked her head. "Why didn't we do that in the first place?"

"I had some silly idea about a cooperative joint testing effort, blessed by a court somewhere. But forget it. Just forget it, Black and Whiteside."

Then Alice stared mesmerized at the Drinkman Foundation website, and the formal photograph of Will Drinkman, anxiety growing by the minute. His face showed no human compassion. Trying to read his eyes, she saw—"I will crush you. I will outspend you. I will humiliate you."

Oh, come on, Alice. He's just a rich guy. Just another guy who, as Ann Richards and others famously said, was born on third base and thought he hit a triple. Is that what unlimited money does to someone? No, she corrected herself. Not necessarily. It's his look of total entitlement. That's not just money talking. And you are just speculating, you're just nervous about that TRO hearing. Pull up your socks.

Neglecting still to grab her socks, Alice scrolled through more articles. "Will Drinkman outflanks rivals to buy nationwide radio station chain"; "New reach for Drinkmans with heartland channel coverage"; "Drinkmans fill air vacuum in rural areas"; "Will Drinkman gets his message out." Eight years earlier the Drinkman interests had bought a strong privately held chain of FM stations out where local public radio never reached and set up sophisticated talk radio, carrying not just commodities reports for cattle and corn but a steady diet of anti–immigration reform rhetoric entangled with political commentary.

So, he's focused. Let's hope he doesn't focus any longer on Bryce and the letter. Let's keep him focused on the Blue Pool, buy some time with the permit process.

She didn't have a snowball's chance without solid DNA results, though. Time to call the lab. She told the receptionist she was calling about test results. After five minutes a human voice took her off hold: "We're not ready to release results. We're finalizing the QA/QC section of the report now. It's not quite finished."

"But I have a hearing tomorrow at four thirty."

"We never send anything out without the QA/QC. Lab policy."

"Can you tell me the preliminary results?"

Pause. "I'll get someone to talk to you."

A cautious new voice told her the hair samples, including one stuck in the bandana, showed paternity within a certain percentage of likelihood.

"What does that mean?"

"That there's a likelihood of paternity within the stated percentage range based on the hair samples. We're still reviewing, but right now the review is approximately sixty percent. We're still waiting on the blood samples and the saliva samples."

Was this enough to show a substantial likelihood of success on the merits when the injunction hearing rolled around? Maybe not. But hopefully enough to argue for preserving the status quo at a TRO hearing? Maybe yes.

"Can you at least get me the hair report by three Central tomorrow?"

Pause. "Yes. But only as a draft, which we reserve the right to alter; it will be stamped DRAFT on every page."

"Okay." She gave him her email and Silla's. "I'm counting on you." And, she thought, I can always promise the final ASAP. Surely this will fend off a TRO. And Judge Sandoval wouldn't lightly remove initial jurisdiction from the groundwater district, would he?

* * * * *

At 4:25 on Tuesday afternoon, Alice stood in the anteroom of Judge Bernard Sandoval's office, next to his courtroom on the third floor of the Coffee County Courthouse. She had rushed upstairs from the probate hearing downstairs and speed-walked straight to the women's restroom for a few private moments to calm her breathing, before walking steadily into the judge's small suite of offices—receptionist, secretary, and then his chambers, book-lined and quiet, with a door opening directly into the back of his courtroom, just a few feet from his bench. She talked to the judge's secretary.

"Alice! You drafted my mother's will. She told me all about you."

Alice asked how she was.

"Oh, she's fine, Alice. Now she's into chickens. Bought four little *cuatros* of bantam chickens. Sixteen chickens, four different colors. She built a chicken chateau—really a chicken Versailles—under an oak tree in the backyard. Every night she and her dog go out to the pen and corral those chickens and put 'em in their house. And every morning she's out there with the dog releasing the chickens and looking for eggs. She's having a ball." She waggled her eyebrows. "She tells me she's going to change her will to leave a trust fund for their care, after she's gone. Please don't take her call. Or if you do, tell me she can't make me the chickens' trustee."

Alice laughed. "Bet she can."

At 4:29 the heavy old varnished doors opened and in marched what Alice concluded were Whiteside Senior and Whiteside Junior. Whiteside Junior was carrying two heavy litigation briefcases, or "lit bags," bulging with files.

Alice opened the door to the judge's chambers and led the way in. "Judge, good afternoon." She nodded.

Judge Sandoval stood up behind the desk, shirtsleeves rolled to his forearms. "Ms. Greer. Good afternoon." The Whiteside team entered. Alice kept her eyes cool and extended her hand to Whiteside Senior, not leaving what she considered her "key" position just left of center of the judge's desk. Squash-court term, holding the key. One of the important concepts she learned in college. Whiteside Senior gave her a limp handshake, fingers only, no smile, and sagged into the chair on the far right.

Whiteside Junior buffeted her leg with his bulging lit bag. "Oh, excuse me," he said. She didn't budge, just looked at him.

"Okay, what've we got here?" Judge Sandoval leafed through the file.

"Judge, I've just filed this downstairs." Alice, still standing, handed him a courtesy copy of her filed response to the request for a temporary restraining order, and handed another to Whiteside Senior.

"Your Honor, we haven't had a chance to review this!" protested Whiteside Senior, his nose reddening.

"Your Honor," Alice squared up, "these gentlemen cannot protest about timing. They called yesterday at ten thirty announcing a hearing today at four thirty. I told them I had a three thirty hearing in probate court downstairs today but could be available any time next week. They refused any alternate date. I intend to show and will show that they have no standing to pursue the groundwater permit for Blue Pool, much less to prevent my client from intervening in the permit proceedings, which he is entitled to do under groundwater district rules. The relevant rules are Exhibit B to our filing. I will show the groundwater district that opposing counsel's clients have no ownership in the land where they propose to drill a well, and no standing to get a permit, much less to seek a temporary restraining order against my client. And I will show that my client is the rightful owner."

The Whitesides erupted from their chairs, protesting that their clients had paid taxes on Blue Pool and fenced it.

"Ms. Greer?" The judge moved large eyes to her, leaning back in his chair.

"Your Honor, record ownership is still in the name of Alex Drinkman, a young World War I pilot killed in 1919 on his way to visit his father. He had acknowledged my client was his son in a letter before he was killed." Well, maybe "acknowledged" was a slight stretch. "And we have preliminary lab tests confirming the likelihood of paternity."

Whiteside Junior was riffling through the lab report, which was an exhibit to Alice's filing. "Your Honor, this report is just a draft."

"Of course it's a draft, given my opponents' precipitous effort to get a temporary restraining order, Your Honor—there's a final report to come. But you do not need the final report to deny a TRO today—opposing counsel has not met the standard. A TRO should preserve the status quo. Instead, opposing counsel asks you to alter the status quo by preventing my client from seeking to intervene in a permit hearing where, properly, the groundwater district will make the initial determination as to whether he can intervene."

Judge Sandoval pursed his lips, shifted his eyes to the Whitesides. "Gentlemen?"

Whiteside Senior rose, rocking forward. "Your Honor, the permit is very important to my client, which will use the water as part of a golf course resort which will bring many jobs to Coffee County." Ah, the election ploy—reminding the judge of his voting constituents.

"The property involved is very valuable and once developed will be a major asset to the county." Ah, the tax-base ploy. "This Mr., uh, Navarro has no right to keep my client from going forward. This so-called report"—waving Alice's filing—"this is just—just speculation."

The judge's eyes were back on Alice.

"Your Honor, the question of value is indeed important—to my client. Water rights associated with *his* property—not the proposed golf course, but the Blue Pool acreage where the proposed well would be drilled—are *his*, tied to his ownership of the surface. We know his rights are very valuable. Yet opposing counsel offers you no proof of *any* ownership in the Blue Pool acres that are rightfully my client's."

"There's no need!" barked Whiteside Senior.

Alice plowed on. "Nor, Your Honor, has opposing counsel any chance to win a preliminary injunction on the merits. Mr. Navarro is the rightful heir. Finally, a TRO precluding the groundwater district from even considering Mr. Navarro's intervention will not maintain the status quo—it deprives my client of rights in a potentially catastrophic fashion. That is not the purpose of the TRO, as we all know."

The judge nodded slowly. "Gentlemen, I don't see why you were in such an all-fired hurry to come up and see me today. I'm going to deny the TRO, and let the groundwater district deal with what is before it"—he held up a hand—"at this point."

"But, Your Honor, we can dispute this!" Whiteside Senior waved Alice's filing. "We just haven't had time."

"Of course you can file what you want to, but you'd still need to show me why you're entitled to the extraordinary remedy of a TRO." He stood, smiled, nodded.

They all stood, chorusing, "Thank you, Your Honor."

Chapter   Twelve

A Little Home Cooking

With the Whitesides still packing up their bags, the judge stepped out to the anteroom. Alice could hear him talking to his secretary about the outgoing mail. Normally she would try to gather information from opposing counsel. Today?

"You got a little home cooking, young lady," snapped Whiteside Senior.

Alice raised an eyebrow. Young lady? Home cooking? "Nope, Judge Sandoval just applied the law. You didn't meet the test."

"Our expert will shoot your DNA report so full of holes it'll look like—like Swiss cheese!" countered Whiteside Junior.

"And who is that?"

"You'll find out soon enough!"

Alice just raised her eyebrows and smiled. She decided not to ask if she'd see them at the groundwater permit hearing, or if they planned to file anything with its board. Maybe they'd forget. She picked up her briefcase and left them to their feverish repacking, then walked into the anteroom, smiled at the secretary, nodded at the judge. "Judge."

And out the heavy old wooden door into the worn marble-tiled hallway she went, wondering where she would find a DNA expert. And why hadn't she already thought about that? Probably should have nailed down an outside expert before she even delivered the samples. The lab could testify about its own protocols, but what about what had happened to the oiled-silk packet before that? *When I was trying to get the samples out of Dodge before someone grabbed the letter and the bandana and the lock of hair . . .* A wave of nausea washed over her. *What if she'd already screwed up the samples somehow, when she first sat down with Bryce? Getting advice from an expert first would have been so much smarter. Hindsight.*

Back at her office, she dropped her briefcase on the floor with a sigh, called the DNA lab, asked for the manager, finally got her. "Who has defended your work in court? Successfully, in particular?"

Dr. Felix Apple, Boston. Okay. She punched in his number, hoping he wasn't about to announce he had already taken a gig as the Whitesides' mystery expert. Outside she saw Kinsear's old Land

Cruiser pull up and heard him open the door and head straight for the kitchen. She left a message for Felix Apple—damn Eastern time, he was already gone. She found Kinsear in the kitchen with Silla, talking over Silla's chances in the Coffee County Rodeo. "If I can beat that Ginnylou Hammer from Blanco this year with my new horse, that alone counts as success." Silla's new horse, she said, could stop on a dime and make a tight turn look simple. And she still detested Ginnylou, who had beaten her in the College Rodeo Championship by seven-tenths of a second.

"Don't you and Ginnylou ever go out for beers?" asked Kinsear.

Silla flashed her eyes at him. "In your dreams."

Kinsear looked at Alice. "Fierce women in this office." Still stumping along in his orthopedic boot, he followed Alice into her office. "Glad to see you're still alive."

"Of course I am!"

"Unlike Carey Norville. And how's that reporter?"

Yikes. She had not checked further since the Rotonda incident. And where had Rose been that day?

"You have time for supper?" Kinsear asked abruptly.

Alice felt the usual initial resistance—why? work, papers, filings—then felt a sudden desire to escape the office. With Kinsear.

Kinsear headed out the door, unlocked the Land Cruiser, and handed Alice up into the tall front seat. "Let's take Penelope for a ride. Picnic's in the back. Take us ten minutes to get there."

He headed east of Wimberley on the River Road, turning in at the Flag Ranch wedding venue. Alice raised her eyebrows at him. "Owner's a friend of mine, Jan McNair. Sold me my horses. She's got a picnic spot by the river."

He carried the hamper down a wood-chip path. The Blanco, a cloudy blue-green, glimmered between the baroque cypress trunks that lined the river. "Ah." He headed for the wooden deck, partly roofed, next to the river, where a table and two chairs sat side by side in the green shade.

Alice walked onto the deck, listening to the soft rush of river. Clear water, the bottom visible, dragonflies flicking from sun to shade.

She helped unpack the hamper.

"I'm trying M.A.'s pimento cheese recipe. Finally got the secret ingredient out of her." Months earlier, M.A. Ellison had helped Alice and Kinsear and others find a disappeared singer-songwriter.

"What is it?"

"It's a secret. Not telling, unless you provide adequate incentive."

Alice scooted her chair closer, nibbled his earlobe, fit herself next to him.

"Was it the mayonnaise?" he muttered, hands around Alice. "Was it a little shot of hot sauce? Or . . . horseradish?" He leaned down, kissed her. The kiss lasted through several inquiring birdcalls, many seconds of rushing water.

"Uncle!" Alice gasped. "Pimento cheese?"

"Oh yeah. Also some of those crackers you like and my own Sheik Kinsear hummus with red peppers to dip with. And a little cold Prosecco." He lifted it out of the hamper. "And real glasses. And brownies from the Sugar Jones Bakery."

"Oh oh. The kind with extra chocolate chips?"

"Correct."

Alice put her hands around the nape of his neck, leaned in shamelessly, kissed him thoroughly.

"Let's pop the Prosecco." He disentangled himself. They toasted life and the day and ate in silence, with occasional *mm*'s. Then they adjourned to the edge of the deck, dangling bare feet in the water.

"So here's what I'm thinking," Kinsear said.

Alice lifted her head inquiringly, waiting.

"I'm thinking we . . . we . . . I'm thinking you—"

Alice's phone rang. She ignored it. It rang again. She ignored it. The text tone beeped. Deep sigh. *"Alice, call me ASAP. Silla."* She showed it to Kinsear.

"Ignore it. I want to talk to you about the rest of our lives." His phone beeped. She laughed. His phone beeped again. Then his voicemail beeped—a particularly annoying beep. He punched voicemail, listened. Alice could faintly hear: "Dad. Where are you? Call me." "Daughter," he said.

Alice ostentatiously put her phone on the far side of the picnic table, ignoring Silla's directive.

"I'll see your relinquished phone and raise you an ignored voicemail," said Kinsear, placing his phone by hers.

"I'll see your ignored voicemail and raise you—switched-off sound." Alice thumbed the sound off on hers.

"I'll see your switched-off sound and raise you by turning the damn thing off." He did so.

"I'll call and put them both in the hamper." Alice did, and sat back down on the dock. "So. The rest of our lives?"

She was filled with trepidation. How could she leave her office in Coffee Creek? How could he leave his bookstore in Fredericksburg?

They heard a four-wheeler crashing down the gravel drive. "Hey, Kinsear!" Stentorian tones from a blocky woman in gray chinos and roper boots, driving with one hand, a large dog bouncing on the seat next to her. "Kinsear, your bookstore called and said your daughter was looking for you!" She dismounted, stalked toward them, appraised the picnic table. "Jan McNair." Stuck out her hand.

"Alice Greer."

"Glad to meet a friend of Kinsear's. He's been alone too long. Needs someone to keep him busy. If you take my meaning." She grinned. Kinsear reddened. "Don't turn all girly on me, Kinsear." She turned back to Alice. "He and I've known each other a long time. Sorry he lost Betsy, but—life's hard. Got to get up and go on." Not missing a beat, she went on. "I appreciate what you did for Ollie West. That was one fine man."

When Alice's elderly rancher client Ollie had been murdered, at some peril Alice found the killer. "I loved Ollie. I still miss him."

"Hard to compete sometimes," Kinsear said. "With a dead octogenarian."

"He would have liked you and your bookstore," Alice said.

Jan McNair left them, roaring away back up the hill. Picnic over.

"Hey, what about that secret ingredient?" Alice asked.

"I'm thinking you still need to provide me with a little more incentive." He sighed. "Later."

Chapter Thirteen

Not Giving Up
a Single Dime

"**A** Ms. Adele Collins," reported Silla, sticking her head around the door the next morning.

Alice looked up from her monitor, then reached for the phone. "Alice Greer."

"Alice. Yes, John knows I'm calling. I've been thinking about our discussion. It made me visit the attic."

"Your attic?" Alice imagined the top story of the Woodville house, imagined old trunks, dress forms, ancient Christmas ornaments.

"Yes. I went up there recalling a particular box—my mother's college keepsakes. You might want to see it." Pause. "I've thought about it and decided you should see it. Fairly soon."

"This afternoon? I could leave in half an hour. Be there about three?"

"Fine." Click.

What could it be? Alice hadn't expected this from Adele and couldn't ignore it.

She sped out of Coffee Creek toward Bastrop, east of Austin, and angled up to Woodville. At a quarter to three she pulled up to the silent columned house. A first magnolia was opening on a dark glossy pyramidal tree in the side yard.

Again the housekeeper was walking down the wide hall to open the screen door before Alice could knock. "Miss Adele is expecting you." She turned and pointed Alice to the open door of the living room, and beyond the living room to a screened porch. Alice could smell the magnolia.

Adele Collins sat straight-backed at a coffee table. Next to her on the floor stood an open wooden trunk. "Bonnie Drinkman" was stenciled in black on one side. The faint smell of old ink, old paper, old wood, old leather rose from the trunk. Adele gestured Alice to a chair and raised her eyebrows at the housekeeper. "Iced tea?" Without preamble, she began. "My mother, Bonnie, started at Texas State College for Women, or TSCW, at barely seventeen. There was no place in Woodville good enough, Aunt Dee thought. Back then, the girls wore uniforms, blue skirts and little red and blue shoes. I used to play dress-up in hers. Anyway, classes were tough, but it was still a bit 'finishing school' in atmosphere. The girls put on pageants and fêtes, wrote keepsake books and diaries, took photographs with their box cameras, kept scrapbooks with dance programs. We still have mama's graduation cap and yearbook."

Iced tea arrived. Of course, sterling iced-tea spoons. No smile for Alice from the housekeeper.

"I wondered if the trunk had anything about mama's departure from the ranch after her brother Alex—my uncle—died." She took from her lap a pasteboard notebook with speckled covers and lined pages and handed it to Alice. "Look at the marked page, near the beginning."

Alice read:

> *Incipit vita nova!* I am at TSCW—a college girl! No boys here and it's very strict. Shoes must be polished, bed made, and we dress for dinner. So far my favorite classes are the English Greats and European history. I have my own room because Aunt Dee was so sudden getting me up here and everyone else was 'roomed up.' But the girls are friendly. My new best friend Lily showed me the ropes because I missed the first day of orientation. And for posterity, if any, I want to set down what happened. Aunt Dee is still nervous about my safety. Dear diary, you recall I broke my arm falling off Fandango, the day Willy invited me to go ride the north pasture and I'd put him off several times but was bored and said yes. The stable boy thought the girth looked cut and told Aunt Dee. She came out to the stable and looked but that night the saddle was gone and so was the stable boy. Miss Ella said he'd quit. Aunt Dee looked stern. That night after Doc Campbell set my arm (fortunately the left or how could I write this?) she told me we were leaving, and to point out my favorite things to her and not say a word. I sat in bed and pointed—my mama's jewel box, my old doll with the china face, the quilt mama made for me, and mama's silver hairbrush and mirror, and my diaries and poetry books. That's all that would fit in the bag. Aunt Dee said we were traveling fast and light and she'd explain later. Never a smile. The next morning before first light she took me outside, put me up on Fandango and we rode out. I guess she saddled those horses herself. We rode straight north to the Gustleben place and left the horses and Mr.

Gustleben drove us to San Antonio where we took the train to Woodville. On the train she said this, and I will set it down as she said it: "Your sweet father's will was well meant, but it did say that if you and Alex both died without heirs before your father did, the real property would go to Miss Ella. Alex is dead, and I don't like your chances around Willy."

"But he keeps saying he's sweet on me! Though I can't stand him."

"Exactly," said Aunt Dee. "If he can't figure one way through the brier patch, he'll find another, because with Alex dead, as long as you outlive your father, Miss Ella gets half that real property, and I believe Willy has his eye on the main chance. I may be doing him wrong, but I've got to be cautious; your mama would want you safe."

"But who will take care of my daddy?"

"Honey, your daddy wants you safe too. He—he's been worried." Then she said, "You remember how he had that first stroke when he heard about Alex, and then two days later the second stroke, so he couldn't walk and couldn't really talk. I was sitting with him one day when he gave me Alex's letter. He'd hidden it inside the Bible under his pillow. He waited until Ella went downstairs and then fished it out with his good hand and waved it at me, made me take it. I asked him twice, do you mean me to have it? He nodded. I put it in a bag in my nightstand with some things of Alex's. I glued them all under the oilcloth. I'll go back after I get you to TSCW and get that nightstand and my rocker."

So I listened to Aunt Dee and thought of Willy and I said, "What things of Alex's?"

She said, "You recall when the boy from Madrone rode up to tell us Alex was dead? And I rode down there alone because your father still had the influenza?"

I said yes.

"When I got to the Madrone store the proprietor and the foreman had just put Alex's body in the back room. The doctor was down with the influenza like your daddy. The sheriff had it so bad he was in the hospital in San Antonio. I kissed Alex's forehead. Bonnie, he had flesh wounds in his right arm and his right leg, but the gut shot did for him. I took his bandana and a lock of his hair. He was wearing his boots. The boy who rode to get me said, this looks like a bullet hole in the top of his boot. The bullet fell out when the proprietor pulled off Alex's boots and I took it for safekeeping. The foreman had fished out the saddlebag too. He loaded the motorcycle and the saddlebag in the wagon for me to bring back, with Alex's clothes and such. When I got home I saw the saddlebag had a hole in it. I found another bullet, stuck in my Tennyson, which was soaked and ruined." Then she gave me such a look. "After your accident, your daddy tried to tell me. All he could say was 'Bonnie,' and he waved his good hand, like 'shoo-fly,' meaning 'take her away!' I told him I was taking you to Woodville and then TSCW and he nodded and blinked his eyes, smiled on one side of his face and fell back on his pillow. Then he closed his eyes. That's why I left everything there and fled with you. I felt you were in mortal danger and I wouldn't be able to stop it."

That is what she said, dear diary. And when Aunt Dee finished, I remembered something. The day Alex died I was reading my history homework in daddy's office by the kitchen where I always did—the old leather chair by the gun cabinet. I did notice a gap in the gun cabinet, right next to my mother's old twenty-two I was supposed to get on my seventeenth birthday. The gap was where daddy kept the Savage, next to his old Sharps. I didn't think about it because anyone could borrow a gun for varmints. When that boy came riding up to tell about Alex I ran to my room, praying, hoping he was really still alive. After Aunt Dee got home I ran downstairs and the gun cabinet was full and locked. Later on the train I asked Aunt Dee, who shot Alex? She said that at first she didn't think of Willy. When she got back from seeing Alex, Willy was just coming in and said he'd been fixing fence on the north pasture all day. I said, "Fixing fence? Willy?" He didn't usually volunteer for outside work. But I myself didn't start to doubt it until the girth on Fandango broke and the stable boy said it was cut and Aunt Dee whisked me away; she whirled me out of there so fast it would make your head spin—except we were riding hell for leather to Mr. Gustleben, me holding on with my arm in a sling, very uncomfortable.

Aunt Dee planned to come back after she got me in school and help take care of daddy. But then we got a letter from Miss Ella saying daddy had died suddenly and was already buried at the church. I will never forgive Miss Ella for not letting me know about the funeral. Her letter was just cruel: *"I assumed Bonnie would not care to come back given her eagerness to leave the ranch for academic pursuits."* And she flat told Aunt Dee to stay gone. Her letter said something like *"With dear Alastair gone there is no need for you to come back, Adecia. My niece is occupying your room."* We wrote Miss Ella asking her to please send our clothes and furniture and books by Railway Express, we'd pay. But she never did. And as frugal as Aunt Dee was, she never said one word, just bought me all new. She did fret over her rocker and the nightstand, which her folks had brought from Virginia back in the 1830s. And she'd had to leave behind the quilt she'd made for Alex, and all her books, the Dickens, the Henry James, the Swinburne. But I did bring the soaked Tennyson.

So, dear diary, we may never know who shot Alex. Aunt Dee did say once that before we'd left she'd found Miss Ella looking for something in her room. She came upstairs and heard a drawer shut in her bedroom and when she opened the door, there stood Miss Ella, right by her dresser. And all Miss Ella said was, "Just checking to be sure the maid is bringing up your hot water every morning. She's been sloppy lately." Then she swept out past Aunt Dee. Aunt Dee said that was the same day Miss Ella refused to let daddy's lawyer in to see daddy. Apparently daddy had somehow let the foreman know he wanted to see him. Miss Ella turned the man out.

I did ask Aunt Dee about the letter. She said she wrote that Susana Navarro once but never heard back. Of course, back then someone from the ranch had to take our letters to Madrone and bring back the mail, so who knows. One other thing Aunt Dee said. Under the will, when Daddy died, with Alex dead, Miss Ella was only supposed to get half, and I would get the other half. But Aunt Dee pointed out Miss Ella could make it very tough for me, on the rest of the property that should be mine. She said, "You aren't there; she is. So I wouldn't poke her with a sharp stick.

Know what I mean? We know your brother was shot, but not by whom. Ella holds the purse strings. And perhaps Willy's not a danger to you any longer under the will, but if he ever knew we suspected him—well, you must be wise as a serpent, says St. Paul." And I said, "You mean, pick your fights." I guess that means I have to be mercenary, at a distance, dear diary. Sounds like a Restoration comedy heroine. Or Shakespeare's Portia? Clever, but in disguise? The only problem is, I don't see a happy ending unless I stay well away from the ranch. The pine trees in east Texas are all right in their place, but that's east Texas. And I was born under the big sky where trees don't get in the way of the stars. Anyway, that's the tale of how we left and why I was off to TSCW in a frankly frumpy (except for the shoes) uniform. I can't go home again, and anyway, there's no home where Ella and Willy have supplanted my sweet daddy. In fact, I heard Willy even changed his name from Kendrick to Drinkman. I suppose I can still go to the graveyard in Madrone; that's where all my family is: Alex, Mama, Daddy. But no closer to the ranch . . . in case Aunt Dee was right, and the old ranch now houses a nest of vipers. Diary, I should aim to be a writer, don't you think? And now I am alone; no, I have Aunt Dee and she is looking out for me on legal things.

Alice looked up. Adele's steady eyes were gauging her reaction.

"Aunt Dee saved Bonnie's—my mother's—life. But she died right after my mother graduated and got married. So all we know is Aunt Dee at one time saw Alex's body, and two bullets, but we don't know where they are, and we'll never know who fired them."

Alice sat silent. Adele did not know the whereabouts of the bullets, or the hair—or did she? Wouldn't she only know for sure that the letter had been found? She was not going to tell Adele a thing, not today. "But Adele, what's your position in this litigation? Alejandro Navarro has DNA evidence that he's Alex's son."

"He can have the Blue Pool Ranch, as far as I'm concerned. I already had to sue the Drinkmans over one parcel that Willy and Ella got my mother to sell when she was sick. They didn't tell her the adjacent parcel had an oil strike on it. They made millions off the parcel she traded them. And Ella lived until 1964! She was seventy when she died. So all the money she made off her share of the estate after my grandfather's death came to Willy, and now the shale oil play is making him rich."

"You've seen Alastair Drinkman's will?"

"Yes. When my grandfather died, Ella was only to get a life interest in income from the real property my grandfather owned before he married her. Then the ownership of the real property would be split between my mother and Alex. But after Alex died, it was split two ways; Ella would get Alex's half, and Bonnie the other."

"That means Bonnie and Ella got what would have gone to Alex or his heirs." Alice stared at Adele. "Alex's money or personal property also apparently went to them." She watched the rapid calculations behind Adele's eyes. "If he had not been murdered, Alex's descendants would have had their share of Alastair Drinkman's estate. What's your view about that?"

Adele's back stiffened. "I'm not giving up a single dime."

"So why are you showing me this diary?" asked Alice.

"To show you my mother too was in danger! I believe Aunt Dee saved my mother's life. Besides, my lawyer says the diary is not admissible and I can keep you from using it. I'm not about to give up any of my money, Alice. I'm doing precisely what I want with it. I have a private foundation, a charity, which does more good than Alejandro Navarro could ever dream of doing in this world."

"Oh, I don't know," Alice said. "He did a lot of good flying fighters in the Pacific. Raised a fine son."

A flush rose on Adele's cheeks and she bent fierce eyes on Alice. "You have no idea about my foundation. I'm doing great work with it, like scholarships to college that get kids out of a poverty loop, like environmental studies in the Big Thicket. Setting up transport for local truck gardens to get really good produce to small towns. Cooking classes for kids and teens through kitchens at local Ys."

"All commendable. We could use the cooking school for kids in Coffee Creek." But Adele's sanctimony made Alice's ears draw back, made her skull muscles contract. "Still, your *first cousin*—your *only* first cousin?—might do equally well, or better, with his father's money. And whether he does or not, he's entitled to the chance."

"My lawyer says he doesn't get my uncle's share if it all was part of my grandfather's estate."

"He may be right. In that case, it may be that his killer benefited from his death."

"Whoever that was, Bonnie had nothing to do with it!"

"Was she part of the cover-up?"

"Cover-up of what? She was a child!"

"Not for long, Adele. And she got part of Alex's share of Mr. Drinkman's estate."

"It could have been a tramp, a thief, anyone! You have no proof who killed Alex, much less that the person profited from it!"

"But I think I'll get that proof." Alice rose and put away her notes, suddenly sick of greed, complacency, smug snobbery, all embodied in the lovely screened porch, the iced tea, the old house, exuding a century of wealth. On the table by Adele she saw a picture in a sterling frame, one she had not seen before. Vietnam era? Pilot by his helicopter?

Adele went on. "And Sandro Navarro won't get another penny from me."

"You mean your first cousin once removed, who might make a fine president for this country?"

They stared at each other for a long moment. Alice stood.

"I hope we can right a wrong together, and that one day you'll be glad you helped make history. Thanks for showing me the journal."

Chapter Fourteen

Tex-Mex-Czech

On Thursday the Beer Barons descended on Alice's office to brainstorm the new brewery. Leaning on the conference room table, Bill Birnbach, the representative German of the three partners, peered up through spectacles and laid out the financing plan. "We're using Jorgé's place, paying rent to Jorgé. We've got our line of credit at Madrone Bank. We've priced the equipment. There's a brew-pub that went under in Lubbock. Thought they'd be the first in town but were maybe a little too early to the dance. We drove out and looked at their stuff. We're hauling it down here next week."

"Next week? Where will you put it?"

"Out at Jorgé's under cover. Under the pole barn. It's too good a deal to miss. And Other Bill is so eager to get his hands on it—mister Brau-meister—back in Czech hog heaven."

Other Bill was Bill Benke, the Czech member of the German-Czech-Hispanic Beer Baron troika. Tall, gangly, pale, Benke smiled. "Gonna be some great beers, Alice. Got to have a perfect pilsener, of course."

"Right, pilsener—brought to you Czechs by a German," Bill Birnbach pointed out smugly.

"Perfected by Czechs, of course, and now world-famous," retorted Benke. "But also some Tex-Czech beers. Different styles."

"Tex-Czech. I like it," said Jorgé, "but then you'll just be copying the great Mexican beers. Tex-Mex-Czech."

"Hey, where's the Deutsch in that?" groused Birnbach.

"Tex-Mex-Czech-Deutsch? Of course not," said Benke.

Alice grinned. "So the beers at the new brewery will reflect the Beer Barons?"

"Of course. We could name them for ourselves!" Birnbach smirked and the three men high-fived.

"Okay." Alice handed out an agenda with state and local requirements. "Let's work through this and lay out the critical path."

They muttered their way through the Alcoholic Beverage Commission paperwork, state comptroller sales requirements, zoning, an adequate septic system. Birnbach was totting up costs on his calculator and checking them against the spreadsheet on his tablet.

"I know you've kicked this around, but how will it affect the Beer Barn?"

The three men looked at each other. Finally Birnbach shrugged. "We're just ready for a new gig. Benke wants to make beer, Jorgé wants to have people out to enjoy his property, we don't see too much downside. There're some economies and benefits—we can use the same cook and bar staff and give them longer hours if they work lunch and afternoons at the brewery, then come back to the Beer Barn. We think the Beer Barn will keep doing well and that we'll get new folks out at the new place. For which we need a name." All three nodded slowly, clearly thinking of possible names. "Besides, we're getting some competition coming out here from Austin." Alice already knew about the Jester King Brewery and Twisted Oak Brewery near Dripping Springs. "Can't let them steal all our thunder. What we're thinking is, soft opening in September. Grand opening for Oktoberfest. And we mean really grand—make the opening one big party."

"And all the neighbors will be fine with it?"

"The ones we've talked to. Couple of places, though, we couldn't find a human to speak to," Jorgé said.

"If you don't run into neighbor opposition, the timeline will be okay," Alice said. "So, fingers crossed. You'll all need to sign the application, and there's a background check involved, with the alcohol folks."

"Uh-oh." Jorgé glanced at his partners. "Anyone have anything we need to . . . uh . . . expunge?"

"Probably. Got a pretty checkered past, back in middle school. More work for you, Alice. And hey"—Birnbach lifted an eyebrow—"your girl Tessa and Los Guapos are playing next month! Coming back from LA! Need to grab that long-legged bookseller of yours and come do some two-stepping."

"He's wearing a rehab boot right now. Don't want him stepping on me."

"Did you kick him?"

"No, he was playing a manly game of basketball."

"Basketball's a very dangerous sport." Birnbach and Benke had played high school basketball. "Especially when you're past twenty-one."

* * * * *

And where was Kinsear?

Well, she could call him, couldn't she? She didn't have to wait by the phone. Not that she'd ever had one of her own, until she was in college. Only the family wall phone, JA3-5527, years ago, before millions, billions of phone numbers hung in the skies, hung in the airwaves.

* * * * *

Just as she reached for it, the phone rang. Sandro. "Alice. The police want to talk to Tomás. I—it sounds like they think he might have pushed Carey."

"Tomás? Why would they think that?"

"One photographer got a shot of Tomás's hand reaching out for Carey."

"Trying to catch him?"

"I assume, but I don't know. The picture, I mean."

"Well, if he talks to the police, have someone with him. Do you have a lawyer in mind? Criminal counsel?"

"How about Chris Gonzales?"

"Good." She knew Gonzales's reputation. "But, Sandro, what motivation would Tomás possibly have to shove Norville off the balcony? Norville's your mainstay! Was."

"Yes." Sandro expelled a long breath. "But they talked to my staffers. One girl heard Tomás arguing with Norville about the money."

"What money?"

"Drinkman money. She heard Norville tell Tomás he thought going after the money was a bad idea, that he was going to tell me not to do it—that it would wreck my chances for the campaign, wreck my chances for the presidency."

"What did Tomás say?"

"Supposedly he told him to butt out of the money, said it was family business and none of Norville's. Said the Navarros should get what was theirs and it would be idiotic not to go after it. That was the

152

word this girl quoted—'idiotic.' Then Norville told Tomás it would be more idiotic for Tomás to think we could just get a pile of money without thinking of the downside, and for me to louse up my future and the country's future by getting tangled up in court over money we never earned."

"Is that the worst she heard?"

Silence.

"No. The worst is, she said Tomás yelled at Norville that he'd be sorry if he messed around with this—he'd better not tell me not to go after the money or Tomás would do his best to make him sorry he had. 'Mind your own business and stay out of mine!'"

"Call Chris Gonzales."

Alice wished Tomás had kept his mouth shut.

C h a p t e r   F i f t e e n

Blood on the Bandana

On Monday of the first week in May, Alice went to the safety deposit box and pored over the bullet Aunt Dee had found in her Tennyson. What kind of rifle fired it? She rooted around online, staring at ballistics websites. Hopeless. She called Kinsear. "You know anyone in Fredericksburg—or anywhere—who could do ballistics on an old bullet?"

"How old?

"1919." Long pause. "Do I hear you thinking?"

"Yup. I'll call you back."

That night she sank into a bubble bath, armed with her latest set-in-Venice mystery. Despite the bubbles, the dead face that kept popping up was not the Venetian victim's, but Norville's, followed by a vision of Alex Drinkman gearing down on his motorcycle as he slowed for the low-water bridge. The phone rang by the tub. She grabbed it.

"Here it is," said Kinsear, "and it means a road trip."

"To?"

"Santa Fe."

"Oh, please do not throw me in that brier patch. Il Piatto? Gabriel's? Where do I eat?"

"Hasty, hasty," said Kinsear. "Where do *we* eat. *We* are going on the road trip because, one, I'm speaking at the Santa Fe conference of the New Mexico Historical Society about new material on Charlie Siringo, and, two, you need an escort to introduce you to Banana Clip Curtis and Bang-Bang Barker. My friends. They're the best."

Alice giggled. "Who made up those names?"

"Hey! Show some respect. Banana Clip—that's Clip for short—and Bang-Bang are the absolute best ballistics guys in the Southwest, maybe nationally, on certain antique rifles. They're consulted by antiques dealers and crime scene investigators. They've been called to consult on problems with unmarked Civil War graves, and remains in French and Belgian trenches. Even the slaughtered Polish officers at Katyn."

"What made them get into this?"

"Clip is Clem Curtis, who grew up homesteading in Alaska. He makes custom guns and repairs antiques, and is very familiar with

European rifles too. Elliott Barker—we call him Bang-Bang because he's so quiet, but a dead-eye shot. He's expert, especially on sniper rifles, carbines, and long-range guns. They both had other careers— Curtis built houses, Barker taught astronomy—but were fascinated with old guns. They met after retiring to Santa Fe and started a consulting partnership. They've had a lot of fun. And some weird moments, too."

"How'd you meet them?"

"At the Santa Fe Trail Association, one year."

"But can they look at our two bullets and tell me what kind of gun was used?"

"They're pretty sure they can."

Something bothered Alice. "Oh! We have to get the bullet with the blood on it back from the DNA lab. It's a little deformed, but these guys will want it, so they can match it with the non-mashed one, right?"

"Definitely. So get on it, Alice. The conference is only ten days away."

"El Rey? The room with the fireplace? Maria's margaritas?"

"Yes ma'am."

Silla called the DNA lab the next morning. The lab reported it was finished with the bullet and would send it back. Alice had asked for rush results. They thought Alice would like to know that the blood on the bullet matched the blood on the bandana and was consistent with the DNA in the strand of hair with the follicle, and the glue on the stamp and the envelope flap. All of those samples were also consistent with samples from Mr. Navarro. Yes, said Silla, Alice would like to know. After she and Silla finished whooping, Alice called Kinsear.

"That still doesn't prove who shot the gun," Kinsear remarked.

"I know, I know."

"But what about his sister Bonnie's notes?"

"Still tough to prove."

"Are you planning to have an exhumation party in the little Madrone graveyard? Looking for the last bullet, beneath the moon?"

"Maybe. If we get enough evidence piled up, can I get an exhumation order? Maybe . . ."

Then she called Mr. Navarro. "We've got results." She told him.

"I knew I could trust you, Alice." She heard the tension in his voice relax. "It's something to think about, isn't it? It's an odd way to learn who your father is."

Alice told him, "We need to file those actions for recovery of land right away, on Blue Pool and the Frio ranch property and the Madrone lot. I'm sending you the drafts to review. And we'll supplement our motion opposing the Blue Pool groundwater permit." She hung up.

The next day Silla filed the supplemental DNA information for the groundwater district permit hearing for Blue Pool. She also filed actions for recovery of land for Blue Pool, Alex's small lot in Medina County, and the Frio County ranch, all with exhibits and lab reports. "Watch out for incoming," Silla warned. "We're gonna get seriously shelled over this."

* * * * *

During the rest of the week, Alice and the Beer Barons met almost daily, and triumphantly delivered the brewery application on Friday. "Whoo-ee." Sitting at her desk, Alice got off the phone, after confirming receipt by the Alcoholic Beverage Commission. "Done."

Silla said, "Let's go get a beer. We can have a pilsener taste-off. So we'll be prepared when the new brewery opens."

"Sounds great," Alice said. Her phone rang. An unfamiliar voice, deep, sharp. "Will Drinkman here, Ms. Greer."

"Yes." She stood up at her desk, standard operating procedure for dealing with the unknown.

"I wondered if you would come by my office on Monday afternoon or Tuesday. I thought it would be helpful to meet."

Well, well. "It might be. But aren't you represented by counsel? If so I need to meet with your counsel."

"We're not at that point. I haven't lawyered up yet on this and I've told our general counsel I prefer to go ahead and talk to you now."

Hmm. "In that case I'd be glad to talk to you too. Monday afternoon is fine."

She agreed to be there by 2:00 p.m.

"I can't believe that man makes his own calls," Silla said.

"Doesn't want to leave a record, maybe?"

"Are you going armed? At least with a tape recorder?"

"What could possibly happen?"

They headed to the Beer Barn.

Chapter Sixteen

Clearly Just a Shakedown Attempt

The Drinkman Foundation building overlooked the landscaping at the McNay Art Museum and the leafy Alamo Heights part of San Antonio. Alice glanced up at multiple security cameras on the entry portico. A doorman opened the tall doors. Then at the information desk a male receptionist, coat pulled tight over muscled shoulders, asked her name and whether she had an appointment.

"With Will Drinkman."

He pushed a button on the phone, turned his back, whispered into the receiver, nodded and got up and took her to the elevator. She jumped when he got in with her. "It's keyed," he said. He inserted the key and pushed the top button.

The doors opened on silence—blue carpet, dark wood, wide windows. In the big reception area, glass-fronted cabinets held plaques, awards, some old books, old maps, and some very old pistols on display. Another smiling receptionist, name tag "Orinda."

"Alice Greer," said Alice, not smiling back. She was still trying to figure what Will Drinkman might say, and what she could or could not reveal.

"He's expecting you but he's on the phone. Should be just a moment."

Alice wandered over to the windows, looked out at the leafy view. Down in the parking lot she spied her truck. Why was that guy staring at it? A man in black jeans and a black jacket, arms akimbo, stood near the front, checking his phone. Then he turned and walked away.

"Would you follow me?" said Orinda. "And would you like iced tea, or coffee?"

"Tea, please." Alice followed her down the hall, staring at the lighted display cabinets on each side. Rifles. Carbines. "What a collection!" she said, slowing her pace a little, trying to read the cards propped by each gun.

"Oh, the Drinkman collection is very well known," said the young woman. "This one, for instance, is the gun issued to Teddy Roosevelt's Rough Riders." She pointed.

Alice stared, trying to memorize. Winchester . . . "How interesting!"

"And some are even Civil War vintage. I think that cabinet?"

Alice moved a bit closer. She read, Sharps . . . something.

Then an empty cabinet, no display. A forgotten card lay on the bottom shelf. Alice read, "Captain Alex Drinkman, WWI Pilot." "Hey," she called. "What about this cabinet?"

The receptionist smiled over her shoulder. "My favorite. Must be out for cleaning." Ahead a door opened. "Oh, he's waiting," she said, and scurried down the hall. Alice tore her eyes away and girded her loins for the meeting.

"Come in, come in. Have a seat." Will Drinkman was standing just inside the door. Not quite six feet tall, iron-gray hair, tall narrow forehead, big blank blue eyes in a stony face. He bowed slightly, not offering his hand, and pointed her to the chair in front of his desk. He lifted one eyebrow at the receptionist, who backed out and shut the door.

Alice sat down and waited, looking around the office. Great view. Huge desk. His chair—vast. Hers—small. Quite strategic. She would ignore that.

"Let's talk about this letter someone sent the San Antonio Express, supposedly from 1919. Are you representing this Alejandro Navarro?"

"I am. How did you get the letter?"

"Someone from the paper leaked it. It's clearly a forgery. Clearly just a shakedown attempt by your client."

"No. I believe it's genuine," Alice said.

"Of course it's not."

Alice stood up. "Mr. Drinkman, if you plan to abuse my client, we have nothing to talk about." She turned to leave.

The door opened and the receptionist sidled in with a silver tray, ice cubes clinking in tall glasses.

"Ms. Greer, one moment. If you would." He gestured at her chair. Perfectly tailored blazer, immaculate French cuffs, large gold cufflinks.

Leaving the tray on a side table, the receptionist scuttled out, glancing curiously at Alice.

Alice didn't budge, standing stiff and silent, staring at Will Drinkman, who stared back at her above half-glasses. This man had no right to insult Alejandro Navarro. She'd checked him out. Unlike Alejandro, Will Drinkman, born to Willy Kendrick Drinkman in 1930, and now in his eighties, had never seen military service. She was confident he'd never had to work his way through school, never had to work the night shift while studying for his actuarial degree. Oh come on, Alice, she thought, not his fault he got the silver spoon. Maybe he has redeeming qualities buried somewhere.

"Yes?" She remained where she was.

"Please sit down. I was rude. Forgive me."

She sat, mistrustful, poised for departure.

"What does Mr. Navarro want?"

"His father's property."

"I don't think a court's going to let you undo the transactions that were part of probating Alastair Drinkman's estate."

"I'm not so sure of that. In any event, Mr. Navarro wants what he would have inherited."

"If—very big if—if he is Alex Drinkman's son, he still wasn't legitimate. Nor adopted. You have no proof."

"I will have more than sufficient proof."

"I'm expecting the court will say, 'Ms. Greer, these are unfortunate circumstances; Alex Drinkman was killed by parties unknown, and this is no reason to undo what the courts have already blessed when Alastair Drinkman's will was probated. The statute of limitations has run.'"

"And I expect the court will follow the law. Limitations has not run, given the very particular circumstances here." And more than that I shall not say, Alice decided.

"Litigation is expensive and the Drinkmans will stand on principle for as long as it takes."

"Meaning a scorched-earth policy? Wear us out with your money? Mr. Navarro will stay the course. He missed knowing his father, and he now knows his father cared deeply about him."

"Back to the letter, which is a mere forgery."

"You will learn that it is not."

"Who the hell are the Navarros! We're the Drinkmans! We've been here for over a century!"

"The Navarros have been here for over two hundred and fifty years."

He folded his hands before him, staring at Alice. She stared back. "Well, I wanted a chance to meet you. Right now you clearly don't recognize the facts and the total failure of your case. Perhaps at some point you'll want to talk. You'll need to talk."

"And perhaps at some point you will figure out you need to talk too. For example, when your inept ninjas get hauled into the Coffee County Jail for breaking and entering. Twice."

"I don't know what you're talking about!" His face slowly purpled. He must have pressed a button: the door opened and there stood the receptionist, holding it for Alice.

On the way down the hall she slowed down, walked close to the cabinets and paused at one, where she read the card: "*Mr. Alastair Drinkman's Savage Model 99, .250-3000.*" And "*Mr. Alastair Drinkman's Buffalo Soldiers (Ninth Cav.) Sharps Carbine, .45-70.*"

"Ms. Greer?" said the receptionist, now standing close to the elevator, the tiniest edge of impatience in her voice. Behind Alice, Drinkman's office door swung open. "Orinda!" he yelled. The elevator opened, and the stone-faced man with the key stood facing her. She quick-stepped to the elevator, smiled and nodded at Orinda and, down the hall, Will Drinkman.

She held her breath all the way down in the elevator, expelling it on the ground floor, and marched straight to her truck. No more time for parleys. Time to crank up the legal machinery.

Chapter Seventeen

Road Trip

Ultimately, the proposed road trip to Santa Fe turned into a plane flight into Albuquerque, and a stay at La Posada instead of El Rey, since Kinsear's meetings were just off the Plaza. Driving up to Santa Fe in the rented Jeep, Kinsear went over the itinerary. "I've got a meeting this afternoon with the historical society board and then make my talk tomorrow morning at nine. Then we have a date in town with Bang-Bang and Banana Clip. And maybe they'll invite us out to their place on Rowe Mesa."

"I can entertain myself this afternoon." Alice had planned it. O'Keeffe Museum. A walk around the Plaza, and maybe a new Navajo bracelet for her niece, bought from the sidewalk sellers under their traditional portal at the Palace of the Governors. Just strolling by herself, sniffing the cool dry air, flavored with a little piñon smoke. What she really wanted, if she wanted anything at all, was a numbered print by Gustave Baumann, of trees, with wavy lines and unexpected color, in that particular apricot-pink he used. But I need to build the client list before that happens, she told herself.

"You can go prowling, but only until dinner. We're having dinner at Maria's with the historical society people. You might actually enjoy them, and at any rate I'll get you a Maria's margarita."

"You haven't invited me to come to your talk tomorrow morning."

"Didn't think you'd be interested. Will you come?"

"Of course! I love Charlie Siringo."

"It's just a little dry talk on some new papers about him, but come ahead and then we can go see the gun guys. And they've got the bullets?"

Eternally cautious, Alice had decided it was safer to express-mail the bullets to the "gun guys" than to carry them with her on the plane. Otherwise, if the plane went down, she wouldn't be able to explain to Mr. Navarro that she'd unfortunately melted his key exhibits. Kinsear had rolled his eyes.

"Well?" she had challenged. "Have to think of my client!"

Before dinner Alice had a bubble bath, which was interrupted and joined by Kinsear with predictable but pleasant consequences. "We're going to be late!" He was pulling on his chinos, scuffing into his chukkas. Alice, still flushed, felt unrushed. "Maria's has been there a long time. Just call your buddies."

* * * * *

After Kinsear's talk on the new research on Charlie Siringo, which stirred the historians to a welter of appreciative questions, he and Alice piled into the Jeep and bounced up past Museum Hill to a small adobe building deep in the piñons and cedars. It was unprepossessing, isolated, quiet, with heavy bars on the windows, security cameras on the eaves, and a barred iron gate locked over the keypad-entry door. Kinsear rang the bell.

The inner door opened and a smiling tall gray-headed man said, "Excuse me, excuse me, this takes a moment" as he opened the iron gate and ushered them in.

"Bang-Bang, this is Alice."

"Elliott Barker," he said, shaking Alice's hand. "I'm almost grown up, you know. Alice, so nice to have you here. This is my colleague Clem Curtis." Curtis was slim, with a white goatee and piercing eyes.

Curtis, Barker, and Kinsear shook, hugged.

"Follow us," said Curtis. "We're really tickled with your project, Alice."

They turned into a large rectangular room lit by clerestory windows and fluorescent lights. Next to a long granite-topped counter stood something like a microscope out of *Star Wars*, nothing like the ancient ones Alice used in college anatomy. "Wow."

"Oh, that's a comparison microscope," said Curtis. "They are kind of impressive. And fun."

"Alice, come sit on this stool and let us show you what we think," said Barker. "By the way, before we get started, is there anything else we should know?"

"Oh"—Alice swung around on the stool. "This might help. I had an appointment at the Drinkman building. There's a display of old guns in the cases along the hallway. Of the older rifles, one was a Savage Model 99 and the other was a Sharps Carbine, .45-70. The card for the Savage said '.250-3000.' Also there was a Winchester of the sort issued to some of the Rough Riders."

Curtis nodded. "Great. You remember any other details, at all?"

"The card for the Sharps said 'Buffalo Soldiers' for sure; I think it said 'Ninth Cav.' I made some notes when I got to the truck. Sorry I couldn't write it down or take a picture right that minute—they were definitely hustling me out of there."

"All good. Someone in Texas could have had those guns in 1919. Not common, but not really rare. That's very encouraging given what we're hypothesizing. Right off the bat, we can eliminate the Winchester and the Sharps. Anyone who knows guns would know these bullets didn't come from those guns. You can tell just by looking that your bullets are a much smaller caliber."

He pointed to a small laptop hooked up to a big monitor. On the left side of the screen popped up two bullets, at magnification. One was still pointed. The tip of the other was mashed and stained. "Those are yours," he said. "First, without reference to the general rifling characteristics, we've narrowed them down by size, or caliber. By the way, the owner could have ordered ammunition out of a catalog, back in the 1870s and later. Now, we think these are .250-3000 caliber. As you know, we don't have the firearm itself, so we can't fire bullets from the firearm and see if they have the same pattern as your bullets. But maybe we can get close. Let's walk through the options, on the right side of the screen." He paused. "By the way, Alice, just so I don't sound repetitious, do you know anything about guns?"

"Nope."

"Only her flare gun," Kinsear said.

Barker nodded, in a mildly puzzled way. "Okay. There's a big FBI database showing the general rifling characteristics or marks left on bullets fired from various commonly used guns. We've picked the time frame for the gun manufacture between, say, 1875 and 1920. We picked that time frame from the database because people keep favorite guns a long time, and certainly did in that era, on ranches."

Curtis clicked the left side of the screen to high magnification. "Here's the bullet that wasn't distorted. Look at the rifling, the grooves, around the bullet. Now we are going to look through the database for similar patterns. We'll focus on the Savage Model 99 .250-3000."

On the right popped up a bullet labeled "*Savage Model 99 .250-3000.*"

"See the grooves from the rifling?"

"Looks awfully similar," said Kinsear.

"Right. So we're thinking Savage Model 99 Savage, with a .250-3000 bullet, which was introduced in 1915. That bullet was popular because it was the first bullet to travel three thousand feet per second. And the rifle is a nice size, not too heavy, doesn't kick too much, but you can certainly kill with it. The Sharps would certainly have been available in Texas after Reconstruction, and the Winchester after the Spanish Civil War," Barker said. "The Savage Model 99 came out about 1899. They could easily have all been in the gun cabinet at this ranch."

Curtis added, "One thing we wanted to check was that both bullets were fired by the same gun, Alice. Just in case you run into a problem of proof. For that, one thing you could do is look at the brass cases, if you had them. They get marks on them from being loaded. But I hear you don't have the cases, right?"

"Right."

"So, let's look at your two bullets. We've already looked at your bullet that hit the book, which is less damaged, on the left side of the screen, with the database bullet for the Savage Model 99 on the right. You saw how similar they are? Now let me put up on the left screen the more deformed bullet that had the bloodstain."

Alice and Kinsear peered at the screen. Alice could see the similarities, the tiny grooves on each bullet.

"So we think we can say that both bullets were fired by the same gun, and that the gun was a Savage Model 99," said Barker.

"Let's assume you had your choice of the guns in that gun cabinet, including the Savage Model 99 and both the Sharps Carbine and the Winchester, and you wanted to kill someone, someone you knew would be riding a motorcycle slowly down onto a low-water bridge," said Alice.

"And you're on the other side of the water? How far? A hundred yards? Two hundred?"

"Between one and two hundred." Alice imagined the crossing. "And the most important thing—"

"Yes?"

"You've got to be sure he's dead."

"Various guns would work well," Curtis said. "You could certainly fire multiple rounds from your Savage Model 99 very quickly, and it's a very accurate gun. So, if you're a pretty good shooter, you'd like that one. You'd like your chances."

Barker nodded in agreement.

The lab was silent.

Alice hopped off the stool. "So, you know what I need? I need an expert affidavit from you two. And I might need you to come testify about what you think."

They looked at each other. Barker said, "Now here's the deal, Alice. The way we work, I have to do the testifying for depositions and trial; Curtis refuses. So for purposes of expert testimony, he demands that he be designated as the lab assistant."

"Right," said Curtis. "I'll talk to you all day long but I won't testify at trial."

"So we'll produce a single report and I'll testify about it," Barker said. "And I'm going to sign as Bang-Bang. Always wanted to."

"So you can get your affidavit drafted," said Curtis. "But Alice, don't you want to get hold of that gun, and test it? Wouldn't that be more definitive?"

"Well, you always have to be careful what you ask for. Right now with the database comparison we have a nice strong affidavit pointing to the gun in the gun cabinet. But of course the other side will argue that any old Savage Model 99 could have fired those bullets, right? So are you sure enough that I should ask for the gun to be produced and fired?"

Barker and Curtis nodded.

"What if they say it's a valuable antique? Or that it's too old to fire?" asked Alice.

"At least it's corroborative evidence," Barker said. "We can look at the rifling and confirm it's like the one in the database. But I'll bet the court will let us fire it. We've never been denied, so far."

"How many courts have you testified in?"

"I've testified about forty times, but been named as an expert at least twice that when I didn't have to give a deposition or testify at trial," Barker said.

Alice nodded. Then she sighed, happily. "I feel so much better."

"Alice, we should try to educate you a little bit more. Just so you know what we're saying. You two want to come out to our range and shoot a little bit, tomorrow morning? It's about forty minutes away. We've got a Savage Model 99, and also a replica Sharps carbine you can try out. And that Rough Rider Winchester. Plus you can participate in our Ballistic Arts Project."

"Irresistible," she said. She made the experts lock the bullets in their safe.

* * * * *

The next morning, Alice and Kinsear headed east out of Santa Fe for Ribera, with the long piñon and cedar covered ridge of Rowe Mesa rising steadily to their right. Past Glorieta Pass, site of the last battle of the Civil War, and past the pueblo ruins at Pecos National Park, to the Ribera exit.

A tiny post office. Pink-orange rock, pink-orange gravel everywhere. "Where's the town?" Alice said.

"A lot of it's hidden," said Kinsear. "Unless you know, you won't even notice the ruins of the old customs house, down at the Pecos River crossing. It's still there, all adobe, from when it was the eastern entry into Spanish territory from the Santa Fe Trail."

They passed a school and then the Sonrisa Café, with cars and pickups all over the parking lot, and a gorgeous metal sign depicting a beautiful woman in a rebozo. "Let's eat there!" said Alice. "Maybe Bang-Bang and Banana Clip will join us."

They lurched onto a rocky road heading up onto the lap of the mesa, driving closer and closer to sheer rock faces speckled with determined piñons and cedars. Kinsear punched in the gate code and they bounced along the gullied road to a sign: "*Clip-Bang Range. No trespassing. Forewarned is forearmed.*"

Bang-Bang and Banana Clip were leaning against a pickup when they drove up.

Barker approached with mugs. "Ready, Alice? How about some coffee? Kinsear?"

They followed the pickup in their Jeep, around a curve in the cliff to a level range about three hundred yards long. Toward the end stood targets at various distances. An odd sort of zip line swooped from the cliff down past where they had parked. "For moving targets," Barker explained.

A gun table was set up facing the targets. Curtis reviewed the safety rules. Stay behind the table. Wear ear protection. Only one person at a time has the gun. The gun must be returned to the table and unloaded. Et cetera. "Lots of musts and no's," said Alice, relieved.

"This one first," said Barker. "This is the Sharps I mentioned. Not too heavy, quite accurate. Remember about breathing. How does the sight look?"

"Good."

"Now, here's the ballistic art part. You see that odd metal box out there?"

Alice squinted. What was it?

"It's the steel box inside a dryer, an ordinary clothes dryer. We're trying to filigree it with holes. It'll be art. So, see if you can hit it. You will know if you do."

They all stood behind the table and Alice squinted, stared, and squeezed. *Whang!*

"You hit it!" said Kinsear, grinning.

"It's art! It's more artistic by the minute!" said Curtis.

Kinsear took a turn. *Whang! Whang!* Then the two experts. Then they all tried the Winchester and the Savage.

"Which did you like better?"

Alice voted for the Sharps. Kinsear voted for the Savage.

"Okay, now we have naming of parts, as the poet said. You can't let us testify unless you know at least the basics."

So Alice had to point at and repeat the names of the muzzle, hammer, receiver, bolt, rear sight, blade front sight, straight grip, lever, loading port, stock, and so on. "I want a cheat sheet."

"We'll send you one."

"What are you going to call that?" Alice pointed at the perforated steel box.

"'Thirty-six Views from Rowe Mesa.' Sort of Hokusai-ish, neh? Or not?"

They poured coffee in tin mugs and stared east from Rowe Mesa across the Pecos Valley, to the mesa on the other side. The silence, broken by birdcall, was almost fragrant, almost a presence. Alice sighed. So beautiful.

She and Kinsear bought lunch for their experts at the Sonrisa, sitting in the back room with cold beer and hot cheese enchiladas, watching a chicken peck outside. "Awfully peaceful here," Kinsear said.

"That's why we like it," Curtis said. Barker nodded.

Alice and Kinsear headed for Albuquerque and the flight home. Alice plopped into the old leather chairs in the airport boarding area, totally relaxed. Then she checked her cell phone, and worried all the way home.

C h a p t e r   E i g h t e e n

Lemony

Sandro had called. Tomás had been called in again to talk to the police about Norville's plunge. "Can you come talk to him? Alejandro and I need to see you too."

The four of them met in a small windowless office at Sandro's campaign headquarters in San Marcos. "Alice," Sandro said, "Tomás has good counsel. Chris Gonzales is fine. But I don't like the way the police keep hovering around this. They just keep circling back. Chris said one thing they're wondering is whether perhaps Norville wasn't the target. Alejandro and Norville were both on the second row, both have gray hair, both had on their blazers. Same height, more or less. So maybe someone was after Alejandro. But for that they have no suspects."

"And they heard about my argument with Norville," Tomás said. "I was pretty mad. But not that mad."

"The police also know Norville had an argument with Rose Rayburn," Sandro said. His eyes met Alice's. "Again, one of our staffers overheard him tell Rose something—they didn't hear what—and she said, 'You can't stop me. You won't stop me.'"

"Sounds like Rose," Alice said. "What was the fight about?" She had a theory.

"I'm not sure it was a fight, and not sure what he told her. She won't tell me," said Sandro.

The four sat silent.

"Well," said Sandro, "we just thought, we three Navarros, we could talk through what we saw that day, for you."

She listened.

Tomás led off. "Dad was talking, making his speech. I felt Norville come in and stand next to me, right on the stairs. I would have moved left so he could get off the stairs but the photographers were taking their videos down below and I didn't want to disrupt the picture, you know? Anyway, he suddenly just lurched forward. Like he'd been launched, sort of. I tried to reach him but—it was so fast."

Alejandro nodded. "It was sudden. Tomás was next to me—I was holding his left arm, so I wouldn't wobble up there. Then suddenly— there went Norville. But I will say one thing. There was a lemony smell. I didn't really think of it until later."

"That's true," Tomás said. "Just a whiff. Like when you walk in and the house cleaner's been there."

* * * * *

Alice now realized she'd forgotten to email her video of Carey's fall to the San Marcos police. She left a message for George Files at the Coffee County Sheriff's Department. "Who do I need to send this to? Who's working on the Norville case?"

He called back. "You mean you didn't already send that video to them? I hear they have about a hundred videos, but didn't see anything special. Everyone at the fundraiser must have been using their cell phone."

"I just forgot. It was so horrible, being there, watching him fall."

"Send it to me. I'll get it to the right guy."

She did.

Fifteen minutes later Files called again. "I sent it and explained you were a good person even though you forgot to send your evidence in. They didn't have a video from the gallery level."

Alice hung up. Then she picked up the cell phone, paused for a moment, searched for the video. She watched it, the whole thing, even the end, where she seemed to be filming the floor for thirty seconds before she turned off the phone. Then she watched it again. Here came the mayor. Here came Sandro. Here came Mr. Navarro, with Tomás. Here came Norville. She saw the janitor on the right side of the musician's balcony. He passed behind the wall behind the musician's balcony, then reemerged on the left side. The mayor finished his speech. Sandro started his. And then—the janitor again, pushing his mop from the left side toward the musician's balcony. And then— Norville fell. Wait. She pushed pause. Look again. Norville suddenly flew forward. Was the door opened, then shut? She couldn't tell. She called George Files again. "May I come see you?"

She and Files drove down to San Marcos with her cell phone and pulled into the police station. "Anthony Luna," said Files at the desk. The officer pointed back down the hall. "Third on the left."

Luna, sturdy, crisp, asked her to show him the entire video on her phone. Then he nodded. "That's everything Files sent me," he said. "Had to check you'd sent me the whole thing." He smiled. But after Alice explained what she noticed, he looked at the video again on his monitor. "This is really weird." He rubbed his chin. "You say you saw the janitor pushing the mop around the gallery back where you were standing? Describe him."

"Thin," Alice said. "Had on the La Rotonda uniform, jacket and hat. Smiled at me. Nice smile. One silver front tooth. When I got up to the gallery level, he was coming around on my left. Then I saw him go all the way around behind the musician's balcony area, and come out on the left of that."

"Would you know him again?"

Alice nodded. Luna pulled out a stack of pictures and laid them out in front of her, one by one. Sure enough, there he was.

"Well," said Luna, "that guy has an alibi. He'd gone down to the ground floor on his lunch break when Norville fell. He definitely was in the kitchen."

"But—isn't he the one in the video?"

"We don't know. We've accounted for all the staff whereabouts at the time of the fall. Every single one has a solid alibi."

"But just look!"

"I know," said Luna. "But that doesn't look like the same guy who pushed the mop past you."

Alice asked him to replay her video. Here came a man from the left, pushing something—she had assumed a dust mop. But he was not thin.

"The lemony smell," said Alice. "Alejandro and Tomás both noticed a faint lemony smell. Did you look in the janitor's closet at the mops and brooms?"

"Sure, but . . . those mops are huge."

Still, Luna picked up the phone. He ordered the evidence team to retrieve all the janitorial equipment from the gallery and fingerprint it, and to take another look at the back of Norville's blazer.

"And you're sure it's not one of the La Rotonda employees?" Files said.

"Like I say, they are all accounted for."

Alice and Files left.

When she got back to the office she called Chris Gonzales and caught him up. "Good," he said. "Maybe that helps our Tomás."

"What about Rose? Is she in the line of fire?"

"That I don't know. And just because our friends didn't do the pushing themselves doesn't mean the police can't still suspect them of asking a hired gun to do it. Or a hired pusher, I guess."

"Oh, good grief." She hung up.

* * * * *

"Rose. I need to talk to you." It was Sunday afternoon.

"Where are you, Alice?"

"In the office."

"Can you meet me at the Beer Barn about four?"

"Background noise? Okay."

At four Alice found her favorite back-to-the-wall stool and ordered a Modelo Especial. Rose came in, circles under her eyes, and climbed slowly onto a stool. "Iced tea," she told History. She eyed Alice's beer. "Don't I wish."

"Rose, what's going on?"

Rose's lip quivered, then she pressed her lips together and put the iced tea in front of her mouth. "I've got to finish, Alice. I've got to finish this project."

"What project? And why do you have to finish it?"

"That's what I do! I'm an investigative reporter. You of all people should know I have to finish a project!"

"Is it going to get you killed?"

"I hope not."

"What does Sandro think?"

"He knows I have to finish it."

"Can you tell me anything about it? I'm assuming it involves state contracts. Right?"

"How'd you know that?"

"That packet you sent. One page had classified legal notices about state contracts."

"Ah. An accident. Well, Alice, I have to think about you too. Knowing much more than you do is not safe."

"Do you have legal counsel, for Norville's death?"

"Yes." She mentioned a name Alice hadn't heard of.

"I thought the Carnes firm handled all the legal work for the San Antonio Express."

"Only if you're on assignment."

"Weren't you supposed to be covering the fundraiser at La Rotonda?"

"No. Two other guys were. I was mainly there to watch Sandro.

Of course you were, Alice thought.

"And the police lost interest in me after they found out I was standing right next to one of Sandro's staffers when Norville fell. But when I first got to the Rotonda I did see something interesting. I saw Kelly Cosgrove talking to Norville."

"So did I! I could even hear some of it. Where were you?"

"In the lobby crowd, close to the bar, laying low. I didn't see you. What did they say?"

Alice told her.

Rose's brows drew together. "So Cosgrove might have been worried about Scanlon being in trouble? I guess that would bother Cosgrove—if Scanlon gets knocked out in the May primary, or after it, Cosgrove's got to find another gig. And money was an issue?"

"Yep, he made that crack about how Norville gets mailbox money, but he doesn't."

"I don't know if he really gets much, but Carey Norville's parents did have farmland in East Texas. He's like a lot of people around here; these days with the shale development, he gets—or was getting—a little cushion from Devon or Chesapeake or Citation every month from some fractional share of some mineral acres in some mineral lease."

"Nice work if you can get it." Alice's ancestors apparently had picked the wrong farms.

"Still, that's interesting, Cosgrove talking to Norville."

"Why, Rose? They've known each other a long time, right?"

Rose stared at her iced tea.

"Okay," said Alice. "Tell me about this project of yours."

"You remember, about a year ago, reading about some inmates dying at a prison down in South Texas?"

"Only vaguely."

"Right. We lock 'em up and then they're just statistics to most of us."

"Wasn't it food poisoning?"

"Not exactly. Kind of, but not exactly. You remember when children in China were dying and it turned out there was melamine in the powdered milk? Which was in their baby formula? We're all more likely to remember if it's children than inmates."

That Alice did remember.

"Well, it was about a dozen prisoners," Rose said. "At least a few had kidney stones, renal failure. Not a good way to die. There were a couple of deaths at a juvenile facility as well, also with kidney issues. There was a half-assed investigation by the state but nothing came of it. At about the same time we got the annual flu plus a norovirus episode in the prison, which confused the issue. I started thinking about the kidney impact, which didn't seem right. And I started looking at the prison food contracts."

"How do you do that? Public records request?"

"Partly. You can get the final contract, and it's often been bid out. But then you might want to look deeper at the background of the bid winner, see the economics, including suppliers for the proposed products. That's harder. That's when I left Washington and came back to Texas. Had to start sniffing around the docks, in Houston.

"You remember that the milk episode in China happened in 2008—there was a delay in the government effort to uncover the facts, because China was also hosting the Summer Olympics and didn't want bad publicity. And after the investigation, China set up a food and drug agency. Started testing baby formula, dairy products, and so on. Some babies got kidney stones—hospitals found melamine in the kidney stones."

"I remember. Horrible!" Alice could only imagine a baby suffering with kidney stones.

"And you'll recall that various countries banned import of

Chinese dairy products, right? Anyway, in the next couple of years there were reports of melamine still being found, hidden here and there in warehouses in China. So I started wondering about the prison outbreak. Thinking about milk powder used for milk, or pudding, or cereal.

"The contract for food commodity supplies for the prison: now that was only a couple of years ago. It's not for fresh food, but bulk supplies. Plenty of bidders for the contract. This was not the low bid, but just by a hair—the low bidder is an experienced supplier for the prisons. Then two other repeat suppliers submitted bids that were just slightly higher than the winner. So, it was worth looking hard at the winning bid, and whether it was significantly 'sweeter' than the lowest and the higher."

"And?"

"The winning bidder was called Fair Foods LLC. Its managing member was Fair Star Partners. The general partner of Fair Star Partners is Starfish Supply, Inc., which is registered on the Isle of Guernsey. The president of Starfish Supply is Warren Drinkman."

"Will Drinkman's son? The one whose profitability he doubts, right?"

"You got it. So I started plowing through customs documents for the six months preceding the bid date. Anything with powdered milk, heading for any of these entities. And guess what. A year before the bid date, a shipment came in for Fair Star Partners of bulk nonfat dried milk, two tons, from Hong Kong. Nothing showing origin. And of course that was a couple of years after the scandal."

"How long can you store powdered milk?"

"If it's nonfat dried milk, depending on the temperature, up to three to five years. That requires cool storage, though. This shipment might have been hidden in a warehouse in China until after the investigation died down."

"So here comes this milk to Houston from Hong Kong. How do you know it was contaminated? That it had anything to do with your prison deaths?"

"First, you have to have a sample. Next, you have to have a sophisticated lab that knows what to look for. The prison investigation didn't even think about sampling the powdered milk, though they sequestered all their dried and canned products in a locked pantry just to be safe. But we got someone to get us a sample, at both facilities. No, I'm not telling you who or how. And right now we've got preliminary results, just this past week, and are waiting for the QA/QC, you know, the quality assurance / quality control report on chain of custody, tests run, control sample, etc."

"And the milk is still there?"

"So far as we know. We can't let a single syllable of this out or the milk will get dumped and we won't be able to duplicate the tests. That's why I've been so concerned about secrecy."

Alice sat for a moment. "I was going to fuss at you, but now I'm not."

"Fuss at me?"

"Because I'm worried. I'm just anxious for you to get this finished. You're exposing yourself to danger. And . . ." She knew she didn't need to say another word about a baby.

"If ever the pot was calling the kettle black—Alice, you know damn well you'd take care of your clients. That's your job. Even when you've been at risk."

"I know, I know. I'm not saying you should quit, but . . ."

"But me no buts. And besides, how does it look if Sandro runs against a candidate funded by the very people I'm trying to expose? How does that look? I need this out, this whole investigation, before we go public with our relationship. And I guess I'm going to have to do that pretty soon." She smiled a small tired smile.

"Is that what you argued with Norville about?"

"You heard something, right? Well, I liked Carey. Respected him too. He was a huge help for Sandro, and his faith in Sandro was inspiring. But he was messing with my work, telling me I should drop this investigation. I thought he either wished Sandro would pick a quiet, photogenic woman who wouldn't cause problems for the campaign, or wanted us to go ahead and get married right now so Sandro wouldn't be dealing with questions about date of conception. Sorry! I have got to get this done. Sandro understands."

"He doesn't care when you get married?"

"Of course he cares. But he understands this is important work too. And also, this is key to him: he understands that it's the investigation itself that is compromised if it's tied up in my relationship with him, that people might think he was just using my work to foment an issue about his opponent, which could weaken the impact of the investigation. That's the last thing he wants. So, it was a joint decision. I've got to see this through."

"Well, is it through? Once you get the lab report?"

"No. There's something missing. I'm still puzzled about what swung the bid to Fair Foods, since it wasn't low bidder. I'm still digging on that. I have a couple of ideas, too. And no, I'm not telling you. Seriously, Alice, I probably should not have told you any of this. But I owe you for finding me trussed up at the diner. And to tell the truth, I guess I feel better if you or someone knows what I'm doing. I can't let Sandro know details at all. Too many ears around his place, and it potentially compromises the campaign." She expelled a breath. "I just hope we get it all tied up soon."

"Who's we?"

"Mostly me. My editors know I'm working on the prison death issue but they don't know all the details yet."

When Rose stood up, Alice noticed, for the first time, that she was starting to show a little bump. She felt a wave of protectiveness. "Take care." She hugged Rose, then shook her head and smiled. "Should I slap you on the pads? That's what Kinsear says when he knows I have a tough hearing. Football talk, apparently."

"Yeah. Slap me on the shoulder pads."

"And if I'm supposed to be keeping tabs on you at least a little bit, keep me posted, will you?"

Rose nodded and swung her leather satchel over her shoulder and left her iced tea sweating on the counter. Then turned back and put some money on the counter. Alice sat back down for a minute. So painfully independent, she thought. I'm going to sit here and finish this beer, and say one small prayer for Rose.

Chapter Nineteen

Pulling Out the Big Guns

"Phew!" Silla dropped the Monday morning mail on her work table. Alice was walking back from the kitchen with a fresh mug of coffee. "Look at this." She waved two large brown envelopes, all embellished with the name of Black and Whiteside.

"Must be pleadings in the groundwater hearing," Alice said.

But Silla picked up three more, each bearing the embossed return address for Armstrong and Brast, PC.

"Ah. They're pulling out the big guns. Maybe for the other two proceedings." Alice had dealt with the real estate lawyers at Armstrong and Brast back in her Houston days. It was a big Houston firm with offices in San Antonio and Dallas, and now Austin. "Let's see."

"Lemme get it all docketed first, Alice. You're not allowed to have the originals, you know." Silla kept files in order by refusing to give Alice the originals, knowing Alice's habit of highlighting and annotating every piece of paper she picked up.

By the time Alice was halfway through the coffee, Silla presented a stack of pleadings for her review. The new Armstrong lawyers had already answered the two actions for recovery of the Blue Pool land and the land in Medina and Frio Counties, and counterclaimed for damages, charging her client with putting a cloud on their ownership of the property sought. Armstrong had filed vigorous motions to dismiss, charging that her petitions were frivolous and vague. An accelerated hearing on limitations was already set. In addition, Armstrong had sent voluminous discovery requests, requiring answers to all the interrogatories allowed by rule, requests for admission of facts, requests for production of documents, and a request that Alejandro Navarro be presented for medical tests. Alice sighed. This was why she'd left litigation in the first place. Armstrong's demands would require hours of concentrated attention—she couldn't and wouldn't give short shrift.

"Here's your docket," said Silla. "It's in the computer calendar too but I thought you'd better see it all at once."

Hmm. Reinforcements needed. She called Alejandro Navarro to tell him about the onslaught. "Okay if I get more help from Tyler on this? I've already got him helping on the DNA."

"Yes ma'am." He paused. "Can Tomás help too, at all?"

She thought for just a moment. "Can he type? Will he follow directions?"

"Yes to the first. And he's a good proofreader. Spelling champ, can you believe it? On following directions . . . I promise nothing."

"Send him up this afternoon and he can at least read through and talk to us both about documents you might have. And don't forget we need to get together to talk about the groundwater district's hearing on your motion to intervene. That's this Thursday! Want me to pick you up in San Marcos, then we can drive over? We can talk on the way."

"Sounds good."

Alice called Tyler Junkin. "You have any space in your schedule to help me?"

Tyler was there in ten minutes. They divided up the pleadings. "I'll do the response on the motion to dismiss, and draft shell responses for the discovery," he said, "but you have to provide the substance."

Silla, silent, made copies for Tomás as well.

"You'll like him, Silla!" said Alice.

"We'll see. He can't mess with my computer. Hey, you've got Rotary today, Alice. Don't forget you're introducing the speaker! It's Jane Ann. And Red is picking you up."

Time for Rotary. Alice was printing a list of "ten things you don't know about Jane Ann Olson" when she saw Red's bright red SUV pull up. She planned to use the "ten things" list to introduce Jane, sometime singer with a local band and the highly regarded head of the local title company.

Red's usual smile was missing.

"What's up?"

"You know I had my eye on an expanded location for the rescue ranch?"

"Yes. Find the place?" Red had fled management of a major Houston law firm to open a rescue ranch for abused horses. She dearly loved her work and her blue-jeaned life.

"I did. Alice, it's almost perfect. It's just off the Blanco road, nearly a hundred and fifty acres. Good barn, tiny house, good pastures on a tributary to Onion Creek. Pretty reasonably priced, too; it's part of an estate, and the heir lives in Florida, no interest in coming back. I was working on the offer this morning and was going to bring it to you to look over. If you would."

"Sure. But something's wrong?"

"I just learned someone's trying to put a cement plant right next to it! Alice, that won't work. The noise will scare the horses, and the dust will be all over the pasture."

"How'd you find out someone wants to put a cement plant there?"

"The broker called me today. She said she'd seen a classified in the San Marcos paper's legal section, showing someone's applying for a permit for a cement batch plant there."

"Oh no. You have a copy?"

"Yep." She handed it to Alice.

Alice scanned it. "Hmmph. Usually these just get routinely blessed by the state agency, if there are no interceptors near the boundary."

"Interceptors?"

"Yes, that's what air permitters call things like your nose. Your lungs. Your eyes. And you don't have an interest in the property yet, so you and the horses aren't impressive interceptors. I mean, you're interested, but until you have property near the plant you can't fuss except on general principles. Are the neighbors fussing? Do they even know yet?"

"I don't know."

"We ought to ask Jorgé Benavides if the parcel you're interested in is near his property. I think it is. Let's grab him."

"Whoo, big crowd," said Red, pulling into the last space.

They found Jorgé and put their purses on a table. Jorgé held a place for them in line. "Oh my." Red peered at the steam table. "Back to yoga tomorrow morning." Lunch was fried chicken, collard greens, rice and gravy. "And look, banana pudding! The way I like it, with whipped cream!"

Alice showed Jorgé the legal notice about the cement plant. He scrutinized the description, then looked back at her. "Alice, this is just up the road from my property! Where we want to put the— you know."

"We need to protest it and we need others to do the same thing," said Alice. "Look, the hearing on the permit for the plant is coming up pretty quickly."

"How come the state agency didn't even notify me?"

"Required notification is only for a short distance from the property line."

"But I've got grapes growing out there, and animals, and the pecan orchard, and plans for the—the . . ."

"And I really wanted to make an offer on that place for my rescue ranch," said Red.

"Red, what if you go ahead with an offer, very small earnest money, and write into the contract that your purchase is contingent on no concrete batch plant?"

"Good. I like it."

The table filled up. George the surveyor, who had succeeded in wangling a chair next to Red, smoothed the newspaper clipping, then put half-glasses on to read the small print. "We did this survey last January," he said, looking up. "For some realtor in Houston. He said it was a ranch sale. Then I heard the sale fell through. Nobody's called me about a new survey though. And you know what?" He thumped the clipping. "This is only five hundred twenty feet from the middle school property line on Highway 290!"

"Hey, my girls will be out there practicing soccer this very afternoon!" Joe Banks, a local veterinarian who took care of Alice's donkeys, had grabbed the chair on Red's other side. "Those kids can't be breathing cement dust! And why is this notice in the San Marcos paper and not ours? How come we didn't know?"

They looked at Alice. "Depends on the public notice requirements. Maybe they could have put it in the *Coffee Creek Caller*. But if they had a choice, they might choose to run the notice where fewer people from Coffee Creek would see it and they'd hope not to wind up with a big crowd at the public hearing. Sometimes public notice requirements don't really provide much public notice." Privately she wondered how much good protesters would do anyway. "If the batch plant met the regulations the state agency might just throw its hands up, saying it had no option but to grant the permit. Still, as Sun Tzu said, 'Strategy without tactics is the slowest route to victory. Tactics without strategy is the noise before defeat.'"

"What's that mean?" asked Dr. Banks.

"Well, strategy plus tactics could go beyond just getting protesters to the hearing, and submitting comments by the deadline, which should be done in any event. Consider whether you get more time if you have an expert who submits independent testing. Look at the property interest of the proposed cement plant operator. That entity may just have an option on the property. If so, what's the time limit? Check out other operations by this cement plant operator, and if it's just a shell, other activities of the shell's owner. Have there been any enforcement actions? What about the interests of the current property owner, if that's different from the proposed operator? Of course look at the interceptors within five hundred or so feet—who could be harmed by the plant. Under the regulations, I mean—and the regs may be weaker than we wish."

"I'm talking to the principal today," growled the vet. "And to every member of the school board. We just finished building the addition to that middle school. When's the hearing?"

Red held out the clipping. "Only two weeks away. We need to get going."

"If you agree, we can meet at the Beer Barn. Tomorrow night at six?" said Jorgé. All nodded but the vet.

"I'll be there by six thirty," he said.

"Whoops." Alice grabbed her "ten things" list about Jane Ann, who was now standing next to the lectern, where the president was banging the gavel, ready for Jane Ann's learned talk on details of a new title policy tweak. Alice dashed up to make her introduction. Item number ten: "Do you know the date of Jane Ann's next show?"

Audience, loud chorus: "No!"

"Beer Barn, this Thursday, six p.m.! She says she does have some new lyrics but they're reasonably clean, so bring your families! Now please welcome Jane Ann Olson."

Chapter Twenty

My Raft's Battered, Tossed by Poseidon

These days Alice had a sense of dread every time she opened the office door. When she walked back in from Rotary, Silla called, "Another hearing scheduled." Scorched earth, she thought. Well, nothing to do but forge ahead. She was drafting her own discovery documents for the Drinkmans, asking for an inventory of Alex's property.

Silla appeared in her office door. "Tomás is in the conference room," she said. "I told him to look at the discovery request asking for his family's documents and anything about Alex Drinkman and about Alejandro's birth. He's nicer than I expected. Also, Tyler sent these drafts and is heading over here in a second." The red pony tail swished as she left.

Alice marked up Tyler's draft response to Armstrong's motion to dismiss the land actions and attached the final DNA report. That should avoid either sanctions or dismissal.

Tyler walked in.

She sighed and leaned back, looking at the welter of paper on her desk. "This is absolutely why I left litigation and threw myself into trusts and estates and real estate."

"You knew what you were getting into when you intervened in the groundwater hearing and filed those actions for recovery of land. That was like throwing a grenade over the wall."

"I know. But it's the best route the law gives us, as far as I can tell. Can you tackle finishing our discovery requests to them? We want any documents about the letter, the Navarros, Alex's death, Drinkman claims to the Blue Pool property, and so on."

Tyler nodded.

Time to check on Tomás.

He sat in the conference room, back to the door, sleeves rolled up, staring down at a page of the Drinkman discovery, jotting tiny marginal notes with a pencil. She stood, peering over his shoulder. He turned the page, bent his head again, then sensed her and jumped up.

She'd never seen him sit still before.

"Ms. Greer!"

"May I see?"

She looked at his notes. "*Check SD box. Check little wooden box.*

Books? Army Air Corps records? House fire—newspaper?" She sat down next to him and pointed at the notes.

"You know my granddad has military records. But Alice, otherwise, we don't have much of what they're asking for. We can check the safety deposit box. He also has a little carved box that was his mother's, has a couple of things in it, I don't know what. Not sure about books, but we'll go through what he has. Letters—well, there's the rub. In 1920 his mother—Susana—went back home to live with her parents and their house burned down along with two others over on the west side of San Antonio. I was always told there was a big lightning storm in hot August weather. With those little wooden houses, nothing was left but ashes. If she had letters from Alex Drinkman, I guess they were lost. If you need corroboration of the fire, I was thinking there might be a fire report in the newspaper microfiches. Anyway, she died when my granddad was only five, so his grandmother brought him up. Last, of course my granddad has his birth certificate, but it does not name the father."

"Pretty thorough. Can you check the safety deposit box and the little carved box? And go through to see if there are any old books he didn't buy himself?"

"I can."

"Let's do some preemptive work. Can you also get any documentation of the Pacific flying, the oil field flying? As well as the later military records?"

"Yes."

"He must have been quite a guy. Imagine pushing so hard to get to fly fighters in the Pacific."

"He loved flying. Told me once that when he was airborne, he felt free as a bird. I wonder if that was from some of his aerial mapping, all by himself up over a bare Texas landscape, no one near him at all." Tomás looked at Alice. "Makes me feel like a piker. I like to drive fast, I guess you heard. It's not the same as flying fighters in World War II. You're thinking I need an adventure, right? Need to man up?"

"Not me. Every mother wants her child safe. I'll bet your mother did too."

"On that note"—the smiling mask was back; he stood and

grabbed his blazer and looked at his watch. "Gotta get back to the city. I'll let you know right away about what I find."

"Remember when these responses are due."

And he was out the door, leaving Alice missing her own John and Ann, so far away, but supposedly with tickets home in June. And had she been honest with Tomás? Maybe he did need to man up, as the saying went.

* * * * *

Alice was already at her desk at seven a.m. on Tuesday, trudging through the turgid Armstrong pleadings, when the phone rang. Tomás, so early?

"Alice, the carved wooden box. It has a ring, it has a book, and it has some poetry. You need to see this, I think."

"I'm sitting right here. Bring it over!" She hung up and went to the kitchen to start more coffee.

In an hour Tomás burst in, unsmiling, intense, wide-eyed. He spurned coffee. "Look."

They sat at her antique tea table in the back window, early sun touching the old carved box. Alice picked up the book, a beautiful small leather-covered book, Pope's translation of the *Iliad* and the *Odyssey*, the cover tooled, the letters in gold. And a small square jeweler's box.

Inside the book was a folded sheet, with a penciled note at the top—"*This struck me.*" Below, copied in the same handwriting, was a poem, the title "Spring Offensive." I know this one, Alice thought suddenly, I know this one. At the bottom, a dash, and the name: Wilfred Owen.

She turned the page over. In the same writing, writing she already knew, were other lines:

To Susana:

Like his, my raft's battered, tossed by Poseidon,
Pushing me farther from shore.
My raft's my aircraft, all my moves beaten
At each desperate turn for home.
O my Penelope, wait for me, wait
Till the war-god sinks in the sea,
Forgetting his hatred just for a moment,
Till the clouds part and I see
Something familiar, a turn of the landscape,
A hill I remember, the rough hills of home.
Give me a wind to carry me west,
But will you recognize me?
Let me steer straight to the home of my heart
Let me steer clear of the sea,
Oh if this tearaway wind will let up,
Let the clouds break so I see,
O my Penelope, wait for me, wait for me,
 But will you recognize me?

January 12, 1919.

And a note below:

Grandiose, thinking of myself as Odysseus, but sometimes I feel as old and battered as he.
—Alex

Alice felt tears rise. She reached for a tissue, turned, blew her nose. Tomás looked appalled, then concerned.

"It's when Odysseus is exhausted, trying so hard to keep his raft afloat, the raft he built, the raft he hopes to sail home, and Poseidon won't let up." Alice sniffed.

"Ah."

"But look, Tomás. It's the same writing." She went to the desk, pulled a copy of the letter from her lap drawer.

They stared at the same sharp *n*'s, the same hard downstrokes on the *t*'s. "But even if the writing is the same, how can we prove that 'Alex' is Alex Drinkman? Couldn't we prove it's his handwriting ourselves? From some other writing than the letter?" asked Tomás.

"Yes! You're right. What about certified copies of his military records? He ought to have something handwritten in his personnel file. And then we need an expert." Her mind was racing.

"Maybe prints? What do we have with his prints?" she wondered aloud. "Aha! The uniform. The uniform in the Drinkman display case. Surely on his leather pilot's cap. His jacket. His boots."

"How do we ask for that?"

"Discovery request. Make them produce the uniform! That cabinet was empty when I visited Will Drinkman's office . . . like just emptied." She remembered that Orinda had something about "cleaning." She'd include in her no-spoliation letter to the Drinkmans' counsel that no item of Alex's was to be cleaned or otherwise messed with.

"Now can we look at the ring?" Tomás asked.

She opened the old box. It held a plain gold ring with an oval ruby. She picked it up with a tissue, thinking there might still be a partial print. Inside the gold band ran tiny engraved letters. She reached for the magnifying glass. "*Siempre. A.*"

All of a piece. Ring. Book. Poem. Maybe it would not convince a court. But it convinced her.

"But Alice, what does any of this prove? Isn't the real question whether Alex intended to adopt Alejandro Navarro? And was forestalled by someone who gained from his death?"

"I'm still thinking about that. We've filed actions to recover his land, instead of an application for determination of heirship. Otherwise we might be fighting for years over the four-year statute of limitations, even though there was never any administration of Alex's estate. My understanding is that your granddad doesn't want years of litigation. Also, Carey Norville said a case with good odds would be less likely to create bad press for your dad, and your family." She glanced at his face, watching for any reaction to Norville's advice. "What you're talking about would mean going after what Alex might have gotten under his father's will. We don't yet have all the facts for that. The court might say Alex could have changed his mind about marriage or adoption, before he was killed. And we'd have to prove who killed him. Getting killed right after he stated his intentions in the letter sure makes it look as if someone took those intentions seriously, but the other side will still say that anyone could have pulled the trigger."

"So this—the poem, the ring—is nothing but some sentimental icing on the cake. Only there's no cake."

"I would not say that." Her eyes teared up again. What was this maudlin sniveling, for goodness' sake? She grabbed the tissue, blew her nose. Thinking of Jordie, that was it. Jordie, the helicopter going down, battered by Poseidon, helpless in the North Sea. Jordie, not ever able to find the shore of his own Ithaca.

Identifying with Penelope again, I am, she scolded herself. Not really appropriate at this point. Pull up your socks, Alice.

"Hey, Tomás. Your grandfather and I have a hearing Thursday night at seven, before the Coffee Creek Groundwater District. I can come get him. You want to come too?"

"Huh. Yes, I'd like to come."

"So why don't we meet at six in the Antler Café parking lot? Short drive for you, short drive for me."

"Deal. Thanks for asking me."

Alice raised her eyebrows. "Thanks for coming." Well, maybe he had potential.

Chapter   Twenty - One

Every Right to Complain

A lone, she called her colleagues at her former firm. Best handwriting expert? Ruby Michaels, miraculously in Austin. Alice called and got a recorded message: call her in Maine. She called her in Maine. No, Ruby Michaels had no conflict representing someone adverse to the Drinkmans. Yes, she could help. What could she send her? And how soon? Did Alice know she would be in Maine for a month? Yes, she could fly down if needed. Yes, she'd been deposed before. Her rate? Yikes. But Alice needed her report soon, before the hearing on Armstrong's motion to dismiss. Though when Alice started practicing it had been harder to win a motion to dismiss, the recently amended Texas rules were not plaintiff-friendly. She couldn't risk a bad result. How fast could Ruby Michaels move and how fast could Alice get Ruby Alex's certified military personnel file? And would it hold any handwritten document, and if so would it be clear it was Alex's handwriting and not some military clerk's? Oh, lord. She tried to clear her brain, and asked Silla to work on acquiring a certified copy of Alex's military personnel file. Step by step, Alice. Handwriting expert. Show Alex did write the letter. Ballistics expert. Show what sort of gun fired the bullets. And—giant step here, with a possible bonus, going after more of the Drinkman fortune than Alex's land—show he was killed by a gun in the Drinkmans' possession. That was the goal. So, make them produce the Savage.

* * * * *

Alice and Red met at the Beer Barn for supper Tuesday night, before Jorgé's proposed meeting on the cement plant. Alice had marked up a copy of the standard real estate contract for the property Red wanted and they went over it while they waited for their burgers. "And onion rings," Red had told History. "I need sustenance."

"How fast will you get an answer to this offer, Red?"

"The broker says fast. But I'm skeptical, given this 'no cement plant' condition we've put in. You think the seller has any influence over a cement plant application?"

"Possibly. We'll talk to the broker. Your seller may want to be one more outraged citizen at the hearing. And since your seller seems to be within the regulatory notification distance, that will have more influence on the agency folks. 'You're devaluing my property! I'm losing a sale!' State people hate to hear that."

Joe Banks, Alice's favorite vet, walked in, still wearing his outdoor work clothes: black jeans, Western shirt, and hat. "Hey, if I'd known you two were already here I'd have come earlier!" He sat down by Red, whose cheeks slowly turned pink. The vet, divorced, with joint custody of two daughters, played mandolin very soulfully when not engaged in his large-and-small-animal practice in Coffee Creek. Alice watched, already envisioning happiness for Red, a local hero for her work with abused horses. Red had been single a good long while, and if she ever remarried—well, the cowboys of Coffee Creek would all mourn.

"I'm here as a soccer dad," said Joe Banks. "And I need a Flat Creek Bock, please." History was polishing glasses and pulling beers. Other concerned neighbors crowded in. By consensus they decided to hold their meeting down by the stage. Jorgé stood in front, carrying notes. "Thought we could corral what we all know," he said. "If no one objects, I'll start." No one objected.

"Okay. We now have a copy of the cement plant application. The permit applicant is White Star LLC, which doesn't own the site yet—just has a member with an option on it. And by its terms, the option expires a week after the hearing, unless it's renewed. By mutual agreement." His eyes met Alice's. She nodded. "So if we can make a big splash at the hearing, or if an alternate buyer turns up, maybe the owner will let the option expire. Furthermore, the application mentions supplying concrete for road improvements out on Highway 290, miles west of here. We looked online and found the cement plant submitted a bid to Blake Road Construction, which is in charge of widening Highway 290 down north of Blanco. Then we thought we'd do a little checking on our city council members to learn whether they had any contributions from either party. Guess what? They did. Our own Lane Spencer got twenty thousand dollars in his election kitty from the permit applicant. And that's a pretty big contribution for an incumbent councilman." Groans from the audience. Alice and the Beer Barn had had a dustup with Lane Spencer earlier in the year, when Spencer tried, unsuccessfully, to take away the Beer Barn's key easement to their parking lot. "Anyway, can we get city council to pass a resolution opposing the plant? What would Lane Spencer do if he knows he's going to get some unpleasant publicity?"

Busy discussion. Joe Banks stood up. "The school board and the middle school principal tell me they are going to issue statements opposing the cement plant."

"Here's something else I found out." A local rancher, a burly woman with tight jeans and a no-nonsense face, came forward. "Like you say, the permit applicant is White Star, LLC. And its managing member is Fair Star Partners. And way on up the line, you know who is involved? Warren Drinkman."

Alice sat straight up.

"Who's that?" said Banks.

"He's the son of the head of the Drinkman outfit, the big foundation that gives all the political money. In fact, he gave a lot to Jody McPhil, who's in a tight race in the primary next month. Let's see if we can't get some heat under that race too," said the burly woman. "Unless McPhil agrees to speak up at the public hearing against the plant."

Red leaned over to Alice. "I would not mess with her. If she tells Jody McPhil to do something, I'm betting he'll do it."

Jorgé reminded all of those present about the deadline for comments. Need to send them certified mail; need to state exactly how close you are, need to say precisely how the dust and noise will affect you. Send a copy of your comments to Jorgé because he's going to get the comments to an air expert. Anyone who wants to put in some money to help defray the expert's fee, please do. A couple of people walked up to him with checks.

Then he headed over to Alice. Red was occupied; Joe Banks was monopolizing her, and she appeared to be enjoying it.

"Alice. This Fair Star Partners, and the Drinkmans. What about that? Why are they putting a cement batch plant in Coffee Creek?"

"No idea. I hear the younger guy, Warren, is trying to show his dad he can make money."

"Not off my family's land, he can't. Not off our mini-brewery. We'll have a united front at the hearing."

Alice was not as positive as Jorgé. But the brewery application predated the public notice of the cement plant application. A nascent mini-brewery had every right to complain.

Chapter   Twenty - Two

At a Critical
Point

Staring on Wednesday morning at the ever-lengthening dock-et taped to her desk, Alice confirmed with horror that the Thursday evening groundwater district hearing on the Blue Pool pumping application came the night before the Friday afternoon hearing in Coffee County on the Drinkmans' accelerated motion to dismiss Navarro's action to recover the Blue Pool property. Well, that concentrated the mind wonderfully.

Alice thought her groundwater district pleadings were in pretty good shape. As to the action to recover the Blue Pool property, she intended to throw the whole kit and caboodle at the Drinkmans. She'd already sent their lawyers Tyler's discovery demands for Alex's uniform or other possessions of his, any documents with his hand-writing, and presentation of the Savage Model 99 for testing. That should highlight for the Drinkmans the risks they were running.

She'd made a strategic decision to go ahead and file both a no-evidence motion for summary judgment and a motion for partial summary judgment asking the court to declare that Alejandro Navarro owned and was entitled to possess the Blue Pool property, as Alex Drinkman's heir. The no-evidence motion should make the Drinkmans do some work for a change; they'd have to pony up what-ever evidence they thought should bar her from getting summary judgment. They'd have to respond to the expert report stating that Alex Drinkman wrote the letter and the poem—Ruby had turned it around quickly—and Felix Apple's report that DNA testing showing that Mr. Navarro was Alex's son had been properly conducted. She'd also attached Barker's ballistics report, and one on the paper in Alex's letter. If the Drinkmans or their experts said anything notable at their depositions, she'd amend her motion.

She'd also sent Drinkman counsel her standard no-spoliation letter, demanding that they preserve without any tampering or al-teration all relevant discovery, including documents, rifles, and all items bearing Alex's fingerprints, including leather parts of his uni-form and his papers. She trusted them not at all. On reflection, thinking of Bonnie's trunk and its contents, she sent the same letter to Adele's lawyer.

And she'd sent him copies of the motion with its expert reports.

Maybe the experts' view of Alex's letter and DNA and the bullets would convince his client to adjust her position, and take the side of her cousin Alejandro.

Silla stuck her head around the door. "Good morning. I am ready to turn to." "Turn to" was Silla-ese for moving from zero to sixty in a few seconds.

"Okay. Once the Navarros sign off on the drafts, let's get this motion filed and served."

She expected a flurry of outraged responses from the Drinkman lawyers.

And where was Rose? Despite promising to stay in touch, Rose hadn't. Annoyed, Alice picked up the phone and got a message. "Leave a number and I'll call you back." Hmmph.

She needed a break. She walked over to Bryce's store. He was deep in impassioned conversation with a big-haired blonde customer about a roll-top desk. "It's just perfect for my husband's office," she was saying. "But does it have any of those secret drawers?"

"Not that I've found," Bryce said. "Are you looking for secret drawers?"

"Definitely not." She smiled an expensive smile. "I'm the only one with secrets."

Alice left them and wandered into her favorite niche, the antique linens. So anachronistic, the embroidery, the tatting, the lace-making. So hard, all that ironing with a flat iron, trying not to scorch. And why? Why make life harder than it already was, trying to stock bathrooms with clean ironed embroidered monogrammed linen hand towels? She sighed. Still, there was something about the beauty, the fragrance of ironing, the sheer joy of unfolding a clean capacious dinner napkin . . . She still used some of her mother's linens. And thought, always, about the lot of women.

The expensive customer left, with Bryce smiling her out the door, holding the completed order in his hand. "Alice! Where are you?"

"Lolling in linens."

"Happy to get rid of that roll-top. Nice price, but it's not the right look for the shop. Too . . . too . . . clunky."

"Don't tell her."

"Let's get some iced tea. Are you just visiting? I've got something you might like that just came in."

"Oh no." She'd already bought twin mahogany music stands from Bryce, for her children.

"Yes, it's you. Look." He pointed at a mission rocker, solid oak, with a worn leather cushion on the seat. "It's not the same vintage as your office furniture, but shouldn't you have a rocker in there? And see, it's just your size. Not too tall. Goldilocks size."

"Not sure about the cushion." She sat down, rocked slowly. "Hmm." She rocked some more. She peered around for the price tag. Usually she looked before sitting, not wanting to develop the least attachment before she learned the price.

"You review our wills now that John T and I have built the house, and it's yours," said Bryce.

"Deal!" said Alice.

"But I'll bet you didn't come over here to buy furniture. What's up?"

"No, I needed a break. Where's Rose?"

"I have no clue."

Chuffed about her rocker, but annoyed by Rose's silence—no, admit it, alarmed—Alice walked back to the office. The air was heating up. And there at her curb stood the blue Ford Focus.

Rose sat in the conference room on the edge of her chair, biting her nails. "Alice. I need help."

"What's up?"

"I'm getting stonewalled by the attorney general on my document requests about these prison contracts. Isn't there a resource where I can figure out what the AG has ruled on before, concerning public contracts?"

"Yup. Let's look."

Just then Silla popped through the door, hands on hips. "Alice. Don't forget the conference call at two thirty with the land trust folks." She looked sternly at her watch. "Thirty minutes."

Alice found the archive of the attorney general's opinions and fed it search terms. "What about this, Rose?" She read aloud: "'Minutes of public board meetings discussing bids shall be considered public information.' So you get those. And how about this: 'Correspondence to the officials considering bid proposals from applicants *and others* are public information.' That's my emphasis on the *and others.* Isn't that what you want? All the documents considered, and the correspondence, if any? And the minutes?"

"Yes," said Rose. "And will you write the letter for me, citing these opinions?"

Alice sat back. "Let's talk that through. I'm representing Sandro's father in his heirship application, and in his intervention with the groundwater district over Blue Pool. Why muddy the waters, excuse the pun? And why isn't your employer helping you on this? The lawyers for the newspaper probably knows these AG opinions by heart—they handle public information requests all the time. Probably have a letter in the computer right now they could print out for you in two seconds."

"It's complicated."

Alice cocked her head, considering Rose. She was paler than before, thinner, except for the growing little bump.

"Okay. I think my computer's being hacked. My work account, at a minimum. And who knows what else."

"Why?"

"Weird stuff. In the last week I've made a couple of email dates for lunch. When I get there, someone's watching me."

"Who?"

"It's been different people. At least two different guys. But I can tell, Alice! Maybe someone has hacked my calendar. But I'm afraid it's email, so I'm afraid of sending work emails even to our counsel and certainly to the AG. Trying to use hard copy instead, these days."

"What if the AG wants to send you documents electronically?"

"I'm picking them up myself. So instead of zipping along electronically, I'm stuck with snail mail and trips to the agencies. It's pretty exhausting and it's slowing me down, but I don't think that's the whole point. Someone wants to know what I am doing, step by step. So I didn't email you. Come to think of it, I never have."

"You think your phone is safe?"

"I think it's safer than the computer, but I bought one of those cheapo cells and used cash to fill it up, just in case. You may think I'm nuts, but I also took the SIM card out of my real phone. Keep it in my wallet for emergencies."

"And you think you're at a critical point in your project? Your investigation?"

"Yes, it's beginning to have that feeling, but I'm not exactly sure why. I looked at minutes of an earlier prison board meeting and saw that a couple of members of the legislature had attended, so I had the idea of talking to their staffs, the AA and LA, you know, administrative assistant and legislative assistant. The election came right after the food contracts were awarded, and one of the two members, a senator, lost his election, had to go home. But I tracked down his AA, who's now attending law school. He sounded like he'd be truthful but didn't want to feed me stuff. He said, 'Look up who was on his campaign team and then come talk to me.' Well, that member's team included Kelly Cosgrove. He worked on several members' campaigns that fall, different districts of course."

"Old Kelly, again," said Alice, remembering the pudgy man talking to Carey Norville in the bar.

"Right. Ostrich boots, always." Then Rose was silent.

"So did you call Kelly Cosgrove? Or go back to the law student?"

"I haven't contacted Kelly yet. I want to get my facts right first. The law student is madly studying for his first-year finals, but we're going to talk about four today at the law school library after he finishes with his study group."

"Ah."

"So if you could just print me out a letter—make up some letterhead, just my name and phone numbers and the newspaper mailing address—for me to sign and send to the AG, and I can fax it from the UPS office down the street. Can you do that?"

"Sure. We've got ten minutes before my conference call. And hey, write down that cheapo number for me."

Together, Rose leaning over Alice's shoulder, they invented letterhead, pulled in the AG citations about public information on public contracts, and printed it with a minute to spare.

"Thanks." Rose hugged a surprised Alice.

"Call me if you find out who the bagman is?"

"Yes, on my cheapo!"

Rose pulled out her car fob, gave it a punch.

"What are you doing?"

"It's hot outside! This starts my car remotely and turns on the AC. I do need at least a little comfort these days!" Rose waved and headed out the door to her car.

Alice's phone rang. She picked up the draft easement, reminded herself of the issues left to address, and jumped on the call.

Chapter Twenty-Three

Worth Killing For

About five thirty, her cell rang. Kinsear. "Hi! I've been missing you!" said Alice. It was true, too. What did that mean? "It's quitting time here at the bookstore. I'm turning over open to closed on the front door, even as we speak."

"Are you free for supper at my house? Could we collaborate?"

"I'm free. Expensive, but free."

They batted menu ideas back and forth and wound up with grilled cherry-chipotle sausage, a big salad ("huge," demanded Kinsear), and grilled bread with tapenade ("which I shall make," he announced). "Ice cream sandwiches for dessert. Homemade," countered Alice. "Want anyone else to come?"

"Only if they go home early."

Driving home Alice tuned in to KUT, the local NPR station. "Breaking news. A bomb, apparently a car bomb, has exploded at the UT law school. The area is currently blocked off by barricades. Police and firemen are at the scene and are not permitting anyone to enter the area." She pulled off the creek road and punched in Rose's number, willing Rose to answer. She didn't. SIM card must still be in her wallet. Alice scrabbled in her purse and found Rose's scribbled number for the cheapo cell. Come on, answer! Ten rings. Then a thin faraway voice said, "Hello?"

"Rose? Is that you? It's Alice, Rose. Are you okay?"

"Alice, yes, I'm okay. I'm okay." She was crying. "I'm okay, but I—the car is gone, Alice. I was going to start it with my remote, it's roasting in this parking lot, but then it blew up. And the girl getting in the car near mine—she's okay but her car caught fire too. Thank God she was a space away. Oh, Alice, I'm still shaking."

"Can I come get you?"

"Not yet. There's a very nice officer here who wants to talk to me."

"Okay, quick yes-or-no question: Did you get what you wanted from the AA? The law student?"

"Yes, more than you know."

"Get you closer to the end of your project?"

"Could be. Okay, I'll call you after I talk to this officer."

"Rose, could I just ask him something?"

"Okay."

"Sergeant Kubek here," said a deep voice.

"Sergeant, I'm a friend of Rose's. She sounds pretty shaky. May I give you my number so you could call me when she needs to be picked up? I'm out here in Coffee Creek, but she could stay with me tonight."

"I'll see someone gets her safely out there, if that's where she wants to be. Thanks, ma'am."

When she got home, Kinsear was pitting olives and mashing them with anchovies, olive oil, garlic, lemon, and chopped parsley. "Broke into your kitchen," he said over his shoulder. Then he took another look. "What's up?"

She dropped her briefcase on a chair. "I'm glad we're here and alive."

"Right. What happened?"

"Someone blew up Rose's car. At the UT law school parking lot. But she's okay."

"Lord God. She wasn't in it?"

"She used the remote start, trying to cool off the car before she had to get in. Otherwise . . ."

"What the hell is she working on?"

"Something about the deaths at that prison in South Texas last year. Maybe she'll tell you. She might wind up here tonight." She told Kinsear about her talk with Sergeant Kubek.

Her cell rang. Sandro Navarro. "Alice. Rose told me. I'm picking her up in Austin. The idiot." His voice cracked. "Sorry. She said you'd offered to keep her."

"Yes. Come for dinner. We can talk."

Once Alice had hung up, Kinsear leaned his fists on the kitchen island. "And our cast of characters?"

Alice explained about Rose, how stubborn she was, how she insisted on finishing her investigation before she and Sandro went public.

"Reminds me of someone."

"I'll get the grill going. And make the huge salad," Alice said. "But first—" She got a bottle of zinfandel from the fridge and poured them each a glass. "*Salud*. And I mean it. That woman scares me to death."

"Now you know how I feel." He grinned.

She took a sip of the zinfandel, and stuck her face up toward his. "Wine kiss."

He took her up on that. "How soon are those people getting here?"

* * * * *

Soon, it appeared. Sandro and Rose pulled up in a black SUV. "Ah, the politico-mobile," Alice muttered to herself, walking out with Kinsear to greet them. Gone was Sandro's warm smile. His face was grim, one arm around Rose.

"She just scared the shit out of me," he said. "What are we gonna do?"

Alice hugged Rose.

They decamped to Alice's screened porch with the wine and iced tea and tapenade and bread. "What can you tell us?"

Rose took a deep breath. "You know I told you I thought my email was hacked, or my calendar? Maybe. But there was also a little GPS bug on my car. The police found it—it got blown off the car in the explosion and nearly hit some guy studying out under a tree. He told us it 'really bugged him.'" She giggled. "Only funny thing I can think of." Then tears seeped out of her eyes and her face crumpled up and she sniffed. Kinsear handed her a bandana.

"So someone knew exactly where you were. And you had talked to the former AA, and were getting ready to leave?" asked Alice.

"Yes. If I hadn't used the remote . . . oh, God."

"What did the law student say?" Alice asked again.

She looked at Kinsear and Sandro and shrugged. "Okay. You guys are now in the cone of silence. The prison foods contract carried a big payoff. It was worth millions, but not just to the contractor. He said he was in his boss's office when Kelly Cosgrove came in, with 'a big shit-eating grin,' direct quote. My guy left the boss's office but could still hear some of what they said. His boss got a big check 'to reduce campaign debts,' per Kelly Cosgrove. My guy doesn't know how much, but his boss said something like now he didn't care if he won or lost. And Kelly Cosgrove said that now he was a member of an LLC and then he said something like, 'Bonus time! Retirement may be within reach!' Then on his way out the door, Cosgrove said, 'Yee-haw!'"

"Hey, translate for us," Kinsear put in.

Sandro sighed and shook his head. "Based on what you're saying, Rose, that particular guy got a big chunk after Fair Foods LLC won the bid. And he did lose the election that fall, but, like he said, he didn't care. But also, Kelly Cosgrove is a 'member' of the LLC, sorta like being a shareholder in a corporation. And got a bonus, it sounds like."

"So Kelly was not only paying off the legislator who greased the skids—he was also an investor in the outfit that won the bid. And he was feeling better about someday being able to retire after his company won. Right?" said Kinsear. "This just sounds like typical corrupt politics. What's the big deal?"

Rose sat for a moment. Alice knew she was considering how much she wanted Sandro to know.

"Oh come on, Rose, tell them," Alice interjected.

"It's poisoned powdered milk. Sneaked in from China, with melamine in it. The same stuff that killed babies, poisoned their kidneys, in China," Rose said.

"Aha," Sandro said. "So that's what you've been looking at, Rose? I remember thinking that China milk scandal got hushed up pretty fast. Do you think Fair Foods knew? Did they pick up some of the tainted milk that was not supposed to leave China?"

Rose gave an ambiguous shrug. "We're looking at the bills of lading."

Sandro whistled. "Boy, if this gets out, and if anyone in the chain knew about the contamination, there could be some designated inmates."

"How important is it to confirm Kelly Cosgrove was the bagman?" asked Alice.

Rose looked up. "It's not important in some ways, but it's my link to the Drinkmans. Doesn't it point to the Drinkmans? To Warren Drinkman's companies? I didn't care who the bagman was, just that I got confirmation that the Drinkmans were paying off the lege on the deal."

"So your law student is the only proof on that. How safe is he, after that car bomb?" Alice asked.

Rose shivered. "He's not safe at all. I taped the conversation but he doesn't know that. I don't know what to do to keep him safe now."

"How can we take the heat off him? Does anyone else at the capitol know that his boss and probably another representative got paid off? Does anyone at the prison board know about these payoffs?"

"I don't know. And if the payoffs are just 'campaign contributions'—you see why it's so hard?" Rose demanded.

"What about Cosgrove? Do you have other proof Cosgrove is a member of Fair Foods LLC?" asked Alice.

"Only from the comment the AA overheard. But a copy of the LLC agreement, which would list the members, is what I was supposed to get the night I left you at the Beer Barn. With my french fries."

"You don't have it," Alice said.

"Right. And my contact, my 'innie' at the Drinkman building, got fired and can't be found."

Kinsear said slowly, "Your laptop was taken that night, right? And you have another one now? Someone could at least use your laptop to figure out how to get into the newspaper electronics, email and databases, and from thence they could probably hack your new laptop too. And someone certainly put the GPS bug on your car. So since that night, someone has known where you are, or at least where your car is, and apparently some of what you're doing, who you're emailing."

"I only emailed that clerk at Drinkman's on his personal email."

"Did he check it on his work computer? The IT guys at Drinkman probably monitor all the employee computer use."

"Back to where we are," Kinsear said. "Who benefits from the car bomb? The Drinkmans? Kelly Cosgrove, on his own hook?"

Sandro shook his head. "Kelly can't afford to let the Drinkmans know he's been outed. That's pretty stupid, to let a legislative employee see you handing over the cash."

"But the Drinkmans—at least Warren—also can't be besmirching their organization with poisoned prison food," Rose said.

"Could Kelly Cosgrove do something like this on his own?" asked Alice. "I just can't see him kneeling down in his ostrich boots to place a car bomb under your car."

"I don't see him dirtying his hands. He'd have to hire someone," Rose said.

"Maybe there'll be prints somewhere. The GPS bug? But Alice, let's feed these people." Kinsear headed outside to light the grill.

Dinner was subdued. Alice pressed Sandro and Rose to spend the night.

"Nope. We're going to my house. If she's outed, she's outed. No, Rose, I mean it. No one will see us drive in the garage, and I want you where I can see you tonight."

"But the kids!"

"Isabella is fundraising in Washington and Tomás—who knows. And we'll go find you a new car tomorrow. Let's roll."

Car lights disappeared down Alice's bumpy drive.

"Okay, let's talk." Kinsear folded his arms. "Whoever this is, at least whoever planted the GPS bug, knows Rose was at your office yesterday."

"Possibly. But nobody's going to try to come after me—too blatant!"

"Someone sure invaded Bryce's shop, and then his house."

"Yes, but that was when 'someone' wanted the letter back. And now it's too late, with our filings and the fact that they're taking the legal position it's a forgery. You can't both want it back and claim it's a forgery. Nothing's happened since the battle of El Rancherito, right?"

"Still," he said, "whatever Rose is after must be worth killing for."

Chapter Twenty-Four

Intentional Criminal Acts

A lice spent Thursday morning preparing with Tyler for their Friday afternoon hearing on the Drinkman motion to dismiss Navarro's land action. The groundwater hearing was that night, but she felt fully prepared.

"The case is starting to come together, Alice. Looking good," said Tyler. "I especially like the handwriting report, and the expert report on the paper used in the letter."

Ruby Michaels, the handwriting expert, had compared the letter and the envelope to the note in Alejandro's mother's wooden box, and had compared both to the handwritten application Alex Drinkman had made to the American Flying Service. Michaels was reasonably confident the writer was the same. Alice had also sent Silla to the courthouse in Woodville to get a certified copy of Adecia Bond's holographic will, probated in 1924 (and for good measure, just in case, a copy of Bonnie Drinkman's, probated in 1970). Alice asked Michaels to compare the tiny notes ("Adecia Bond") on the envelope, and on the slips of paper about the lock of hair and the bullets, to Adecia Bond's will. Michaels could not be quite as confident, but said they seemed to be by the same person.

"I like the paper expert," Alice said. An expert on paper from the Blanton Museum had verified that the letter, envelope, and poem were vintage 1919 paper, and that the ink matched that date as well.

"On our demand for access to test the Savage Model 99, we'll be getting real pushback," Tyler said.

"Even if we prove that the bullet was fired by a Drinkman rifle, we won't be proving who fired it," Alice said.

"But remember, this isn't a murder trial where you have to prove facts beyond a reasonable doubt. It's a civil trial, so it's—"

"Preponderance of the evidence," they repeated together. "Except," Alice said, "where some evidence may have to be 'clear and convincing.'"

"If we did want to prove who fired the gun, wouldn't we look at the bullets? Weren't there some partials visible on the photographs?" Tyler wondered.

"They could also be Aunt Dee's, but there may be more than hers. Are we rolling the dice, going down the fingerprint trail?"

"I suppose they could offer fingerprints to prove it wasn't one of the Drinkmans," Tyler said. "Maybe they could exhume Willy."

"Would there still be fingerprints . . . uh . . . available?" asked Alice.

"Yecch. No idea."

Tyler got ready to leave.

"Remember I'm going to be at the groundwater district tonight," Alice said. "But that ought not to be too stressful. So final prep for this hearing tomorrow afternoon—shouldn't be a problem."

* * * * *

It was after four. Time to race to the Antler Café to meet Mr. Navarro and Tomás. One last time she paged through her notebook, scanning the law granting limited powers to groundwater districts; the district rules, highlighted in yellow marker, especially the requirement that applicants own an interest in the property; the Drinkmans' permit application; and finally her petition to intervene. Had they filed anything at the last minute? "Silla, anything else come in from the Drinkmans? Or the groundwater district?"

"Nope. I called the clerk to be sure."

She packed her briefcase. Would she need anything else? No, just her secret weapon: her dignified, steady-eyed client. Out the door she sailed.

Alejandro Navarro and Tomás had already grabbed a table at the Antler Café. Mr. Navarro rose, ever courtly, in his white shirt, bolo tie, blue blazer, sharply pressed chinos. And his beautiful old roper boots, polished to a military gleam. He pulled out a chair for her. Tomás grabbed her briefcase and stowed it under the table. "You didn't leave it in the car?"

"Never, not before a hearing."

"Alice, what can we get you?"

"Just iced tea."

"I don't want supper until after the hearing," Mr. Navarro announced. "But I could have a piece of that coconut pie."

Alice went over the rules. Make eye contact with the board members. Nod at them. Be sure to thank them at the end, whatever happened. Sit quietly. Mr. Navarro should sit next to her. Tomás was to sit in the chair right behind their table, assuming there was a table. Tomás should make notes on a yellow sticky pad—she handed it to him and made him put it in his jacket pocket—of anything he thought she needed to clarify or address; he should just hand her the note, don't interrupt her or she'd lose her train of thought. And don't make faces if the opposition says something you don't like. "Your usual exquisite courtesy, I count on that."

They nodded. "And I think we can just take the back road from here—their office is between here and Wimberley, and we can take Ranch Road 631 straight there without having to drive back to 281. Besides, it's pretty, and there'll still be bluebonnets."

"What if you and Granddad ride together, and I follow you? That way you won't have to bring us all the way back here afterward."

And you can talk on your cell phone without an audience, she thought. "Sounds good." Alice picked up the briefcase and headed outside.

"I'll follow you in just a minute. Got to make a phone call." Tomás waved, heading to his little BMW.

With Mr. Navarro installed in her passenger seat—did he smell faintly of something classic, something from her childhood, like lavender talc?—Alice turned off Highway 46 onto the narrow blacktop leading north. Ranch Road 631 was also classic: not repaved in recent memory; no center stripe; generous old bar ditches on the sides, full of wildflowers. The road ran up a narrow valley. On the right lay pastures with occasional live oak mottes, tilted down toward the hidden stream that had carved the valley, then the rugged cliff above the stream. On the left rose the limestone hills of the Edwards Plateau. "Wine-cup!" Alice pointed at the flowers in the bar ditch. She loved the wine-cup, and it was cabernet—no—zinfandel-colored.

The road rose. "I love the view from the top of this ridge," she told Mr. Navarro. He didn't answer for a moment.

"You see that?" he said. "See that helicopter?"

She peered through the windshield. "Now I do." The helicopter was moving from the far right toward the center of the ridge ahead.

"Think that's the same one we saw out at Blue Pool," Mr. Navarro said. Now it was hovering above the road.

"Looking for something?" asked Alice.

The road rose steeply before them, heading for the top of the ridge.

The sound of the helicopter was louder. Why was it holding steady there? Alice and Mr. Navarro peered up through the windshield. They saw a man, tethered by a belt, step out onto the skids and lift a rifle.

Alice swerved and heard the rifle at the same time. Impossibly loud. Bullets hit the roof and the truck bed. She floored the accelerator, jiggling left and right. The truck flew over the top of the ridge. A mile ahead she saw an overpass. "Get under that," Mr. Navarro said. She scrunched down, hoping the headrest would save her, driving wildly down the empty narrow road. Behind her came the helicopter. Bam! Another shot hit the back windshield. Glass everywhere. As Mr. Navarro scrunched down he said, "Zigzag." She used to do that taking John and Ann to school. Make the car dance, mama, they would say, and she would get the minivan to dance a bit, usually to the soundtrack from *The Big Chill.*

The helicopter was behind, and she was dancing madly, bullets still hitting the truck bed as they neared the overpass.

"You got a gun?" Mr. Navarro asked.

"Just a flare gun, under your seat."

"Flare gun." He lifted the old Verey pistol, checked to be sure it was loaded. "Alice, stop as fast as you can and back up under the overpass."

She braked hard, came out from under, backed up. The overpass gave scant shelter, barely two lanes wide.

"Get down! Down!" Mr. Navarro shouted.

"What are you doing?" she cried, falling across the gearshift. But he was out the door now, crouched behind it, bad leg splayed out. The helicopter came around, about one hundred feet above the ground, Belted Man lifting the rifle for another shot.

Mr. Navarro carefully squeezed off a shot that hit the tail rotor, with a burst of green light. Immediately the chopper started a spin to the right. "Got him," he said in satisfaction. A last burst of rifle shots sprayed wildly, some hitting the concrete, sending chunks flying onto the truck. Alice heard Mr. Navarro grunt. She sat up and stared at the spinning helicopter.

Belted Man tumbled off the skids, dangling upside down by his belt. He dropped the rifle. The helicopter lurched east, the pilot clearly struggling for control. Alice heard brakes skidding and saw in the rearview the little BMW jerking to a stop. Tomás jumped out, cell phone in hand. "Are you okay?" he yelled, panting, face frantic.

"Take the picture!" yelled Alice, jumping out and pointing. Tomás raced forward into the highway, pointing the cell phone at the helicopter, with its dangling passenger silhouetted against the darkening sky.

"Trying to find a place to land it," said Mr. Navarro, standing by Alice. "Good luck, amigo."

The helicopter disappeared over the low ridge to their east. They stood transfixed, listening. They heard a muffled explosion, then saw a column of greasy black smoke rising somewhere beyond the ridge.

Mr. Navarro turned to Tomás and Alice. "Basic rule when a chopper's trying to kill you, hit the tail rotor. Pilot has to gain speed and altitude fast or he's toast."

"Good God, abuelo!" Tomás reached a hand toward Mr. Navarro's head.

Alice looked up. Blood ran down through the silver hair. "Piece of concrete got me. I'll be okay." He dabbed with his handkerchief.

"Let's find that rifle before it gets dark," Alice said to Tomás. "We'll do it, Mr. Navarro."

But it was Mr. Navarro, limping heavily, who moved just past the bar ditch, found the rifle, and used his handkerchief to pick it up. He slid it into the backseat of Alice's truck. "We'll want that."

"We need to call the sheriff," Alice said.

"No cell service. I kept trying to call you guys," Tomás said.

Alice looked at her watch. "Tomás, move where you can get service and keep calling 911 every minute until you get someone. Stay until they come. Your granddad and I have to leave right now. I want to get him in a safe place. We'll likely miss the hearing but we'll wait for you at the groundwater district office. Be sure to tell the sheriff the helicopter was somewhere east of this overpass. And we've got the rifle. Mr. Navarro, there's an old first-aid kit under your seat. Let's go."

* * * * *

"Apparently the purported intervenor is not here, Madam Chairman. Has not even bothered to attend. So I ask you to dismiss the Navarro petition in intervention with prejudice." Whiteside Senior stood at the lectern before the curved dais of the hearing room.

"To the contrary." Alice, pushing through the swinging doors, walked straight to the lectern. "We are indeed here, after an incident—blocking progress for a significant time on Ranch Road 631." The board members were staring at Mr. Navarro, who stood erect behind Alice, a Band-Aid on his forehead, a blood spot on the white shirt. "There was a helicopter crash," she said, arranging her notebook on the lectern. She didn't want them thinking she'd had a flat tire, something she could have avoided by, oh, leaving earlier. "May I begin? It is our petition after all."

"You may," said the chair.

And with Whiteside sputtering beside her she said, "According to district rules, a permit applicant must show he or she has a property interest in the property to be permitted. We've submitted an affidavit showing the property is still in the name of Alex Drinkman, a young pilot who died tragically in 1919. And we have submitted the affidavit of his son, Mr. Alejandro Navarro, who only in the past few weeks has learned the identity of his father, who was killed—shot—trying to get home for Easter to ask his own father's blessing on his wedding to Mr. Navarro's mother."

The audience was rapt. Alice waited one beat, then went on.

"You have copies of the affidavit, showing DNA evidence corroborating that Alex Drinkman is his father.

"You have nothing showing this applicant owns the property. Indeed, you can't, because for whatever reason, Alex Drinkman's estate was never administered. It still owns that property, and Mr. Navarro is the rightful heir, and the only rightful heir.

"At this point, all you have to do is grant our motion, which allows Mr. Navarro to intervene, and puts this permit hearing on hold until the Coffee County courts have worked this out. That's the cleanest solution." She saw two board members nod. "You would be correct in granting our motion because under your rules, the permit applicant's application is defective. You have no obligation to proceed on a defective application." Several board members glanced over at the general manager, who nodded back.

Whiteside returned to the lectern but could not explain the current state of the deed. Gathering the members with her glance, the chair called the question. The board voted to grant the Navarro motion, with only one member abstaining.

"We'll appeal this decision!" Whiteside barked.

Alice tried not to smile. She'd argue the decision wasn't appealable until his application was complete. A chicken-and-egg issue.

The board adjourned. Alice took Mr. Navarro to the dais to introduce him to the chair. "Madam Chairman, we apologize again for being late," she said. Tomás had come in late after waiting for the emergency crew on the road and now joined them. Alice watched him apply his smile to the chair until she melted and asked him whether he was in school.

"I've applied to start law school this fall." He glanced at Alice. Heavens, she thought.

"And what was this helicopter crash?" asked the vice-chair.

"Private bird, I believe," Mr. Navarro said. "We'll be meeting outside with the sheriff to tell him what we saw."

* * * * *

She saw the Coffee County Sheriff's Department sedan outside, door open. George Files was walking slowly around Alice's truck. When he saw Alice he came over and shook her hand. "Once again, Ms. Greer."

"Didn't expect you, detective."

"I was on duty. Besides, this sounded . . . unusual. As usual."

"Can you tell me . . ." Alice hesitated.

"Both dead," Files said. "I'm waiting for the emergency crew to call me with details."

She introduced the Navarros and stood back. Both dead. Who were they?

"Sir, may I talk to you first?" said Files.

He took Alejandro Navarro to the sedan and helped him into the passenger seat. Alice watched Files make notes as he interviewed her client, and saw his eyebrows soar up at one point. Yikes, did she need a permit to carry a flare gun?

Then it was Tomás's turn. She could see him showing the cell phone pictures to Files.

Finally, Alice's turn.

"Well, Alice," said Files. "I've learned a lot. I've learned that the tail rotor on a helicopter is very vulnerable and if you can damage it, it is extremely difficult to continue safe flight."

Alice nodded. "That's what I understand."

"And that after that, the shooter was still dangling from the belt and dropped his rifle."

"He did."

"And then?"

"The helicopter flew over the ridge somewhere to the east of us. We heard an explosion. We looked for the rifle. Mr. Navarro found it."

"And how old is he?"

"Ninety-four." She watched Files's face as he glanced back at Navarro, talking to Tomás. "Bet he didn't tell you he flew fighters in the Pacific, in World War II."

"No, he did not. Guess he knows about flare guns. That's what you carry in your truck?"

"It's the one my husband had in his sailboat. I usually have it in the cabinet by the front door, but I had to get more flares for it, so I had to take it with me."

"Alice, Mr. Navarro said you'd seen that chopper before, when you were looking at some property he owns at the south end of the county."

"It looked much the same, but I was driving, and I don't know helicopters. Same color, though. Same shape."

"So you were out on a lonely road, no one else around—right?"

"Right. We saw no one after we left the Antler Café."

"This chopper was hovering up above the ridge, like it was waiting for you?"

"I think so. Sure looked that way."

"But how could anyone know you were coming at that time on that road?"

That stopped her. She thought of Tomás, wanting to bring his own car, making a call on his cell phone. "Maybe someone saw us at the Antler Café?"

"Why did Tomás not ride with you?"

"He didn't want me to have to drive all the way back to Antler after the groundwater district hearing."

Would Tomás have any reason in the world to call in a chopper attack on his own grandfather? She couldn't think of any.

He pressed his lips together. "You know, with those bullets hitting the back of your truck, it's a good thing the gas tank didn't blow." He shook his head. "I wouldn't have wanted to see that."

Alice shuddered. She remembered her second summer in law school, when she was being recruited by competing firms. A senior litigator at one firm, waving his glass of Woodford Reserve at a Friday afternoon cocktail party, was telling war stories to the rapt summer associates. He had recently settled a wrongful death case where a gasoline tanker had rear-ended a passenger car trapped by the lowered arm at a railroad crossing; the passengers had been unable to escape the ensuing fire, the doors buckled and locked by the impact. He told the students gravely that it took real toughness to handle such situations, referring to the ensuing inferno as a "crispy critters" case. Alice was so revolted that she decided forthwith to join the other firm. Not that she herself was incapable of being callous: she knew she was. She sometimes shocked herself by the cold-blooded bottom-line analysis that was key to her decisions. But being burned alive? She'd had to bury the horror over and over in her head, imagining the passengers trying to kick out the windows, then enveloped in flame. This time, someone had deliberately invited such a fate for Mr. Navarro, and for her.

"Excuse me." Files turned away, took a call, then turned back. "It's confirmed, Alice. Both those guys were killed. Chopper pilot and the shooter. Shooter wound up hanging in an oak tree, couldn't get away from the explosion."

Alice shut her eyes. *Crispy critters*—the words ran round inside her head. Then fury rose at the effrontery of the someone, the shooter, the sender of the chopper. Fury helped. She took a deep breath, straightened her shoulders, and remembered Rose's car.

She asked, "Do you have a flashlight?"

Files came back from the sedan with the requisite enormous Maglite.

"You know there was a bug, a GPS bug, under Rose's car when it blew up at the UT law school?"

"Ah. No, I didn't."

He peered under the truck. "You got a mirror?"

She groped in her purse for her emergency do-I-have-spinach-on-my-teeth-did-my-mascara-run mirror.

He knelt, holding the mirror with one hand, the flashlight with the other. "Aha. Come here, little buddy." He grabbed a baggie from his pocket, put it over his fingers, reached under the left-front wheel well.

"Good call, Alice. You have any idea when this was put on? Or where?"

"I might." She told him about the man in the Drinkman parking lot. "Can you tell who's tuned in to the GPS device's frequency? Like, see who's peeking?"

"We'll see."

"And would you please take this rifle? Will you be able to identify the guy in the tree?" Visions of scorched clothes, burnt flesh, burnt—but maybe he'd had dental work done. Ah, Alice, so cold, so cold.

"Yes ma'am, probably we will." He took a look at her. "Let's go sit down for a minute. You think they still got any coffee in the meeting room?" He sent Tomás in to ask. "Alice, I thought you sat sedately in your office and did wills and trusts. Quiet stuff."

"I do!"

"How'd you get in a situation where you're rolling up Ranch Road 631 being shot at by a chopper? More to the point, is this going to happen again in this, this case or whatever you're on?"

"I'm wondering that. I imagine Mr. Navarro was the target. He's the one who's asking the court to confirm he has inherited Alex Drinkman's land."

"Drinkman as in the Drinkman Foundation?"

"Yes."

"But if he gets killed, he still has heirs himself, right? Getting rid of him wouldn't end your lawsuit?"

"Maybe not, but this sort of event could be discouraging to another heir."

"Well, while we're checking this out, for the lord's sake be careful. And tell Mr. Navarro the same thing. What's wrong?"

Alice was staring at her truck. "Should I make a claim or not? I'm afraid the carrier's going to cancel my insurance. Maybe my insurance doesn't even cover being shot at." She thought she remembered an exclusion for intentional criminal acts.

"At least get the rear windshield fixed. Make it your ranch truck. Just for hay. Don't you want something new?"

"That's what everyone says. But that truck is very reliable."

He rolled his eyes. "Help me out here. You think I got all the bullets? There were three in the truck bed. One in the back of Mr. Navarro's seat. Must be the one that blew out the rear windshield."

"At least one bullet hit the overpass above Mr. Navarro and sent some concrete chunks down on him. He was outside the truck, behind the door."

"Okay. We'll be checking the area in the daylight."

"And I'll bring the truck to the office in the morning and you can come look more if you want. I'm so tired now. Can I go home?"

She puttered up the road north toward Coffee Creek. Tomás and Mr. Navarro sped south. Files followed Alice and didn't leave until she turned in the ranch driveway, parked, and flashed the front porch lights at him. She locked all the doors and checked them twice, then poured a glass of Syrah and headed for the bathtub. Called Kinsear, left a garbled message about a helicopter and a rifle but everything is okay now, she was headed for bed. To her shock, it was only 9:00 p.m. She'd forgotten Kinsear was at a Ransom Center fundraiser. And she had to be in Medina County for the motion-to-dismiss hearing at one the next afternoon.

She lay staring at the darkness, head whirling, and only swam back up to consciousness when the alarm went off.

Chapter Twenty-Five

No Tracks, No Prints, No Nada

S trategy breakfast at the Camellia Diner with Tyler Junkin. "Always brings me luck," he said, spreading still another pat of butter on his biscuit, "to eat breakfast here early in the morning before a big hearing."

"But Tyler, you eat breakfast here every day!" Alice spooned a little more sausage gravy on her fried egg, then, on reflection, added a spoonful of salsa.

"That's what I mean. I'm a lucky guy. Okay, we got any loose ends to talk about? I'm handling the applicable standard on their motion to dismiss, you're handling all the facts in our affidavits, since you know them. And then you're asking the court to enter our discovery order and set an early hearing on the motion for summary judgment. And of course pointing out that we've offered deposition dates for our experts and a proposed discovery order, and they haven't agreed to anything."

"Right. And if we finish fast, we still have time to reconnoiter Madrone Creek this morning. You'll have to drive, since the AC in my truck won't work with the back window gone."

"Alice, what are you going to tell the judge about the little incident on Ranch Road 631?" He leaned back, wiping butter off his mouth and fingers. "Will opposing counsel be a little surprised to see you?"

"Hope not. Surely our fellow lawyer wouldn't have anything to do with the chopper. Or the GPS bug."

"Oh, Alice, the world is changing. I myself have a bug detector. Got to, in the criminal defense line. It works on GPS bugs, and most car bombs too."

"You're kidding!"

"It's a deductible expense."

Alice shook her head. The things she didn't know. Then she wondered—why didn't Rose have such a device?

"Really, what do you plan to say about the chopper?"

"Not sure what to say, until we hear from Files."

"Come on. You've got a dramatic opportunity in front of the judge today. Look at the parallels! Alex Drinkman gets killed, coming home to ask his father's blessing on his marriage and mentioning his wish to adopt little Alejandro! And a chopper tries to take out little Alejandro and you, ninety-odd years later, on your way to a hearing intended to establish Alejandro's heirship! And if that little chopper ploy had worked, you'd both have been shot—leaving no tracks, no prints, no nada. Sound familiar? Doesn't that resonate a bit with the past?"

She had not thought about it quite like that, had not realized that if the shooter, belted into the chopper, had succeeded, the police would have had virtually nothing to go on, unless another car, a witness, had suddenly turned onto the lonely road. "Tomás," she said at last. "He got pictures. But if not . . ." If the chopper guys had seen another car coming, they could have waited, taken their time, hovered behind the nearby hills, and tried again when there were no witnesses.

* * * * *

The hearing on the motion to dismiss Mr. Navarro's action to recover the Blue Pool property was set before Judge Carmen Harrison at the Coffee County Courthouse. Alice felt a strong need, before she stood in front of Judge Harrison, to reconnoiter the crossing where Alex had been shot. She and Tyler headed south. They stopped briefly at the old Madrone general store, which still held cabinets full of old merchandise, but now sold antiques and collectibles. After a few missteps, they found the low-water crossing over Madrone Creek. Alice got out of the truck and gazed across the little creek, imagining her boy angling the motorcycle down the bank, western sun in his eyes, wondering how the family visit would go, thinking of Susana and baby Alejandro. Well, maybe it had been like that. She took pictures from both sides of the low-water crossing. Turning back, she and Tyler found the cemetery at the old Madrone Presbyterian Church, and the Drinkman graves behind an ornate iron fence, once painted white, now peeling. Alice pushed open the iron gate and stepped through the overgrown grass to Alex's headstone. It bore only his name and dates of birth and death. In contrast, his mother Adeline's stone was large and ornately carved. She had died in 1913.

"Doesn't look like anyone's tried to dig him up recently," commented Tyler.

"Not yet."

They headed back north to Coffee Creek. Almost showtime. Tyler and Alice loaded their briefcases and a file box into Tyler's truck and drove the short block to the Coffee Creek Courthouse. They grabbed their briefcases and a file box and headed past the flag flapping on the tall pole by the entry. Tyler held open the door. "Onward and upward."

Alice was fond of the limestone staircase, and the handrail, doubtless unsanitary, but polished by generations of hands. She always felt both anxious and at home in the courthouse, with its smell of old paper files and floor wax, and the sound of voices echoing from the district clerk's office on the ground floor. They toiled up the stairs and pushed open the big wooden doors to Judge Harrison's courtroom. Theirs was the first hearing after lunch, so Tyler chose a counsel table and arranged their belongings. They checked out the lectern height, arranged their pleadings and exhibits, put the requisite yellow sticky notes and yellow legal pads on the table, poured water. Alice went to the bathroom to check her hair and take a couple of deep breaths. Tyler went outside to meet Mr. Navarro and Tomás.

When Alice pushed open the courtroom doors again, Armstrong and Brast were in full cry, with two silver-haired partners and intense young associates arranging boxes on an entire long wooden pew behind the other counsel table. She took a deep breath, marched up to the partners, made herself smile, and stuck her hand out. "Alice Greer."

The silver-hairs looked only slightly surprised.

Duly noted.

The taller one said "Haverty Armstrong" and extended his hand. Oh, hell, another finger crusher who refused to actually shake her hand. The shorter one, mild-mannered and bland, shook only her last two finger joints. "Hampton Rhodes. Probate counsel." Alice grinned, started to say "Naval counsel?" but decided name jokes were in bad taste.

"Um, you're here without your client, I see," said Haverty

Armstrong.

"Oh no. He'll be here. Now, I'm going to have to tell the judge I've offered you deposition dates for our experts, sent over a proposed scheduling order, and offered hearing dates for our motion for summary judgment, and still you've given me no response whatsoever. I'll be asking the court to enter my scheduling order and set the hearing on summary judgment."

Armstrong frowned. "I'm sure that's an oversight, but you're rushing us, and we haven't—we want our motion to dismiss decided first."

"I've not even had the courtesy of a response on the offered dates. And your motion to dismiss is facially defective under the rule."

Armstrong puffed up. "We disagree, and we're sure the judge will see it our way. This case should be entirely barred by limitations. Furthermore, our research shows, and we're sure the judge will agree, that your client loses. You have zero chance on the DNA—you have a laughable chain of custody. Your ballistics claims are useless—there's no proof any family member fired at Alex Drinkman. Current law does not apply and under prior law we believe we win."

Oof. He was hitting some vulnerable spots. She lifted her chin. "We think the court will conclude without doubt that Mr. Navarro is Alex Drinkman's heir and entitled to possession of Blue Pool. And more."

Tyler, Tomás, and Mr. Navarro walked up. Could you possibly ask for a better client? Alice wondered. Just look at him! Alejandro Navarro stood erect, his white shirt gleaming, starched to a fare-thee-well. His blue suit, slightly old-fashioned, was perfectly pressed. His boots gleamed. Tomás had emulated his granddad, though Alice suspected an Italian label on his suit. Tyler looked exactly like what he was: a highly experienced courtroom lawyer. She took a quick glance at the Armstrong team. They were staring at Alejandro Navarro. Surprised, boys? The door opened and the bailiff cried, "All rise!"

Judge Harrison entered without fanfare. "Good afternoon, counsel. I've read all your papers, so no need to review them for me. We'll hear first the motion to dismiss, then the petitioner's motions." She looked down to be sure her court reporter was ready. "Introductions?" Alice introduced Tyler and the Navarros, who stood with her behind the table.

Haverty Armstrong introduced his three colleagues, but no client was present.

Armstrong then strode to the lectern and began describing requirements of the rule governing motions to dismiss. "I'm familiar with the rule, counsel," the judge finally said. "Please show me how your motion complies. I have a concern as to whether you've adequately stated a basis for dismissal."

Oh goody, thought Alice. Tyler, next to her, had arranged their motion and his copy of the rule and his notes and sat like a leopard ready to pounce.

Armstrong rephrased and repeated his argument.

"But Mr. Armstrong, while you are correctly stating the rule, your motion does not show how the allegations of the petition, if true, would not create a cause for relief."

Armstrong shifted gears, claiming that marriage or actual completed adoption was necessary for Mr. Navarro to be Alex Drinkman's heir and that the statute of limitations had run decades ago.

"Thank you." She looked at the Navarro table. Tyler walked to the lectern. After five minutes Alice began to feel almost sorry for Armstrong as Tyler walked through Mr. Navarro's petition, establishing that it met all requirements and that a motion to dismiss should be denied. Alice then stood and reviewed cases saying that the four-year statute of limitations did not apply to an action to recover land. Armstrong's reply was interrupted, after two minutes, by the judge. "I'm denying the motion to dismiss. Ms. Greer, prepare an order for my consideration. Petitioner will recognize, however, that escaping a motion to dismiss because your allegations state a claim still requires you to prove your claims before me. Furthermore, I have remaining concerns about what law should apply, and will require briefing on that by both parties." She looked at Alice, then Tyler, over her half-glasses. "Now, we also have pending procedural motions asking me to enter a scheduling order and set a hearing on the motion for summary judgment. The petitioner's draft scheduling order appears simply to track my standard order on the court website."

"Yes, Your Honor," Alice said.

"Any objection to the standard order?" The judge stared at Haverty Armstrong.

Armstrong stood. "We need more time."

The judge looked at Mr. Navarro, straight-backed in his seat next to Alice. "How old are you, sir?"

He got to his feet. "Ninety-four, Your Honor." He sat again, carefully.

Alice stood. "Your Honor, last night in Coffee County Mr. Navarro and I were shot at by a private helicopter." How much to say? Not much. The judge raised her eyebrows.

Alice continued. "The helicopter crashed. The police are investigating. I raise this solely to say that given Mr. Navarro's age, we will do all in our power to avoid delay."

The judge said, "Mr. Armstrong, I'm entering the standard discovery order. We don't want Mr. Navarro to wait forever. Petitioners state they have already answered your discovery and offered expert dates. If you have a serious problem with a particular time requirement, you can ask for a specific delay."

Armstrong nodded, speechless, then leaped to his feet, said "Thank you, Your Honor," and sat back down.

"Ms. Greer, you've asked for your summary judgment to be heard two months from today. That date is available, according to the court coordinator. Mr. Armstrong, you have three counsel with you. Looks like a capable team. Any reason you can't take their experts' depositions and get your own experts designated and get dates to Ms. Greer within the required time frame?"

"No, Your Honor."

"Go ahead and get your briefing to me, sooner than the deadline in the order if you can. Anything else, counsel?"

"No, Your Honor," they chorused. She stood. "All rise!" cried the bailiff, and the judge swept out.

Alice maintained her expressionless courtroom face. Tomás whispered, "Aren't you happy? Isn't that what we wanted?"

She turned her head to face away from defense counsel and whispered back, "Yes, but you can't show it. Think of it as poker."

Armstrong's minions were silently packing up boxes, heaving

them onto a dolly. Armstrong and Rhodes stood by their table, hissing at each other in low tones. Alice slowed her packing but couldn't quite hear them. She figured the combined billing rates for Armstrong and Brast that day were close to two thousand an hour.

Armstrong walked over. "We'll depose your handwriting and paper and ballistics experts on the first dates you gave us. We may need more time on the DNA expert."

"I understand from the Whiteside guys that you already have your DNA expert. Why would you need any more time before you depose Dr. Apple?" said Alice. "We're ready to go on this summary judgment schedule. Delay won't do your clients any good in the news media."

"Are you threatening to go to the media—?"

"No." She pointed to the young man in the back row, scribbling on a tablet. He'd come in late, after her chopper comment.

Armstrong and Rhodes fled out by the other side aisle, trying to escape the courtroom before the young reporter looked up and saw them.

"That was a piss-poor motion to dismiss," Tyler said.

"Don't get cocky."

"I thought for a minute you pulled your punch too much on the chopper, but the judge picked up on at least part of it."

"Hope I planted a seed, anyway. We can paint a vivid picture later."

Mr. Navarro, walking down their aisle, smiled when the young reporter popped out in front of him. "Sir, did you really fly fighters in the Pacific in World War II?" He poised his pen.

"Yes sir. What would you like to know?"

Alice and Tyler put down their briefcases, stood back and listened.

Twenty minutes later the reporter raced off to write up his story. They pushed open the courtroom doors and hit the elevator button with the usual post-hearing relief. Mr. Navarro was still standing straight, but visibly tired, swinging the game leg as unobtrusively as possible when he walked, leaning a bit on the wall. Tomás, following, said to Alice, "I just learned some amazing stuff. He ought to write a book! He never told us the stories about New Guinea or crash-landing on that deserted island!"

She looked at him hard, wondering if he'd ever sat still long enough to hear all his abuelo's tales of hair-raising flights far out in the Pacific.

"Hey, Alice, I said not one word to that reporter. I just listened!"

She laughed. "The beginning of wisdom!"

Then she sobered. The judge was no cream puff. That was a sharp warning about proof and the applicable law.

Chapter Twenty-Six

Heartless as We Are

On Monday morning as Alice arrived, Silla sang out, "Call George Files."

Alice complied.

"Hey, Ms. Greer. Just an update here, on your chopper situation."

"Whose was it?"

"Registered to Fair Star Flight, LLC, a Cayman Islands company. Its managing member, whatever that is, is Fair Star Partners. That's also the managing member of Oak Motte Links, LLC. That's your permit applicant. Looks like the ultimate owner of Fair Star Flight may be Drinkman Holdings, which is the holding company for a bunch of entities."

"Ah. And the pilot and the dangling man with the rifle?"

"Employees of a company with no assets but two employees."

"Did they have a contract with the chopper owner?"

"We're still looking."

"Did you identify them? Who are they?"

"Not necessarily sweet guys. The shooter has some history but has never been sentenced. Veteran, about fifteen years out. Sniper. The pilot recently finished a stint as a mercenary, i.e. security contractor, in Saudi."

"Did you interview the Drinkmans?"

"They're disclaiming any involvement."

Alice exploded. "How can that be? They or their people put a GPS bug on my truck and then tried to kill me and my client!"

"We're not sure about the GPS bug yet. We might have a partial of the left hand, but the person who put it on your truck wore a disposable glove on the right hand."

"Is the bug the same kind that was on Rose's car?"

"Good question, I'll check."

"Did they have a flight plan, any kind of communication with air control? Were they based at Blue Pool? What about the rifle—any prints there?"

"Yes on the prints. Yes, the chopper was based at Blue Pool. We don't know about ground communications. Hang on, Alice, we'll get there. And I wanted to tell you something else. Tomás?"

Her heart thumped. "Yes?"

"Just in case you were worrying . . ."

She said nothing, but she had worried.

"We interviewed him, as you know. Also we checked out his phone. His last calls, after you left the Antler Café, were, in chron order, to his dad; to his sister, Isabella; and to a young lady named Cecilia Ruiz, also called Cissy. He begged us not to out him on that last call. Says he likes to keep his love life secret, or he gets nagged by both his dad and Isabella. He actually said, 'She's a game changer, that girl.'"

"Game changer, huh?"

"But, heartless as we are, we did check out Miss Ruiz. Very bright young woman. She's taking a combined MD/Phd program in forensic pathology."

"Good heavens."

"She did acknowledge she and Tomás were on the phone that night. Indeed, he pulled off the road to talk to her because he was losing cell service. That's why he wasn't right behind you."

"Ah. I did wonder."

"So, at this point, we know who shot at you but we're low on proof as to why."

"And are either of those two guys the same ones who invaded Bryce's shop? Or his home?"

"I don't know about his home. Tell me."

Alice explained, but when she got to the throwing stars and the Filipino fish spear, Files had to cover the phone, he was laughing so hard.

"Obviously no one at the department made the connection with this home invasion. But I'll find out who took the call, and we'll see what we can do about identifying those men in black. Did the sheriff not even come out to investigate?"

"Ask Bryce. He was pretty lighthearted on his so-called report to the sheriff's department. Still on an adrenaline high, chasing those men off."

* * * * *

"I left litigation because of depositions," grumped Alice. She and Tyler had spent Monday prepping the handwriting expert, Ruby Michaels, for her deposition the next day. On Wednesday the paper expert would drive over from Austin to get ready for her Thursday deposition at Tyler's office. Alice was puzzled why Armstrong was setting these depositions in Coffee Creek instead of his downtown Austin office, but she finally concluded he was either thinking of retiring to the Hill Country or planning to stop for excellent barbecue. He'd first proposed her office; she'd insisted on Tyler's. She'd gotten cautious about visitors earlier that year, after a murderer visited her late one day, trying to retrieve an incriminating letter from her mail. Also, there was better taxidermy at Tyler's office, including the trout with fur and fangs.

Before the deposition, Alice and Ruby Michaels, a slightly round woman with round spectacles and dimples, met in the bathroom. The expert looked at Alice's set face. "Hey, don't be nervous," she said. "This is not my first rodeo! This is a pretty clear-cut assignment."

Then she sat at the end of Tyler's conference table, cheerfully facing the video screen, as if she sat for depositions daily. She made an unflappable witness, cautious but confident, firm in her opinion that, based on all the materials she had reviewed, Alex Drinkman had written the application for flight school in his military personnel file, the poem found in Mr. Navarro's wooden box, and the letter to Alastair Drinkman. Repeated efforts by Haverty Armstrong, flanked by two associates, to make her alter or at least shade her conclusions failed. When his questions included embedded assumptions, she teased those out, attributed the assumption to him, and calmly noted in her response that he was making an assumption with which she disagreed, based on the observed facts.

Armstrong and his team marched out of the office. The handwriting expert shook hands with Alice and Tyler, waved a cheerful good-bye, and left. Two days later, the paper expert's deposition was also a nonevent. "I've seen over a hundred examples of similar paper from correspondence in 1919. This letter is clearly on paper that was widely available in Central Texas in April 1919. The ink is also of that vintage." Armstrong looked unhappy when he left.

"Whew," said Alice once the Armstrong team was gone. "Two down, two to go. DNA next Tuesday, and Bang-Bang on Thursday."

"Both of those could get heated."

They arranged to split the prep work, with Tyler taking the laboring oar on DNA, Alice on ballistics, which (she admitted to herself) might make some people smile. She would study.

But she felt tired, cranky, oppressed.

What kind of life was this?

Her children were in Scotland, doing lord knows what. She was making a living, not starving, but not hitting the lottery. She'd made friends in Coffee Creek, and she loved her quiet house on the creek, but sometimes . . . it was lonesome. Yoga wasn't enough. Taking care of burros wasn't enough. Playing the piano with no one to listen wasn't enough.

And Kinsear? Kinsear had his own life. He had a ranch outside Fredericksburg, a bookstore just off Main Street, two daughters still requiring attention. Probably had his own favorite bars, his favorite lunch place, probably saw his buddies there, flirted with the round-cheeked German ladies at the bakery. And who knows who else he flirts with, Alice thought.

Alice climbed into her battered truck. At least it now had a rear windshield. But inside, it was too quiet. She plugged her cell phone into the Rube Goldberg device she'd managed to assemble on the truck dashboard, chose a playlist, turned the volume to a dangerous level, and sang with Janis all the way down the creek road. Her phone rang.

"Alice?" It was Kinsear. "Can you hear me, Alice?"

She almost ran into the ditch, trying to turn down the volume.

"Yes. Was singing along."

"That's good for you. Listen, what about a very short road trip?"

"Where?"

"Overnight trip to Bandera and Cypress Ranch. Friday and Saturday night. Leave early Sunday. I know you have big depositions next week."

She thought for only a nanosecond. "I'm in."

"How early?"

If she finished her draft of prep questions tomorrow morning . . .
"Eleven?"

"Meet you at your place. Gotta go before you change your mind."
He hung up.

C h a p t e r   T w e n t y - S e v e n

The Real People

The road Alice loved almost the most, and never mentioned to anyone lest she find it covered with wine vans taking flatlanders through the Texas Hill Country, was the road from US 281 to Kendalia. Not quite as rocky as her territory, her ranch, this road was a little more generous with pastures crowned with oak mottes, a little more promising of wine grapes trained on their wires, a little more frequent with low-water crossings over cypress-lined spring-fed creeks. A few bluebonnets and wine-cups still painted the pastures.

The Cypress Ranch lay along a big creek, with rope swings hanging from the cypresses over the bigger pools. Kinsear parked the Land Cruiser in front of the old ranch house. Alice walked in with him, admiring the 1940s wrought-iron wagon-wheel chandeliers and the mission furniture and the enormous limestone fireplace at one end. She heard the perky receptionist, ponytail bobbing, chirping to Kinsear: "You two are signed up for the activities you requested. Here's your schedule. And your dinner is at seven thirty. We've reserved the table you asked for. What else may I help you with?"

Activities? She walked back. Kinsear handed her the schedule.

"Skeet shooting today?"

"Yup. Aren't you the queen of ballistics next week?"

"Ah."

"But first, the queen has lunch on the terrace."

After lunch, jeaned and booted, Alice and Kinsear showed up at the skeet range. Their cowboy tutor, Rodney, had heard all of Alice's worries before: "I'll jump. I'll miss. I'll shoot myself. I'll shoot you. I'll kill an innocent bird."

"You'll be just fine. Now let me show you how to stand . . . now how to sight . . . now . . ."

And before she knew it, random reinforcement occurred. She missed five times, then hit twice, then missed three times, then hit twice more.

She stopped in moderate triumph to watch Kinsear. Clay bird bits flew everywhere. The cowboy tutor nodded approvingly.

Alice sidled over, bumped him with her hip. "Hey. You're pretty good." He tried unsuccessfully to mask his satisfaction.

"Okay. Now our friend Rodney is going to walk you through naming of parts again, Alice. Ask whatever you want. Rodney, you know she has to look generally familiar next week."

"Well, Alice, of course you know this is a shotgun, not a rifle. And you're dealing with rifles, I hear?"

He took her into the bunkhouse gunroom. For the next hour he drilled her on parts, cartridge calibers, lever action, and other details. He showed her all the bullets in his locked cabinet. He unlocked the gun cabinets and let her heft and sight the old guns. After two hours Alice's brain was fried.

"No more. I just hit the wall."

"Go buy her a drink," Rodney told Kinsear. "She's worked hard."

"Actually, don't I get a massage too?"

She did. A sturdy Central Texas girl with pigtails turned the lights down in the massage room, warmed her hands up, stood at Alice's head, and slowly slid her powerful forearms down Alice's back. Alice let out a long oof of all the breath she'd held all week, and gave herself up to the forearms. An hour and a half later she rolled off the massage table, groped her way into a robe, stuck her feet in slippers, and blissfully trotted off to find their room.

Kinsear was standing in the shower, holding a can of Tecate with a lime wedge.

"The fabled shower beer, I see," said Alice.

"You can still talk?"

"Barely. Can barely enunciate."

"Need someone to help you remove that pesky massage oil?"

"Hmm. Maybe yes. You have a proposal on how to do that?"

"Is it food-grade?"

* * * * *

They did make it to dinner by seven thirty. Barely.

Saturday they were floating down the cypress-lined creek. Kinsear had done three cannonballs off the rope swing, splashing

Alice. Alice had finally done her own big swing, all the way out over the biggest pool, and emerged puffing and spluttering. Now it was quiet. She waggled her toes, sitting in the float chair, watching a small green heron on the shallows in a bend up ahead. Far behind she heard children squealing on the tall slide. She'd told Kinsear more about the chopper attack.

"So," said Kinsear, "I did call the next day while you were at the hearing to grill Silla for the details. And here's my question. It's about the recent helicopter encounter."

Uh-oh.

"Why didn't you call me for help?"

"Right. While we were zigzagging down the highway? Or while Mr. Navarro was crouching behind the door with my flare gun?"

"Did your parents bring you up to behave this way?"

"No. And honestly, I don't understand how it happens. He's ninety-four, for goodness sake! How could I guess this would happen?"

"I guess I should be grateful he knows how to shoot at helicopter tail rotors with flare guns."

"He deserves to know, and for other people to know, who his father was, and that his father loved him. He deserves respect. That's what we're after. Also, he deserves the Blue Pool property."

"Seriously, I do worry about you. I do want to know when you're in mortal danger."

Alice nodded. "I feel the same way about you, but so far you've avoided murderers in the bookstore." She sat up, suddenly anxious. "Haven't you?" She overbalanced and fell into the water, then dragged Kinsear off his float chair. Underwater the world was green, cool, with a Guadalupe River bass hiding at the bank. She could see the spring water bubbling up from the bottom, feel the force of the water tickling her feet. May in the Hill Country, before the world got far too hot, grass got brown, sky turned brazen blue. She kicked back up to the surface and dunked Kinsear again.

"This always happens when we are having a serious discussion of our future."

She crawled back into the float chair. "Okay."

"What are we going to do? Should we buy a helicopter? Shuttle back and forth from your place to mine?"

"What would your girls think?"

He parried. "What would your children think? What are you telling them? They'll be back here in six weeks."

They looked at each other. "I like having secrets from my children," Alice said. "But you have become a fact."

They thought awhile about that, then paddled to the bank and walked back to their casita. Alice was not sure why getting out of a bathing suit was so erotic. What transformed a struggle with clinging wet material into an opportunity for exploration of wet skin?

They had dinner on a screened porch off the ranch dining room, kerosene lamps on the tables, moths hitting the screens outside. "So how are you feeling about the ballistics expert?" Kinsear asked.

"You know the problem, right?"

"You have no brass cases."

"Right. We have the two bullets that Alex's aunt brought back and hid in her bag, along with the bandana and a lock of his hair. But no cases."

"So," Kinsear said, "you may be able to show that the bullets were fired from that very Savage Model 99, if the judge lets your guys test the rifle. But your guys have to find similar bullets first, if you're permitted to test."

"Right."

"Even assuming you could actually show that your two bullets came from the Drinkman rifle, you still haven't found a way to prove who fired it. Maybe it was Willy Drinkman. But it could have been another ranch employee, or another family member. Right?"

Alice sighed. "This is why I lie awake in the middle of the night. We can show Willy had motive. We can show opportunity. But we can't prove his finger was on the trigger." She thought of Adele Collins. "We could try to prove that Alex's sister Bonnie saw the rifle was gone, then saw it was back, when Willy came back that day. But of course Bonnie died decades ago. We only have her diary, and the Drinkmans will challenge it as hearsay."

Back in their room, Kinsear opened his backpack and lifted out a stack of books. "Take a look at these."

Alice hefted the first volume, *Hill Country Ranchers*, flipping to the publication date. Nineteen nineteen. "Where'd you find this?"

"Secondhand store in San Antonio. Check out the pictures."

In the middle of the volume, twenty pages of old black-and-white photos, mostly posed. Captions listed the ranchers, the year, the ranch name: Starks, Johnstons, Craigs. And then, in 1917, the Drinkmans. The caption read, "Bonnie Drinkman, Alexander Drinkman, Alastair Drinkman, Willy Kendrick." Bonnie, shining hair tied back, sat very straight on her horse, smiling at her brother. Alex, eyes bright, cowboy hat slightly tilted, glanced at someone near the camera. Alastair Drinkman, broad-shouldered, rancher's hat firmly on his head, stared straight at the camera, almost smiling. And, sitting his horse just a little further back, Willy Kendrick, straw hat pulled down, turned his eyes toward Bonnie.

"Goodness." Alice's eyes were only four inches from the page. "The real people."

"Turn the page."

The half-page photograph showed Alex Drinkman, Alastair Drinkman, and Willy Kendrick. Caption: "Twelve point buck, Christmas 1916." All three wore heavy jackets. Alex and Alastair stood smiling in the background, rifles on their shoulders. In the foreground, Willy Kendrick knelt on one knee, next to a dead buck. With his right hand he held the deer's head up by the antlers so it faced the camera. With his left he held a rifle, stock on the ground.

Alice pulled the book closer, squinted at the rifle. "I can't tell," she breathed.

"Show it to your guys. If you're in luck, maybe you can at least prove he got to use that rifle. And in this picture he's still named Kendrick. Did Alastair Drinkman adopt him later?"

"No. According to the county records he just changed his name to Drinkman later."

Alice picked up the second book, *History of Medina County*, with a bookmark sticking out at a chapter called "Holidays and Festivals." Out jumped the description of a 1916 fall roundup at the Drinkman Ranch: "Mr. and Mrs. Drinkman delighted the assembled multitude with a band playing 'Ragtime Cowboy Joe' and dinner on the grounds served by the well-known Cookie Kubecka and his Chuck Wagon." A slightly out of focus black-and-white photograph showed a line of people posed and smiling for the camera, men in cowboy hats and broadcloth coats, women with Gibson Girl hairdos and long skirts, holding plates and waiting for Cookie to serve them. Alastair Drinkman stood left of the chuck wagon, next to a woman with curly bangs, who held his arm. Ella Kendrick Drinkman?

Alice wished she could be there, hear them talking, know their voices.

"These books are incredible! Thank you!"

He handed her the third book.

"Oh!" said Alice. It was *The Zimmermann Telegram*, by Barbara Tuchman. She peeked in. "Ben, it's a first edition!"

"You can keep thinking about how the world would be different if there had been no Zimmermann telegram," he said.

The alumni photographs of her two great uncles, in scholarly cap and gown, materialized before her. Yes, she'd think about them. No heirs . . .

Kinsear handed her the last little volume.

"You were wondering what poems Ivor Gurney had published, what Alex might have been bringing Aunt Dee, in April 1919," he said. "This is *Severn & Somme*, published in 1917. He was a musician, you know. You should listen to his music. *Gloucestershire Rhapsody* is lovely."

"Where did you find that?" Alice wondered, touching the small ancient book.

"Hey, that's my business."

Alice knew the poems of Wilfred Owen, and Siegfried Sassoon, but Gurney was new to her. Her eye was caught by "Bach and the Sentry," and Gurney's poet-musician question about how he'd feel about that music after the war: "Shall I feel as I felt . . . ?" And by "Strafe," and its first line, "The 'crumps' are falling twenty to the minute." And then inevitably, almost, a poem titled "Scots." Oh the horror. "Earth's best and dearest turned to red broken clay"— she shut the small book. She hoped Jordie's Scottish mum had not seen it; her favorite uncle had died in the trenches on the Somme.

She forced her mind back on Alex, coming home. Alex had wanted Aunt Dee to understand where he had been, what he had seen, whom he had lost in his generation. She found her backpack and pulled out a copy of the poem Alex had written for Susana and handed it to Kinsear. "She kept this in the little carved wooden box that Mr. Navarro still has."

"Alex's poem is like a dream, isn't it," Kinsear said, after a minute.

"What do you mean?"

"The dream we sometimes have where we are trying to get home, trying to get back to the one we love, dealing with obstacle after obstacle."

"Horrific waves."

"Scylla and Charybdis."

"Shipwreck."

"Sea monsters."

"Thunder and lightning."

"Land wind, blowing you ever away from the shore."

"Poseidon, all wrath and revenge."

"He was an interesting guy, your Alex," said Kinsear. "Worth the fight. At least he got home. But only for a few days."

"Yep."

* * * * *

On Monday Alice went to Rotary, again without her red sweater, but with Red. At the door stood the entire Beer Barn troika: Bill, Other Bill, and Jorgé.

"What is this? Are you three running for office?" asked Red. "Is this a receiving line?"

"They're lobbying against the cement plant," guessed Alice.

"You got it!" said Jorgé. "Free beers for you! Yes. We're also making a presentation today at Rotary about our proposed new enterprise. We'll be explaining the Pilsener Protagonists Contest, with the ongoing battle for supremacy there over Tex, Mex, Czech, Deutsch, or some combination thereof, culminating in a vote for the winning beer and of a big drawing at Oktoberfest at the new brewery. The drawing will be for a truck, of course. And while talking up our idea and mentioning the economic opportunities this presents for Coffee Creek, such as our needs for a geo-tech survey, landscaping, septic system, construction, music venue, meet-and-greet spot, et cetera, et cetera, we'll be identifying and flushing out the opposition."

"Clever, no?" said Other Bill.

"Brilliant. Maybe better not to use 'septic system' and 'flushing out the opposition' in the same sentence. Are you our featured speakers today?" asked Alice.

"We are! So we want you two at our table, which is right by the speaker's lectern. We've got your chairs saved."

"Okay, boys. Smile at all these people lining up behind me." Red glanced behind her, flashing an especially bright smile at Dr. Joe Banks.

After lunch the Beer Barons began their presentation, discussing pilsener, the new facility, Oktoberfest, and the big drawing for the truck.

Query from the floor: "What about the cement plant? Oktoberfest won't be so great if we're all covered with cement dust." Cheers from the floor. The mayor, standing by Birnbach, nodded, brow furrowed in concern. She said, "I share concerns that the cement plant is proposed for a location that will affect middle school athletes and impact the growth of Coffee Creek enterprises."

Good warm-up for the public hearing on the cement plant, Alice thought, looking around at the Rotarians. The Beer Barons would be prepared. Would no one speak a word for the permit applicant? Birnbach looked around, eyebrows interrogating the crowd. Everyone turned back to the last crumb of dessert, and he and the mayor sat down.

Alice left to pick up her DNA expert at the airport.

Chapter Twenty - Eight

A
Cold-Blooded
Dissection

D r. Felix Apple was the dry, cool, crisp Bostonian Alice had imagined from their phone call, with an academic fillip here and there—tweed coat, button-down oxford, chukkas. She picked him up at the Austin airport on Sunday night, waiting for him at the bottom of the escalator. She took him to Shade Tree for barbecue, then drove him out to a B&B on Bell Springs Road. "This little cabin is really special," she told him. "Hand-built from cedar rounds. But there's good Internet, you can hear the creek from the porch, and breakfast will be superb."

Apple looked around the little cabin, gave one approving nod.

"I thought you might like a break from the usual," she said. "I'll pick you up at eight."

She took him straight to Tyler's the next morning, where he lifted his eyebrows at the office jukebox, pool table, and taxidermy. Then he took off his coat, rolled up his sleeves, and set to work, asking only for coffee.

Tyler walked him through prep questions. Alice knew these were intended by Tyler as much to beef up his own knowledge of recent DNA advances as to be ready to question his own witness on redirect after Armstrong got through. "Given your opinion that the blood on the bullet and the saliva on the stamp on the envelope match as to DNA, and that results show Mr. Navarro's cheek swab is consistent with a father-son relationship with the bullet-letter samples, what are the hardest questions the other side can ask you?"

Apple leaned his elbows on the table, chin on his clasped hands. "Don't forget I'll also say the hair sample is consistent with the bullet-letter samples, based on the hair with a follicle that was stuck in a fold of that bandana. But opposing counsel can ask me where the bullet, envelope, and bandana were from 1919 to the present, and how various temperature and humidity conditions might have affected the samples. Of course I am assuming that those items were, as your friend—Mr. Sheridan, I believe—indicated, sealed under the oilcloth in a nightstand for a number of years, and I do not know all the locations that nightstand might have been. I'd say the provenance questions and the possibility of sample contamination are areas of uncertainty for us."

"How about the sampling itself, and the procedures at the lab?" Tyler asked.

"There we're in pretty good shape. I talked to the lab to double-check the procedures. They reported no problems with the samples, and I saw no problems with the lab procedures either. I've worked with those folks before; they're very careful."

On Tuesday morning at nine, Alice and Apple convened at Tyler's office. Armstrong was already in the conference room; he shook hands and introduced his entourage—associate, paralegal, and the Drinkman DNA expert, Blair Reilly. On one end of the conference room table Dr. Apple had stacked all the materials he had reviewed, including the lab reports themselves, the video of the sampling process for Mr. Navarro, photographs taken by the lab of the Navarro sample and of the bullet, envelope and hair before tests were run, recent journal articles on refinements in DNA sampling (including his own articles), manuals on laboratory procedures, his emails with the lab confirming the lab's procedures, his engagement letter from Alice, his résumé, and his report. The envelope sat all alone, in archival paper.

Alice had looked up the Drinkman expert's background and printed out his résumé for Dr. Apple's reference. But she saw there was no need after Apple walked over and said, "Hi, Blair. Ready for another go-round?" Blair Reilly's smile was a little stiff.

The videographer hooked a lapel mike on Apple and the court reporter swore him in. They were off. Armstrong ran through Apple's résumé and then asked him to explain everything he had done during the preparation of his report. Apple carefully left an opening for himself, saying at the outset, "I may leave out a step here and there, so I'll need to check my report to be sure, but I recall the sequence as follows." Then he embarked on a detailed but succinct description of his initial contact, initial research, review of the documents provided, confirmation of details with lab personnel, review of recent articles on DNA testing, development of his conclusions, and drafting of the report.

"Did you draft the report yourself?"

"Yes."

"Did you send a draft to counsel?"

"Yes."

"What changes did counsel request?"

"None."

Armstrong turned a page, face reddening slightly. Blair Reilly leaned over and whispered something to him. "Are you ready for a short break, Mr.—Dr. Apple?" Armstrong asked.

"No, I can continue."

"Well, let's take a short break."

Ha, thought Alice. She, Tyler, and Apple left for Tyler's office so the Armstrong team could stay in the conference room to strategize.

Armstrong was ready with another technical question challenging sample preservation, apparently suggested by Blair Reilly, who leaned forward in a proprietary way as Armstrong posed it.

Apple: "The lab indicated that Mr. Navarro's cheek swab was preserved in accordance with the lab's instructions and that the lab found no issues with the sample. Of course the lab took its own samples from the bandana, bullet, envelope, and stamp. So your question is inapplicable."

Reilly sagged back in his chair. Armstrong regrouped. "Sir, the lab has no way to conclude that the blood or hair or envelope saliva samples did come from Alex Drinkman in 1919, does it?"

Apple: "The lab is not charged with making that determination, although there does appear to be corroborating evidence. The lab's conclusions relate to the relationship of the samples you mentioned with the sample from Mr. Navarro, which do indicate paternity."

Noon approached. Armstrong had not rattled Apple. Apple had acknowledged that the bullet and hair and letter had apparently been secured for years under the oilcloth inside the old nightstand. Yes, he had talked with Mr. Sheridan about how Mr. Sheridan had found the oiled-silk packet, and about the day he had first unfolded the bandana, in his shop. Yes, Mr. Sheridan had described his actions on that day. Apple understood Mr. Sheridan had provided an affidavit as well. Mr. Sheridan had told him that once he saw what the bandana contained, he had called Ms. Greer. Given the advanced techniques used by the lab and the variety of materials sampled, even given the unusual history of the oiled-silk packet, he was confident in the lab's results. Also, the single hair with a follicle, which the lab had discovered tightly folded in the bandana, and had tested, was visibly inconsistent with Mr. Sheridan's hair. Mr. Sheridan had reddish hair with a touch of gray. Oh, Dr. Apple had talked with him online. Yes, the video screen was quite clear. No, he did not think it likely that the person representing himself as Mr. Sheridan on the video screen was an impostor. However, it could be checked, since Mr. Sheridan's shop was two blocks away, if he was in today.

Tyler and Alice scribbled notes to each other. Looked like Armstrong was running out of steam. If no one asked for a break for Apple, maybe they could push Armstrong into finishing now, without coming back after lunch. Did they even have any cleanup questions to ask Apple? Alice didn't think anything required cleanup; his testimony was glorious. Sitting next to Alice, Tyler leaned back, relaxed, arms crossed. Meanwhile, Dr. Apple sat quietly, looking interested and rested and alert, apparently ready and willing to continue answering questions for hours.

After a pause, Armstrong said, "No more questions."

"No questions here," Tyler said. He wasn't going to open the door for Armstrong to have any more follow-up. "We're done, then."

Alice stood. Three down, one more to go. Guns.

* * * * *

Back at Alice's office, Silla stuck her head into the conference room, where Apple was packing up his papers, ready to head back to Boston. "Alice, call Bang-Bang and Banana Clip," she said. "Here's their number." Apple lifted an eyebrow.

"Your fellow experts," Alice answered, walking back to her office.

Alice made the call and found that Banana Clip Curtis and Bang-Bang Barker had already landed. "We rented a car and we're heading down to Madrone. We decided we should view the site. Want to come meet us?"

Alice grabbed her phone and notebook and headed south. If she didn't run into construction on the back roads south of Coffee Creek, she'd find them before dark. She'd sent them a copy of the gazetteer map for the area, ten kilometers to the inch, and pictures she and Tyler had taken on their own foray to Madrone.

Alice pulled up by the rental car parked on the east side of the low-water crossing. Banana Clip, phone in hand, stood at the top of the embankment, where the road dropped down. He grinned. "We're all set, Alice. We've got accurate distances and lines of sight the shooter would have had from various points over there, including up the hill"—he pointed—"behind that big limestone outcrop. But the easiest thing for him would have been right in that little copse, just behind where you see Bang-Bang." Bang-Bang, also holding his phone, was planted on the west side, at the edge of a copse of live oaks and persimmon and juniper. He waved and started back across the bridge.

"So, you have everything you need? Whatever that is?"

"Yup, Alice. And we're starved."

"We can fix that. Anyone object to barbecue? Just sixty minutes if we're lucky."

No one objected. Curtis rode with Alice, and the group headed north back to Coffee Creek.

Shade Tree was still open. "Let's sit outside," Alice said. They picked a table on the deck overlooking the creek, then walked back into the smoke-blacked interior on the prescribed route past stacks of oak, hickory, and mesquite, past the hulking iron smokers, to the chopping counter, where Big John stood ready. "These gentlemen are visitors from New Mexico," said Alice. "Do your best."

Big John stuck a long fork into the dark, crusty brisket and sliced across the grain, revealing the interior. The red smoke line, the black crust, and the smoke-fragrant meat, so tender the slices were collapsing. Alice salivated.

"And maybe some of your grilled sausage, just so they can taste it?"

He made his own. Alice thought it was better than anyone else's: not too fat, balanced spice, sneaky lingering heat on the aftertaste.

Curtis and Bang-Bang were rapt, watching every move of the knife. They held up their trays and John laid the beautiful slices on the butcher paper. They acquired cups of beans and slaw and headed outside. "I'll bring your beers," John called.

Night was falling. Crickets were tuning up. Spring peepers made *chink-chink* noises down the hill.

"Alice, tomorrow we'll walk you through everything. We've only got one worry," Bang-Bang said.

Her heart sank. What worry? This deposition was critical.

"Is this place open again tomorrow night?"

* * * * *

"The hardest question they can ask me," said Bang-Bang, "is how many Savage Model 99 .250-3000s there were in Central Texas in 1919. I'll respond that we can't know that, but that the model was available."

"And although you actually saw a rifle labeled 'Alastair Drinkman's Savage Model 99' at the Drinkman headquarters, another tough question is when the Drinkmans got that gun and whether it's the one in the picture. We've looked at that picture in your book," said Curtis. "The way your boy Willy is holding the rifle in his hunting picture, the bottom of the stock isn't completely visible. But we think that gun has the shape and features of a Savage Model 99. So, it's a reasonable surmise."

Alice had forwarded the picture to opposing counsel, since she had to provide whatever she'd given her expert. She counted on Tyler Junkin to handle Armstrong's inevitable objections. So far Armstrong had objected to all their discovery questions on the Savage Model 99 (such as where and when acquired) as irrelevant, and was opposing her motion to compel the Drinkmans to produce the gun itself. But she didn't want to put off this deposition.

Alice and Bang-Bang pulled up to Tyler's office Thursday morning, ready to go. Mr. Navarro and Tomás were already there. Bang-Bang was to testify on history and availability of the Savage Model 99 .250-3000 and on ballistics.

Once again the Armstrong team marched in. Their ballistics expert, a young man from Atlanta, sat next to Armstrong. Armstrong had lost a bit of what Alice called his "puff." He looked about an inch shorter. His shoulders sagged. Right off the bat, on the record, Alice challenged Armstrong's failure to provide requested information on the Drinkmans' Savage Model 99 and said she would seek sanctions, including making Armstrong's clients pay the cost of continuing the deposition.

After a heated skirmish (the printed typescript would not reflect the red spots on Armstrong's cheeks or Alice's narrowed eyes and out-thrust jaw) the court reporter swore in Bang-Bang. Armstrong made final arrangements to his legal pad and notebooks and forged ahead, asking Bang-Bang to describe his education and work history. Finally he started digging into Bang-Bang's record as an expert witness. Over a hundred engagements; active testimony about forty times; yes, both federal and state court; yes, he had advised the US Army; yes, he had advised the State Department; yes, he had been asked to identify weapons used on victims at Kosovo; yes, his opinions had been accepted. In addition, he had advised government agencies in investigations of bodies across the Southwest, including from Indian fights and wagon trains, and at the site of the battle of Glorieta Pass in New Mexico. No, he had never been disqualified as an expert in any proceeding. Yes, he had produced all of his file, including the documents that Ms. Greer had provided to him. All of his file documents were included in the box at the end of the table, the one the associate was looking through.

"Dr. Barker, please state your opinion completely and the basis for it," Armstrong asked. Bang-Bang was off and running, in a mild scholarly way ticking off his longtime familiarity with that gun and with others ranging back to the Civil War, the various ways the Savage Model 99 rifle could be distinguished from other guns, the scope of his research, and how he had concluded that the .250-3000 Savage cartridge was available for the Savage Model 99 in Central Texas beginning in 1915. Armstrong questioned him about the pictures Alice had taken of the low-water crossing where Alex Drinkman was shot. "Yes, Ms. Greer had sent those. Yes, he had only her word as to where she took them. However, he and his assistant had also taken pictures there." Tyler shook his head in disgust at the question but Alice remained true to her law school moot court training ("Do not make faces, Ms. MacDonald"). Maybe, she thought, her professor said that only to the women students.

Now Bang-Bang was discussing a blow-up of the picture of Willy and his buck from the history Kinsear had located about Central Texas ranch families. "Yes," Bang-Bang concluded, the gun in the picture was a Savage Model 99; no, he had no confirmation that that gun had been used to shoot that deer but the conventional practice was for the hunter to pose with the animal and with the gun used to shoot the animal; it certainly would be unusual for a hunter to pose with a different gun in the photograph recording that shoot. He had never known that to happen in all his years of hunting. In addition, the combination of the Savage Model 99 and the .250-3000 cartridge was considered a good choice for youths because of the killing capability combined with light recoil, and of course the bullet itself was considered a good choice for deer hunting. Yes, he was very familiar with the Savage Model 99 and the available ammunition. In his opinion Alex Drinkman was shot using a .250-3000 cartridge that was likely loaded in a Savage Model 99. Yes, it is possible a second shooter could have been involved; the bullet from Alex Drinkman's reported abdominal wound had not been seen or tested. Possibly exhumation of the body would permit such testing. Could the .250-3000 cartridge have been used with a Savage Model 99 to kill a grown man? Yes, in his opinion. Then he moved to the elevations and locations at the low-water crossing where Alex Drinkman had been shot. "Though the terrain immediately next to the creek may have changed, due to occasional floodwaters, there are a number of rocky outcrops that would allow an excellent field of fire for a target crossing the creek." Yes, from several of those outcrops multiple shots would be possible using the Savage Model 99. No, he did not know how fast the motorcycle could have been going. He understood from the available clipping that the motorcycle had fallen in the creek at the crossing itself, and if that was accurate, the motorcycle could not have been going particularly fast. But in any event, multiple shots would have been possible. Yes, it was possible that in 1919 the foliage was different at the creek. However, he considered that the variety of outcrops on the hill on the west side would have permitted a shooter to choose a site where he could see the target.

Armstrong moved to ballistics. Bang-Bang spread out the pictures from the comparison microscope showing the markings on the standard used for comparison, then the blow-up of the deformed bullet and the book bullet, as he called them. The similarity was overwhelming. Armstrong couldn't shake him. Armstrong and his ballistics guru wanted a ten-minute break.

The Navarro team decamped to the kitchen. "Kinda fun," said Bang-Bang. "But these people don't seem very well prepared. I can think of a number of questions I would have asked myself."

"Well, for goodness' sake don't mention them," said Alice. She looked at Mr. Navarro. No smile. "How are you holding up?"

"It's odd to be sitting quietly in a conference room listening to discussion of the bullets that killed my father."

Bang-Bang nodded. "It's a cold-blooded dissection of a hot-blooded terrible death, isn't it. Doesn't seem respectful. But that is precisely what it is."

They reconvened. Armstrong asked a long complicated question with many embedded assumptions, to which Alice objected. "But you can answer," she told Bang-Bang. In his scholarly way, Bang-Bang dissected the question, clarified the flaws in Armstrong's assumptions about ballistics, explained the use of accepted standards in comparative examinations of bullets, and restated his own conclusions. Then came twenty more minutes of tortuously worded questions. Armstrong was running out of gas. Alice secretly rejoiced that she had pushed for this schedule. She knew she'd face at least as much time pressure with Armstrong's experts, given the push to meet the deadline for filing summary judgments. She reminded herself it was her own fault, this deadline . . . as usual.

"Have you told us all your opinions, Dr. Barker?"

"All I can think of at this moment." Ha, he'd left the door slightly ajar for himself.

Alice's turn. "Dr. Barker, assuming the blood on the deformed bullet came from Alex Drinkman's body, was Alex Drinkman shot with a Model 99 Savage using a .250-3000 bullet?"

"Based on the evidence, yes."

More skirmishing, then Armstrong said, "No more questions." His associate began packing up the file boxes.

"Let's talk schedule, Haverty," Alice said, staring across the table at him. "You know we're deposing Will and Warren Drinkman Tuesday. I need the requested documents at least twenty-four hours in advance."

"Um, I'm not sure about the documents. I'll call you tomorrow."

Alice frowned. Something shifty here. "Look, Haverty, we can't let this schedule slip. We need their depositions and those of your experts for our amended motion for partial summary judgment, since any amendment is due the following week under our agreed order. Your guys are under subpoena."

"Well, I'll call you." And he was out the door.

"Something's up," she told Tyler.

"He's afraid his client will be under arrest for funding a helicopter assault."

Kinsear joined Alice, Bang-Bang, and Banana Clip for supper at the Shade Tree. "Alice, can you get us more gigs around here?" Curtis held up a slice of brisket. "I love Santa Fe. I'm reasonably fond of Hatch chiles. But it's quite alluring, this powerful Central Texas barbecue tradition. Bang-Bang and I sense that you need more ballistics experts here. We're available."

Chapter Twenty - Nine

A Note in a Bottle

On Friday morning Alice called Armstrong. "Your documents need to be here at nine a.m. Monday." She wasn't going to remind him his discovery responses were due as well—she'd love it if he missed the deadline for the requests for admissions, since they would be deemed admitted.

"We're still getting them together. We may need to postpone the deposition."

"Haverty, this is an agreed date under the order. I'm not moving it. You've got three other lawyers so far working on this case. No reason you can't comply."

Maybe Tyler was right. Maybe Will and Warren Drinkman were facing serious trouble on the helicopter investigation—perhaps taking the Fifth?—and didn't want to answer questions at the deposition. Maybe there was a small breach in the high wall around Drinkman headquarters.

* * * * *

The four deposition transcripts arrived. Alice sent all four to Adele Collins's lawyer, with a note that she asked him to send to his client. "*Adele, I hope you'll read these and see that your cousin Alejandro's claim is solid,*" the note read. "*I would like to have an affidavit from you about Bonnie's diary, if you can see your way to it. Please let your lawyer know if you'd be willing.*" Sending this felt like putting a note in a bottle and dropping it in the ocean. But perhaps hearing that the experts were confident the letter was authentic, that the DNA tests confirmed Alejandro was her uncle's son, and that the bloodstained bullet her great Aunt Dee had so carefully preserved was a .250-3000 fired by a Savage Model 99, the same sort Bonnie mentioned in her letter, the same sort held by Willy as he crouched next to the dead buck—perhaps that would slowly persuade Adele which side she should be on. Also, Alice really wanted Adele to see the Drinkmans under oath. What if . . . Adele came to the Drinkmans' depositions? They were theoretically open to the public.

* * * * *

On Monday at ten Alice called Haverty Armstrong. "Where are the documents, Haverty? They're late. I'm deposing your clients tomorrow." She'd subpoenaed both Will Drinkman and Warren Drinkman, individually and as representatives of their companies.

"I was going to call you, Alice. Okay, here's a proposal. What if instead of a deposition tomorrow we have a settlement conference?"

"Nope. I need your clients' sworn testimony before the amendment deadline for my summary judgment motion."

He paused. "I understand your position. Here's mine. One or both likely will take the Fifth Amendment. I'm going to have to advise them not to respond."

"To any question?"

"No, but to anything related to the, uh, helicopter matter. In fact, you won't get answers to anything where there's a potential criminal count."

"I will be asking them about Alex Drinkman's ownership of the Blue Pool property or other real property, about any defenses they have to our actions to recover the Blue Pool or other property and our evidence on heirship, about any counterclaims you have, and about any ownership right they think they have to pursue the Blue Pool groundwater permit. I do intend to ask about the 'helicopter matter' as you so delicately call it; you can object, of course. I'll limit my questions tomorrow to those issues if you give me the documents on every topic I've named and agree to present them for deposition later on other matters, again before our deadline. We can limit time to three hours if you get me the documents this morning. Then we could have an informal settlement conference immediately afterwards, but I expect it will be preliminary only, pending receipt of more financials from your folks." She wouldn't give up any Navarro claims until she knew what the Drinkmans had.

Silence. "Okay."

She and Red, a certified public accountant, worked feverishly Monday afternoon and evening over the sketchy production of Drinkman financials. Red said, "You need the following additional documents," handing a neatly written list to Alice. Silla made a spreadsheet of the properties and deed records it looked like either Alastair or Alex owned in 1919, which did include the small Medina property and the Frio County ranch. The finances especially looked like a tangled mess to Alice. She could barely imagine what trial would be like.

On Tuesday morning they convened at Tyler's office. Tomás brought Mr. Navarro. Sandro was speaking at the LBJ School at UT but could be available by phone if needed.

When Haverty Armstrong entered Tyler's conference room with Will and Warren Drinkman, Mr. Navarro rose, his face impassive. He nodded when introduced, but said nothing. Nor did he extend his hand across the conference room table. His dark eyes were staring at the son and grandson of the man he believed murdered his father, the father he never got to know.

The conference room door opened again. John Frierson, Adele Collins's lawyer, nodded at Alice and took a chair in the corner, legal pad on his lap. Well, well.

"We're ready," Alice told the court reporter. As Will Drinkman swore to tell the truth, she speculated whether for him that meant telling the truth ninety percent, or thirty percent, or ten percent of the time . . . or only if convenient.

"Your father changed his name from Willy Kendrick to Willy Kendrick Drinkman when?" And they were off.

Two hours later Alice stopped.

Will Drinkman had acknowledged the outlines of the Drinkman empire, admitted that he knew of no record of any administration of Alex Drinkman's estate, admitted that the Blue Pool Ranch was still in Alex Drinkman's name, as was part of a ranch in Frio County and a small property in Medina County. He admitted that if Alex Drinkman had not died before his father, he would have inherited half of the children's share of Alastair Drinkman's real property. No, he did not know what that share was worth at the time. Then Drinkman added, "Of course, Mr. Alastair Drinkman could have changed his will. Who knows how it could have read later on?" But he then admitted he knew of no other will. As to what Ella Kendrick's share was worth in 1919, he could not estimate. Alice made him read the counterclaim filed by Armstrong in the Navarro land action case and asked what basis he had for disputing Alejandro Navarro's claim that he was Alex Drinkman's son. He asserted there was no proof that the DNA samples actually came from Alex Drinkman. Even the letter? "Some unknown person could have licked the stamp and licked the envelope shut!" But he grew red-faced when Alice asked whether he would consent to exhumation of Alex Drinkman's body so that additional samples could be taken. "Certainly not!" He also could not explain why a Drinkman entity had any right to drill for groundwater at Blue Pool. Ah, Alice thought. They know they don't really have a good shot at claiming adverse possession.

"This is on the record too," she told the court reporter. "I reserve four more hours to depose this witness, including on the following topics: the break-in at Mr. Sheridan's shop; the break-in at Mr. Sheridan's ranch; the helicopter attack by Drinkman employees on Mr. Navarro and me; history of use and current location of the Savage Model 99 and other guns that were at the Drinkman ranch in 1919; and the current location of Alex Drinkman's personal property, including whatever was or had been in display cases at Drinkman headquarters."

"Those aren't relevant to this land recovery dispute!" said Armstrong sharply.

"They are highly relevant. We don't just claim Alejandro Navarro is Alex Drinkman's heir; circumstances show that Alex Drinkman was killed for the benefit of Ella Kendrick Drinkman and Willy Kendrick and his heirs, who should no longer be permitted to benefit from Alex Drinkman's murder. I intend to go into all of these matters in the reserved four hours."

"We'll take that to the judge," Armstrong said. "Alastair Drinkman's will was clear! Alex died before his father. You can't possibly claim that Alex's supposed heir would have any rights to Alastair Drinkman's estate. Even if you thought you could prove it, which you can't!"

His fury gave Alice an idea.

Now Warren Drinkman had to take the seat facing the videographer, with the microphone clipped to his tie. In his early fifties, broad-shouldered but soft around the middle, he still glanced anxiously at his father's set face. His father never looked at him.

Alice asked him about Drinkman connections to the Oak Motte Links and the proposed golf course. "Objection!" barked Armstrong.

"Basis for the objection?"

"Relevance!"

"It's relevant to the Blue Pool groundwater permit application."

Warren answered. Yes, Oak Motte Links was a Drinkman company. Alice went on with her questions. Warren dodged and darted like a pig in a pen trying to avoid the final road trip to the livestock auction, but ultimately admitted that Oak Motte Links held no deed to Blue Pool. "Oak Motte Links does not own it right now," he said. "But we've bought a pipeline easement to it. And I believe we paid some taxes." He acknowledged that the Blue Pool property was still shown on deed records as owned by Alex Drinkman. He acknowledged that Oak Motte Links had started fencing around the Blue Pool property a little over a year ago.

"Why did you do that?"

Warren glanced at his father. "I don't remember," he said. "I believe it was legal advice."

"Don't answer about legal advice," Armstrong ordered.

Alice was itching for an opening on the helicopter. "Your assets include a Bell Huey Two, the civvy version of the old military UH-1?"

"No, that's on dad's side of the company."

"Objection!" Haverty Armstrong was red-faced. But the damage was done.

"Was it hangared at the Blue Pool site?"

"I think so."

"And it was flown from there?"

"Believe so."

So they admitted using Alex's property for their own purposes.

"Whose permission was sought before using Blue Pool as a helicopter base?"

"Objection!" Armstrong again.

"You can answer," she told Warren.

"I don't know of anyone."

This time Will Drinkman shot a look of hate at his son. Alice shifted gears.

"Is Kelly Cosgrove a member of Oak Motte Links?"

"Yes, I believe so."

"You know so, don't you?"

"Yes."

"Does he own an interest in any operations connected to Oak Motte Links?"

Warren's forehead wrinkled. "He has some ownership in land we plan to use for some operations."

"What land and what operations?"

"It's in Coffee Creek, off Highway 290. Cement plant operations."

"What's Cosgrove's land ownership?"

"He's got an option on the land we plan to use."

Alice saw light glimmering ahead. "Has Kelly Cosgrove provided services to Oak Motte Links?" Armstrong was now objecting to every question.

"Yeah."

"As a PR man, advance man?"

"Yes. He smooths the way, you know."

"Does he do the same for the proposed cement plant?"

"Yes."

"And is he being compensated by having you lease back the property for the cement plant?"

"That's right. He calls it his retirement plan."

"He's getting ready to retire then?"

"Yeah, kind of shifting gears away from the political gigs. Don't think they've been so lucrative lately."

"Have you fired the Savage Model 99 that is kept in the display case at Drinkman headquarters?"

"Yes."

"When?"

"When I was a kid."

"When did you last shoot it?"

"Oh, about three years ago. Took some guys antelope hunting out in New Mexico."

"Did it work okay?"

"Oh yeah. Got some pretty nice antelope."

"Has anyone else shot it lately?"

He glanced at his father. "My father did, a couple of weeks ago."

"Has it been reworked, or revamped, to your knowledge?"

He looked disapproving. "No. It's a classic. You wouldn't want to mess with it."

She looked at Armstrong. "Obviously the gun can be fired. We demand its production for testing."

Alice ended the questions and reserved four more hours with Warren Drinkman. The court reporter and videographer left, with Alice demanding a rush transcript: "I need it right away." In other words, don't lowball me on settlement, Haverty; we're gearing up for a fight. Frierson stood up in the corner, nodded toward the hallway, wanting to talk. Alice excused herself and took him into the kitchen. "Yes?"

"Ms. Greer—Alice, if I may. Are you planning to sue my client too, for what she may somehow have of Alex's estate?"

"Haven't decided." This was interesting. What would Alejandro Navarro want her to say? She went on, "It would be nice if somehow they could cooperate. My client is Adele's only first cousin. And they are both very strong characters."

"I agree. They seem to hold fairly similar beliefs."

"Are you making any kind of proposal here?"

He shook his head. "Not yet. I just hope we can figure out a way forward for them, and I don't know how you'll resolve things with the Drinkmans. Could you keep me posted?"

She nodded. "Yes. To the extent I can. In terms of cooperation, I expect you've thought about whether, if Adele proves that Ella or Willy killed Alex, she may also have a claim that their share of Alastair Drinkman's estate should be forfeited to Bonnie and her heirs?"

He smiled but didn't respond. Instead he said, "In terms of cooperation, Adele wanted me to tell you that she does have the Tennyson."

"Oh!" Alice thought back to her meeting with Adele. She'd bet that Adele had had the copy of Tennyson, bullet hole and all, right there in the trunk that day. Adele could play poker, for sure. She remembered something. "John, the young pilot by the helicopter, the photo in Adele's living room?"

"That's Adele's only child. Rob Collins. He was killed in Vietnam, in 1970."

Alice stood stock-still, transfixed. "Oh," was all she could say. Another pilot.

She went back to the conference room. "Instead of reconvening after lunch, we thought it would make sense just to send out for lunch and then go straight into a settlement conference," Alice told Armstrong. "This is your party, Haverty, the settlement portion. I don't know what you plan to talk about but let's don't waste time, since we've got this opportunity. We look forward to hearing what you have to say. You guys stay in this conference room, and we'll be in Tyler's office, and we can get together in the conference room after we have a bite."

Haverty agreed. Tyler had already sent out to Shade Tree for barbecue and sides, and the irresistible smell of oak and smoked meat was wafting under the conference room door.

As the Navarros and Tyler and Alice sat around his desk, Tyler said, "I've found that barbecue enhances settlement potential greatly. Wish they could try it in the Middle East. Get all the parties together around some Shade Tree beef brisket, maybe there could finally be a meeting of the national minds."

"Peace through barbecue. Provided you observe food taboos." Alice dabbed at her mouth. She did feel more serene. But time to reconvene. They marched back to the conference room.

Haverty Armstrong, standing, leaned his arms on the table. "We're here to see if we can resolve this dispute now. We'll offer you the Blue Pool property. You relinquish any claim to any other asset."

"Nonstarter," said Alice. She stood up. "Blue Pool and the Frio Ranch are clearly Alex Drinkman's. That's not even an offer. We're going back to Tyler's office. Let us know if you have something else to say. And I mean something serious, or we're done. We'll see you at summary judgment."

She and Tyler and the Navarros picked up their papers and walked back to Tyler's office.

"That was an insult," Mr. Navarro said.

"I'm getting more iced tea," said Tomás. "Anyone need anything?"

In five minutes came a tap at the door. Haverty Armstrong peered in. "Alice? May we talk for a moment?"

Alice and Tyler walked with Armstrong into the office kitchen. "What do you really want?" asked Armstrong.

"We aren't bidding against ourselves and you're the one who asked to talk settlement. That said, we've had folks looking at what Alex Drinkman's share of Alastair Drinkman's estate is now worth. Mr. Navarro is entitled to that."

"No way you could get that in court. Anyway, it's Ella and Willy and Will Drinkman who built the fortune."

"Not so. They just sat back and reaped oil revenues when oil was discovered on the ranches Alastair Drinkman bought before he got married. Anything they built with oil revenue came straight from Alastair Drinkman."

"So you want a third of the Drinkman holdings? That's ridiculous!"

Alice cocked her head at him. "Look, Haverty, we can do the math another way. Just divide by two, not three. After we prove Alex Drinkman was deliberately killed by people who directly benefited from his death, since they apparently got part of his share of Alastair Drinkman's estate, we can just split the estate with Adele Collins, Bonnie's daughter. At a minimum, the two children would have inherited all the real property that Alastair Drinkman already owned when he married Ella."

"Sheer speculation! You have no proof Ella Kendrick Drinkman was involved!"

"We'll see," Alice said. "Her son was a minor, and she was responsible for him."

Armstrong said, "Make me some kind of offer I can take back to my folks."

"Not until you've made us a real offer, and you still haven't

284

made one."

"Okay, I need to talk to them." Armstrong left.

Alice and Tyler told the Navarros about their conversation with Armstrong. "Alice," said Mr. Navarro, "I don't want to spend a year of my remaining time on this earth dickering with people like Will Drinkman. You lie down with dogs, you get up with fleas."

"I hear you. Asking for any of Alastair's estate has problems, unfair though it seems. Also, it's an accounting and probate nightmare. We'd have to figure out what was Alastair Drinkman's community property, what was his separate property, especially his real property he owned before he married Ella. The battle could go on for years, and there have been cases lasting decades."

"I won't be here for decades."

"Right. So despite what I told Haverty, let's do come up with a demand. You do want Blue Pool and whatever real property Alex owned?"

Mr. Navarro nodded.

"What else?"

"How much are all the radio stations worth?"

"We don't have exact figures. It's also hard to estimate the total future oil and gas revenues, and we don't understand their accounting yet—they have so many investment entities. However, the radio station systems, including station properties and contracts, seem to be worth about twenty percent of their holdings." Into Alice's mind flashed the possibility of future headlines in the *San Antonio Express-News* on the fallout from the prison food scandal. "We should be careful what we ask for and what they try to foist off on us. We don't want to wind up with anything tainted, anything that comes back to bite you or Sandro and Tomás and Isabella."

Tomás made a sour face. "Like the tainted milk. Imagine delivering that crap to a captive audience. Helpless! Including juveniles in detention." He saw Alice's surprise. "Rose told me!" he said.

Mr. Navarro cleared his throat. "My father's land. A one-third share of mineral interests on the land my grandfather owned at his death. The radio stations. Those look relatively clean."

"You're not going after past revenue?"

"I think not, Alice. But I'm not going to bargain on any of this. It's take it or leave it."

Alice worried. "We don't even have a full picture of their holdings yet."

"You want to close off discussion and just go after summary judgment?"

That would be irresponsible, thought Alice. What does my client really want?

"Oh," said Mr. Navarro. "There's a bit more. I want every item of Alex Drinkman's effects. Everything. Papers, books, furniture, clothes. Everything on display at the Drinkman headquarters. His saddle. Anything those people have that belonged to him, I want. Furthermore, I plan to set up my own foundation. The Alex Drinkman Foundation. Will Drinkman has to change the name of his foundation and agree not to use the Drinkman name in any future entities."

Tyler, Tomás, and Alice stared in open-mouthed admiration.

"Makes me feel cleaner, if they do that," said Mr. Navarro, shooting his white shirt cuffs.

Alice walked back to the conference room and made Mr. Navarro's demand. She thought Will Drinkman might die of apoplexy right then and there.

"What effrontery!" His face was a dangerous purple.

She watched Haverty Armstrong put his hand on Drinkman's sleeve.

"Let me know if you have any questions about our offer," Alice said. She met complete silence. So she walked out of the room.

* * * * *

Haverty knocked and walked in. "Um, we need to talk to our financial folks. I don't think we can finish this today."

"If you leave and we don't reach agreement, we're going forward with summary judgment, full tilt boogie."

"We can't get there today, Alice. You guys are asking for way too much."

"See you in court." She stood up.

"Seriously, we are trying to put together a response. We just need some more time. Can we reconvene later this week? Friday morning?"

"We'll talk about it. But not for long. You asked for this party and you haven't even made a serious proposal. If we make no progress Friday morning, I'll be deposing your clients that afternoon. And if you're leaving today, we are not promising our demand won't be higher on Friday. And I want that agreement in writing."

"I understand. Just send me the agreement. We'll be here Friday morning." He left.

Mr. Navarro got to his feet. His face looked carved from mahogany. He walked out of the conference room.

"Uh-oh," said Tomás. "He is furious."

"I can tell," Alice said. "So am I."

* * * * *

Rose called Alice an hour later. "Just checking in."

"Hey, how come you didn't have a bug-checking gizmo?" Alice asked. "Tyler Junkin says he has one, which amazed me. Don't investigative reporters have them too?"

"I do have one, Alice! Rather, I did. It's toast, along with the car. But its battery was dead and I hadn't checked it. Was more worried about bugs on the phone and the computer."

"Okay, what are you up to?"

"Gonna go talk to Kelly Cosgrove. He'll be at a fundraiser for the governor today at Texas State in San Marcos. He's hoping someone will hire him for a gig in the reelection campaign, I hear."

"Rose, does he know who you are or what you're doing?"

"Don't think so."

"Who was listening to your phone and watching your email then? Who put the bomb on your car? Police figured that out yet?"

"I'm guessing Warren Drinkman's buddies, at Fair Star. But so far the police don't seem to know."

Alice shook her head. "Rose. You don't know either."

"Well, Cosgrove is my last interview. He wanted to meet last week but I was hammering the last nails into this story, which is finally in the editor's hands at the *San Antonio Express*. I've got hard copy locked up in my safety deposit box with the supporting documents, and everything's on a couple of thumb drives too. We're planning to go with it this Sunday, but I really want to interview Cosgrove, get comments in person."

"Why in person? Can't you just call him on the phone?"

"That's not my way, Alice. You get a lot more, watching someone's eyes. Those eyes tell you what the next question should be. Such as, 'Mr. Cosgrove, how do you feel knowing that the deal you helped fund resulted in the deaths of twelve helpless prisoners?' Of course, maybe he thinks if you're already in prison you aren't a person anymore."

"Rose, aren't the police looking at him for the car bomb?"

"Last I heard, his alibi checked out. He was down at the capitol doing something."

"Was the car bomb on a timer?"

"Yes. That makes it even harder to prove."

"Take someone with you."

"Oh, come on, Alice! We're going to meet at a Starbucks right off the interstate in San Marcos, if you must know. And then we're done, the story's done, and I might just get married."

Alice smiled. Sandro would find he had lassoed the wildest mustang in the herd. "I guess you can't tell me details, but how—how powerful is the story?"

"Well . . . I'd say it's about a nine point two on the Richter scale. It shines a bright, bright spotlight on the Drinkman empire, with sharp focus on little Warren Drinkman and his prison profits."

"Wow. I'll watch for it Sunday morning. Be careful, Rose. Stay in touch, okay?" Lord, she sounded like Rose's mother. Stop it, Alice.

Chapter Thirty

How to Tie a Pigging String

Alice and Red had planned their own road trip for Wednesday: long-standing joint appointments for facials with Gerda, the Mittel-European skin genius of San Antonio. Some said it was easier to get an appointment with the pope than with Gerda, but once finally there, your face became her property, to be assessed and analyzed, cleaned and anointed, until you emerged gleaming into the South Texas sunlight. Today Red was driving. "She'll tell me, 'Now we must make your eyebrows look less moth-eaten!'"

"And she'll tell me, 'Now we must remove all that dead gray winter skin! Get you ready for spr-r-r-r-ring!'"

When they emerged from Gerda's, each carrying a bag of secret ampoules for eternal beauty, Alice said, "I'm starving. What about stopping at La Rotonda for late lunch? I'll show you the scene of the Norville murder."

"Oh my. Okay. You think the cook still makes those chiles rellenos with the sour cream and raisins and pecans?"

The La Rotonda parking lot had plenty of empty spaces. "Sorry, cook doesn't come in until three. I can get you tortilla soup here in the bar. Really good," said the bartender. "Cold draft beer?"

"First I'm going to show my friend the ballroom." Alice took Red down the hall to the circular ballroom. Red admired the domed ceiling. Alice led the way up the stairway to the gallery. They stood by the gallery railing, looking across at the musician's balcony. "I thought this would be a great view, looking right across at the dignitaries instead of standing in a crowd downstairs craning my neck. First came a janitor polishing these tiles, pushing his mop around the gallery. Then I saw Sandro walk down into the musician's balcony with the mayor, and Tomás with Mr. Navarro, then finally Carey. He came halfway down the stairs and just stood there." She looked down at the floor, where Carey's body had scattered the reporters and TV cameramen.

"It wasn't the janitor? The janitor, in the hallway, with a push broom—as in Clue?"

"Huh. Wasn't the janitor because he was in the kitchen when it happened. Although it seems like he got there awfully fast." Alice turned right, walking counterclockwise around to the other side of the gallery. Red followed, trailing her hand along the balcony rail.

Alice tugged at the door to the musician's balcony. Locked. Well, it should be—it was a deathtrap that didn't meet code. Although back in the day the low railing was apparently safe enough for those mariachi players, with nothing barring the view from below of their gorgeous uniforms, big hats, bright instruments.

Behind Alice, just past the musician's balcony and on the other side of the hall, a door marked "STAFF ONLY" stood slightly open. Alice glanced around the silent gallery. No one. She pushed the door gently and peeked in. No one here either. She and Red surveyed the staff sanctum sanctorum. A couch. A small table with two battered chairs. A wall with small lockers and a row of hooks holding jackets and hats labeled "LA ROTONDA STAFF." At the far corner was a small service elevator. Of course, Alice thought. That's how the kitchen staff brings up carts for room service on this floor. And how janitors get down to the kitchen for their break, without having to go down the gallery staircase and walk back through the ballroom to reach the kitchen hallway. She opened a closet door. Lemon-oil smell. Hooks for dustpans. One long-handled mop with a wide woolly mop head. A shelf loaded with unopened bottles of lemon floor cleaner, dusting mitts, and packages of woolly mop heads. A push broom. And standing in one corner, several spare mop handles with the bare wire holder at the other end.

Alice backed out of the closet. Red had already left, continuing the gallery circuit. She was disappearing into the next room. The brass plate above the imposing French doors read "BILLIARD ROOM." Red stuck her head around the door, waggling her eyebrows. "Alice, here's where the big boys go play pool after dinner and port!" The air held a faint hint of cigar smoke. Oversized dark leather couches and chairs were grouped against the walls, under slightly erotic paintings of the September Morn variety. "So amazing, how these young women consistently forget to bring their clothes to the creek," Red said. "Only a sheer wrap. So improvident."

Ah, thought Alice. Maybe this is where Kelly Cosgrove was going when I saw him standing by the balcony. Or had he already been in here? Looked like the very place for a lobbyist to invite a target he needed to buttonhole for a particular deal. Alice leaned back in a club chair, imagining the scene.

Red chose a pool cue from the wall rack, hefted it in an experienced way, then began chalking the tip, eyeing the cue ball. She leaned over the green baize, face intent, getting ready to break, when Alice heard a low murmur outside. "Shh!" She raised her finger to her lips and tiptoed to the open French doors. Red followed, pool cue in hand.

Twenty feet away in the hall stood Rose, watching Kelly Cosgrove unlock the door to the musician's balcony. "How do you come to have a key?" she heard Rose ask. Ah, the whispering gallery.

"Oh, I worked my way through school here," he laughed. "And somehow—after all these years, I always manage to have the master key. Come on, let's go in." He slipped the key into his left pocket.

Rose held back. "I'm fine looking at it from here."

"No, you need to see this. Hey, you're an investigative reporter." Now he had his hand in his right pocket.

Rose tensed up, clutching her leather bag. "No. I'm staying here. I don't like heights."

Cosgrove grabbed her arm. "You need to see this."

Rose pushed him away with the other arm, but her face froze when Cosgrove pulled a black pistol. "In you go, Miss Reporter."

Alice and Red glanced at each other. Alice mouthed, "I've got Rose!" and ran left, diving for Rose's legs. Red charged at Cosgrove, the butt of the pool cue aloft. He turned to his right at the sound of flying feet. Red swung the pool cue down hard on his gun arm. The pistol fired and tumbled to the floor. Cosgrove bent to grab it. Rose planted her feet, and swung the pool cue like a baseball bat at Cosgrove's head.

Sickening thump. Cosgrove fell heavily by the balcony rail, moaning.

Alice was clambering off Rose, hoping not to see blood. Rose stood up.

"Think you knocked him out, Red," panted Alice.

The three gathered around Cosgrove, collapsed on his back, eyes closed. Blood oozed from his right boot. "Oh no," said Red. "Got himself right in his Lucchese. And ostrich too! Five hundred dollars at least!"

Cosgrove's hand twitched. He groped for the pistol again but missed, sending it careening through the metal balcony rail onto the ballroom floor. Bang! An enormous crash below.

"Oh, God." Alice leaned over, peering down. A terrified busboy holding an empty tray stared up at her, wide-eyed, broken plates and glasses all around his feet. "You okay?" she asked. He nodded. "Call the police!" He ran across the ballroom floor toward the lobby hallway, tray waving in his hand.

Cosgrove was rolling over, grunting, trying to get up. Rose and Alice each grabbed an arm, yanking him onto on his belly, then bent his forearms back. He howled. Red pulled his tie loose, then sat down on his rear end and thighs so he couldn't kick, tied his wrists together with his own tie, and used the long ends to tie him to the balcony rail. They stood back, considering the result. Then the three women high-fived. "I rode quadrille in rodeo, but my high school boyfriend did calf-roping, and he taught me how to tie a pigging string," Red said, head tilted, admiring the knot. Cosgrove thrashed in a discouraged way.

Across the ballroom they saw the bartender racing in, holding a phone, staring up open-mouthed. "We're fine, don't worry," Red called. "But we're ready for that cold draft beer now. This ol' boy up here, though, he probably needs an ambulance. And a police escort."

"And don't let anyone touch that gun. It's got fingerprints on it," called Alice.

The bartender shook his head. In a moment the manager came huffing up the staircase by the musician's balcony. "But that's Mr. Cosgrove!" he said, horrified.

"Used to work here, didn't he?" said Alice.

"Yeah! He told us that all the time. Good customer, too."

"Not this time. This time, he was a very bad boy."

The police followed. Alice asked them to call the Hays County detectives who were working the Norville murder. Then she called George Files. "I think you need to see this scene too, before Cosgrove gets lugged off to the hospital," she told him. "Can you coordinate with Hays County?" He grunted, said he'd try.

The patrolman kneeling by Cosgrove said to Red, "You do this?" He pointed to the growing lump on the back of Cosgrove's head.

"Yeah. With this pool cue."

"Pretty good wallop."

"I played high school softball," Red explained. "In East Texas. San Augustine."

"Oh, the Lady Wolves."

"She really put her hips into it," said Alice.

"That's what the coach taught us," said Red.

"I really can't think of an appropriate response," said the patrolman, getting to his feet. "But I'd like to be on your team."

Files arrived just as the Hays County detectives did. Cosgrove was being wheeled out on a gurney. "Here's what we found when we searched his jacket and pants," said the patrolman.

He held out a plastic bag with wallet, watch, cell phone, car keys, loose change, and a folded note.

"What's the note?" Files asked.

He and the detectives read it together, then looked at Rose.

"Let me see if I have this straight," said Files. "You were interviewing him for a story."

"Right. We met at the Starbucks by the outlet mall on the interstate, then he wanted to sit and do the interview in the La Rotonda bar. He said it was more confidential. I followed him in my car and we went up to the gallery. He got out his key and was opening the door to the balcony. I didn't want to go in—he was scaring me—then he pulled that pistol."

"And then you two jumped in," said Files, looking at Alice and Red.

"Right."

"Then the pistol went off?"

"The man shot himself in the foot," Red said. "I think that was about the same time I whacked his gun arm. Then I beaned him."

"Then you all tied him up with his own tie."

"Right. After he tried to pick up his pistol but he knocked it through the balcony rail, where it went off again, we're not sure where."

"And you did not at any time touch the gun or search him?"

Surprised, they all shook their heads.

"Rose, did he have his coat, his blazer, on the whole time? At the Starbucks, and then here?"

"I think so. Yes, I know so, because it wasn't that cool in the Starbucks and I noticed he kept it on."

"Okay. I know we need signed statements." He looked at the Hays County detectives, who nodded.

It was another hour before the three women made it downstairs to the bar. The bartender looked at them. "You ladies do this all the time?"

"What do you mean, sir?"

"Have this kind of afternoon?"

They laughed a little. "Not exactly." He brought Alice and Red their beers, and an iced tea for Rose. "She's not drinking these days," Alice explained. Red raised a knowing eyebrow.

Rose stood at the other end of the bar, talking intently into her phone. She walked back over to Red and Alice. "Had to phone in the grand finale for the story. But it's not really final, is it?"

"I'd wait," Alice said. "We're going to hear more about that note. And have you called Sandro yet?"

"He's not picking up his cell, but I'll try his office." Rose walked back to the other end of the bar. Alice heard her say, "I'm just fine, just fine, but here's what happened." Alice tried not to eavesdrop; rather, she tried to try not to eavesdrop. But she was relieved when Rose came back with a smile, picked up the iced tea, toasted them. "You saved me. Can we be friends forever?"

"May it be so! *Salud!*" Alice lifted her glass.

"Watch out, Rose. The old adage says when you save someone's life, you're responsible for them forever. So, we're on your case." Red lifted her glass, clinked it on Rose's iced tea.

"All right. Like the man said, I want to be on your team."

Chapter   Thirty - One

It's Not about Norville

Early on Thursday, George Files called Alice. "Okay, the note in Kelly Cosgrove's pocket? It was a supposed confession by Rose Rayburn. Typed on a computer and printed out, with space for a signature, but unsigned."

"A confession to what?"

"Norville's murder."

"But she has an alibi!"

"I don't think Cosgrove knew that."

Alice remembered seeing Cosgrove over to her left, staring down at Norville. She remembered the janitor, pushing the broom back . . . "George, did the Hays County people look at my video?"

"Think so."

"Did they identify the janitor? Not the one I saw, but the one in the video, pushing back toward the musician's balcony?"

"I don't think so."

"Couldn't it be Kelly Cosgrove? He has a master key. He knows the janitors' staff room on that floor. He could have grabbed a jacket, grabbed a hat . . ."

"What did he do with his own coat, then?"

"Left it in the billiard room!"

"But how could he knock Norville over the balcony with an enormous woolly mop, and no one saw it?"

"It wasn't a woolly mop. It was just the empty mop stick without a woolly mop head. Maybe that was the lemony smell. Why didn't I get this before?" demanded Alice.

"There were some prints we didn't identify on the mops and brooms in the staff room closet."

"One of them has got to have Cosgrove's. Got to."

"But why, Alice? What's his motive for knocking off Norville?"

"It's the same reason he had that note in his pocket. He killed Norville because he thought Norville was going to link him to the tainted-milk investigation. He must have thought that when Norville accused him of 'milking the public'! He was going to push Rose over, put the note in her bag, drop it over, as if she had it on her when she committed suicide out of guilt, and try to pin Norville's murder on her. Then he'd get rid of both the people he thought could link him to the milk mess. So it's not about Norville. Though he hated Norville. It's about the Drinkman contracts for contaminated milk. So it ties into the car bomb too. That didn't work and he still needed to get rid of Rose so he's trying to make it look like suicide and then frame her. It's all about the prison contract for the melamine-contaminated milk!"

"Okay. Can you come over here and look at some pictures?"

* * * * *

"So the shooter was this man." Files pointed to the picture of Dark Man. "Seen him before?"

"Yup." That man had stared at her, standing in the street by the Audi in the dawn light. And then he had tried to kill her and Mr. Navarro. She stared back at the picture. Was it just a job?

"Who flew the chopper?" Alice asked.

"We think it was this man."

Blond Man.

"This pair was after the letter at Bryce's store and then Bryce's house," said Alice. "And up on the gallery at La Rotonda."

"But you said they didn't seem to know what Cosgrove was doing."

She nodded. "Maybe because he was off on a frolic of his own, and they were maybe focused on Alejandro. They said someone 'screwed it up.'"

"I should be hearing from Austin police later today. They've got some leads on the car bomb."

* * * * *

Alice was leaving the office late Thursday when the phone rang. Haverty Armstrong. "Alice," he said. "Glad you're still there! Got a moment?"

Alice heard a note of anxiety. "You have a proposal or are you and your clients going to be here tomorrow at nine?" she asked.

"Well, here's where we are, Alice. We agree to your terms with one addition, and one exception. The addition is that we need your client to agree not to pursue criminal charges against my clients or the Drinkman companies about the, uh, helicopter incident."

Alice had expected that. It was the leverage she needed, given how hard it would be to prove who pulled the trigger on April 19, 1919. "And the exception?"

"We need some more consideration for those radio stations. Twenty million. They are worth several times that."

"You know the Navarros don't have that kind of money!"

"Well, that's where we are. And Alice, it took some real work to get there. You don't know . . ."

"I assume you're saying Will Drinkman is hard to deal with."

No response.

"I'll talk to my folks, but you'd better tell your clients to show up tomorrow at nine wearing whatever they want the videographer to see."

Damn it, Alice thought. She didn't want the Navarros to have to offer back the anticipated future oil revenue, iffy as it could be, as a source for the twenty million—even if the Drinkmans would accept it. And Mr. Navarro wanted those stations.

She sat, thinking. Then she called Alejandro Navarro. Then she called John Frierson. The phone rang again. Thinking it might be Armstrong with another idea, she picked it up. A cultured voice, a voice used to having its way. "Alice? Adele Collins. May we speak?"

"Since you're represented, I should be talking to John Frierson, Adele."

"Oh, he knows I'm calling. We've talked. You know John watched those depositions."

"Yes."

"And he's told me all about them. His notes are exemplary."

Where was this going?

"Alice, I'd like to buy a share in the radio stations, and I'd put up the twenty million I hear the Drinkmans are asking. I'd like to be on the board, but not with a controlling interest. We'd have to agree I guess on some basics— is it going to be a nonprofit with some stated goals?"

"It could," Alice said.

"May I talk to your client about those goals?"

"You may."

Chapter Thirty-Two

Let Us Drink Beer!

Theer Barn's portable sign read "Friday night—Tessa
and Los Guapos!" and added: "Whoever drinks beer, he is
quick to sleep; whoever sleeps long, does not sin; whoever
does not sin, enters Heaven! Thus, let us drink beer!" The
sign attributed the quote to Martin Luther.

She and Kinsear climbed out of his Land Cruiser. They were
meeting Bryce, John T, Tyler, Silla, Red, Rose, and the Navarro
party at the Beer Barn for supper before the Friday-night show.
Alice had helped clear Tessa of murder the preceding fall and was
curious and anxious as to how growing fame would affect her passion for Johnny Garza, the lead singer of Los Guapos, and her singing and songwriting.

Kinsear had picked Alice up at her place. He'd abandoned the
orthopedic boot and was wearing his Goodson Kells boots and jeans.
"You look excellent, Alice."

She'd sauntered out in her own beloved and newly reheeled
Goodson Kells boots, surprised and tickled as always at the immedi-
ate boot swagger that took over her walk. With her jeans she wore the
embroidered rodeo jacket, with sequined yellow roses, that she sometimes thought might be over the top—until she caught a glimpse of
herself in the mirror. "Rodeo festive, that's me."

He cocked his head, looking at her face. "But I detect that you
don't feel totally festive yet? Even with the Drinkman deal done?" The
negotiations had been fierce, but were now final. Alice had pressed
even harder after Sandro reported the rumor that recipients of Drinkman campaign contributions were hinting there was a downside to
the Drinkman's high-handed treatment of the Navarro claim. Alejandro had what he wanted, signed, sealed, and delivered. Afterward,
Haverty had suggested Alice might also give up "any claim she might
have." She hadn't answered yet, though the prospect of a new truck
crossed her mind. Even so . . .

"Files was showing me pictures of those guys. Blond Man and
Dark Man. They were the ones in the helicopter, too. Sizzled and
dead."

"Not as comical as when they were inept foes at the battle of El
Rancherito, then?" He looked at her hard. "That was more like a

game, but being shot at on the highway . . . not to your liking?"

"I think it's just hitting me. Excuse the pun. Not a good feeling." She brushed it away. "'I vant to live!'"

He wasn't deflected, hugged her, stood back, pursed his lips. "Beer and a Pancho Villa might give you the will to live. And some two-stepping. Let's go."

* * * * *

The Beer Barons had placed a "RESERVED" sign on a big round table by the stage. Tyler, Red, and Silla were already there with Bryce and John T and Sandro and Rose when Kinsear and Alice arrived. Alice was the first to see Mr. Navarro, white shirt gleaming, slowly walking down toward the table, followed by Tomás and an alert, bright-eyed young woman, radiating intelligence. Tomás had his arm around her. "Everyone, I'd like to introduce Cecilia Ruiz, my—my very good friend." He was blushing.

"Please call me Cissy." She shook hands with everyone. "So glad to meet you."

Tomás pulled a chair out for her, fussed until he had her seated, got her a menu.

Alice smiled at Mr. Navarro, who sat with one eyebrow raised. "And, everyone, let me introduce Tomás Navarro, the new general manager of the formerly Drinkman radio stations. He'll have his plate full, doing that and heading for law school this fall." They all applauded. A small smile twitched Mr. Navarro's lips. Maybe the boy would turn out after all.

The Beer Barn was still quiet, though patrons were starting to stream in from the parking lot—the calm before Los Guapos ignited the crowd. Tyler said, "Okay, Alice, we're all here. Fill us in. What's going on with the criminal investigation?"

"Rose may know more than I do. George Files says the Austin police have found the guy who put the car bomb on Rose's car."

Rose nodded. "He's a longtime lowlife named Buddy Holtz, in and out of prison in Louisiana, did seriously bad stuff for the New Orleans mob, moved to Houston after Katrina and announced his availability. Kelly Cosgrove's phone shows they were in contact. Buddy Holtz is in jail, no bond."

"But Rose, was he the one who bopped you on the head? He doesn't sound like he'd have left you alive," asked Alice.

"I know." She shivered. "No, the Old Spice head-bopper was actually the guy I thought was my 'innie' at Drinkman's. Kelly Cosgrove knew he was talking to me and paid him to grab my computer so Kelly could figure out how much I'd figured out about the milk deal, and assess how dangerous I was. He's already pled and turned state's evidence. I'm just glad Kelly used him and not that Buddy Holtz."

"And I'm so glad that Rose has finished the tainted-milk investigation. We have an announcement," said Sandro. "And I know this is the Beer Barn, but we're having champagne. Rose, show them."

Rose, pink from forehead to chest, held out her left hand. The third finger sparkled. Tomás got up and kissed his dad and offered a hug to Rose, smiling over her head at Cissy. Cissy smiled back.

"And you're all invited," said Sandro. "Tomorrow evening at Our Lady of Guadalupe, after five o'clock mass. You hear? Tomorrow. I'm not waiting another day, now that I finally have Rose corralled. Be there or be square."

"Biggest congratulations, you two!" Alice was mortified to find tears threatening. She turned her head and pretended to watch Bill Birnbach and Other Bill pouring and serving champagne in flutes.

Mr. Navarro slowly stood up, one hand on Sandro's shoulder. "*Salud! A nuestra familia!*" They all cheered and drank.

Sandro stood up. "And to the missing one we won't forget. To Carey Norville." They raised their glasses in silence.

Bryce stood up. "I want to give you your first wedding present." He took a deep breath. "Alex Drinkman's letter. It belongs to your family."

"Bryce, Bryce, do you mean it?" Sandro asked.

"I mean it. However . . . I would like to keep the nightstand."

They all laughed. Birnbach circulated with the champagne once more. "Champagne's on the house," he said. "Thanks to our lawyer getting involved in still another death-defying mess, we're gonna have a mini-brewery! Because there's gonna be no cement plant!"

"What?" said Red.

"Tell 'em, Alice," said Birnbach.

"Well, oddly enough, the option on the proposed plant property was held by Kelly Cosgrove. But it expired without renewal day before yesterday. He was too busy talking to the police. I called the owner today to double-check. She's relieved to be out of that deal and thinks she may keep the property now. She's excited about Red's expanded rescue ranch and the mini-brewery. She thinks you guys are upping her property values."

Tyler jumped back in. "Alice, you didn't tell us yet: What about the helicopter? Do we know for sure who was involved?"

"It was the same two guys who broke into Bryce's shop and El Rancherito. George Files says the helicopter company they work for is owned by the Drinkmans. Even though it was leased to Warren's company, Oak Motte Links, he's pretty sure Will Drinkman was calling the shots, excuse the pun. But it may be hard to prove he gave them those specific orders."

"So Will Drinkman first used the two men just to try to get the letter back, but then decided he couldn't afford to let Alice and Mr. Navarro take the case to trial," said Kinsear.

"Right. And it helped us settle. He knows we don't have all the pieces yet, and that there are problems with the case, but he doesn't want to run the biggest risk, even if it's unlikely: for some jury to decide the Kendricks were never entitled to any of Alastair Drinkman's estate. At least that's my read," Alice said.

She felt a warm arm slide around her neck followed by a kiss on her cheek. "Alice!"

"Tessa!"

Alice stood up and hugged her, held her shoulders, looked at her. Tessa was still pigtailed, still freckled, but a settled depth shone in her eyes. "Gotta run," she said. "We're on."

Tessa and Los Guapos rocked the hall. After the first song, an electric silence, then wild cheers from the crowd. Dancing was breaking out between the tables, in the aisle, and down next to Alice's table. Kinsear grabbed her hand. "Let's show these children how to two-step," he said, one hand on the small of her back, the other turning her smoothly across the old wooden dance floor. Alice said, a little breathless after the first dance, "It feels so good to be alive, to dance."

Kinsear nodded. "Yep. Beats being dead in your pickup out on Ranch Road 631. Alice, I wish you'd tone your practice down. I'm getting awfully attached to you." He swung her out toward the edge of the floor. "Seriously attached." He swung her back. "Let's go outside for a minute."

They walked outside, the drums and guitar fading as the double doors shut. In the parking lot, a nighthawk swooped around the lights, catching spring bugs. Alice kissed Kinsear.

"When do your kids get home? Is it Monday?" he asked.

"Monday."

"I'd like to meet them, Alice."

She nodded.

"You feeling okay?" he asked.

"I have a knot in my chest, for some reason."

"Yes. There's something about Mr. Navarro, behaving with all that dignity for all those years, never knowing his own father, and then finding just a bit of him, so many years later."

"Right. That's part of it."

They went back in. Red was dancing and laughing with Joe Banks, the vet. Sandro and Rose were dancing, interrupted from time to time by constituents coming over to shake hands. Tomás and Cissy were still sitting at the table, heads together, talking intently. Mr. Navarro, with a small smile, watched his grandson. Alice felt odd, like she was there and not there, watching herself from afar, as if she were watching a movie. She felt splintered in time and space. One practical voice in her brain said, you just need a good night's sleep. But she felt she was waiting to hear another voice. What was it?

Chapter Thirty-Three

Take Love Easy

Alice stood at the bottom of the Austin airport escalator, waiting for the precious children to come around the corner and down. And there they were—different, but hers. What made them look different? Scottish haircut for John? Quirky braid for Ann? Wilder clothes? Alice waved frantically, a load off her heart. They were home! Hugs, more hugs. A wait for the baggage, as her children shrugged off jackets, scarves, sweaters. Then outside, into the summery Austin air, and into the car, all talking at once. "Of course we're stopping at Maudie's, right?" they demanded. Of course. The stop at Maudie's Lake Austin was obligatory, as were queso, nachos, and fajita salad. Gazing fondly at her offspring, Alice asked about final papers, final exams, and their last gig at Sandy Bell's. "Pretty jammed, Mom," said John. "And you know who joined us on bodhran? That ancient lady, Maura McBride. She's incredible."

"And did you sing, Ann?"

"I did. 'The Bob o' Dunblane.' Brought down the house. Gran loved it. She taught me that one, you know."

"Wish I'd been there."

The siblings glanced at each other. "We need to talk to you about that, Mom. Gran asked us to ask you. She needs some help. Something about Dad's land. Some guy up there is trying to grab it and Gran doesn't know what to do. She knows you're busy but she asked if you could fly over this summer 'just for a bit.'"

"And I'd go back with you," said Ann. "If you wait until August I'd go back with you, after summer school's over."

"Tell me about Gran's issue."

"Something about an expired lease or an expired easement or something. He claims she's lost her rights. Didn't quite make sense to me." John finished off the queso, heaved a blissful sigh, then leaned forward. "Mom, Gran does need some help. She's getting older. We could tell she was upset, though lord knows she's got that stiff upper lip."

"Okay," said Alice.

"And when we get home we've got a surprise for you."

"Okay! Also, there'll be barbecue tonight. Ben Kinsear wants to meet you two and he's bringing some Shade Tree brisket." Across the table she caught Ann raising eyebrows at her brother.

At home the kids stripped off their airplane clothes, jumped into swimsuits, and raced for the creek. Later they fed carrots to the burros. Alice waited.

Kinsear showed up looking stiff and anxious. To her relief, John stuck out a firm hand and Ann smiled. When the stars were out, they slid into the living room. John carried his fiddle.

"Mom, we've learned a new song. It's by this guy we hadn't heard of, an English composer named Ivor Gurney."

Her heart skipped a beat.

"It's a different version of the Yeats poem that we know—'Down by the Salley Gardens.'"

The two musicians glanced at each other, nodded, and were off, Ann's soprano so warm and clear, John's fiddle unexpectedly sonorous. "Down by the salley gardens, my love and I would meet . . . she bid me take love easy . . . but I was young and foolish and now am full of tears . . ." The bow rose and fell, Ann's voice soared and curled back, soared and curled, and the tears rose in Alice's eyes. She blinked, but couldn't stop the tears. Oh, Ivor Gurney, writing in the unending mud of the Somme trenches about his beloved Gloucestershire regiment; oh, Alex Drinkman, who with so many others crossed the Atlantic to join Gurney, Sassoon, Owen, and the rest of that lost generation, and did not quite make it home again.

"Mom?"

She blew her nose. "It's just beautiful." She blew her nose again. "I'm just so glad you're home." So that was it. I "now am full of tears," she thought, though nearly a century away from the mud and blood of 1918 and the blood in the water of 1919. And way too close to Norville's blood on the floor, and the echo of shots hitting her truck out on Ranch Road 631. But here were her precious children.

She jumped up. "Would you sing 'The Bob o' Dunblane'?" Robert Burns's bawdy words rang out, the magnetic melody captured them, and Alice laughed at Ann's raised-eyebrow delivery of the importunate lover's words: "The dinner, the piper and priest shall be ready, and I'm grown weary with lying alone . . ." Hmm, too close to home? She wasn't quite yet thinking of piper and priest. Kinsear shook hands again with John and Ann, hugged Alice and left.

She and the kids took the requisite nighttime walk out to the gate, the caliche road glimmering white under the summer stars. She hummed the first line: "Life let us cherish while yet the taper glows . . ."

"Oh, Mom. So sentimental. So last century. No, so century before last."

"I know, I know."

So, Scotland in August. Get it all straightened out, whatever it was. She would not think, "What fresh hell?" No, she would not.

"Look at the stars!" said Ann.

THE END

Daniel D. Arreola, *Tejano South Texas*, The University of Texas Press, 2002. Arreola describes the Tejano territory of South Texas ("larger than the state of Pennsylvania"), including its ranchos, towns and cities, foodways and culinary history, and political history.

Ivor Gurney, *Severn & Somme*, originally published in November 1917. Gurney named this volume of war poems for two rivers: the Severn of his beloved Gloucestershire, and the Somme, where he served at the front with his Gloucestershire regiment and was wounded and gassed. In 1985, Gurney was included as one of Sixteen Great War Poets commemorated on a stone in Westminster Abbey's Poet's Corner. Born in 1890, Gurney was prodigiously talented. He wrote poetry, drama, and vocal and instrumental music such as *A Gloucestershire Rhapsody*, 1919-21. His mental health was fragile; he was institutionalized from 1922 to his death in 1937.

David Kahn, *The Code-Breakers: The Comprehensive History of Secret Communication from Ancient Times to the Internet*, Scribner, 1996. Kahn presents a chronology of true detective stories solved by cryptography and cryptanalysis. See 282-297 for his riveting account of the affair of the Zimmermann Telegram. At 297: "The Texans blinked in astonishment: the Germans meant to give away their state!"

Henry B. Thoreau, "Walking," Part 2: "My needle is slow to settle — varies a few degrees, and does not always point due south-west, it is true, and it has good authority for this variation, but it always settles between west and south-south-west. The future lies that way to me, and the earth seems more unexhausted and richer on that side. The outline which would bound my walks, would be, not a circle, but a parabola, or rather like one of those cometary orbits, which have been thought to be non-returning curves, in this case opening westward, in which my house occupies the place of the sun. I turn round and round irresolute sometimes for a quarter of an hour, until I decide for the thousandth time, that I will walk into the south-west or west. Eastward I go only by force; but westward I go free."

Barbara W. Tuchman, *The Zimmermann Telegram*, Random House, 1966: this slim riveting tale, first published in 1958 and revised with new material, begins, "The first message of the morning watch plopped out of the pneumatic tube into the wire basket with no more premonitory rattle than usual." You are immediately drawn into the heart of Room 40, Whitehall, the cryptographic office where in early 1917 a motley group will unravel "a key to the war's deadlock." As to the telegram's impact on sentiment in the U.S., see generally 184-187. As to Texas, at 186, "The San Antonio *Light* asserted 'with quiet modesty and simple truth' that if a German-Mexican-Japanese army overran Texas, not a Texan would be left alive unless he was across the border fighting his way back."

THANKS AND MORE THANKS

This book would not have taken shape without the collaboration, brainstorming, and support of Larry Foster, Sydney Foster Schneider, Drew Foster, Fritz Schneider, Amanda Foster, and my sister Grace Currie Bradshaw. Nor could this book have hatched without the creative and generous comments and encouragement from friends and family: Carol Arnold, Ann Barker, Dr. Ed Barker, Dr. Megan Biesele, Bill Bradshaw, Boyce Cabaniss, Pat Campbell, Elizabeth Christian, Ann Ciccolella, Curt Clemson, Keith Clemson, Dr. Mark Currie, Floyd Domino, Grant Hines, Mary Keeney, Tom Welch, Suzanne Wofford, David Wofford, Virgil Yarbrough, and Stephenie Yearwood. What friendship! Heartfelt thanks to all of you. Any errors are mine.

For superb advice from Bill Crawford and Aaron Hierholzer (editor nonpareil) and for Bill Carson's cover, layout, craftsmanship and sheer professional brio, thanks and more thanks!

Helen Currie Foster writes the Alice MacDonald Greer Mystery series. She lives north of Dripping Springs, Texas, supervised by three burros. She is drawn to the compelling landscape and quirky characters of the Texas Hill Country. She's also deeply curious about our human history, and how, uninvited, the past keeps crashing the party.

Find her on Facebook or at www.helen.currie.foster.com.

Made in the USA
Middletown, DE
04 February 2016